VIR
MODERN

Angela Thirkell (1890–1961) was the eldest daughter of John William Mackail, a Scottish classical scholar and civil servant, and Margaret Burne-Jones. Her relatives included the pre-Raphaelite artist Edward Burne-Jones, Rudyard Kipling and Stanley Baldwin, and her godfather was J. M. Barrie. She was educated in London and Paris, and began publishing articles and stories in the 1920s. In 1931 she brought out her first book, a memoir entitled *Three Houses*, and in 1933 her comic novel *High Rising* – set in the fictional county of Barsetshire, borrowed from Trollope – met with great success. She went on to write nearly thirty Barsetshire novels, as well as several further works of fiction and non-fiction. She was twice married, and had four children.

By Angela Thirkell

Barsetshire novels

High Rising
Wild Strawberries
The Demon in the House
August Folly
Summer Half
Pomfret Towers
The Brandons
Before Lunch
Cheerfulness Breaks In
Northbridge Rectory
Marling Hall
Growing Up
The Headmistress
Miss Bunting
Peace Breaks Out
Private Enterprise
Love Among the Ruins
The Old Bank House
County Chronicle
The Duke's Daughter
Happy Returns
Jutland Cottage
What Did it Mean?
Enter Sir Robert
Never Too Late
A Double Affair
Close Quarters
Love at All Ages
Three Score and Ten

Non-fiction

Three Houses

Collected Stories

Christmas at High Rising

THE OLD BANK HOUSE

Angela Thirkell

VIRAGO

This edition published in Great Britain in 2024 by Virago Press
First published in Great Britain in 1949 by Hamish Hamilton Ltd

1 3 5 7 9 10 8 6 4 2

A CIP catalogue record for this book is available from the British Library.

ISBN 978-0-349-01868-3

Typeset in Goudy by M Rules
Printed and bound in Great Britain by
Clays Ltd, Elcograf S.p.A.

Papers used by Virago are from well-managed forests
and other responsible sources.

Virago Press
An imprint of
Little, Brown Book Group
Carmelite House
50 Victoria Embankment
London EC4Y 0DZ

An Hachette UK Company
www.hachette.co.uk

www.virago.co.uk

I

Edgewood Rectory is a comfortable early nineteenth century house in the small market town of Edgewood, over Chaldicotes way. Up till the middle of last century the name Edgewood fitted it well, for it lies on the confines of what is still by tradition called Chaldicotes Chase. But through various causes, among them the gambling debts of Mr Sowerby, a small remount depot between 1914 and 1918 and a very large camp during the last war (or Second World War to end War), the forest in which Kings of Wessex and later Kings of England had hunted has dwindled to scattered woods and thickets which lose ground year by year under the saw or the tractor. Edgewood is now almost entirely surrounded by arable or grazing land and only to the north does a piece of forest approach the town. The Rectory stands at the north end of Edgewood, and just outside the far end of its large garden which no Rector since the beginning of the century has quite been able to afford to keep up properly, is a very large oak far gone in age and decay, with gaunt, bare, skeleton branches sticking up like giant antlers among its summer green, a relic of the days when Chaldicotes Chase was a royal hunting lodge. No one knows its age and probably when it becomes so dangerous that it has to be felled it will be found rotten to the core, so that no one will ever be able to count the rings. That part is rotten is well known, and each generation of Rectory children has poked with sticks or excavated with its maiden pocket knife a large gaping hole on the north side, trippers have put the revolting paper and broken meats of their picnics into the hole and set fire to them, but the oak still stands.

'It makes me think of Falstaff,' said Eleanor Grantly, elder daughter of the Rectory, looking from the breakfast table one Saturday morning in June.

'What makes you think of Falstaff, and why?' said her father, 'which,' he added, 'sounds like Mangnall's Questions, whatever they are.'

'They sound rather like Eno's Fruit Salts,' said her younger brother Henry who was daily expecting what he wittily called his subscription papers, or in other words his calling-up papers for military service, and was quite old enough to know better.

'Why Eno anyway?' said Grace Grantly, younger daughter of the Rectory, who was a weekly boarder at Barchester High School. 'Eno isn't a real word.'

Mrs Grantly, who had created for herself a myth that she was the stupid one of the family on no grounds at all, said there was a place called Arnos Grove at one end of one of the London Tubes and she was sure that wasn't a real word either and when one got there it wouldn't be in the least like what one expected and she really must go and telephone to the butcher.

Or, said Tom, the eldest of the family, who had gone back to Oxford after demobilization and was trying not to feel too old to be an undergraduate, it might be an anagram, though he couldn't at the moment think of an anagram of Arnos that made sense.

'Roans,' said his sister Grace scornfully.

Henry rashly said it wasn't a word.

'Well,' said Grace, who dearly loved to dogmatize and was Secretary of the Barchester Girls' High School Senior Debating Society, 'if you had a lot of roan horses and you wanted to talk about them I suppose you'd say roans, whatever roan is,' she added.

The four young Grantlys then explained simultaneously each his or her own views on the word roan, which led to a very ill-informed argument on piebald and skewbald and a good deal of noise.

'I do wish,' said Mr Grantly, who was tall and handsome with a kind gentle expression like the portrait of his great-great-grandfather Bishop Grantly which hung on the dining-room wall, 'I do wish that you children wouldn't have such jumping conversations. They make my reason totter. How did we get from Falstaff to skewbald?'

'That's like the unravelling game,' said Grace. 'You all sit in a circle and someone says a word and the next one says a word it reminds her of and the next one says a word the other word reminds her of and then when you've been round about ten times you have to go backwards and say the word that reminded you of your word. We did it at Miss Pettinger's party last Christmas and I was the only one that remembered the word that reminded Ruby Alcock of *Paradise Lost*.'

'And what was the word?' said her father, with the kind courtesy he used to young and old alike.

'Mouthwash,' said Grace.

'The point is beyond me,' said the Rector, slightly dejected.

'It isn't beyond you, father, it is just silly,' said Eleanor, who had from her earliest years constituted herself her father's protector. 'There is a mouthwash called Milton, and Milton wrote *Paradise Lost*.'

'Very ingenious,' said Mr Grantly admiringly. 'Are you going to Barchester to-day, Eleanor?'

'Lady Pomfret said I could take to-day off,' said Eleanor. 'There isn't much to do at the office to-day. Oh, who do you think came in yesterday? Susan Belton.'

'Do I know her?' said Mr Grantly anxiously, for he felt it his duty as a clergyman to remember people and was perpetually falling short of his own standards.

'Of course you do, father,' said Eleanor. 'She was our Depot Librarian. Susan Dean she was. You know her father over the other side at Winter Overcotes and her sister Jessica Dean the actress. She's going to have a baby in August you know.'

'I don't know,' said Mr Grantly. 'Or rather, I do know now because you have told me, but I didn't know. But I am very glad. I like babies,' he added thoughtfully.

'I shall have five before I am thirty,' said Grace.

'Don't you boast, my girl,' said Tom. 'I don't suppose anyone will want to marry you. I wouldn't.'

Grace said being married didn't matter now. Look, she said, at Edna and Doris, and then she fixed her reverend papa rather fiercely with the look that had quelled members of the Barchester Girls' High School Senior Debating Society who spoke out of their turn.

The Rector looked and felt a little uneasy. Life had been very hard at the Rectory during the war with the house full of evacuees and very little help to be got and he had felt both unhappy and guilty, though for this latter feeling there were no grounds at all, when he thought of the hours, days, months, and years that his wife had not only borne the brunt of evacuees and her own young, but also slaved in the kitchen. Then, soon after Peace broke out, Providence in the guise of Sir Edmund Pridham who knew more about the county than anyone alive had intervened with the offer of Edna and Doris Thatcher, handsome young women from Grumper's End with various children of shame; which offer had sorely exercised Mr Grantly.

'I know we ought not to cast the first stone, nor indeed any other stone,' he said to his wife after all the washing-up was done, 'but on the other hand, would having them at the Rectory be – dear me, what is the word I want?'

His wife suggested eyesore.

That, said the Rector, was a very good word, but not exactly what he meant. He meant something more like a bone of contention, though that wasn't exactly it either.

'You mean stumbling block, darling,' said Mrs Grantly. 'But I really don't think they would make anyone stumble. Mrs Miller, the Vicar's wife at Pomfret Madrigal, has known them for a long time and says they are very nice. Besides the house seems rather empty without any children and Mrs Miller says they are very good mothers and Edna is a very good cook.'

Mr Grantly was about to say, as charitably as he could, that one might be a good cook and yet give scandal to the congregation by one's manner of life. But he looked at his wife and his heart smote him as he noticed, which he often did and every time with a fresh pang, for he was not unobservant, how completely tired she looked and how much harder she had worked than he had ever worked in his life. So he swallowed all his doubts as to the propriety of having unmarried mothers as domestic helps and expressed to his wife his complete approval of, nay enthusiasm for, Mrs Miller's plan. And if he expected a reward for this he was the more deceived, for Mrs Grantly did as most women in her place would have done and instead of saying 'Thank you, darling, how splendid,' she broke down for the first time since 1939 and cried till she had not a tear left to shed, nor could her husband succeed in calming or comforting her till he thought of asking if he could have a cup of tea before he went to the meeting of the Parish Council.

So Edna and Doris Thatcher took up their abode in Edgewood Rectory and brought with them youth, health, zeal and good spirits, and if they had the kitchen wireless on from 6.30 a.m. to 11 p.m. and joined lustily in everything from Lifting Up Their Hearts to Old Favourites of the Halls, it was all from joy of life. And the winter when Eleanor had pneumonia very badly they kept silence themselves and smacked their children of shame into hushed voices and made them wear their woollen stockings over their boots in the house.

Edna, the elder of the sisters, had contented herself with one boy, Purse, called after an Army Service Corps corporal named Percy who had dallied too often and too long with Edna Thatcher and vanished when his regiment left Barsetshire. Purse was now about twelve years old and quite stupid at school which he despised, preferring to frequent the local garage where the proprietor said he was as good as two men when it came to taking down a car. But Doris, not content with Glad, or Gladys, whose father she had never quite been able to place, had continued a career of being quite incapable of saying No to any gentleman (for so she artlessly called the probable fathers of her young) and had since produced Sid, Stan and Glamora, this last called after the famous film star Glamora Tudor. All five children were beautiful, healthy and very well brought up on the family system of alternate sweets and smacks, and all were useful about the house and in the large understaffed garden. It had taken Mrs Grantly some time to get used to being greeted with a smile in her own kitchen and enthusiastically pressed to have cups of tea instead of spending her life making them for other people who despised her for doing it, but gradually she got used to it. And if ever she wondered whether the peculiar household seemed quite normal to her children, she told herself not to be silly and put the thought where it should be, out of sight and out of mind.

So there was a silence, very brief but just long enough to give a slight feeling of uncomfortableness, when Mrs Grantly came back from telephoning the butcher who was being obliging enough to have liver and sending her up a nice piece only it did need thoring out first a bit coming straight out of the fridge, he said; a remark which to the housewife needs no explanation.

'Anything wrong?' said Mrs Grantly, who was very brave.

'Nothing mother; really,' said Eleanor.

'Well, what unreally then?' said Mrs Grantly.

'It was my fault,' said Tom, who had his father's kind and gentle nature. 'Grace said she meant to have five children by the time she was thirty and I said perhaps nobody would want to marry her and Grace said Look at Edna and Doris, and then father looked anxious. But I don't think it mattered much,' he added.

'Not in the least,' said Mrs Grantly calmly. 'Edna and Doris are very nice, good girls and that's that. But let it be clearly understood,' she added, looking round her family with the air of a benevolent lecturer, 'that the middle classes still get married before they have their families. And I think you will find,' she continued, interested in the field of speculation opening before her, 'that it works better in the end. And Grace will have plenty of time to think about her family when she has passed her School Certificate. Though why,' said Mrs Grantly thoughtfully, 'people should have to pass that silly thing I cannot tell. I'd like to see the Government passing it themselves. Which reminds me that we *must* have that defective ball-cock in the storage tank seen to, Septimus. And I do think and always shall think, though I daresay I don't really understand these things, that it was silly to christen you Septimus when you were an only child.'

The Rector said he was extremely sorry and if he had been in a state to give an opinion when he was christened he would certainly have made a protest.

'But it is extraordinary,' he added, 'how used one gets to one's own name over a period of sixty years or so. Of course my great-great-grandfather Harding *was* a seventh child, though as the other six all died before he was born it doesn't seem quite to count.'

'Well, I'm glad you didn't call any of us after the multiplication table,' said Eleanor. 'I think it makes people rather frightening to have mathematical names. Like Mrs Needham, the one that her husband's Vicar of Lambton and only has one arm. If she weren't called Octavia she wouldn't be so frightening. She came into the Red Cross the other day and quite bullied me about books for the Cottage Hospital.'

'So what did you do?' asked her father, amused, but secretly very proud of having a daughter who was Depot Librarian of the Barchester St John and Red Cross Library in succession to Miss Susan Dean, now Mrs Freddy Belton and a happy mother about to be made.

'I temporised,' said Eleanor. 'And then Lady Pomfret came in and said about two words and Mrs Needham stopped roaring and did what she was told. It's an extraordinary thing how Lady Pomfret always seems to come at the right moment. Oh, and she said would I come to the Towers one week-end, mother.'

Mr and Mrs Grantly were pleased to hear this news. They were very fond of their elder daughter and very proud of her and possibly felt that their Eleanor was quite as good stock as Sally Wicklow, sister of the Pomfret Towers agent, though whether Eleanor could have filled the position of Countess of Pomfret as the present holder of the title did was another question. But even if Mrs Grantly was conscious of good county blood it was none the less pleasant that her daughter should be asked to stay with the Lord Lieutenant of the county and to know that she was asked on her own merits.

'Good girl,' said Tom approvingly, at which Eleanor almost blushed, for praise from Tom had been one of her greatest pleasures ever since nursery days. 'I'll come and hang round the back door and you can give me beef and ale. Oh bother, I can't,' he added. 'I've got to go back to Oxford to-morrow night. I must get through these wretched Schools somehow, though I must say it seems silly at my time of life and being a Major to have to do lessons again.'

His parents both looked anxious but said nothing and Tom blamed himself for depressing them, and wondered if he would ever have the courage to face them if he didn't take a first, or at any rate a very good second in Greats. And then Doris came in, with golden hair, blue eyes, a rose-petal flush on magnolia skin, and an air of dewy, candid innocence, accompanied by Stan and Glamora who were in a fair way to being a most accomplished butler and parlourmaid, and began to clear away the breakfast things with such zeal that the family were routed.

'When breakfast is over the day is practically done,' said the Rector sadly to his eldest son as they walked over the lawn towards the ha-ha. 'There must be something in the Bible to that effect, but I cannot put my finger on it.'

Perhaps, Tom said, in Ecclesiastes. One got some jolly good depressing things in Ecclesiastes, he added.

'It is curious,' said his father, 'how cheerful being depressed makes one feel. In dark times I have often read Ecclesiastes and come away refreshed.'

Tom said, diffidently, for he loved and respected his father and would not for the world have hurt him, that perhaps it was because Ecclesiastes was rather pagan and people often felt a bit pagan themselves.

'Not pagan,' said his father thoughtfully. 'Not even in a Pecksniffian sense. I think what you mean, Tom, is heathen, which is rather different.'

'How exactly, father?' said Tom.

'I don't quite know if I am clear in my own mind as to what I mean,' said the Rector. 'One is so often in a muddled way of thinking. But I think – mind you, I only say think – that whoever wrote or collected Ecclesiastes was far more like a Norseman than an inhabitant of the Middle East. If you read the sagas you will find much the same attitude to life and a feeling of the inevitability and the coldness of death. Real ice and icy winds and black desolation. But I daresay,' said the Rector, 'that the Bishop would think quite differently.'

Tom, rather glad of this change of subject, said whatever the Bishop thought would be wrong anyway and had his father heard what Sir Edmund Pridham said about bishops.

If, said Mr Grantly, it were not too disrespectful to gaiters and aprons he would very much like to hear it, as Sir Edmund had a great deal of sound common sense.

'It was when the Bishop made everyone have a kind of celebration because he had been a clergyman for twenty-five years,' said Tom. 'And Sir Edmund came up to a Gaudy at Paul's and he said being a clergyman for twenty-five years was quite common and if the Bishop had been a *bishop* for twenty-five years there would be something to boast about. And then he said that whenever any man he knew personally became a bishop he always seemed to lose any sense he had previously had.'

The Rector smiled and said Sir Edmund certainly had the root of the matter in him, but he hoped Tom had not repeated the story.

'Well, only to people like the Dean and Bishop Joram,' said Tom, naming two of the strongest supporters of the anti-Palace faction. 'But I think Sir Edmund was rather pleased with saying it and told everybody. And Charles Fanshawe, my tutor you know, turned it into a nice elegiac couplet.'

He then repeated the verses which owing to our ignorance of Latin we are unable to reproduce.

'Very neat, very neat,' said the Rector. 'And what does Fanshawe think of your chances, Tom? Or oughtn't I to ask?'

Tom said nothing. There was a great deal that he wanted to say, but he did not quite know how to say it and he was afraid of hurting his father. Not that his father would ever be annoyed, or even show it if he grieved, but Tom could not bear the thought of possibly grieving him, let alone annoying him. So he remained silent and wondered if one could burst or go mad through sheer inability to speak.

'I have been wondering if I made a mistake when I let you read Greats,' said his father. 'Did I, Tom?'

'I really don't know, father,' said Tom, the words forcing themselves out of his mouth in a kind of desperation. 'I did want to, father. Really. I mean I did love Latin and Greek at school, especially Greek. But only the poetry kind and the plays and historical things. It's the philosophy that gets me down. It all seems so silly. I mean I don't really know anything about philosophy but I think one has to make one's own as one goes along. I mean one tries to behave decently and all that, but I can't see why one should make such a fuss about it. I'm most awfully sorry, father.'

'Then I take it that Fanshawe thinks poorly of your chances on the philosophy papers?' said Mr Grantly, who much to his son's relief appeared to be more interested than disturbed.

'Absolutely,' said Tom. 'And if I'd tried that stupid P.P.E. I'd have come a cropper just the same and not had the fun of the literature.'

'P.P.E.?' said the Rector. 'What is that?'

'Philosophy, Politics, Economics, father,' said Tom.

The Rector was silent for a moment.

'The only comment I can make,' said he in a quiet measured voice, 'upon that school, if school one can call it, is in the words of the prophet Haggai, the favourite writer of my dear old friend Dale of Hallbury. You never knew Dale,' he added accusingly.

'No, father,' said Tom.

'The words,' the Rector continued dispassionately, 'are, "I smote you with blasting and with mildew and with hail in all the labours of your hands." And even that is really hardly adequate treatment for such a so-called school.'

'Yes, father,' said Tom.

'Don't worry,' said the Rector. 'It will be all right.'

Tom felt much comforted but rather at a loss.

'It is,' said the Rector, apparently embarking upon a perfectly new train of thought, 'extremely lucky that my great-grandfather was a very wealthy man.'

'Yes, father,' said Tom.

'And although the wealth has been divided and each share has decreased in accordance with the wishes of the present Government,' continued the Rector, 'I am very comfortably off.

When I die there will still be pickings, unless the people whom His Gracious Majesty has to call His Government, which must be a sore mortification to His Majesty, decide to confiscate all the property of the dead. Do your best, Tom. If you want to earn your living in some way that we haven't as yet tried, you might let me know. I daresay you haven't really thought about it. This peace has made things difficult for us all and very difficult for the young. And if you change your mind more than once I am prepared to back you. But the sooner you decide the better, because at your age you need work and work and work.'

'Thank you, father,' said Tom. 'Lord! I do seem to have made a hash of it.'

'We all do,' said Mr Grantly mildly. 'And then we pick ourselves up and go on again.'

'I say, father,' said Tom, encouraged by his father's words, 'it's rather awful, you know, being so much older than the others. It makes one feel no end of a fool.'

'That is exactly what I felt,' said the Rector.

'But there wasn't a war when you were at Oxford, father,' said Tom. 'You went up at the ordinary age, didn't you?'

'I did,' said the Rector. 'But I had no idea of going into the Church then. I meant to be an estate agent. But I suppose having two great-grandfathers and a great-great-grandfather in orders was rather infectious and at last I felt the Church was really my place. So I went to a Theological College and was one of the oldest there, not counting of course the old men with beards who had failed every year for the last fifty years. I felt rather foolish at times, but it was well worth it. And I must say,' he added reflectively, 'that my people were extraordinarily kind about it.'

'Well, so are you, father,' said Tom, going red in the face.

'Why not?' said his father. 'By the way, Tom, do *you* want to be an estate agent by any chance?'

Tom looked across the glebe, examined a little piece of moss on the stone balustrade which divided the garden from the ha-ha, straightened his tie and made a noise which might have meant anything.

'Because if you do,' said his father, apparently unconscious of his son's peculiar behaviour, 'there is a great deal to be said for it. Do as well as you can in your Schools, and then we can consider the matter. One thing at a time. Which reminds me,' he added, taking out of his waistcoat pocket the gold watch that had belonged to Archdeacon Grantly, 'that I have to go down to the Old Bank House. That man Adams at Hogglestock has an idea of buying it and old Miss Sowerby asked me to come and support her. I think she feels that a Labour M.P. might confiscate her house at sight.'

'Thanks awfully, father,' said Tom. 'Eleanor says the lawn-mower isn't working too well. I'll have a look at it, because she wants to mow the croquet lawn.'

In a kind of happy embarrassment, or embarrassed happiness, he went off to the old stables where no horses lived now, nor any brougham nor wagonette nor open carriage, though a faint smell of oats and leather still hung about the stalls and loose-boxes and harness-room making a nostalgic atmosphere of a life that was dead. The Rectory car, shabby but useful, was the only inhabitant of the coach-house and here were also kept various garden implements including the lawn-mower which Eleanor Grantly was examining.

If Tom had thought to come as a deus ex, or rather pro machina, he was the more deceived, for Master Percy Thatcher was already in charge with an assortment of tools and needed no help at all.

'Hullo, Purse,' said Tom, who always felt ashamed of himself for so truckling to the slip-shod speech of the Thatcher family but could not bring himself to be so peculiar as to say Percy. 'What's wrong?'

'Everything, I think,' said his sister Eleanor, almost crossly, for half an hour's wrestling with a machine that set its teeth firmly when she tried to propel it had made her hotter and crosser than she had been since the Hospital Library took over another storey of the house where it lived and about five hundred books had to be moved by hand up two flights of stairs and the shelves weren't what the carpenter would like, or so he said, shelves to be; and most of the staff weltered among books and sawdust and a window stuck and one of the junior helpers put her hand through a pane and bled all over a nice new six foot length of beading that the carpenter had set his heart on nailing into place before all them heavy books went in; evidently looking upon books as agents of wrath specially directed against bookshelves.

'Let's have a look,' said Tom, squatting beside the unfriendly machine, which Purse, who had his mother's wide tolerance of the gentry, allowed him to do. 'There's something queer here, among these cogs.'

'I know,' said Eleanor. 'It's a beastly little bit of metal that won't stay in its place. I've tried for half an hour to put it back and it falls out every time and gets all entangled in the machinery.'

'You did ought to treat her koind, miss,' said Purse, who much to the Rector's pleasure remained pure Barset in his speech, unmoved by school to which he paid little or no attention or the wireless which only interested him as a machine, the more especially when it went wrong as the kitchen wireless not infrequently did owing to a rooted belief held by Doris and Edna that if it went wrong the best treatment was to throw something at it: possibly the remains of some primitive belief in exorcising evil spirits by violence. 'Let her feel your fingers, miss, loike. She's all roight.'

Under Tom's and his sister's fascinated gaze he felt delicately among the machinery with his small, very dirty fingers and by what seemed to the onlookers a miracle everything fell into place. Purse gave the machine a slight push to which it responded with a smooth movement and a happy purring sound. He then produced an oil can from a wooden shelf, carefully oiled the machine and wiped off any superfluous oil with the cotton waste which he habitually carried in the front of his jersey owing to his pockets being full of other useful things.

'You run her easy, miss,' said Purse, 'and she'll be all roight. Me and Sid's going to the pictures this afternoon, Mr Tom. It's a lovely film about motor races and there's a bad lot and he puts sand in the hero's bearings, miss, to stop him winning the race, but the hero's girl she dresses up like a man and she's got a car just loike her friend's and she droives it and wins the race. Me and Stan sor it at the Barchester Odeon, miss, and Sid croyed ever so because he didn't go, so Oy'm taking him to the threepennies.'

'Suppose you take him to the ninepennies,' said Tom, these being the most expensive seats at the Edgewood Cinema which only had films on Thursday and Saturday. And he took some money from his pocket and gave it to Purse.

'Please, Mr Tom,' said Purse, 'if Oy was to take Sid to the threepennies Oy could boy mint gums with the rest.'

'All right, Purse, you do whatever you like,' said Tom and Purse, stuffing the cotton waste back into his jersey so that he bulged in an alarming way, went off to the kitchen to tell his mother, while Tom pushed the lawn-mower over the cobbled yard and round to the croquet lawn and began to unroll the carpet of green striped moiré silk, while the machine purred gently and the grass and the daisies flew before it.

'Do you suppose we'll ever play croquet again?' said Eleanor, as her brother stopped to empty the grass-holder or whatever is the correct name for the thing the grass flies into; though heaven knows that as a rule almost as much flies outside as goes inside and has to be swept away afterwards, rather spoiling the striped pattern.

'I don't know why not,' said Tom. 'The tennis court won't ever be fit to play on again as far as I can see, and anyway it would cost an awful lot to get it really put right. Quite a lot of people do play croquet. Let's get the things out when I've finished mowing.'

Eleanor said, with a slight bitterness unusual in her, that it served people right for trying to be patriotic and mother could just as well have grown potatoes in the glebe field instead of digging up the tennis court.

'Well, if it hadn't been potatoes it would have been something else,' said Tom philosophically. 'Remember the Dreadful Dowager,' for so the Dowager Lady Norton was known to most of the county. 'She kept her tennis court that she never used and the army dumped about a million tons of corrugated iron sheets on the top of it and most of them are still there. Let's have some croquet parties in the Long Vacation. Oh Lord! there won't be any Long Vacation for me any more. I say, Eleanor, father was awfully decent. He said to do my best but if I didn't get a first he wouldn't mind.'

'But if you don't get a first you won't get a job, will you?' said Eleanor anxiously.

'Not an Oxford job or a good schoolmastering job, I suppose,' said Tom. 'But father did ask me if I wanted to be an estate agent. I wonder how he knew.'

'He usually does,' said Eleanor. 'I must say it seems frightfully unfair that you have to find a job and I've got one. Does one have to do lots of exams to be an estate agent?'

Tom said he didn't really know. And anyway, he said, the girls seemed to get all the jobs now. But he said it without any bitterness, merely as a fact of nature.

'Perhaps,' said Eleanor. And then she stopped.

Tom asked perhaps what. But Eleanor said she had forgotten and Tom did not press her and then they got out the old croquet things from their box in the harness-room and found the little marking machine.

'They all look pretty mouldy,' said Tom eyeing the mallets and balls and posts, all much the worse for years of use followed by years put away in a dusty corner. The marking machine seemed to be stiff beyond repair, but Eleanor said she was sure Purse could get it going and then they found some half used tins of enamel paint and some brushes in fairly good repair and repainted the red, black, blue, and yellow till it was time for lunch. They worked in friendly silence, each occupied with private thoughts, Tom wondering if he would scrape through with a second and Eleanor thinking that when she went to Pomfret Towers she might be able to talk to Roddy Wicklow, the earl's brother-in-law and estate agent, to some useful purpose.

Meanwhile Mr Grantly had walked from the slight rise on which the church and rectory stood down the High Street of the little town. Before 1914 the High Street had been almost untouched; red-brick houses like Caldecott pictures and small friendly shops. But during the succeeding years progress had made alarming strides. Most of the old houses had become shops; a large multiple store had brought its own special red which clashed with the mellow red brick round it; the old coaching inn had put concrete all over its front garden and set up petrol pumps, the smaller inns and public houses had put plate glass in the place of their square window panes; the early nineteenth century Congregational Church, a not unpleasing stone building with windows set high in the wall the better to prevent the congregation being distracted by worldly sights, after being derelict for some years had been converted to a cinema and very badly converted too, so that the Society for the Protection of Ancient Buildings and the Georgian Society went nearly mad with rage and wrote letters to *The Times*: to which the chairman of the company who owned that and many other local cinemas replied that if anyone could prove that the amenities of Edgewood had been in any way lessened by turning an empty building to educational and cultural purposes and serving the Workers as well as the Privileged Classes, he would be glad to listen to what they had to say. But after this *The Times* very rightly lost interest in the affair in favour of a very boring correspondence about the need for a College of Empire Economics in Borioboola Gha, and Edgewood went to the pictures every Thursday and Saturday. Though, as Sir Edmund Pridham said, what They meant by Privileged Classes he didn't know, and to his mind the only Privileged Classes in Edgewood were the thirty or so allotment holders who had been allowed to dig up during the war and keep during the peace the field which had from beyond living memory been a football and cricket ground for the boys of Edgewood and a pleasant walking place for perambulators, away from the main road. After which the dispute became personal and acrimonious and languished to death in the back page of the *Barchester Chronicle*.

Among the few eighteenth century houses that had survived the Revolution was a fine red brick house known as the Old Bank House because it used to be a private bank when such places still existed. It stood right on the High Street with a few steps up to a white front door with a brass knocker and surmounted by an elegant shell canopy. It was three storeys high with well-proportioned sash windows. On one side of it was the doctor's house, on the other a stable yard with a wooden gate and behind it a biggish garden which ran down to the stream. For many years it had been a kind of House of Refuge for the Sowerby family who used to own Chaldicotes and had received various widowed or lonely relations, and for the last ten years or so had been inhabited by an elderly Miss Sowerby whose property it had become. By the time Peace had got well into its stride Miss Sowerby's income, which was mostly trust money in gas and railways, had sadly dwindled and with each piece of so-called nationalisation of important industries it grew less. Also Miss Sowerby did not grow any younger and after a winter of semi-freezing and semi-starvation at the hands of a very unpleasant cook-housekeeper she swallowed her pride and accepted the invitation of a widowed sister to go and live with her at Worthing where there were two good servants and central heating. As we have already heard, Mr Adams the wealthy ironmaster from Hogglestock had made an offer for her house and it was to meet him that the Rector took his way down the High Street.

In spite of progress Edgewood was still in the habit of walking into each other's houses, which, though the grammar defies our analysis, explains why the Rector walked up the four stone steps, turned the brass handle and went in. He looked to the left where the mahogany dining table and sideboard were shining with cleanness, for Miss Sowerby had views on polishing and always did it herself. He looked to the right where the long drawing room ran from front to back of the house, with its elegant shabby Chippendale furniture and its faded Chinese wall-paper. Both rooms were empty, so he went down the wide hall, pausing as he always did to admire the square staircase of perfect proportions in miniature, and so through the garden door and down a flagged path to where Miss Sowerby was doing useful things in her herbaceous border, which border was the pride of her heart and the cause of great jealousy from other gardeners, especially from the Dreadful Dowager who had never been able to grow Palafox Borealis in spite of all her gardeners and glass even before the war.

Though Miss Sowerby was elderly her hearing was remarkably acute and even as the Rector stepped onto the flagged walk she emerged from the border, straightened herself and came towards him. Dressed in an old black frock covered by a hessian apron with as many pockets as a herd of kangaroos and each pocket dripping raffia and secateurs, in gum boots, a very old felt hat with a dirty silk scarf round it and wearing old white kid gloves, she may have looked like a scarecrow, or Judy, or a female Guy Fawkes, but there was no doubt that she was County.

'Good morning, Mr Grantly,' said Miss Sowerby. 'How very good of you to come. It isn't any good my taking my glove off to shake hands because I'm just as dirty underneath. The seams rot, you know, with all the damp, and the earth gets through. Luckily I still have a few pairs of these left. My dear mother always bought everything by the dozen, or the six dozen, or the twelve dozen. I remember so well when my widowed sister was married, not that she was a widow *when* she married though she unfortunately became one as years went on, my dear mother gave her six dozen of everything and all beautifully hand marked in white linen thread. Quite useless now of course, because the laundries do such dreadful things. It was bad enough when they marked in red cotton though one could always pick it out, but now you will hardly believe me when I tell you that they have a rubber stamp with indelible ink and take no notice at all of my complaints.'

The Rector said his wife would sympathise fully with her, for her best nightgown which had been sent to the wash by mistake had come back with GRANTLEY in purple ink right across the front and he did think they might at least have spelt the name correctly.

'And how is Palafox?' he inquired.

'Ah,' said Miss Sowerby in a very knowing way, and plunging into the border again she beckoned the Rector to follow her, holding a large clump of lupins aside for him to pass. 'Look.'

The Rector, following the direction of her pointing finger, gazed with as much show of interest as he could muster on a clump of rather ugly serrated leaves, fleshy and covered with a kind of whitish bristles as if they had forgotten to shave, from which rose a short grey-green stalk crowned by a sticky knob from which depended, apparently, three strips of housemaid's flannel.

'So this is Palafox,' said the Rector, for once at a loss for a suitable pastoral comment. 'Most unusual, Miss Sowerby, *most* unusual.'

'Palafox Borealis,' Miss Sowerby corrected him. 'Anyone can grow Septentrionalis, even Victoria Norton. But mine is, I believe, the only Borealis in the county. The Royal

Horticultural would give their eyes to have one like it. When I let them show it last year,' said Miss Sowerby with the air of a queen conferring a favour, 'I was inundated with requests for the seeds. But I didn't part with any. They wouldn't know how to grow them.'

'Where are the seeds?' said the Rector.

'Aha!' said Miss Sowerby. 'They live in that knob at the top. But Palafox only flowers once in seven years. There won't be any seeds till 1955. And that's what the Horticultural *don't* know. There's the bell.'

And indeed from the house the little-used front door bell was jangling loudly, being one of those bells created to make callers ashamed of themselves and quite uncontrollable. Miss Sowerby released the Rector from the clump of lupins and went back to the house, the Rector following her, and opened the front door. On the doorstep was the powerful form of the Member for Barchester.

'Adams, that's my name. Sam Adams,' said that gentleman. 'And I may say I'm sorry I pulled your bell so hard. That wire wants a bit of tightening. The bell pull nearly came out in my hand.'

'Like Brugglesmith,' said Miss Sowerby, holding out her capable but dirty hand. 'How do you do. Come in.'

'I admit I don't quite take the relusion,' said Mr Adams, stepping into the hall and looking admiringly at its proportions and the square staircase beyond, 'but my little Heth would, that's my daughter, Miss Sowerby. She's a great reader and anything literary she's down on like a pack of wolves.'

'Kipling,' said Miss Sowerby. 'This is our Rector, Mr Adams. Mr Grantly.'

The two men shook hands.

'Glad to meet you, Rector,' said Mr Adams. 'That's a nice church you've got up there. I saw it as I was driving past and I said to myself, "If Miss Sowerby's house is as good as that church then Sam Adams is the man for it." And a lovelier house, Miss Sowerby, I may say I have seldom seen,' said Mr Adams looking round with a respectful admiration that made Miss Sowerby feel more at ease; for if she had to sell her house she would wish to sell it to someone who would love it. Otherwise she would almost have preferred to remain in it and die in a corner of cold and want of proper food.

'I expect you would like to see over it,' said Miss Sowerby, suddenly shedding the gardener and becoming the chatelaine. 'The dining-room and drawing-room I think you have already seen when you came with the agent. Let us go upstairs. Will you come too, Mr Grantly?'

The Rector said he ought to be writing his sermon for to-morrow but he would far rather look at the house, and if need be read one of his great-great-grandfather the Bishop's sermons.

'Quite right,' said Miss Sowerby approvingly. 'It does the people good to listen to something they can't understand. I have no patience with pap-feeding for congregations.'

'Give me a sermon with some Latin and Greek in it,' said Mr Adams unexpectedly. 'I never had much schooling, but it stands to reason if the Bible was written in Latin and Greek, well, Latin and Greek it was and I daresay they knew what they were about.'

The Rector said apologetically that the Old Testament was in Hebrew.

'Or Hebrew either,' said Mr Adams. 'It's all one. Now your staircase, Miss Sowerby. That would be about the beginning of the eighteenth century, I take it.'

'Sixteen-ninety, to be precise,' said Miss Sowerby. 'The top flight is later and is more elegant, but less handsome. Come up.'

She led the way to the first floor where Mr Adams truly admired the bedrooms and dressing rooms and told Miss Sowerby exactly where he would put bathrooms, a piece of information which that lady, who had never lived in a house with more than one bathroom and had spent most of her childhood in a house with none, far from taking amiss seemed to find interesting. They then went up the more elegant upper flight to the top floor where Mr Adams arranged for servants and for a nursery.

'You see, Miss Sowerby,' he said, 'my little Heth she's thinking of getting married this autumn and she'll want to visit her old Dad with the children when they come along. Forewarned is fourarmed as they say,' said Mr Adams, apparently envisaging a kind of Briareus, 'and Sam Adams likes to look ahead.'

'My widowed sister lived here during her early married life,' said Miss Sowerby, 'and these two rooms were her nurseries. You'd better make the kitchen-maid's room next door into a pantry and bathroom for your daughter's family. It has two windows and would make two nice little rooms.'

Although Mr Grantly had known Miss Sowerby for a good many years, he had never come across her domestic side and was rather touched by it. So evidently was Mr Adams, for he thanked her almost humbly and then they all went downstairs again and visited the kitchens which were built out at the side, behind the stable yard.

'Fine times the girls must have had too,' said Mr Adams, 'with the grooms and all so handy. I'll have to alter them a bit, as I'll only have my housekeeper and a couple of girls.'

'And where, pray, do you get girls?' asked Miss Sowerby, incredulous of such words.

'Well, Miss Sowerby,' said Mr Adams, 'it's this way. My works are at Hogglestock and Hogglestock's a big place now and most of the young girls go into my works. But there's always some that want to go into service and their mothers know Sam Adams will give them a fair deal. So one way and another I manage.'

'By the way, Mr Adams,' said the Rector, 'my grandmother's people came from Hogglestock. Crawley was the name. But I don't suppose anyone remembers them now.'

'That's right,' said Mr Adams. 'I've never heard the name myself though I was born and brought up there. Still, it takes all sorts to make a world and I'm glad to know an old Hogglestock family, and you can count on me, Rector, to put my hand in my pocket if your church needs anything. Me and my Heth we used to be chapel, but after the way the Reverend Enoch Arden talked at Hallbury the summer my Heth and me were there, mixing up politics and religion and saying Jack was as good as his master, well, we went up to the Old Town to the church there and the Reverend Dale was as nice an old gentleman as you would wish to see and he *was* a gentleman if you take my meaning, though he's dead now. And to cut a long story short,' said Mr Adams, suddenly shooting his left hand out of its cuff and looking at a solid wrist watch, 'Timon Tide waits for no man and I must be off. Miss Sowerby, it has been a great honour to see your house and my lawyers will be writing to yours – not but what they're all a lot of sharks,' said Mr Adams reflectively.

By this time they were in the hall again and moving towards the front door when, to the Rector's horror, Miss Sowerby who had hitherto stood up manfully against Mr Adams's personality, suddenly sat down on a seat of lacquered wood and cane and taking a dirty bandanna handkerchief out of some recess of her apron, wiped her eyes.

'My dear Miss Sowerby,' said the Rector, who had never seen his hostess show any of the softer emotions.

'It's talking business,' said Mr Adams. 'I've noticed it always upsets the ladies. Miss Sowerby, if you feel you don't want to part with this house, say the word. Sam Adams is a home bird himself and I wouldn't like it having to leave a house I was fond of. Say the word and I'll call my lawyers off,' he added, as though lawyers were a peculiarly savage race of bloodhounds.

'It's not that,' said Miss Sowerby, wiping her eyes and choking a little.

'If it's the money,' said Mr Adams, 'name your price. I know a good thing when I see it and Sam Adams is a warm man though he made it all himself, and he won't haggle over a matter of five hundred pounds or so with a lady.'

'It's not that,' said Miss Sowerby, making a great effort to control herself. 'I wasn't thinking of the money. I think your offer was very fair, Mr Adams. But when you said you would tell your lawyers to write to mine, I was afraid you didn't want the house.'

'I do want it,' said Mr Adams. 'And if I wasn't talking to a lady I'd say I do want it and I'm going to have it. I've paid the deposit to the agent. But if you don't want to sell that's that. I wouldn't if it were mine,' he added, looking lovingly at the plaster of cornice and ceiling.

'Can I help you, Miss Sowerby?' said the Rector, who having come in answer to Miss Sowerby's appeal felt he ought to do something, though he didn't quite know what.

'I *don't* want to sell the house,' said Miss Sowerby, who had regained her composure. 'But I can't afford to live here and if I can't live here I want you to. You understand about the house, and the house will take to you. The sooner you can arrange the business the better I shall be pleased. I can be out of here in a week. My sister at Worthing is quite ready to receive me. *Please*, Mr Adams.'

To this appeal there was but one answer. Mr Adams, more touched than he liked to admit, promised to do all in his power to expedite matters and Miss Sowerby almost kissed his hand as she said good-bye.

'There is just one thing I must tell you about the house, Mr Adams,' she said. 'It likes a mistress. I hope your daughter will love it.'

'If she is my daughter she will,' said Mr Adams in a Roman manner. 'But my Heth won't be mistress here for long. She's going to be married, as I think I mentioned before. Still my housekeeper Miss Hoggett, she's an old Hogglestock family too, will keep everything nice, so don't you worry, Miss Sowerby. Good-bye.'

The wealthy ironmaster got into his car and was driven away.

'Well, may I congratulate you?' said Mr Grantly to Miss Sowerby. 'We all wish you weren't going and we shall miss you very much, but I believe the Bank House will be in safe hands.'

'It will,' said Miss Sowerby, adding 'Thank God,' though as she told her widowed sister later, it seemed presumptuous to use such an expression before the Rector, but something made her feel she had to say it. So the Rector went back wondering, as he often did, whether it was really an essential part of his duties to rally to elderly female parishioners in their hour of need when one always found one wasn't really wanted. Then his truly kind self told him that readiness to help was never wasted even if the help were not needed and he laughed and went on with his sermon.

Miss Sowerby watched him go up the High Street. Then she went into the Bank House and shut the front door. Alone in her beloved home she straightened a few things that Mr Adams's passage had moved and then stood at the foot of the stairs, reflecting on the morning's work.

'Housekeepers!' she said. 'What this house needs is a mistress.'

2

Lunch could not be liver because of the thoring out advised by the butcher, but was the Sunday joint instead, and a fair-sized joint too with six ration books in the kitchen and five in the dining-room, for Tom's ration book had been confiscated by his college where the college servants did very nicely out of the young gentlemen's books and the young gentlemen had to go several times a week to British Restaurants.

'I don't know why,' said Tom, who had been harrowing his mother by telling her what a rush it was to get food and how one usually felt hungry in spite of parcels from home, 'British seems to mean something rather horrid now. Anyway British Restaurants aren't much fun.'

His sister Grace, who was a keen if ignorant and bigoted politician, said it was because Lord Woolton wasn't running the food. And anyway, said Eleanor, Civic Restaurants were just as bad, because she knew a girl who ran the Barchester one and no one would believe the hours she had to work and quite often had to take things home at night to make cakes and things for next day and really not enough fat, because the meals had to cost so little.

'You ought to learn logic,' said her brother Henry, on which subject Grace was prepared to argue quite indefinitely with no premises at all, had not Tom, returning to the subject of the word British, said what about British Railways.

'I must say,' said Mrs Grantly, 'it all seems very silly, because when you said Great Western you knew which railway you meant, and now you don't.'

It was not so much the confusion, said Mr Grantly, that he deprecated, as the hideous lettering of the words British Railways on the innocent locomotives. The kind of lettering, he said, that cheap printers used for trade cards.

'If I were an engine and they painted that on me,' said Henry, 'I'd run off the line and kill the Minister of Transport, whoever he is,' which remark led to a discussion as to who the principal holders of Cabinet rank were, which discussion combined ignorance with an almost total lack of interest, and talk veered to the far more interesting topic of when the croquet season should be inaugurated. Grace and Henry wanted to start at once, but as the balls and mallets and posts would not be dry for twenty-four hours or so, it was agreed to christen the lawn as it were on Sunday afternoon and collect some friends. This was not so easy as it sounds, for nearly all their young acquaintances seemed to be married or away on jobs.

'What we want is two other men and two other girls,' said Henry. 'I say. What about Charles Belton? He's a schoolmaster, but he often gets a Sunday off. And then we could have – no we couldn't. Gosh! there doesn't seem to be anyone left now.'

'Why not those nice young Dales from Southbridge?' said Mrs Grantly. 'He's a schoolmaster too, so he and Charles would have something to talk about.'

'I say, father,' said Grace. 'If we can't get another man, will *you* play?'

'Tact, tact, my girl!' said her brother Henry.

'Oh, shut up,' said Grace. 'You know I didn't mean it like that, father. Oh, do.'

'I am not proud,' said Mr Grantly, 'but do you happen to remember, Grace, that there is a special Mothers' Union service at three o'clock?'

His daughter's lips formed the words, How ghastly, but she so far controlled herself as to say anyway they could play after tea, which was agreed to by all parties, the only objection lodged being by Tom, who had to get back to Oxford on Sunday evening. But the difficulties of others are light in comparison with one's own and his brother and his sisters said they were sure there was a six something that went as far as Didcot and there must be trains from Didcot to Oxford.

'Not on British Railways, my girl,' said Tom. 'Do you realize that it is quite difficult now to get a through train from Paddington to Oxford unless you go by that nice little toy line that passes through Princes Risborough?'

But no one else was interested in through trains from London to Oxford and the subject dropped.

'I say!' said Grace.

'What do you say?' said her father.

'Does anyone know where the old book of croquet rules is?' said Grace. 'We've got the marker going and some white stuff, but how long ought the sides to be and those lines that run down parallel into the other lines?'

No one knew. So as soon as lunch was over a kind of treasure hunt took place in all the most likely places, such as an old tin trunk with mouldering straps in the attic, a disused corn bin in the stables, and various tallboys and presses in the unused bedrooms. A great deal of valueless material was turned out and Mrs Grantly garnered a rich harvest for her next jumble sale, but nowhere were croquet rules to be found, till Grace thought of looking in the drawers of the kitchen dresser, because she said she distinctly remembered Doris showing the booklet to her and saying Purse had found it in one of the attics and might he keep it. And under a collection of rather repellent bits of material, known to the kitchen as the cloths, the book was found. A second hunt then had to be made for the measure, joy of all Grantlys when young, which lived in a flattish round leather case and after use was wound up again with a kind of brass double-jointed handle. Which description will be perfectly clear to those who know the measure in question, and as for those who do not, their state is the more to be pitied.

The whole paraphernalia having been at last assembled, the young Grantlys set themselves to measure the oblong of the croquet court. It is hardly necessary to describe the result of their amateur efforts, for most of us have in our time tried to mark a croquet or a tennis lawn, and most of us have had the mortification of seeing our oblong come out as a rhomb, or what we can only describe as a sort of scalene rectangle. After about an hour and a half of this exercise, during which no tempers were quite lost, a halt was made for tea.

'Look here, Eleanor,' said Henry, 'it's really quite easy. I know what we ought to have done. You take a bit of string the length of one side and peg it down at the corner and make a circle, at least a semi-circle; and then you do the same thing at the other corner and where they cut each other is the middle of the width of the court.'

He paused to admire his own ingenuity.

'Anyway,' said Grace, 'the place where the bits of circles met might be in the middle of the lawn from side to side but it wouldn't be any use for up and down. I wish Marcia Yates were here. She's awfully good at geometry.'

Her mother asked who Marcia Yates was.

'Oh, a girl in the fifth,' said Grace. 'Her father keeps greyhounds and she's going to a finishing school near Oxford where they only have ten girls and her mother took her to the Derby and then wrote an excuse to Miss Pettinger to say it was cultural to see the Derby and the Pettinger was furious.'

Her father asked her how she knew her headmistress's reaction to Mrs Yates's ideas of culture.

'Oh, one of the prefects reported me for talking in prep three days running,' said Grace. 'I was only asking Jennifer Gorman if her mother was going to let her have a perm and she didn't know till the last day, so I had to go to the Pettinger's room to have a talk about the honour of the school and while I was there the letter came from Marcia's mother and Miss Pettinger forgot I was there and went right off the deep end. Come on, Henry, let's have another go.'

Mr and Mrs Grantly also came to see how things were going, prepared to interfere with theories of their own, but during tea Purse, who had previously been watching them, had taken the matter in hand, and on the lawn lay a white oblong of impeccable rectanglitude.

'How on earth did you do it, Purse?' said Mrs Grantly.

Purse said he took the two pieces of string that was the longness that Mr Tom said and put those little things for the corners in the ground and drawed the loines.

'Absolute pitch, if you take my meaning,' said Tom reverently. 'Look mother. It's as square as – I mean as oblong as – well anyway Purse has done the job.'

The Rector said it reminded him of Joseph Vance and the equal sides of the triangle, but as none of his children had read the works of William de Morgan they failed to take the allusion, considering it to be the sort of thing father was apt to say.

After supper Henry rang up the school at Beliers Priory and secured Charles Belton, and his sister Eleanor rang up Southbridge School to ask the Robin Dales.

'Oh dear,' said the gentle voice of Anne Dale. 'Robin is on duty to-morrow. I could come, because I've got some petrol, but I don't expect you want an odd woman,' to which Eleanor replied truthfully that they would love to see Anne whether they got another man or not, and anyway her father would play if nobody else did. But all efforts to find a disengaged fourth man were vain that evening.

Next morning, between breakfast and church, the Rector tried to ring up Mr Wickham, the Noel Mertons' agent, about a cow. Mr Wickham was out, but Mrs Bunce the cowman's wife who came in to oblige after breakfast said he was over at Northbridge Manor. So the Rector rang up the Mertons' house and was answered by Mrs Noel Merton, formerly Miss Lydia Keith.

'I'm awfully sorry, Mr Grantly,' said Lydia, 'but Mr Wickham isn't here. He did look in, but he has gone over to the Crofts at Southbridge to do some bird exploring with Mrs Crofts. Was it anything important?'

Not very, said the Rector, only a cow, and added that they had been marking the croquet lawn and wanted a fourth man or else he would have to play himself which he didn't want to do.

'You wouldn't like Colin, would you?' said Lydia, alluding to her dearly loved brother who was a very successful barrister in London, famed for his knowledge of railway law. 'I have to be in with the children this afternoon and Noel has promised to go to the Brandons and Colin has nothing to do, and he's leaving us this evening anyway.'

The Rector accepted the loan of Colin Keith with pleasure and reported the news to his family. It was received with gratitude, if not with enthusiasm, for Colin Keith was secretly considered a bit too much of a Londoner by Barsetshire. But a man was a man.

All being settled and the croquet lawn marked, there was nothing to do but to sleep through Saturday night, have breakfast on Sunday morning, go to church, have lunch (which was the liver, quite beautifully cooked by Edna with lots of onions) and set out the croquet things which had dried nicely during the night. The only member of the family who was not quite enjoying himself was Tom, for the thought of the train to Didcot which might connect with a train to Oxford lay on his mind. He had attempted to find out from Barchester Central: but here he met his match, for though the Barchester line and the Oxford line were both British Railways by Tyranny of Parliament, each still thought of itself as superior to the other. And long may this state of things remain and long may the little mineral railway between Ravenglass and Eskdale, with its equipment by the great Hornby, run backwards and forwards with the engine-driver sitting outside his engine. Barchester Central had been kind but not hopeful, rather implying that once one got to Didcot one was on such a barbarous railway system that no man alive could predict with accuracy which trains would run whither, nor when. However several years in the army had taught Tom patience and to rely on his own resources, so he did his best to forget the gloom ahead.

The first guest was Anne Dale who brought with her apologies and regrets from her husband.

'And anyway,' said Anne to Mrs Grantly, whom she secretly found more sympathetic than her children, 'Robin isn't very good at games because of his pretence foot. Do you know, Mrs Grantly, he still wakes up sometimes in the morning and thinks his foot has come back, poor darling. I'm so glad Tom didn't get badly wounded or anything.'

'So am I,' said Mrs Grantly. 'The chief worry now is that he wanted to do classics when he got out of the army and of course we agreed, but we have found that his heart is really in the land, and it is all rather dispiriting.'

'Robin says,' said Anne, whose friends occasionally laughed at her, though very kindly, for beginning so many sentences with those words, 'that the classics are the most useful thing you can learn, because whatever you do they come in useful. He used to say Virgil and things to himself when he was in hospital after his foot was blown off at Anzio. And if anything worries him in the House, he always takes some Greek or Latin to bed with him. I am sure if Tom gets a job on the land he will find Latin just as helpful,' which piece of special pleading if it did not entirely convince Mrs Grantly did cheer her a good deal, and she blamed herself for not being grateful enough to a Providence which had brought her son back with all his arms and legs.

Then Colin Keith arrived in his car for which he had got some extra petrol, though why nobody quite knew, least of all Colin himself who was quite happy to profit by the mistake. The two younger Grantlys were at first a little suspicious of a man who lived in London when he might live in Barsetshire, but his wholehearted admiration of the re-painting conquered their distrust and Grace in particular attached herself to him with the uncivilised ardour of a sixth form girl. And then Charles Belton came on his bicycle, a little late because a boy called Addison had offered to pump the tyres up for him and forgotten to do it, so that Charles had to dismount and do it himself. But his native cheerfulness was unimpaired by this misfortune and he too fell into ecstasies over the new paint.

'It's a tournament,' said Grace who had, unasked, constituted herself a kind of General Manager. 'First four of us play and then the other four, and then the two ones that have won play against each other. I bag Charles.'

'And I bag Anne,' said Henry, who felt he would be safe with her.

'I say, mother,' said Tom. 'We forgot to get another girl. I bag having you for my partner. Oh do, mother.'

It was so flattering to be appealed to by her elder son that Mrs Grantly quite overlooked the fact that she was but a last moment substitute and expressed her willingness to play.

'Then that leaves Eleanor and Colin,' said Grace. 'Bags I playing first, against Anne and Henry.'

But her mother said Tom ought to play first as he had to leave early, so she and Tom with blue and red took the field against Charles and Grace.

'Is it real croquet, or golf croquet?' said Charles Belton to his partner.

'Golf,' said Grace. 'We did have an old set ages ago for real croquet, with those lovely wide hoops you can't miss.'

Charles said his people used to have one too, with a kind of triumphal arch of crossed hoops in the middle and a bell depending from them which jingled when a ball went through, and everyone was allowed to put their foot on the ball while they hit the other and everyone lost their temper, which information so captivated Grace's virgin heart that she told Charles all about how beastly the French mistress was and how awful it was that she had a terrific crush on Miss Floyd, the maths mistress, but never got more than B for geometry and quite often B minus or

C; to all of which Charles, whose own school days were not so very distant and who liked schoolgirls, lent an attentive ear, with results almost as fatal as in the case of Desdemona and Othello, except that Charles had fair hair and blue eyes.

Charles and Grace were dashing and unreliable, now and then bringing off brilliant coups by sheer luck, and were mostly yards apart. Tom and his mother were more steady and played as far as possible a mutually supporting game, so that they had opportunities to talk, which in the busy crowded life of the Rectory did not often occur.

'I'm sorry about your classics, darling,' said Mrs Grantly, while her opponents were at the other end of the lawn. 'But I'm sure they will always be a help. My father learnt Greek and Latin at Eton and he always read his Greek testament in church. He said it helped him to get through the sermon. I do wish you had known him,' for her father, a hard-working landowner in the Omnium country, had caught pneumonia from a very chilly ride home after a long day's hunting and died, soon after his daughter had married Major Grantly's grandson. 'You are rather like him sometimes.'

'Perhaps it's him that makes me love the country,' said Tom, with more earnestness than grammar. 'I can't think why I was silly enough to think of being a don or a schoolmaster. I'm awfully sorry, mother.'

But whether that last remark expressed regret for having elected to read for Greats, or for having missed a hoop by several inches, we do not know, and it was not till Grace and Charles had knocked the balls all over the field that red and blue came together again.

'Never mind, darling,' said Mrs Grantly, continuing their conversation. 'As soon as you have done your exams we will think of a plan, and I am sure something to do with the land is the most sensible and patriotic thing one can do now.'

'My dear mother,' said Tom, carefully destroying as he spoke Charles's hopes of the next hoop, 'you know you would say that even if I became a trades union leader or a saxophonist at a night club. But I do value it all the same. And I swear I'll work at whatever it is as soon as I'm through Schools.'

'Of course you will,' said his mother, thinking all the while how she could never even begin to understand what her eldest son had experienced during the war; and that is what no mother, no wife, no woman, will ever understand, try as she may.

Meanwhile the Rector had escaped from the Mothers' Union and came out to watch the croquet. Anne Dale, who had a kind heart and gentle manners, came and sat with him in case he needed company, so that Henry had to attach himself to Colin and Eleanor.

'And how is your father, my dear?' said Mr Grantly.

Anne said very busy, as he always was, and so was her mother, but she hoped they were getting abroad in July. And then she said, in her rather grown-up way, how glad she was to see all the Grantlys again. And what were the children doing?

'Child yourself,' said Mr Grantly affectionately. 'You must be the youngest Housemaster's wife on record,' to which Anne said rather proudly that she was of age. But having thus asserted herself she relented and prattled away to the Rector about Southbridge School and the masters and the boys and how nice the Headmaster and his wife Mr and Mrs Everard Carter were. The Rector asked after her husband.

'Oh he is very well, thank you,' said Anne. 'His foot does bother him sometimes, I mean the one that isn't there, but he manages to do pretty well everything. Do you know, Mr Grantly, I think the classics are a great help to him. When his foot hurts in the evening he reads Virgil and things and feels much better. He says they are a kind of armour against horrid things. What do you think?'

'I agree with your husband, my dear,' said the Rector, 'though I admit that this Government have invented things against which even the classics are not a certain shield.'

'Still they *are* a sort of shield,' said Anne. 'And Robin was so glad that Tom was doing classics, because they will always be useful to him, whatever he does.'

The Rector, who had known Anne Fielding as she was before her marriage all her life, was interested and amused by her talk. Undoubtedly little Anne had changed, had come out, a great deal since she became Mrs Robin Dale. The timid, rather delicate child, girl, young woman was still there, but with an air of slightly precocious assurance combined with the real, though impersonal kindness of a Housemaster's wife. That her parents' daughter should be kind and competent was not surprising. Both Sir Robert and Lady Fielding were hard workers, giving time, brains, energy, and human feeling to every city or county job they undertook, and Anne must have inherited much from them. Something she had gained from the old governess, Miss Bunting, who had helped her through a difficult year and encouraged her to read and love the great heritage of English writing. By Miss Bunting her natural sweetness had been strengthened to a kind of universal courtesy and from Miss Bunting she had learnt quickly an old-fashioned but none the less important quality of appearing at any rate to give her whole attention to the person or the subject in hand. Mr Grantly would have wagered a golden sovereign (a few of which he had illegally hoarded to show his grandchildren, while quite aware that they would probably not take the slightest interest) that Anne was deliberately telling him that the classics helped her husband so that he might feel that Tom was also laying up treasure; for Tom's affairs had been discussed at Southbridge School, where the Rector had many friends.

'All the charm of all the Muses often flowering in a lonely word,' said Anne Dale, ever mindful of her favourite poet Lord Tennyson.

'Yes indeed,' said the Rector thoughtfully, and seeing that he had retired into his own thoughts Anne Dale quietly retired into hers; which were chiefly how much she loved Robin, and what fun the boys were, and a thought and a hope for the early days of the spring when the earth began to turn from darkness to the lengthening days.

The game had now come to an end with a triumph for Mrs Grantly and her elder son whose quiet and solid play had routed the brilliant but erratic fooling of Charles and Grace, and the ground was free for the second round of the tournament. Anne was ready. Colin Keith and Eleanor were sitting nearby on the stone parapet above the ha-ha. Only Henry was missing.

His brother and his younger sister were raising their voices in yells for him when he appeared round the corner from the stable yard looking rather hot.

'Hurry up,' Grace shouted. 'We're waiting for you. Where have you been?'

Henry, looking slightly confused, said nowhere. He just went for a little turn on his bicycle, he added, and then he came over to Anne, his partner.

'You do look hot,' said Anne. 'Will you take black or yellow?'

Henry said he felt like both and didn't care which he had,

so Anne, who knew one should not ask men questions till they were disposed to answer them, placidly knocked the yellow ball to its starting point. Colin, who imported even into a Sunday game of croquet an accurate and painstaking mind, at once got his ball into a position peculiarly annoying to his opponents.

'Dash!' said Henry, as his ball took matters into its own hands and rolled to the wrong side of the hoop, and his temper was not improved by Grace saying in a loud voice to Charles that the little depression where the ball had settled was known as Mug's Home.

'Never mind,' said Anne. 'We had a place just like that in father's garden at Hallbury. I always got into it.'

Henry was grateful for this sympathy and felt how right he had been to bag an understanding person like Anne for his partner.

'As a matter of fact,' he said, 'I really went down to the post office. Mrs Goble there is a friend of mine and I thought perhaps there might be a letter and she'd let me have it.'

Anne said there wasn't a post on Sunday.

'I know,' said Henry. 'But I thought a Saturday letter might have got left behind or something, so I thought I'd just ask.'

This Anne seemed to think a very reasonable idea, which so encouraged Henry that he took advantage of their opponents being out of earshot to say to Anne, 'It's my papers. I'm waiting to be posted to the Barsetshire Yeomanry and I might hear any day. It's *awful* having to wait from lunch time on Saturday till breakfast time on Monday.'

'How *awful* for you,' said Anne, her large serious eyes growing dark at the thought of a letter delayed.

'Most people don't understand,' said Henry. 'It isn't everyone's luck to get into the Barsetshires. I saw the Colonel, he's an old friend of father's, and he as good as promised me when I was through my OCTU. Do you think he's forgotten?'

But Anne, though entirely ignorant of the military world or its ways, was so certain that everything would be all right that Henry's spirits rose again and his ball went where he wished and presently he was away at the far end and Anne found herself by Colin Keith. The Fieldings and the Keiths, both connected with the legal world, had always been on good terms, but between Colin and Anne there had been no particular link, for Colin was fifteen years older than Anne and spent his working life in London.

'And how is law?' said Anne.

'You know you don't care in the least,' said Colin. 'Don't come the Housemaster's wife over me, Anne. Lord! To think that when I was an assistant master at Southbridge you were in the nursery. All eyes and beak you were then.'

'Were you a master at Southbridge?' said Anne. 'Robin never told me.'

'Because he didn't know, my love,' said Colin. 'It was well before the war when Birkett was Headmaster, and I must have been far more trouble than I was worth. Only for a term.'

'Well, I hope you will come to see Robin and me,' said Anne with her usual grave courtesy. 'You will find things changed a good deal, I expect.'

At which Colin burst out laughing, though in a very friendly way so that Anne could not be hurt, and they got on very well. So well indeed that Eleanor Grantly, whose partner Colin was, had to call him twice to come and play his ball.

The thought of tea expedited the finish of the game which was won by Colin and Eleanor; entirely, so Eleanor said, by Colin's play. And then they all went indoors, for this was not one of the summers when meals out of doors were any pleasure at all; as indeed they very seldom are, for if there isn't a wind there are gnats and mosquitoes; and if there is a wind no one wishes to sit in it, except the Dowager Lady Norton who had been a Lady in Waiting to Queen Alexandra and was impervious to every kind of discomfort. During the meal the Rector described his experience at the Old Bank House and how Mr Adams seemed determined to buy it.

'Oh dear,' said his wife. 'Will that be a good thing?'

The Rector said he saw no reason it shouldn't be, adding that personally he liked Mr Adams and if one had to have new rich, Adams was an excellent sample.

'Of course I have heard a lot about him,' said Mrs Grantly, 'but I've never come across him. Does anyone know anything about him?'

As so often happens when one throws a question into space, replies came from quarters most unexpected by Mrs Grantly. Charles Belton said Mr Adams was a great friend of his mother's, and Heather Adams came two or three times a year to spend a few nights at Harefield though he didn't much care for her himself. And if it were not surprising enough that Mrs Belton, herself a Thorne and pure county, should have the rich iron-master's daughter to stay with her, Anne Dale volunteered the information that the Adamses had been at Hallbury for a whole summer during the war and first she thought they were rather horrid, but now she liked them very much, especially Mr Adams, who often came in to see her mother if he was near the Close.

'And Heather is being married this autumn,' Anne continued. 'To young Mr Pilward, the brewer's son.'

'Not Ted Pilward?' said Tom Grantly.

Anne said that was his name.

'Lord!' said Tom. 'We were in Iceland together and we tried putting soap down a geyser, but it didn't work. Rum things one did in the war. I must look him up. Perhaps he'd give me a job in the brewery. One of our men at Paul's who got a First in Greats last year got a job straight away in a big firm in Liverpool or somewhere that picks over the dumps where the corporation dust bins are emptied. Some people do have luck.'

Feeling the slight bitterness in his voice his sister Eleanor looked at him anxiously, but the mood passed and all the younger people planned a croquet tournament in which the Bishop and Lady Norton were to be caught cheating and disqualified, till Eleanor said they had better play the finals, which were herself and Colin against Mrs Grantly and Tom.

'I say, mother,' said Tom, looking at the grandfather clock which had belonged to Archdeacon Grantly. 'I'll have to go if I'm to catch that train at Barchester Central.'

'You haven't much time,' said his mother anxiously. 'The bus passes the corner in five minutes.'

'No it doesn't, mother,' said Grace. 'They took that bus off last week. Didn't you see the notice at the bus stop in the High Street?'

'That's torn it,' said Tom and darkness fell upon the party till Colin Keith asked if he could help.

'I've got my car and some petrol,' he said. 'I can take you to Barchester.'

'Oh, I say, that's marvellous. Thanks awfully,' said Tom.

Mrs Grantly, with the insane desire to make unnecessary trouble that besets us all from time to time, said wouldn't it be taking Colin rather out of his way.

'Not a bit,' said Colin. 'I was going to cut across by Crabtree Parva and Framley, but I can just as well go by Barchester.'

'But Framley's the wrong way,' said Grace, eager to show her knowledge. 'Northbridge is bang south and Framley's bang north.'

'But I'm not going to Northbridge,' said Colin, amused. 'I'm going to Oxford to spend the night with the Fanshawes.'

Upon which the whole Grantly family talked at once, some saying What a piece of luck, others Wasn't it Mr Fanshawe who married Jessica Dean's eldest sister, others again Then Tom could stay for the finals after all.

'Will you have supper with us, Colin?' said Mrs Grantly.

Colin thanked her but said he had promised to get to the Fanshawes for a late supper, so if Tom didn't mind he ought to be going as soon as the croquet was over, and the party went out again to the lawn. By now it was decidedly chilly, like nearly all that summer, and to sit and watch the game was no particular pleasure. Anne said she must go home or Robin would miss her and she would ring up later on to hear who had won. So she said her good-byes and her thanks and Henry took her to the stable yard and opened the gates for her car.

'It's been splendid,' said Henry, alluding we think rather to Anne's encouragement than to a peaceful game of Rectory croquet.

'I loved it,' said Anne. 'Oh, and Henry, I don't think that letter will come just yet. I know several of our old boys who are waiting for their papers and they nearly all had to wait longer than they expected, but they all came in the end. Do try not to worry. Could you do a job of some sort, or some reading?'

'I say, you *are* a schoolmistress,' said Henry, in a kind of grudging admiration for her organising powers. 'The trouble is I don't know what jobs I *do* want. And if I thought I wanted something I'd probably find I didn't, like poor old Tom who wanted to do Latin and Greek and now he wants to go on the land. I don't know. All very unsatisfactory, that's what it is. I wish there were a war and then they'd have me quick enough.'

'Well, don't wish that, Henry,' said Anne with her little air of wisdom. 'It might happen. Come and see Robin one week-end and you'll feel much better,' for she still believed and probably would always believe that in her adored Robin lay the panacea for every human ill.

'I daresay you're right,' said Henry. 'But I do wish that letter would come.'

'It will,' said Anne. 'I promise you it will,' and she drove away, leaving Henry a little comforted. So he went back to the lawn and found Eleanor and Colin winning and presently they won.

'I say,' said Grace, 'there ought to be a prize.'

Her brother Tom said Nonsense, this was a strictly amateur affair, but Grace insisted on giving the winners some of her chocolate ration which touched Colin very much, and so pleased was Grace by his pleasure that she hung about him in a quite embarrassing way, with the simple adoration which she had up till now kept for a favoured mistress or a hockey captain. No one appeared to object. Mrs Grantly had decided some years previously to leave her children alone unless they were being outrageously rude or deliberately giving pain, and as Grace's behaviour did not come under either of those headings she thought it best to pretend she didn't notice it. Her elder son guessed her feelings and caught her eye, saying 'schoolgirls, schoolgirls' in a mock-elderly way that made her laugh. Then Mr Grantly said Good Gracious it was nearly time for evening service and Colin said he really must go, so Tom collected his luggage, which consisted of an army kitbag and a long woollen scarf and a very dirty mackintosh, and the whole party went to see the travellers off.

'Do let's do this again soon,' said Colin as he thanked his hostess.

'Certainly,' said Mrs Grantly, speeding the parting guest as much as politeness allowed, for it was almost half past six.

'It won't be so nice next time,' said Eleanor.

Colin asked why not. Things weren't, said Eleanor, without trying to explain, and possibly she was right.

'Then we'll do something else,' said Colin. 'If you ever come to town, let's do a theatre. I expect you stay with an aunt or a friend to shop. People mostly do, except my sister Lydia who clings to Northbridge like a limpet to a rock. That's settled then. Good-bye.'

He drove off with Tom while the rest of the family went to the evening service and thought their various thoughts. For though there may be people who think of nothing beside the immemorial words (when not revised or deposited or otherwise defaced) and the familiar, friendly, if uninspired hymns (for as for *Songs of Praise* and their like we cannot away with them) and the noble music of the psalms (which we are glad to say Mr Grantly caused to be sung as the *Book of Common Prayer* intended, refusing to cut and mangle them), to most of us church is rather like Grace's game of unravelling and after a period of day-dream or coma we come to with a jerk and try not to look as if we had lost ourselves. And we hope these things may be forgiven to us and do it all over again next Sunday.

Mrs Grantly had tried to school herself to concentrate and attend, but the flesh, or rather the mind, is weak and so much did Tom's future in civil life and Henry's future as a conscript occupy her thoughts, not to speak of wishing Grace's maiden affections for young men, though Colin Keith was not so very young, were more restrained, and fearing on no grounds at all that Eleanor would never get married because she did her Red Cross work so well, besides the usual thoughts about rations and getting the coal allocation before the next rush began and determining that at her age she need not bother about the New Look, that she might almost as well have stayed at home and worried there, alone. But not quite, for in spite of all the kaleidoscope of thoughts and anxieties some of the peace of the evening service flowed into her mind and heart. And also, which is quite important though in a different way, she saw Edna and Doris and the two elder children of shame all behaving very well, and she knew if she had been lazy about the outward act of church going, Edna and Doris would also have lapsed, and the cheerful children of shame would have been cheerful heathens and not learnt to keep still. So she made a kind of general act of contrition in her heart without being able to put it into words and determined to do better next time: knowing well that she would do exactly the same thing over again next Sunday.

And now, the labours of the day being over, the county turned to its Sunday evening amusement of telephoning, which was also the amusement of the various young ladies at the telephone exchanges, for except within Greater Barchester which now includes Hogglestock in its area, there were no automatic telephones. Now was Miss Palmyra Phipps (called after Mrs Palmer of Worsted) in her element as telephone queen, helping callers whom she liked, deliberately obstructing Lady Norton, listening to conversations and making helpful suggestions, telling Mrs Birkett at Worsted it was no good her trying to get on to Mrs Everard Carter at Southbridge because Mrs Carter's Nannie had been speaking to young Mrs Brandon's Nannie and said Mrs

Everard Carter had gone away for the week-end to Mr Carter's mother in Devonshire.

Eleanor Grantly had tried several times in vain to get on to Mrs Freddy Belton at Harefield to ask her about some detail of Hospital Library work, for Mrs Freddy (so called to distinguish her from her mother-in-law) was formerly Miss Susan Dean the extremely efficient Depot Librarian. But it was a bad cross-country connection and after several vain attempts she begged the exchange to put her through as soon as they could, which they very obligingly promised to do and entirely forgot, owing to the joy of hearing Lord Stoke and Mr Palmer, who were both deaf, deliberately misunderstanding each other about a heifer. Then Henry rang up a friend who was also waiting for his papers and talked for what Grace, who wanted to speak to Jennifer Gorman and find out when her mother was going to let her have her perm re-set, considered an unconscionably long time; though it was no longer than the conversation Grace had while Eleanor was waiting to get her connection to Harefield. At last Henry, after having said the same thing several times in much the same words, rang off and even while he was looking up the number of yet another friend in the same position, the bell rang.

'It's for me,' said Henry. 'Hullo, Bonky. What? Oh I say. I'm frightfully sorry. Here, Eleanor! it's your boss,' and he handed the receiver to his sister.

'Lady Pomfret speaking,' said that lady's voice, for she had not a secretary and did most of her husband's telephoning as well as her own. 'Is that you, Miss Grantly.'

Eleanor said it was.

'Lord Pomfret and I would be very glad if you could come to us next week-end,' said Lady Pomfret's voice. 'I shall have the car and will take you back with me on Saturday morning. And I hope your brother will come too.'

Eleanor accepted for herself and said, with unfeigned regret, that her brother was still at Oxford, but would be down in about a fortnight.

'Then you must both come later,' said Lady Pomfret. 'And you will come next week-end. I shan't be at the office on Monday as I have to go to London,' and she gave Eleanor a few instructions about letters to be written, said good-night and rang off.

Eleanor at once took the news to her parents, who were playing picquet. They were glad to hear that their daughter was to have a treat or reward for all the hard work she did, and speculated as to the kind of life she would lead.

'It was about 1937 that we last went to the Towers, wasn't it?' said Mrs Grantly to her husband. 'Old Lord Pomfret was rather overpowering but a very good host and his wife was still very beautiful. And they had that nice secretary, Miss Merriman, who went to Lady Emily Leslie afterwards.'

'Was it great fun?' said Eleanor.

'It was,' said her father. 'It is a revolting and uncomfortable house, but when you have dozens of servants it doesn't matter. There was no central heating of course, but we had huge fires everywhere and the housemaid lit your bedroom fire before you got up. That was the year old Major Foster, who was Lord Pomfret's heir, died abroad somewhere and his son came to the Towers to learn how to be an earl, poor young man.'

Eleanor asked if that was the one that was Lord Pomfret now, because he seemed exactly like an earl when she saw him once at the Depot.

'And he married Sally Wicklow whose brother was under the old estate agent, cross old fellow called Hoare,' said the Rector, taking up the story, for he dearly loved county history and maintained that one could not talk about it too often because the spoken word kept old things alive. 'He resigned soon afterwards and Wicklow has been agent ever since. How Pomfret gets through the work he does I do not know. I have a strong suspicion that he couldn't get through it without her. She has a head on her shoulders and good health and old Lord Pomfret used to say she had the best hands in the county,' said the Rector, musing over the past. 'Well, enjoy yourself, my dear.'

Eleanor said she was sure she would, and spoke in praise of Lady Pomfret who appeared to have every detail of the Hospital Library Depot at her finger tips, although she could only come in two or three days a week. Then she kissed her parents good-night and went upstairs. On her way up she met her brother Henry coming down.

'I thought you had gone to bed,' said Eleanor.

Henry said he thought he would just go out for a little walk because it was so hot.

'It seems pretty cold to me,' said Eleanor. 'Are you going into the wood? I'll get a coat and come with you.'

Henry did not show any marked enthusiasm for her suggestion and waited with some impatience till she got the coat. They went out of the house and Eleanor turned towards the garden, at the end of which a door led to the wood.

'I thought it would be rather a good idea to go down the High Street,' said Henry, with unusual diffidence. 'I mean it might be rather jolly just to walk down, about as far as the Post Office.'

Eleanor was quite agreeable to this and they began to stroll down the hill. At least that was what Eleanor intended, but her young brother gradually quickened his pace till she was hard put to it to keep up with him, though they were almost of a height.

It was still very light, owing to Double Summer Time, but there were not many people about in the street. The Post Office was more than half-way down the High Street and on their way they passed the Old Bank House, where a light shone in the hall. Eleanor lingered, but her brother impatiently urged her on till they came abreast of the Post Office, where Mrs Goble the post-mistress was airing herself on the pavement with her cat.

'Oh, good evening, Mrs Goble,' said Henry with an ill-acted air of surprise.

'It's you is it, Mr Henry?' said Mrs Goble. 'Hasn't she written yet?' and she laughed a Dame Quickly-ish laugh.

'Hasn't who written, Mrs Goble?' said Eleanor, mystified and a little curious.

'His best girl,' said Mrs Goble, winking heavily at Eleanor. 'Gives me no peace, he doesn't. Expects me to bring him a letter like a rabbit out of a hat. You know what I told you, Mr Henry. His Majesty's Mail comes in to-morrow morning and if there's a letter you'll get it. Why don't you phone her up? Poor girl, I expect she's setting by the phone waiting for you. You're a bad lot, that's what you are.' And Mrs Goble's fat form quivered with laughter.

All this was Greek to Eleanor, who was pretty sure that her young brother was not at the moment in love, or he would have been boring his whole family and especially his kind elder sister quite dreadfully about it. But being a kind and fairly wise elder sister she held her tongue.

'Oh, thanks awfully, Mrs Goble,' said Henry. 'I say, Mrs Goble, if there's a letter for me to-morrow it's sure to come to the Rectory, isn't it? A kind of long letter I'm expecting.'

'Well, I don't open no one's letters, so I don't know if they're short or long,' said Mrs Goble, evidently taking the adjective long as applying to the amount of written matter and not to the shape of the envelope. 'You go along home to bed, Mr Henry. Good-night, Miss Eleanor. Come along in, pussy.'

Eleanor and Henry turned and retraced their steps up the High Street. Eleanor would have liked to ask Henry for an explanation of the scene, but he was so obviously unhappy that she felt it would be kinder not to. As they passed the Old Bank House, Miss Sowerby was at her open door surveying the street. There was nothing for it but to stop and greet her.

Miss Sowerby, who was now in a neat black dress with some old lace round her head and a jewel flashing at her neck, asked them what they were doing. Eleanor said just having a little walk before they went to bed.

'And very nice you look,' said Miss Sowerby approvingly. 'Will you give your father a message for me? Mr Adams, who as you know has been looking at my house, rang up this afternoon, or at least his secretary did, to say he has deposited part of the price with my lawyers and everything was going ahead. Quick work, but I like quick workers.'

Eleanor said she would tell her father and was sure he would be glad and then felt confused.

'Only glad because you do want to sell it, Miss Sowerby,' she said. 'But we do all wish you weren't going. It won't seem like the Old Bank House without you.'

'That is very nice of you, my dear,' said Miss Sowerby. 'And I believe you mean it. But one must face facts. I am old and I am not well off and I have a home with my widowed sister. The one thing I couldn't have borne would be for the wrong person to buy the house. It is used to being kindly lived in and I think Mr Adams will live in it very kindly and give it treats and pleasures that I have never been able to give it. This is the end of our family and now the new world must come in and I have been lucky in finding the right kind of new world. I hope your father and mother will be friendly to my successor. I know they will. There is only one thing that my house needs, apart from money spent on paint and repairs, and that is a good mistress. As soon as I hear from my lawyers I am going, and I don't want a fuss, so good-bye my dear.'

She bent from her step to kiss Eleanor very affectionately, shook hands with Henry and went back into the house.

'Is she a bit mad, do you think?' said Henry in a hushed voice.

Eleanor said she didn't think so and fell silent as they walked home and went quietly to bed. Lying awake for a time, thinking of the croquet party and how nice it was of Colin Keith to take Tom to Oxford, she then thought of her evening walk and Henry's mysterious letter, to which however she attached no particular importance. And then she thought of Miss Sowerby, old, poor, but undefeated and she came to the conclusion that Miss Sowerby with her readiness to accept and understand the new world, and her hopefulness for its future in good hands was probably more modern than any of them and so, with a sudden pleasant recollection of Colin's suggestion of a theatre evening, she went to sleep.

3

After the stirring events of Saturday and Sunday the Rectory and Edgewood relapsed into their normal condition. Mr and Mrs Grantly did their thousand and one jobs. Eleanor went to Barchester by the bus every morning, worked at the Red Cross and came back by the bus in time for supper. Henry did various jobs about the garden and haunted the Post Office till Mrs Goble nearly lost her temper with him in earnest, so that he had to confess to her why he was so anxious.

'Now don't you commence to worry, Mr Henry,' said Mrs Goble. 'There's my younger sister's boy over at Courcy and he's been waiting to be called up these last three months. I daresay he'll not be took after all. It does seem a shame taking young gentlemen like you,' said Mrs Goble, with the large charity of the countrywoman for the gentry, nor would any explanations convince her that Henry longed to be away with the Barsetshires and wished he had lived in the days when a shilling from a recruiting sergeant with ribbons in his cap made one a member of His Majesty's forces on the spot. As for Grace, she resumed her studies at the Barsetshire High School and was able to report to her uninterested parents that Jennifer Gorman had had her perm re-set and looked ghastly and that Miss Pettinger had told Imogen Arbuckle to go to the cloakroom and take that red off her nails at once, and Imogen had obeyed, but subsequently put blue ink on her nails and been given a Bad Conduct Mark.

In Edgewood itself little of importance occurred. It was known by the small town secret service that Mr Adams rang Miss Sowerby up every day, and Mr Mould, the undertaker, carrier, and general remover told his driver that they'd be carting Miss Sowerby's little lot any day now. Strangers were seen at the Old Bank House with tape measures and yardsticks. Representatives of The Gas, The Drains, The Electric Light, and The Plumbing Interest were seen going in and out and lunching at the Cross Keys. From all of which omens the little town, putting its head or heads together, surmised that Mr Adams would soon be moving in.

'Ar,' said Mr Mould's foreman, 'if I'd as much money as Mr Adams I'd buy a nice new house. I see one over Framley way that I wouldn't mind having. Rounded corners and chromium taps and built-in cupboards and a nice stainless steel sink,' to which Mrs Mould, who happened to be in the yard at the moment, said it stood to reason built-in cupboards took up just as much room as built-out cupboards, only being flush you didn't notice them so much, and if anyone offered her a steel sink she wouldn't thank them for it, nasty things breaking the china as soon as look at it and clean they might look but clean they weren't no matter how much Vim you used, because it stood to reason steel wasn't clean, not like a nice porcelain sink. To which the foreman's wife, who had come into the yard to take her husband's clothing coupons away from him because she was going to Barchester, said that rounded corners weren't healthy neither, or else the horspitals wouldn't have them; evidently looking upon hospitals as collectors of germs for professional purposes.

'Ar, that's as you look at it,' said Mr Mould's foreman. 'But

I'll lay an even half-crown that Miss Sowerby's stuff'll be in the vans within a fortnight.'

And then he wound up the engine of the big van so that further talk became impossible.

On the following Saturday Eleanor took a small suitcase to the Red Cross Hospital Library Depot and put it in a corner of her room while she did her work. At a few minutes to one Lady Pomfret rang her up on the house telephone to ask if she was ready. So Eleanor went downstairs with her suitcase and in the hall she found Mrs Freddy Belton, the former Depot Librarian.

'I'm so glad I caught you,' said Susan Belton. 'I couldn't answer your letter properly before because I was away. But I've made a list of all the things you wanted to know and as I had to come to Barchester I thought I'd come and give it to you. If there's anything else, let me know.'

And then Lady Pomfret, incredibly neat and tailored in her uniform, joined them and kissed Susan affectionately and told her to take care of herself.

'I do,' said Susan. 'And so does everyone else. I mean they all take care of me like anything at Harefield. I'd sometimes almost like to jump off the kitchen table and see what happened.'

Lady Pomfret smiled and asked how Captain Belton was, and turned to give some instructions to the telephone girl in the little glass box by the door.

'Everything all right?' said Susan.

Eleanor said yes, except that she thought her mother was a little worried at the idea of Mr Adams buying old Miss Sowerby's house. Susan asked why.

'Well,' said Eleanor after a moment's thought, 'I really don't know. I think she thinks he will turn Edgewood into a kind of Hogglestock.'

Then both young women laughed and Susan said so many nice people liked Mr Adams that he must be nice, which may not have been logic but satisfied Eleanor, who then accompanied Lady Pomfret to her car and was driven away.

Doubtless in normal times the Pomfrets would have filled their great house with friends and the children of friends every week-end, and the young Grantlys would have known the mystery of tea in the housekeeper's room and made friends with the third footman and adored the keeper at a distance. But for ten years the Towers had been for the most part dismantled, the great reception rooms dust-sheeted, the state bedrooms dark behind their shutters except for a weekly airing, the huge kitchens full of Red Cross Stores, and the whole family with nursery and a small staff were living in the West Wing where the rooms were smaller and less oppressive and the still-room took the place of housekeeper's room, servants' hall and butler's pantry.

No longer did guests drive up the immense ramp and enter by the majestic portico. Lady Pomfret guided her little car by a narrow drive to the far end of the gigantic pile, built by the sixth Earl of Pomfret in pious imitation of St Pancras station, drew up at what used to be the entrance to the housekeeper's apartments, and took Eleanor through a stone passage, up a flight of stone stairs, into a comfortable small sitting-room looking to the south over the Italian garden, which was brilliant with colour between the little box-hedges.

'How *do* you manage your bedding-out, Lady Pomfret?' said Eleanor; to which Lady Pomfret replied briefly, 'Nasturtiums. Penny packets. At least they used to be a penny and then they vanished completely, and now they are back and rather expensive. It was Gillie's idea. Here he is. This is Eleanor Grantly, darling, from Edgewood. She is our Depot Librarian.'

Eleanor had seen Lord Pomfret more than once at meetings but never before at close quarters, and a wave of compassion for him rose in her kind heart because he looked so tired, so conscientious and, though this was quite illogical, because he shook hands with her so charmingly and asked after her parents. Eleanor said they were quite well and sent their kindest regards and remembered staying at the Towers when old Lord Pomfret was alive.

'Yes, I remember them,' said Lord Pomfret. 'It was in the winter of '37. How good-looking they were. And Sally tells me you are such a help at the Hospital Library. I hope you will be happy here. Is Roddy coming up to lunch, Sally?'

Lady Pomfret said he was and almost at once in came Roddy Wicklow her brother, who had been the Pomfret agent for a good many years now, with a gap made by the war. They went to lunch in an adjoining room, also looking over the formal garden and its brilliant red and yellow lovers' knots and geometrical figures, and the lunch was casserole of rabbit and vegetables and a semolina pudding and strawberries and real cream. Also oatcake and butter if anyone was hungry for it. Much the same as the Rectory lunch in fact, thought Eleanor, only we haven't so much cream. And while they ate Lord and Lady Pomfret and the agent talked about estate matters; whether Lord Mellings would enjoy going to his prep school in the autumn and if Lady Emily Foster would need her front teeth straightened and the chances of getting a small safe old pony for the Honourable Giles Foster from the local pony-copers who were gypsies and lived over towards Allington. So that Eleanor, recovering from a slight fit of shyness, thought again how very like home it was.

'This afternoon,' said Lady Pomfret, as she poured out the coffee, 'I expect you would like to go for a walk, Miss Grantly.

Roddy, do take Miss Grantly round the Home Farm and you might see about the pony. I told Jasper to bring it round about three. What about you, Gillie?'

Lord Pomfret, who spoke in a very gentle voice as if he were husbanding his strength, said he must go over to Starveacre Hatches and later he must do some boring County Council stuff and decide whether he would go to Hartletop or to Silverbridge as they had unfortunately chosen the same day for their Conservative Fête in July, and with a kind smile to Eleanor he got up and went away. Lady Pomfret looked after him.

'We all kill ourselves in our own way,' she said, speaking to nobody in particular. 'See you at tea, Roddy.'

This appeared to be in the nature of a dismissal, so Eleanor asked the agent when they would start. He said now, if she was ready, so they went off together, leaving Lady Pomfret at her large desk with a table at right angles to it on which were a number of baskets and files.

'Poor old Sally,' said Roddy Wicklow to Eleanor when they got into the garden. 'She used to ride to hounds better than anyone in the whole county. And now she is at work all the time. Would you like to see the stables?'

Without waiting for an answer he took Eleanor to the stables, some hundred yards or so from the house. Here where noble hunters had champed and stamped, where each horse had its own name over its stall or box and a neatly plaited edging to its straw, three horses stood rather disconsolate.

'That's mine,' said Roddy, stopping before a chestnut. 'He'll take me anywhere. And that's Sally's mare and that's Gillie's horse. Dull for you, old fellows, isn't it? I take them out when I can. Gillie never hunted, but he likes riding about the place. It does him good. Do you ride?'

Eleanor said she loved it but hadn't much chance and had nothing with her to ride in.

'It's a pity,' said Roddy. 'I'd have taken you round by the obelisk and Hamaker's Spinney. The drives are looking very pretty. Never mind. We'll go down to the Home Farm. I expect my wife and the children will be there.'

Accordingly they walked through the shrubbery, the Italian garden, the walled garden, up a rising ground where the last bluebells still lingered under scattered beeches and down again by a wide green grass path that wound its way to a small wrought-iron gate in a beechen hedge.

'Old Lady Pomfret had this grass walk made,' said Roddy. 'They called it the Green River. Here we are.'

He opened the gate and Eleanor found herself near a group of farm buildings, with pleasant comfortable noises of clucks and quacks and moos and grunts, and an inspiring smell of good straw manure. On the far side of the great farmyard was a large barn with both doors wide open. Through this Roddy led the way and they emerged in a field where a little knot of children and grown-ups were standing near a gate. As they caught sight of the newcomers shrieks of 'Daddy, daddy' and 'Uncle Roddy' rent the air and some of the children came tilting at full speed towards Eleanor, while those who were restrained by their mother or nurse, or by being strapped into a perambulator, added agreeably to the general clamour without quite knowing what they were shouting about. Rather like Gulliver with Lilliputians clinging to his legs, Roddy Wicklow made his way to the gate followed by Eleanor.

'This is my wife,' he said, as a slight creature with large brown eyes came forward rather shyly to shake hands. 'And these are Guy and Phoebe, and young Alice in the pram.'

Eleanor, who really liked children, even in their muddiest or jammiest moments, at once was friends with the young Wicklows who recognised in her a kindred spirit, at which Mrs Roddy Wicklow gave Eleanor a sudden and unexpectedly brilliant smile, so that Eleanor thought how good-looking she was.

'And this is Nannie Peters. Her brother used to be butler here. This is Miss Grantly, Nannie. She helps Lady Pomfret at the Hospital Libraries.'

Eleanor was about to put out her hand when she realized, with the sixth or county sense that sometimes comes to the rescue, that in Nannie Peters's eyes she was but as a new nursery-maid on probation, and that probably Nannie thought poorly of young ladies who worked at offices instead of settling down to produce Nannie-fodder. So she contented herself with saying 'How do you do, Nannie. What a nice day it has been,' in what she hoped was not too bright a voice.

'And here's Ludovic,' said Roddy Wicklow, presenting Lord Mellings who was so like his father that Eleanor expected him to say he must go and answer some letters, 'and Emily and Giles,' which last two were sturdy and rather bumptious-looking young people of tender years. 'Is Jasper here, Alice?'

His wife said he had promised to meet them at three.

'Then he'll come,' said Roddy, and turning to Eleanor he explained that Jasper was the gypsy who was to bring a pony on approval for the Honourable Giles. 'Emily has a pony and is shaping quite well, but Ludovic has never got any confidence,' said Roddy, 'so I am giving Giles a pony and perhaps that will make Ludovic want to try. It's tough luck on Ludo, but it can't be helped. Jasper's uncle is a kind of keeper over at Beliers, and his grandmother was a witch who used to turn into a black hare. She was rather a nuisance till Uncle Jasper shot her with a silver button off Lydia Merton's coat, only she was Lydia Keith then,' at which interesting mixture of social and anthropological information Eleanor's brain reeled, though she quite realized that Roddy was speaking the truth and these things had really happened.

'When old Jasper says he'll bring a pony for the little gentleman, the pony he does bring,' said a slow voice from the lane.

'Old impostor,' said Roddy to Eleanor. 'He does love to show off. But he knows about horses. Bring your pony in, Jasper,' he called.

Jasper opened the gate, led a small pony through it and shut the gate behind him. Alice Wicklow shook hands with him and all the children who were free clung to Jasper's legs shouting, 'Pony, Pony!' while the youngest Wicklow in its perambulator and the Honourable Giles who was firmly held by Nannie Peters shrieked and struggled to get loose and join the Laocoön group.

'You do look younger every day, Miss Peters,' said Jasper, addressing Nannie and adumbrating a wink to the rest of the party. To which Nannie Peters replied That was enough from him and it was a good thing her aunt by marriage, his poor mother, died when she did, as it saved her a lot of trouble.

'Now, where's the young gentleman Jasper's brought the pony for?' said the gypsy. 'Is it his little lordship?'

But Lord Mellings, so like his father, so unlike his country-bred mother, shrank to Eleanor's side, which so touched her that she put down her hand and felt his small hand clutch it.

'It is for Giles,' said Alice Wicklow, with an authority that surprised Eleanor. 'All right, Ludovic, you shan't get on the pony. I think Giles had better come and talk to the pony, Nannie.'

Eleanor expected the sky to open and a thunderbolt to fall

on Alice, but to her surprise Nannie let go of Giles's hand and he came running to Jasper's side.

'Afternoon, young gentleman,' said Jasper, assuming a perfect gypsy whine. 'Here's a fine pony for a fine young gentleman. Look at him.'

Everyone looked at the pony who was a small determined person with a rough coat and a forelock that he tried all the time to toss away from his eyes. Giles took a biscuit out of the front of his jersey, laid it in his flat open hand and offered it to the pony who examined it, suddenly blew all his breath out with such violence that the biscuit was nearly whiffed away, and then neatly picked it off Giles's hand with soft lips and crunched it.

'Where did you get that biscuit from, Giles?' said Nannie Peters.

'He gave it to me,' said Giles, pointing to his elder brother.

'Did you give Giles your biscuit, Ludovic?' said Nannie.

Eleanor, who felt sorry for little Lord Mellings, though she did not quite know why, watched his face, while he looked anxiously from side to side as if he were seeking for help and at last nodded his head.

'He didn't give it me. I took it,' said Giles. 'And then he said I could have it.'

'Then you're a naughty boy,' said Nannie, 'and next time you won't get one at all. Nor you neither, Ludovic,' a piece of good nursery treatment of the finer shades of justice.

'Then when I do get a biscuit I'll give Ludo mine,' said Giles, suddenly becoming virtuous.

Eleanor felt a tug at her hand and looked down on Lord Mellings's anxious little face.

'I didn't say Giles could have it,' said Lord Mellings in a whisper which, so Eleanor felt, was not far from tears. 'But I don't mind him having it really, only I *did* want to give it to the pony.'

By the greatest good luck Eleanor had in her bag a bit of that month's chocolate ration which she offered to her small friend. His anxious face became radiant as he offered the chocolate in his open hand to the pony, who snuffed at it and took it without a word of thanks.

'Now say thank you to Miss Grantly,' said Nannie.

Eleanor could feel Lord Mellings's little hand, rather unpleasantly covered with chocolate and the pony's licks, slipped back into hers and looking at him saw in his face an attack of severe obstinacy.

'Did you hear me, Ludovic?' said Nannie.

'He did say thank you, Nannie,' said Eleanor, thus imperilling her immortal soul. 'Are you going to put Giles on the pony, Mr Jasper?'

'Old Jasper he knows what he's doing,' said the gypsy, producing an old sack which he flung over the pony's shaggy back. 'Coming up, Master Giles?'

'Give us a leg, Jasper,' said Giles, and in a trice his strong little form was firmly seated on the improvised saddle, the rope reins in his hand.

'Now, take the little gentleman for a walk,' said Jasper.

The pony thought for a moment and then ambled gently up the field and back.

'And now give the little gentleman a trot,' said Jasper, and the pony trotted nimbly round the field.

'Now gallop!' said Giles, intoxicated with the movement.

'If his little lordship gave you the biscuit, young gentleman,' said Jasper, 'you'll stick on. If you took the biscuit from his little lordship, you'll fall off. Gallop!'

Away went the pony at a rough canter, while Giles held on

with his strong little legs and his easy balance till just as the pony reached Nannie it stopped dead and Giles rolled over on to the grass, but immediately scrambled to his feet and said, 'Again, Jasper.'

'That's not the way to speak,' said Nannie. 'Say thank you to Jasper.'

'Thank you, Jasper,' said the Honourable Giles. 'And I did take Ludo's biscuit. But I'll give him my red and blue pencil to make up. Uncle Roddy, is it really my pony?'

Roddy had a short conversation with Jasper, from which each emerged battered but with an amused respect for the other. Some pieces of paper changed hands and Jasper touched his villainous old hat to the company.

'Groom him yourself, young gentleman,' he said to Giles. 'His name is Pillicock. And don't forget old Jasper when you want a bigger one. Good-day my honourable ladies and gentlemen. Good-bye Miss Peters. Be good, be honest; see you again before then.'

Before the outraged Nannie could gather her wits to blast him he had slipped into the road and gone swiftly if unromantically away on a battered bicycle.

'I'm sure I never!' said Nannie.

Nothing would then please Lady Emily Foster but to have a ride, which with great condescension her younger brother allowed. His Uncle Roddy put her on the pony which she sat as fearlessly as her brother, though with less grace, and both the nursery parties walked back to the Towers, Lord Mellings still holding tightly to Eleanor's hand. At the garden gate the Wicklows said Good-bye, got into their car with the children and drove home to Nutfield, while the rest of the party went on to the West Wing.

'Her ladyship must have gone to fetch his lordship from Starveacre Hatches,' said Nannie. 'The car's gone. Will you have tea in the nursery with us, miss? There's a nice home-made cake and we've plenty of milk.'

Eleanor accepted with pleasure and was conducted to the nursery, a pleasant room above the little sitting-room, with some leads outside and a stone stair that led to the garden.

'Now, you sit down on the sofa, miss,' said Nannie, 'while we get ready for tea. Come along and wash your hands, Ludovic.'

Lord Mellings unwillingly relinquished her hand and followed Nannie to the bathroom whence noises of expostulation from Lady Emily Foster were heard as Nannie flattened her face with a damp sponge. Presently his lordship came back and sat beside Eleanor, slipping his hand again into hers.

'Now, don't you bother Miss Grantly, there's a good boy,' said Nannie bustling about with a great show of zeal.

'I'm not bothering her,' said Lord Mellings. 'I'm only holding her hand because she was frightened of the pony. Weren't you?' he added, looking at Eleanor with a mute appeal to her to back him up in this untruth.

Nannie said She was the cat's grandmother and where were his manners. Miss Grantly was the lady's name. But Eleanor said Miss Grantly was only her name in the office and she was called Eleanor at home, and the nursery felt so like home that she would like to be Eleanor. Which tribute to the nursery placated Nannie who graciously said it was ever so nice to have a young lady to tea who knew what a nursery should be and would Miss Grantly like to pour out. But Eleanor knew her place. Nannie poured out with a generosity of milk and sugar that Eleanor could well have done without, all three children behaved well and when they had finished tea she told them about the big oak at the end of her father's garden and how it had a hole so big that ten people could squash inside it. And then they played Heads, Bodies, and Legs and made so much noise that Lady Pomfret coming in was not at first noticed, till Lord Mellings suddenly caught sight of his mother and upsetting his chair ran to meet her.

'Eleanor was frightened of the pony, mother,' he said, 'so I held her hand.'

'I wasn't frightened,' said Giles. 'I trotted and cantered and galloped and fell off and didn't mind a bit. He's called Pillicock and Jasper says I'm to groom him.'

Then Lady Pomfret took Eleanor away, with promises of coming up at bath-time, and they went down to the sitting-room.

'Were you really frightened of the pony?' said Lady Pomfret.

Eleanor wondered if she ought to tell the whole story or not, and decided it would be better not to.

'I really couldn't have been frightened,' she said, 'he was so small. But I think Ludovic was frightened, so I let him hold my hand and I expect he wanted you to think he had been protecting me. What a dear he is.'

Lady Pomfret sat silent and Eleanor wondered if she had annoyed her till Lady Pomfret said,

'Thank you, my dear. Poor little Ludovic – such a name too, but old Lady Lufton offered to be his godmother and she's such an old friend, so we couldn't refuse. He is so like his father. Gillie is the dearest, kindest, most generous creature in the world with ten times more courage than I will ever have, but he has never been very strong and he is always over-anxious and takes things so hard. If only Ludovic were like me, without a nerve in my body. And now Gillie will come back from Starveacres too tired to rest and too tired to enjoy his dinner and talking to you. He wouldn't come back in the car with me because some tenant wanted to see him about repairs. And all these awful County Council papers to be gone through. I wish the Pomfret title had never been invented. I sometimes think it will kill him and I see Ludovic growing up so like Gillie. Oh dear.'

Eleanor sat mute with astonishment and pity. The County Organiser who was so capable, business-like, cool, sure of herself, impersonal, had suddenly vanished and left instead a woman in distress for a dearly loved husband, anxious for a dearly loved child. She would have liked to comfort her and did not know how. A thought came to her.

'Lady Pomfret,' she said. 'Those papers. I don't know much about County Council, but I did do my secretarial course before I came to the Hospital Libraries. Do you think I could help? I've nothing to do this week-end except enjoy myself here. Would Lord Pomfret mind?'

'He can mind until he is black in the face,' said Lady Pomfret with a vehemence very unlike her usual poise. 'Bless you, Eleanor. I'll keep Gillie amused till after dinner if you will sort those papers. They have been accumulating and he is so busy and he *won't* have a secretary. Roddy is an angel, but he has his hands quite full with the estate business and he has Alice and the children to consider. I'll show you the papers and then we'll go and look at the children in the bath.'

She led the way across a passage to a little room looking out over the drive, with a large office table to the right of the window and a smaller one in the middle of the room.

'The real estate office is at the far end of the house,' said Lady Pomfret, 'and we can't heat it properly, so we made one here. I wanted Gillie to have one of the rooms facing south, but he wanted this one. I think he likes to see who is coming or going. These are the papers.'

She showed Eleanor a number of files of letters, forms, memoranda on the smaller table.

'It's Housing Schemes and Electricity Schemes and Homes for the Aged and what not,' said Lady Pomfret. 'I would do it, but I literally haven't time. Can you really deal with it? If Gillie had a kind of précis of each paper and how they fit in with each other if you see what I mean, it would save him a whole evening's work. He is rather slow, poor darling, because he is so very conscientious. Oh dear.'

She looked so unhappy that Eleanor could hardly bear it. To see the firm, competent, omniscient County Organiser of the St John and Red Cross Library so baffled, so at the end of her tether, was a shock to her, for she was still young enough to believe that really grown-up people, and to her Lady Pomfret had always seemed a grown-up though there were not more than ten years between them, always knew exactly what to do. Now this illusion was shattered and Lady Pomfret was human and in trouble. Eleanor's kind heart warmed to the superior officer whom she had always liked, and putting aside any private doubts she might have had as to her own competence, she said with perfect composure that she was sure she could get them straight.

'Bless you for it,' said Lady Pomfret. 'It's still rather early for the children's bath-time. Perhaps you would care just to look at those files. Not unless you feel like it.'

But Eleanor said she felt exactly like it, and would Lady Pomfret let her know when the nursery was ready to be visited. So Lady Pomfret went away and Eleanor sat down and began to go through the files, making notes of the contents as she went and putting things under their right headings, in fact the work that a competent trained secretary ought to have been doing for Lord Pomfret. She had a quick intelligent mind and was fascinated by the ramifications and wheels within wheels of county life, and so swiftly did the time pass that she could hardly believe it was half past six when Lady Pomfret came to summon her. Lady Pomfret looked over the papers and Eleanor's neat lists and sighed with relief.

'I don't know how to thank you,' she said.

'I'll tell you what I'd love,' said Eleanor, childishly delighted by being a conspirator with her superior officer. 'If you could keep Lord Pomfret away from this room till after lunch to-morrow I think I could get it all straight. That is if you don't mind my not going to church,' she added.

'I shall say I am keeping you in bed because you have worked too hard at the office,' said Lady Pomfret, to whom such a lie appeared natural, nay commendable, if it was to help her husband, 'and you can spend the morning here. It's the Litany to-morrow and Gillie always goes round the farm with Roddy before lunch, so you'll have nearly three clear hours. Now come upstairs.'

The nursery party were by now bathed and smelling very nice, with their hair slightly damp. Giles had already been put to bed and Emily and Ludovic were having a rere-tea of biscuit and milk in their dressing-gowns. Emily shrieked with joy at the sight of the guest, which produced answering shrieks from Giles and in a minute his pyjamaed form came dashing from the night-nursery.

'Go back at once, Giles,' said Nannie scandalised. 'What will Miss Grantly say,' but by this time Giles had got onto Eleanor's lap and Nannie gave in and went away to tidy the bathroom while Eleanor told the three children the story of the Hobyahs, which was such a success that she had to tell it three times running, till Lady Pomfret said they mustn't tire Eleanor.

'Bed now,' said Nannie re-appearing and in a voice which

even Giles recognised as an ultimatum. So the children were collected and put into their beds, Emily and Giles with Nannie, Ludovic in a little communicating room by himself. Eleanor kissed Emily and Giles and promised to tell them the Hobyahs again next day, and then followed Lady Pomfret into the little room. Lord Mellings sat up in bed and patted his blankets, looking at Eleanor as he did so, which she rightly took to be an invitation to sit on his bed.

'Good-night, darling,' said Lady Pomfret, hugging her first-born.

'Good-night,' said Lord Mellings. 'Oh, mother.'

Lady Pomfret waited.

'Hurry up, darling,' she said. 'Daddy will be back and I must go.'

'It's only a kind of hurting thought I had,' said Lord Mellings his little face more than usually anxious. 'About holding *her* hand,' and he nodded his head towards Eleanor.

'What about it then?' said Lady Pomfret, giving, as Eleanor remembered she always did at the Red Cross, the impression of having nothing in the world to do but the business in hand.

'It was about saying I held her hand because she was frightened of the pony,' said Lord Mellings, his forehead puckered in a soft frown of concentration on a difficult talk. 'She wasn't frightened, mother, really she wasn't. I was holding her hand because – because – oh, mother, *need* I ride a pony?'

Then Sally Pomfret understood. That anyone should not want to ride was a mystery to her, born to the saddle. But that her elder son was really terrified of riding was only too plain and with the same adoring care that made her understand how her hard-working husband hated the social life that she would have loved, she understood that to Ludovic, so like Gillie in looks and spirit, a pony was nameless terror. All the love in her flew to arms to protect her little boy from the child's fears which are perhaps almost worse than grown-up fears, because it cannot hope far enough ahead.

'Of course not,' she said, in a matter-of-fact voice, though for a pin she could have cried. 'Next time Emily and Giles have rides, Nannie shall take you in the donkey cart. And then if Pillicock is very good, you could let him take you round the stable yard on his back, for a treat for him, and Nannie will hold the reins.'

Lord Mellings considered and Eleanor, so close to him, felt the tension of his little body relax.

'Only *once*,' he said. 'You see Pillicock might be tired.'

His mother agreed that once would be quite enough for Pillicock and kissed him good-night. Eleanor also had to kiss him and was almost choked by the grasp of his thin little arms round her neck.

'I like you,' he said and then pulled sheet and blanket right over his head, which his visitors interpreted as their congé and went downstairs.

'You see,' said Lady Pomfret when they got back to her sitting-room.

'The *little* thing,' said Eleanor.

'Two of them,' said Lady Pomfret. 'I am sometimes so afraid of how the world will treat Ludovic that I wish I were dead. And much good that would do,' she added.

Eleanor, more sorry than she could say for her hostess, said hesitatingly, for she did not wish to presume and she was not quite sure whether she was saying something sensible or something foolish, that she imagined from what Mr Wicklow and Lady Pomfret had said that Lord Pomfret had found his position and his work far from easy, having been forced without his own wish into being an earl and having to do a great many hard dull things without being particularly thanked for them. And she felt sure, she added, though secretly wondering if Lady Pomfret would think her a horrible meddler and presumer, that Ludovic would be just like his father in all the best ways as well as in the unhappy ones, and turn into a very good man and be very brave. And having said this, she wished she hadn't and waited to be sent home in disgrace.

'Thank you, my dear,' said Lady Pomfret, coming over to her and kissing her impulsively. 'I expect you are right. And we won't say a word to Gillie. I hear him coming. Did you settle old Wheeler, darling?'

'Yes I did, ungrateful old scoundrel that he is,' said Lord Pomfret. He then inquired courteously whether Eleanor had had a pleasant afternoon and looked so tired that Eleanor made a pretext to escape to her room and leave her host and hostess alone together, till dinner time.

During dinner some chance remark led to a question about picquet and Eleanor, who had played with her father since she was a child, gave her views.

'Do you play, Miss Grantly?' said Lady Pomfret. 'That is perfect. Gillie adores it and I have no card sense at all. You must have a game after dinner.'

Lord Pomfret looked pleased.

'Gillie has a running game with Mr Barton, Roddy's father-in-law,' said Lady Pomfret, 'but the Bartons have gone to Italy and he has no one to play with. What is it you are playing for, darling?'

Lord Pomfret said ten thousand, by which he meant points, not pounds, and the game usually lasted him for several months, as he had so few free evenings. So after dinner Lady Pomfret put up the card table in her husband's little sitting-room and found the cards and then went back to her own writing-table and her telephoning.

Lord Pomfret played well. So did Eleanor and they were pretty fairly matched and both became absorbed in the game, though Eleanor was not so absorbed but that she noticed with pleasure that Lord Pomfret appeared to be enjoying himself.

'Sally tells me,' said Lord Pomfret while Eleanor was dealing the cards, 'how kind you were to Ludovic this afternoon. He finds life hard, poor little chap. I wish he didn't hate riding so much. Still I daresay we shan't have any horses left soon.'

'I think he is rather brave,' said Eleanor. 'He was frightened of the pony, but he told Lady Pomfret that he had really held my hand not because I was frightened but because he was frightened. At least he didn't exactly say that in words, but he made Lady Pomfret understand. I call that distinctly brave. And very honourable,' she added, in case her host did not fully grasp the implications of the story.

'Thank you very much,' said Lord Pomfret and took up his cards. But Eleanor guessed that he meant a good deal more and was satisfied that her small friend had pleased his father. And presently Lady Pomfret came in and said they must go to bed and would Eleanor like to look at the children asleep. In the two night nurseries all three children were deep in the abandoned slumber of the very young, Giles sprawling across his bed, Emily in a complete ball. In the inner room Ludovic was lying on his side, his face turned away from the late summer-time light, one hand clutching what looked like a piece of painted wood. His mother stooped to look.

'Bless him, he has taken a pencil to bed,' said Lady Pomfret.

Eleanor looked and saw that the pencil was parti-coloured, blue and red.

'It's Giles's special pencil, red one end blue the other,' said Lady Pomfret. 'I expect there will be tears about this.'

Giles had honourably redeemed his promise made before Jasper to give his brother his red and blue pencil because he had taken his biscuit for the pony. But this the grown-ups could not know.

4

Lady Pomfret was as good as her word (as indeed she always was) and sent Eleanor's breakfast to her in bed, which was a delightful lazy treat for the hard-working daughter of the Rectory, though she found the wait till nine o'clock very trying, being used to early hours. But when the breakfast did come the coffee was scalding, the butter and the egg fresh from the farm, the toast kept nicely warm in a napkin and the fresh home-made straw-berry jam excellent. She had hardly finished when there was a knock at the door and in burst the three children demanding the story of the Hobyahs again, so she asked Lord Mellings to put her tray on the floor and invited them all to sit on the bed.

'Can I draw?' said Lord Mellings. 'I've got Giles's red and blue pencil and some paper.'

Eleanor said of course he could, so he lay on the floor on his stomach and drew, while the other two children sat on Eleanor's legs till she had pins and needles, and she told them the story of the Hobyahs six times running till Nannie appeared.

'Well really good morning miss what a way to behave come along and get ready for church now,' said Nannie all in one breath.

Emily and Giles tumbled themselves off the bed and their brother said, 'Oh, *need* I, Nannie? I'm drawing a Hobyah.'

But Nannie bustled him up and sent him to wash his hands.

'You have a nice rest, miss,' she said as she left the room. 'No wonder you're tired, working in an office all day. How her ladyship does it I don't know. I'd be tired if I was to work in an office.'

Eleanor said she would be tired if she had three such lively young people to look after and rather despised herself for using such a form of speech. But Nannie appeared to take it kindly and gave several instances of the liveliness of her young charges, from Giles being found in the pig-sty experimenting on the pigs' food to Emily shutting herself into a cupboard in one of the unused bedrooms and being lost for two hours.

'Ludovic's a good boy,' said Nannie. 'He's no trouble at all except his fancies, miss, and the way he always gets those nasty heavy colds in the winter. Dr Ford said something about a specialist, but I don't hold with them,' said Nannie. 'Now you do understand children, miss. Wouldn't you say with a boy like Ludovic going to London and seeing a strange doctor would upset him? As it is he screamed at Dr Ford's stethoscope till I thought he'd burst a blood vessel and he was only two and a half then,' said Nannie proudly.

Eleanor rather agreed but did not wish to compromise herself in any way, so she said that time would show, again despising herself. However Nannie seemed to think well of the remark and went away. Not long afterwards Lady Pomfret looked in to ask how she had slept and say the coast would be clear in a few moments.

'Right,' said Eleanor. 'I'm nearly dressed really, only I've got my nightgown on. I'll be down as soon as you're gone.'

Lady Pomfret smiled and went away.

*

From about a quarter to eleven Eleanor worked steadily at Lord Pomfret's papers and after two hours' hard work had reduced them to a very orderly condition so that her host could see at a glance what was what, and beside each file she laid a neatly typed précis of its contents, having to that end taken the little portable typewriter from Lady Pomfret's room. As she was shutting it up the agent came in.

'It's you, is it,' he said, but in quite a friendly way. 'I've just been round the Home Farm with Sally and the children. Sally said I might find you here. She was rather mysterious about it.'

Eleanor blushed as fiercely as if she had been caught stealing.

'I hope I haven't done anything awful,' she said. 'The papers were in rather a muddle and Lady Pomfret said I might tidy them. I did do a secretarial course.'

'It needs more than a secretarial course to get the guts out of all these blasted forms,' said Roddy with some vehemence. 'I only know one woman who could do what you've done. Miss Merriman who was old Lady Pomfret's secretary. She had a genius for getting things straight. You aren't looking for a job, are you, Miss Grantly? It would save Gillie's life to have someone like you. All this filling in forms and stupid routine work will kill him on top of everything else and half his time wasted when Parliament is sitting.'

Eleanor said apologetically that she was the Depot Librarian at the St John and Red Cross Library.

'Of course you are,' said Roddy Wicklow. 'Sorry. One gets so wrapped up in this place that one forgets what's happening outside. If you ever hear of anyone who could do this kind of friend-secretary business and would be a help when she was wanted and vanish when she wasn't, like Miss Merriman, I'd pay her anything. I mean Sally would.'

'I suppose,' said Eleanor diffidently, 'a man wouldn't do?'

'Might,' said Roddy. 'Only we don't want one of those professionals who start by ordering a new typewriter. And it must be someone who wouldn't get on Gillie's nerves and knows the county a bit. I'd take it on if I weren't doing everything else.'

Eleanor, with increasing diffidence, then said she had a brother, a very nice brother she added, who had been all through the war and was demobilized and went to Oxford and did classics because he thought he would be a don or a schoolmaster, only now he wanted to do some kind of estate work.

'Well, a good classical education doesn't seem to hurt people,' said Roddy. 'I still read a bit of Greek myself sometimes, with a crib.'

'The awful thing is,' said Eleanor, overcome by the particular form of self-consciousness or shyness that makes us run down what we most wish to praise, 'that Tom thinks he's done very badly in his exams.'

'Lord! that's nothing,' said Roddy cheerfully. 'I was ploughed in pretty well everything and here I am with a wife and three children and a frightfully interesting job. If your brother could come over here sometime, I'd like to talk to him.'

Our formerly lively neighbours the Gauls have a saying La joie fait peur, and this is a not uncommon feeling. After so much worrying over Tom and his changes of mind and his anxiety to start doing real work, the sudden prospect of finding for him what he wanted almost unmanned Eleanor. But being a very sensible girl she got the better of her temporary emotion and thanked Roddy Wicklow. And then they saw the family coming up the drive, so Eleanor shut up the typewriter and took it back to Lady Pomfret's room.

Roddy Wicklow left alone surveying Eleanor's handiwork

decided, for he wasted little time on haggling over things in his mind when he knew what he wanted, that he would interview Miss Grantly's brother as soon as possible, and then went home to his wife and family.

When Lord and Lady Pomfret came in they found Miss Grantly seated by the sitting-room window doing the *Sunday Times* crossword not very successfully. Lord Pomfret said he hoped she was rested and it was just as well she hadn't come to church because the Litany was even longer than usual and the locum who was taking their parson's place appeared to have no roof to his mouth.

During lunch, which Lord Mellings and Lady Emily Foster were allowed to attend, the telephone rang several times which meant that one or other of the hosts had to answer it, and Lord Pomfret said they had better have lunch at half past twelve or half past two on Sundays and then people wouldn't run them to earth so easily. When the bell was heard for the fourth time he barely controlled his feelings and language, but after a few moments' absence he came back in a much better mood.

'It's Agnes,' he said to his wife. 'Cousin Emily wants to come over this afternoon, so Merry will bring her.'

Lady Pomfret said she loved having Cousin Emily, but she was always afraid she might think she still lived at Pomfret Towers, her childhood home, and refuse to go back to Little Misfit where she had for some time lived with her daughter Agnes Graham.

'You know Sylvia told me that Cousin Emily thought she still lived at Rushwater when they had the party for her last year,' said Lady Pomfret to her husband, 'and Agnes found it quite difficult to persuade her to go back to Little Misfit. And Lord Stoke is coming and he is deafer than ever. Oh dear. Well, we've got a cake and I suppose we'll manage.'

After lunch Lord Pomfret took his two elder children for a walk, his usual Sunday custom, while Lady Pomfret showed Eleanor the house including the chapel with its carved and gilded chairs and ornaments brought from Italy by old Lady Pomfret and the lapis lazuli and marble floor laid down by the sixth Earl and the incredibly uncomfortable attics on the top floor where earlier generations of young Fosters had had their nurseries and footmen had staggered up with nursery meals, and Eleanor couldn't help thinking that the Towers was more comfortable now than it could have been then. But we are not sure that she was right. So much was there to see and so interesting did both the ladies find it, that it was four o'clock before they knew where they were and from one of the inconvenient Gothic windows in a housemaid's bedroom with three iron bedsteads forlornly commemorating the happy days of overcrowding and plenty of company, Eleanor saw a car coming up the drive and told Lady Pomfret, who said they must go down at once and catch the visitor at the door, because if they didn't Lord Stoke (if it were he) would go to the farm and never be seen again and Lady Emily (if it were she) might do *anything*, which gave Eleanor, who had never seen Lady Emily, a rather alarming idea of her.

The visitor turned out to be Lord Stoke who was over eighty and in excellent health, troubled by nothing but his increasing deafness which he attributed largely to the perversity of other people, and with him was a lady whom her hostess did not recognize, not young, in ordinary country clothes, from whose head as she got out of Lord Stoke's car a large tortoiseshell pin fell onto the ground.

'Well, my dear,' said Lord Stoke to Lady Pomfret. 'I'm pleased to see you. Mrs Morland was lunching with me and time passed, talking of one thing and another. You know the way time passes.

Queer thing time. My old father had a joke about it. If anyone said to him "I haven't time to do this or that", you know people *do* say it, say it myself sometimes, my old father always said, "Well, you've got all the time there is." Quite right too. Now what was I saying? Oh yes, time passed and my car was at the door, so I said "Look here, Mrs Morland, I'll drive you home." You know Mrs Morland, don't you?'

Lady Pomfret, who never lost her head whatever the social emergency, said she was a great admirer of Mrs Morland's works but somehow hadn't met her and shook hands.

'Unfortunately for me I haven't met you either,' said Mrs Morland, slightly tilting her hat to put the comb into its place. 'Would that be mutual or common?' she asked anxiously.

Lady Pomfret, whose varied activities did not include a close study of the deeply lamented H. W. Fowler's *Modern English Usage*, was a little perplexed but avoided the question, which in any case appeared to be rhetorical, addressed to Mrs Morland by Mrs Morland and not requiring an answer, and said she was glad Mrs Morland had been able to come.

'Now don't rush your fences, Sally,' said Lord Stoke, who had very annoyingly chosen to hear the whole of this pointless interchange of civilities. 'Steady does it. I was telling you how Mrs Morland was lunching with me and then my car came to the door. I meant to come in the dog-cart, but the mare has a swollen pastern, so I told my man to bring the car round. Nasty things those swellings. I remember my old father had a mare in about '95 and she had a very nasty swelling. But we got it down again. Rest does it.'

Lady Pomfret whose life until she became chatelaine of the Towers had been almost bounded by horses, expressed polite interest, and asked her guests to come in.

'So,' continued Lord Stoke, using his deafness to the best advantage, 'I said to Mrs Morland, "I'll drive you home," because she hadn't got enough petrol and I sent the car to bring her to Rising Castle and promised to see her back. And then I said, "Why not come to the Towers with me? Sally likes people coming to the house."'

'I simply couldn't help it,' said Mrs Morland, breaking in with desperation upon Lord Stoke's monologue. 'You know what Lord Stoke is, Lady Pomfret, and I knew you couldn't want me and I really ought to be getting on with a book because my publisher,' said Mrs Morland in an aggrieved voice, 'seems to think I have nothing to do but write books for him, but it was one of those days when Lord Stoke doesn't hear what you say. So I hope you don't mind,' she added.

Lady Pomfret hastened to assure Mrs Morland that she was delighted to see her, which happened to be perfectly true, for though Lady Pomfret was by nature almost incapable of reading fiction, Mrs Morland's novels were so much in demand in the Hospitals and so much talked about by the Librarians and other Red Cross workers, that she had gone so far as to borrow one from the Barchester Library though after keeping it for three months she had had to return it unread. And by dint of shepherding Mrs Morland firmly into the house, she trusted that Lord Stoke would follow.

Eleanor meanwhile had stood aside, a little out of it and amused, till Lady Pomfret made her known to the newcomers and said she was her right-hand man at the Hospital Libraries.

'Grantly,' said Lord Stoke, planting himself in an armchair. 'Now wait a minute. Your father must be Septimus Grantly. My old father used to talk about his great-grandfather the Archdeacon. And your father married, now don't tell me, I've got it at the tips of my fingers, yes, he married Mary Carter. Her father rode to hounds. Rode to hounds once too often and got a chill and died, eh? Bad plan to get a chill. I always have my man there with a second horse and a mackintosh. Can't take risks at my age,' said Lord Stoke, who was well known in his younger days as a hard rider and had taken as many risks as most. 'Glad to meet you, my dear. And what are *you* doing?'

Lady Pomfret repeated her explanation of Eleanor's work in what for her was almost a bellow, though not at all impatiently.

'Librarian, eh?' said Lord Stoke. 'Good girl. The Archdeacon had a very fine library. My old father bought some of his books when he died. Fine bindings they have. You must come over and see them, my dear, and bring your father – and your mother too,' said Lord Stoke, who had a courteous heart.

Eleanor was just trying to penetrate his deafness and thank him, when the nursery party came in followed by their father and they all sat down to tea in the dining-room.

'Oughtn't we to wait for Cousin Emily?' said Lord Pomfret.

If Lady Pomfret's vocabulary had included the word unpredictable, she would have used it to explain why she was not waiting, but her husband understood her and smiled. The children all behaved excellently, though Lord Mellings boasted rather too loudly that he had patted Pillicock's nose. Lord Stokes suddenly became undeaf and inquired about the pony, giving it as his opinion that though Jasper was a rogue he knew as much about ponies as any man in the county, and told Lord Mellings he must come cubbing that autumn. His parents felt acutely uncomfortable for their elder son, whose little face at once assumed the anxious look which so rent their hearts. Eleanor, with great courage and skill, managed to tune her voice to what we can only describe as a low clear bellow and explained to

Lord Stoke that Giles was the horseman and his elder brother did not, so far, like riding. She rather expected Lord Stoke to excommunicate the little boy and was prepared to defend him, when to her great relief Lord Stoke, looking intently at him, said,

'Yes, yes. I see. He's all right though. You mark my words, Pomfret, and don't push that boy of yours. He'll push for himself when he wants to. First time my old father put me on a pony I screamed myself black in the face, so my mother used to tell me. My old father never stood any nonsense. He gave me a leathering, then and there, and I've ridden ever since. Your youngster'll be all right. He's got pluck, my dear. Impossible not to be plucky with you and Pomfret behind him,' and he made a courteous little bow to his host and hostess. Lady Pomfret looked quickly at her son to see whether the talk of leathering had alarmed him, but it did not appear to have made any impression.

'You ask Laura,' said Lord Stoke to Lady Pomfret. 'She has four boys. She ought to know. Three of them married too.'

It was obvious that the three married sons of a stranger could not be of very great interest to the Pomfrets, and Mrs Morland wished, as she often did, that her old friend Lord Stoke had more tact. However she made the best of it and answered Lady Pomfret's civil questions as intelligently as she could, curbing as far as possible her natural instinct to divagate at every turn.

Lord Pomfret, manfully bearing his part, said it must be very delightful to have daughters-in-law, and for them to have Mrs Morland for a mother-in-law, he added.

'Oh, do you think so?' said Mrs Morland, clearing the decks for action by pushing a loose piece of hair behind her ear and ramming a hairpin home. 'I thought people weren't supposed to like their mothers-in-law. Luckily I never saw mine,' which remark brought the conversation to a temporary stop, but Lord

Pomfret picked it up and asked whether she had any daughters, to which she replied no, adding thankfully but foolishly that daughters-in-law were just as good.

'Your son's your son till he gets him a wife, eh?' said Lord Stoke, who usually heard what Mrs Morland said.

'As for that, I do not agree,' said that lady in her most impressive voice. 'What I say is Your son's your son till he gets him a wife, but you'll find he'll go on expecting you to do everything for him and for his wife and for his children all your life,' which modern version of a respectable proverb so stunned her audience that there was a temporary silence.

'Eleanor told me about the Hobyahs,' said Lord Mellings, who felt that Mrs Morland would be a safe and understanding person to talk to. 'Do you know about the Hobyahs?'

And of course Mrs Morland did, and what was more she knew about Mr Miacca, and Drumikin and Lambikin, and all the delightful stories of mystery and terror which give the young so much pleasure and apparently do not alarm them in the least, and when she had for the third time repeated 'Fallen into the fire and so will you, On, little Drumikin, tum-pa-tum-too' and the wolf had torn open Drumikin and eaten Lambikin, the nursery party were in such roaring ecstasies of pleasure that their mother had to say it was really time they went to Nannie, upon which they recovered their manners, shook hands gravely and went away.

'Very nice children,' said Lord Stoke approvingly. '*Very* nice children. Never had any of my own. Can't think why.'

As he was unmarried and over eighty, this fact had long been common property in the county and appeared to his audience less remarkable than it seemed to appear to him.

'Cousin Emily is late,' said Lord Pomfret, to which his wife replied reassuringly that Merry would have telephoned if they weren't coming and in any case she would have to order fresh tea so they might as well go into the Italian garden, whither they accordingly went and sat in a little box arbour with chairs in it, in the full western sunshine, while Lord Stoke and Lord Pomfret talked cattle and pigs, and Lady Pomfret asked Mrs Morland about the High Rising W.V.S.

Eleanor, listening quietly, suddenly thought of her own home. For more than twenty-four hours it had gone out of her mind as if it had never been there at all, so do new scenes overlay one's real daily life, and she felt a little homesick and laughed at herself for being such a goose. It was not that she was unhappy, for she had enjoyed her stay very much and particularly the nursery life, but it was all different. Her own parents worked hard and ceaselessly, and they had plenty of worries with Tom's choice of career and Henry going off to the army and Grace's boringness about the Barchester High School and doubtless about herself, though she felt that she was so much less interesting than her brothers and her sister that her parents could not be anxious about her and might even think her a bit dull, though they were very fond of her. But they had not the larger anxieties that the Pomfrets had, and the great responsibilities of an estate which they could barely keep up. Her father, though sometimes tired or annoyed, especially after going to any meeting at which the Bishop was present, was able to sit back in his own home and enjoy the society of his family and his books, and his county friends. Lord Pomfret, it was very plain, was incapable of rest or loosening his too taut nerves. His wife did more than her share with, added to it, a ceaseless ill-ease about him. As for their elder son, Eleanor could not forget his terror of the very harmless Pillicock and his uneasy mind about the most natural and innocent lie he had told when he held her hand.

Emily and Giles were all right and would go their way through life, tanking over and through all obstacles with complete equanimity. Eleanor envied them, for competent though she was and mistress of her jobs, she sometimes had immortal longings in her and the thought of being a good Librarian for ever did not fill her life. Susan Dean had been a good Librarian, though Eleanor did not underrate her own abilities, and Susan Dean had left her job and married Captain Belton and was going to have a baby in August. Eleanor had no particular wish to have a baby in August, nor at any other time, perhaps owing to a too close view of Venus gripping her prey as exemplified in Edna and Doris, but to be a Librarian for ever made her think of a wet Sunday in Barchester, where she sometimes stayed with an old aunt and watched the rain on the Close and heard the cathedral bells jangling and wondered how early she could go to bed. Perhaps she could transfer to London, where she had many friends. In London one met more people, newer faces.

She wondered when Colin Keith would ask her to the theatre so that she could tell the friends she usually stayed with that she wanted to come, or if she ought to arrange her visit to London first and then tell him she was coming. And would Lady Pomfret give her leave, for though she felt entirely at her ease with her County Organiser at the Towers, Lady Pomfret was a disciplinarian in the office. If Colin did suggest Aubrey Clover's new play, what fun it would be, because everybody said Susan Belton's sister Jessica Dean was more clever and charming than ever. And so deep were her daydreams about the joys of London that she did not notice the approach of Lady Emily Leslie in a kind of royal procession with her granddaughter Clarissa Graham as outrider, Miss Merriman as bodyguard, flapper and bearer of impedimenta, and the whole nursery party in attendance with Nannie generally disapproving in the rear.

'Dear Cousin Emily,' said Lady Pomfret as she rose and hurried forward, 'we were afraid you weren't coming.'

'But I was,' said Lady Emily triumphantly, 'and I have. Only things do seem to get in one's way. Dear Gillie, how are you. And Lord Stoke. And Mrs Morland. And who is your new friend?'

Lady Pomfret introduced Eleanor, with a brief explanation of her position and antecedents.

'But of course I know your father, my dear,' said Lady Emily, enveloping Eleanor in a kind of lasso of scarves as she spoke. 'He is a great-grandson of the Archdeacon whom my people knew very well and one of the most handsome men I ever met. You are so like him, my dear. Is he as good-looking as ever?'

From anyone else these remarks might have been embarrassing, but so genuine was Lady Emily's interest and, we may add, her ladyship's curiosity, that Eleanor was able to answer quite easily and truthfully that her father was very well and looked a great darling, thus avoiding the question of family good looks.

'And tell me all about yourself and your work,' continued her ladyship, extricating herself with her granddaughter's assistance from her cocoon of scarves and taking a seat in the arbour. 'You are a librarian? My father made a most beautiful translation of a poem by Ronsard and had it printed. I must give you a copy. And what other children has your dear father got, because the clergy always seem to have large families, though the Bishop has no children at all, but then one cannot call him a *real* clergyman,' which piece of anti-Palace criticism gave intense pleasure to the whole party and even Lord Pomfret almost laughed aloud.

Under Lady Emily's benevolent inquisition Eleanor told her

about the Rectory; how Tom was at Oxford and wanted to be an estate agent, how Henry was champing to get into the army and how Grace was at the Barchester High School and meant to go to college.

'I know, I know,' said Lady Emily. 'Clarissa is at college, only she is having a kind of half-term holiday and my grandson Martin is his own estate agent and Agnes's eldest boy is in the army now. The young are all alike. They do what they wish and we watch them and can't help much. You must come and stay at the Towers some day soon, my dear.'

Lady Pomfret and Miss Merriman looked at each other, for of late Lady Emily had been living more and more in her own past and especially at the Towers which she had left when she married Mr Leslie some sixty years ago. But luckily Lady Emily's eye fell on Mrs Morland to whom her ladyship said, very truthfully, that she had not yet read Mrs Morland's last book and never could tell one from another and liked them all, to which that worthy creature, who had a very fair idea of her own value, replied that it was all she could do to tell her own books apart herself and was always getting them mixed up. And then, having satisfied Lady Emily's curiosity, she felt the family party might be happier alone and asked Lord Stoke if he was ready to go. Lord Stoke, whose mind had been running on a favourite heifer who might calve at any moment, seized the opportunity for escape.

'We never know at our age if we will meet our old friends again,' said Lady Emily, taking Lord Stoke's hand, 'but it is always pleasant to meet and I know Papa will be sorry to have missed you,' at which allusion to the seventh Earl of Pomfret, long laid to rest among his fathers, Lord Stoke looked alarmed, and Mrs Morland with great presence of mind said good-bye to Lady Emily and took him away.

The children who had for some time been showing signs of insubordination were now unleashed and surrounded Lady Emily, begging to be allowed to look at her ivory-handled stick and to examine the contents of her large bag, with both of which requests her ladyship good-naturedly complied, and also favoured them with delightful stories of her childhood and how the third footman once fell down the steep nursery stairs with all the nursery lunch and how her sister Lady Agnes kept a toad in a cardboard box and fed it on flies.

Lady Pomfret asked Miss Merriman to walk round the Italian garden with her and look at the nasturtiums which, as both ladies knew well, was merely a pretext to talk about Lady Emily.

'She is keeping quite well, Lady Pomfret,' said Miss Merriman, 'but she forgets more and more. At least she remembers her early life more and more and lives so much in the past.'

Lady Pomfret said it must be difficult for Lady Graham and Miss Merriman sometimes.

'It is,' said Miss Merriman, and they walked in silence, for there was really nothing to say and she knew and Lady Pomfret knew that a time must come, though no one could say how soon, when the past would claim Lady Emily for ever. Then Miss Merriman said she ought to be taking Lady Emily back to Holdings as she got so tired if she did not rest before dinner.

With some art Lady Emily was persuaded to reassemble her belongings and return to the house with the children in close attendance. Clarissa followed with Eleanor, who in spite of her greater age and her position was slightly in awe of Clarissa's poise and assurance.

'You are doing the job that Susan Belton used to do, aren't you?' said Clarissa.

As soon as Eleanor remembered that Susan Belton meant the ci-devant Susan Dean, she said yes.

'Do you know Charles Belton?' said Clarissa. 'He's quite charming, but too, too young,' but Eleanor had thought Charles quite an ordinary age, so the conversation languished.

If Lady Pomfret had hoped to get Lady Emily through the house and into her car without any further trouble she was the more deceived, for as they walked through the Italian garden Lady Emily took the path leading to the big garden door which led into the back hall.

'This way, Cousin Emily,' said Lady Pomfret. 'That door is locked.'

'Papa likes that door left open in summer,' said Lady Emily, not criticising, merely stating a fact.

Lady Pomfret exchanged a glance with Miss Merriman who said perhaps Lady Emily would like to see the alterations in the West Wing, a suggestion which her ladyship accepted eagerly, as giving her an opportunity to meddle, saying that the housekeeper's room was always a difficulty and she would like to see what had been done. When they got into the family's present quarters she showed some surprise at the furnishing of the rooms, but said it was all very nice and she was sure Mrs Blackett would be delighted, to which Lady Pomfret who had never heard of this person said non-committally that the rooms were very comfortable indeed and looked round for help. Her husband was as much in the dark as she was and Miss Merriman who was trying to control her gifted employer's efforts to alter the position of several very heavy pieces of furniture did not hear the words.

'I am not so young as I was,' said Lady Emily, flashing a mischievous regretful smile at the company. 'I think I will go to my room now, Merry.'

It had become increasingly obvious to everyone that Lady Emily was, in her own mind, back again in her girlhood's home and that little short of wild horses would keep her from going up into the main building, climbing the great slippery polished oak staircase and making for the room which Lady Emily Foster had inhabited till her marriage. Lord Pomfret made a step forward, which Lady Emily understood as a request to accompany her and took his arm, saying that the grasshopper was a constant burden and she would like to be helped upstairs. Lady Pomfret, for all her competence, was temporarily paralysed and Clarissa, the precocious, the worldly-wise, completely at a loss and a little frightened, while Eleanor, who did not know what was wrong, felt vaguely alarmed. It seemed that no human power could stop Lady Emily, and what effect the gaunt dismantled hall and the sheeted rooms might have upon her no one could guess, when Miss Merriman, the utterly reliable, said in a very matter-of-fact way,

'Conque has packed your things, Lady Emily, and they are in the car, so there is no need to go upstairs. I am afraid we shall be late if we don't start and Lady Graham will be so disappointed. She is looking forward so much to your visit to Holdings.'

The thought of her daughter Agnes being disappointed at once deflected Lady Emily's thoughts, and when Miss Merriman added that she had brought the car round to the side door to save Lady Emily trouble, her ladyship was quite ready to go. Clarissa, not quite understanding, still rather frightened, said to Lady Pomfret, 'Darling Gran. Too, too Mary Rose,' at which Lady Pomfret could willingly have slapped her young cousin by marriage to relieve her own anxiety. Lady Emily on Lord Pomfret's arm went slowly to the door, kissed everyone very affectionately, and then said to Lord Pomfret, 'I didn't say good-bye to Papa.

Will you give him my love? Where is he?' to which Lord Pomfret with great presence of mind and a kind of compassionate affection for Lady Emily said Lord Pomfret was somewhere about the place and he would give him the message. Lady Pomfret and Miss Merriman exchanged a look which meant many things, a subdued Clarissa got into the back seat and the car drove away with wavings and shoutings from the children.

'There is a word used in French novels,' said Lord Pomfret, 'which I always thought unreasonable; Ouf! But now it exactly expresses my feelings. I don't know how we got through it.'

'You pulled us through,' said Lady Pomfret, 'as you always do,' and Lord Pomfret's tired face lit with the deep affection that he had felt eleven years ago for Sally Wicklow when he was plain Mr Foster, an affection which had deepened with every year though he was not very good at expressing it. 'Poor darling Cousin Emily.'

Lord Mellings, who had been gently tugging at his mother's hand, now said, 'Mother.'

'Well, darling?' said Lady Pomfret.

'Mother,' said his lordship, 'I want to tell you something. Pillicock said he didn't want to take me round the stable yard today, but he said next Sunday. I couldn't ride on him if he didn't want me, could I, mother?'

This was an obvious lie which Sally Wicklow would probably have pounced on at once, but Sally Pomfret, looking to her husband for support, said that was quite right and Pillicock must do as he liked.

'But mind you make him keep his promise next Sunday, old fellow,' said Lord Pomfret and Emily and Giles boasted so awfully about their proficiency in horsemanship that the subject of next Sunday was dropped and then Nannie collected the children for supper and bed. Eleanor followed them, for she felt that after the events of the afternoon her host and hostess would probably wish to be alone and the atmosphere of the nursery was something safe and normal after Lady Emily's gentle wandering fancies. So she told the children the story of the Hobyahs and Mr Miacca and Lambikin and Drumikin and the fisherman's wife who wanted to make the sun rise and found herself back in her mud hovel, to all of which they listened with the joyful excitement of Cortes in Darien, for romance, which is also the fairy-tale or house-tale (to use Grimm's name) is being rapidly displaced by the crude new educational substitutes which are provided by modern progress and the march of intellect, and the common prose children of England are being defrauded of their inheritance. They learn nothing now in the way that all generations, including those of the enlightened eighteenth century, learned their ballads and fairy stories. These things may come to them by way of books; they do not come as part of their real life, from the mouth of their nurse or grandmother, and so the child is taken away from his native home and is turned into an abstract educational product. Or, equally bad, they think that the stories of Hobo Gobo and the Fairy Joybell are real fairy stories, which these vapid, common, rootless things most emphatically are not.

'Now that's what I call a nice story,' said Nannie approvingly, when Eleanor had recited the dialogue of the Cat and the Mouse with its awful end of the pouncing cat and 'I'll eat you, good body, good body,' at which the children shrieked with joy. And we think Nannie was right.

So much noise did the nursery make that Lady Pomfret came up to look and was delighted to find such harmony reigning.

'Now we must ask Miss Grantly to stop,' said Nannie, 'or

we'll be too excited to go to sleep. Say good-night and thank her nicely,' upon which Lady Emily and the Honourable Giles wound themselves round her legs, beseeching her to live at the Towers for ever.

'That's enough. Miss Grantly's got plenty to do without telling you stories,' said Nannie, not with any ill-will but on the general principle of seeing what Master Alfred was doing and telling him not to. 'She helps your mother at the Library.'

Lord Mellings said mothers didn't need helping, which touched Eleanor, as implying their perfection and universal capability as seen through his young eyes.

'I've got to do my work,' she said, 'but perhaps your mother will let me come again and tell you some more stories. And we will have a secret.'

'What?' said Lord Mellings, clutching Eleanor's arm in his excitement, with his anxious little face turned up to hers.

'Will you write me a letter next Sunday and tell me if Pillicock kept his promise?' said Eleanor, rather wondering if she wasn't playing the part of didactic or moralizing spinster aunt.

Lord Mellings looked searchingly at her.

'Say Yes, like a nice young gentleman,' said Nannie severely, and it speaks volumes for the essential sweetness of the young gentleman's nature that he merely cast a passing scowl at Nannie and, without speaking, nodded his head violently at Eleanor.

'I'll draw you a picture of Pillicock,' said Lady Emily, who already bid fair to inherit the older Lady Emily's gifts with pencil and brush.

'And I'll whack Pillicock like blazes if he doesn't give Ludo a ride on Sunday,' said the Honourable Giles, putting a protecting hand on his elder brother's shoulder.

But at this point nursery ethics became so involved that Lady

Pomfret took Eleanor away, the loud farewells of the nursery following them down the passage.

'Oh dear,' said Lady Pomfret, when they got to her room. 'Saturday afternoon is really the only good moment of the week. One is always thinking of Monday morning on Sunday. I'm not going to the office to-morrow, but Gillie has to go to Barchester early and he will take you in,' which news rather depressed Eleanor, for though she liked Lord Pomfret she was a little frightened of him. Not that he had been anything but kind and courteous in his own gentle, abstracted way, but she felt that an almost unknown young woman would be a great nuisance to a busy Earl on a Monday morning.

They then talked of various library matters and Lady Pomfret said how sad they all were at the signs of age in Lady Emily and Eleanor tried to think of the right thing to say but couldn't. And indeed in these matters there is no right thing to say except to speak according to one's own heart or one's wish to please, which second can be at a pinch a substitute for the first, and remember that on the whole our friends do not listen to what we are saying, any more than we listen to what they are saying.

'Gillie ought to be back soon,' said Lady Pomfret. And even as she spoke her husband's steps were heard in the passage and Lord Pomfret came into the room with an expression that Eleanor could not account for.

'Sally,' he said. 'Who on *earth* has been arranging my papers?'

This was the end. The blow had fallen and if there had been a table large enough Eleanor would have got under it. Lord Pomfret would now certainly refuse to take her to Barchester next morning and she might count herself lucky if he did not turn her out that evening, or throw her into a dungeon, though it must in fairness be added that though the cellars at Pomfret

Towers were terrifying in their depths and their gloom and owing to the late Lord Pomfret's precautions against fire had neither gas nor electric light so that a row of flat candlesticks lived at the entrance and more often than not there were no candles, or alternatively no matches, they had never been used for prisoners.

'Who do you think, darling?' said Lady Pomfret, not in the least appalled by her husband's question.

'Someone with a much clearer head than mine,' said Lord Pomfret sitting down. 'Was it Roddy?'

'Of course not, you goose,' said his wife. 'Roddy is a hard-working angel, but you know what he is like with papers. He always knows where everything is, but no one else does. It was Eleanor, of course.'

Eleanor felt her face burning as if it would never cool again.

'I'm so sorry,' she said.

'I really don't know why,' said Lord Pomfret, who was always scrupulously fair. 'Sally must have asked you to and I can't stop her when she gets going. I nearly lost my temper when I saw someone had been re-arranging my stuff, but when I saw how well it was done I was extremely grateful. Thank you very much indeed, Miss Grantly.'

'Eleanor, darling,' said his wife. 'We are very formal at the office, but all friends here.'

'Then thank you, Eleanor,' said Lord Pomfret, smiling. 'And the result of your meddling, my love,' he added to his wife, 'is that I shall have time to play picquet with Eleanor again to-night, while you grapple with Mothers' Unions. And I hope that will teach you a lesson.'

Lady Pomfret looked her gratitude at Eleanor and then spoke to her husband about Lady Emily, at which Eleanor felt uncomfortable and as if she were eavesdropping against her will, and looked questioningly at Lady Pomfret as if asking leave to retire. But Lady Pomfret laid her hand on Eleanor's arm and saying, 'You are one of the family now,' continued her talk, while Eleanor, to show that she was not listening turned the pages of the late Lord Pomfret's book *A Landowner in Five Reigns* which had been snatched by its publisher, Mr Johns, from the very jaws of Bungay and Hobb, who handled Mrs Rivers's popular novels of Female Middle-aged Romance. Seldom had a worse book been written by a peer and even Horace Walpole, if hard up for another titled author, might have been excused for passing it over, but it was in its way the portrait of an age and will have its value as a footnote to history when better autobiographies are dead. So absorbed had Eleanor become in his lordship's account of an incredibly dull visit to Osborne that she missed part of the conversation and Lady Pomfret had to say her name twice to call her attention.

'I am so sorry,' said Eleanor guiltily. 'I was reading the bit where Queen Victoria asked Lord Pomfret what he thought of Dean Stanley's *History of the Jews* and he said, "The Bible is good enough for me Ma'am, or bad enough."'

'I believe he might have been a Marquis if he hadn't said that,' said Lord Pomfret. 'Not that Uncle Giles would have minded. He never held much with Marquisates. I think it was because he disliked the Hartletops so much. You are connected with them, aren't you?'

Eleanor admitted that she was, feeling that it was not in the best taste for her, a kindly treated guest, to be a relation of people her host disliked.

'Father's great-aunt, Griselda Grantly, married Lord Dumbello who turned into Lord Hartletop,' she said. 'Father nearly called my younger sister Griselda, but then he called her Grace after his grandmother.'

'Then you,' said Lord Pomfret, one of whose hobbies in his rare intervals of leisure was relationships in the county, 'are called Eleanor after old Mrs Arabin and she was – now don't tell me for I almost have it – she was Archdeacon Grantly's sister-in-law, so she was, or would have been, your great-great-aunt-in-law.'

'That's it,' said Eleanor, who shared her host's passion for families. 'And my brother Tom that's at Oxford was called after mother's father and Henry is after my great-grandfather, I mean my father's grandfather.'

'And I am called Giles after my uncle,' said Lord Pomfret, 'which is the only name the Pomfrets ever seem to have been able to think of,' to which his wife said it was just as well, because when you got people called Alured or Cedric Weyland, like Lord Bond and his son, it rather put you off names.

And then they had dinner, and after dinner there was picquet and if they had been playing for high stakes Eleanor would have risen from the table owner of Pomfret Towers and the estate, for his lordship's mind was on his papers and he played very badly.

'I'm sorry, Miss Grantly,' he said. 'I am afraid I didn't pay attention. I think, Sally, I ought to go through those files again. It's a sub-committee to-morrow,' to which his wife answered with what was for her almost irritation that if he couldn't stop working on Sunday evening she would go to the villa at Cap Martin for Christmas, and there was no need to say Miss Grantly when Eleanor was helping him and being so nice to the children.

'Sorry, darling,' said Lord Pomfret. 'But you seem to be doing a good deal of work yourself,' at which Lady Pomfret laid down her pen and laughed and said he might have one hour if Eleanor would help him, and then they must all go to bed because of Monday morning.

Next day Eleanor woke with the depression that Monday morning on a visit always brings, unless we are staying till Tuesday and are in a position to jeer at the departing guests. Breakfast was quiet, her host and hostess reading a great many letters most of which looked very dull. At a quarter to nine the car was at the door.

'I shall see you to-morrow at the office,' said Lady Pomfret, kissing Eleanor affectionately, 'and I can't thank you enough for all you have done for Gillie. Here are the children,' and down came the nursery party with such demands for stories that Eleanor promised, though it seemed to her rather forward to do so unasked, to come again and tell them more stories.

'About giants cutting people's arms and legs off and eating them?' said the Honourable Giles hopefully.

'There aren't any giants really,' said Lord Mellings contemptuously. 'I want a story about a prince with a magic pony that he couldn't fall off,' on which Lady Emily Foster's comment was, we regret to say, Cowardy Custard, so that as the car drove away Eleanor's last view of the Towers was a kind of Laocoön group of Nannie among her three charges who were trying to fight each other, though in quite a friendly spirit.

Lord Pomfret drove in silence, though a pleasant silence, down the long drive and so onto the Barchester Road, and Eleanor, who with the Monday morning feeling strong in her was not quite sure whether one ought to disturb a busy Earl when he was driving his own car, also sat silent, though quite comfortably so. At Starveacres Hatches Lord Pomfret got out and with an apology went into a cottage.

'That's all right,' he said, when he came back and started the car again. 'Old Wheeler is an arrant impostor, but his family have been imposing on us for hundreds of years – in fact they were in Barsetshire long before the Fosters. It is all his own pig-headed fault that his cowshed is falling down, but I'll have to repair it for him. Sally tells me that your work at the Hospital Library is perfectly splendid, and I want to thank you, because she never spares herself and it is a great comfort to me to know that you are there.'

It is difficult to answer direct praise to oneself, but Eleanor did her best and said quite truthfully that everyone liked working for Lady Pomfret.

'It seems to me that you don't spare yourself either,' she said, again a little nervous of presuming.

'One has one's work to do, you know,' said Lord Pomfret, 'and that's that. Roddy does ten men's work on the estate, but we do really need a helper for him. You know his leg was hurt in the war and he gets nasty bouts of pain sometimes.'

Eleanor, noticing that Lord Pomfret spoke of help for his agent, not for himself, asked Lord Pomfret if he was really looking for someone.

'Do you know the right person?' said Lord Pomfret.

'I don't know,' said Eleanor, 'because it's my elder brother and one always thinks one's own family are perfect.'

'I can assure you one doesn't,' said Lord Pomfret. 'Look at the de Courcys. If any one of them can do another a bad turn they'll do it. And I know my uncle and my aunt thought poorly of me till the day of their death, though Uncle Giles had to put up with me. If it hadn't been for Sally I'd have gone to Australia or Canada. I hope Ludovic won't hate me for making him heir to all this worry and difficulty, poor little chap.'

Eleanor said she was sure he wouldn't and then summoning up all her courage she said, 'When Tom comes down from Oxford, do you think he might come and see you or Mr Wicklow? He wants to do estate work more than anything. My grandfather, mother's father, farmed and I think Tom inherited it. Of course,' she added, with the fatal propensity of the too scrupulously honest to underrate their own goods, 'he hasn't been to a land agent's school or anything, but he works terrifically hard and he would do his very best, he really would. And he did frightfully well in the war, though I don't suppose that helps,' she added sadly.

Lord Pomfret was silent and Eleanor knew she had mortally offended him.

'If your brother can deal with people half as well as you dealt with my little chap,' he said presently, 'I shall be glad to see him. Sally told me how you helped Ludovic about the pony and I would do a good deal to show my gratitude. I haven't anyone in mind, nor has Roddy. If you will let me know when your brother comes down from Oxford I will see him and get Roddy to have a talk with him. I can't promise. But if he can tackle things as you tackled those papers, Eleanor, he will be the man for us,' to which Eleanor could only say, like a schoolgirl, 'Oh, Lord Pomfret.'

'Say, Oh Gillie, and it's a bargain,' said Lord Pomfret.

So Eleanor, though with some diffidence, said, 'Thank you, Gillie, very, very much,' and then the Barchester traffic lights appeared and Lord Pomfret had to concentrate on his driving and presently put her down at the Red Cross Library Depot.

5

With considerable self-control Eleanor said nothing of her plans for Tom at home and the next few weeks passed quietly, for Tom had gone to France with some friends on a bicycling tour as soon as Oxford came down, with the reasonable hope of forgetting for the time being about his Schools and the unreasonable hope that somehow by getting out of England he would make the gods think he wasn't worrying about his results and therefore they would treat him favourably. All of which is quite illogical, but very human.

Henry managed to get a good deal of fun out of life in the intervals of worrying about his military papers and Grace was in the throes of that very anti-educational affair the School Certificate, without which it will soon be impossible to get employment of any kind. She had also twice again been sent up to Miss Pettinger by the Head Prefect for talking to Jennifer Gorman in the cloakroom about the horribleness of Jennifer's mother who had made her re-perm conditional on her passing her School Certificate, and though Miss Pettinger would dearly have liked to deal faithfully with Grace for her good, she reflected that the Honour of the School came first and that it would be a pity to upset Grace who was almost a dead certainty for several credits; and so refrained.

Colin Keith was as good as his word and asked Eleanor to dine and go to the theatre on a Saturday, saying that he would then drive her down to Edgewood afterwards, so long as she didn't ask unintelligent questions about petrol. This invitation came at a most opportune moment, for there was a good train to London early on Saturday afternoon and the excitement of London and a play would help Eleanor not to think too much about Tom's Schools. The play was to be Aubrey Clover's latest success, *If Turnips Were Watches*, with Jessica Dean its star as usual.

'I do hope Colin will drive carefully,' said Mrs Grantly for at least the sixth time that evening, as she and her husband were seated at their evening meal by the hard unsympathetic light of Summer Time.

'Now do stop worrying, my dear,' said Mr Grantly. 'Just think how nice it is to be alone for once,' for Henry was playing tennis and spending the evening with the Deans at Winter Overcotes and Grace had gone to the Barchester Odeon with Jennifer Gorman and would not be back till the last bus.

'It is, it is,' said Mrs Grantly, 'which reminds me that Miss Sowerby asked us to go down for coffee. She will be leaving Edgewood very soon so I think we ought to.'

The Rector agreed, but was in no hurry to move, for he but rarely had his wife to himself and Edna had provided an excellent supper of pig's fry and bacon quite illegally procured by her from the local Black Market at Grumpers' End where her parents lived.

'Do you know what I was thinking about while I was finishing my sermon this morning?' said the Rector.

'*Not* Tom's results. They aren't out, are they?' said his wife. 'I couldn't have missed them, though goodness knows one could miss *anything* in *The Times* now with all the nonsense they print and putting it all on the wrong pages.'

'Don't worry, my dear,' said her husband kindly. 'I am quite certain he will take a good class, though we can't expect a first. No,' he continued, with the expression of Christian when he beheld the Celestial City from the high hill called Clear, 'I was thinking of a real loin of pork with rich, crisp crackling and kidney under it and roast potatoes and pease-pudding and fresh greens and real gravy. If I saw it, I could almost sing my Nunc Dimittis.'

'How *beautiful*!' said his wife. 'But I'd rather have a real porterhouse steak, well browned outside and blood simply *gushing* out of it when you cut it and fried potatoes. That's all.'

'What I'd like,' said Doris who had, for such was her method of parlourwork, put a raspberry pie askew in front of Mrs Grantly before she removed the pig's fry and the dirty plates, 'is reel fish and chips. There's Bunce's in Calf Street at Barchester isn't too bad, but the fish now it always seems to repeat. S'pose the Government like it that way. When I took Glamora to Weston-super-Mare to auntie's we had lovely fish. Just come out of the sea it had and you never got the taste of it afterwards. But they do say that Mr Strakey or whatever his name is likes his fish a bit off. Well, it takes all sorts to make a world.'

'So it does,' said Mrs Grantly as Doris crashed out with the dirty plates, 'but how very nice it would be if it didn't. There are so many sorts one could willingly dispense with,' as example of which she named several gentlemen of Cabinet rank.

Her husband said these things were sent to try us, to which his wife replied that Things was exactly the word she would use and she only wished somebody or something would try Them, for she did not think it fair that all the trying should be on Their side and all the triedness on the part of the great, patient English nation.

'There's a ever so nice piece on the wireless,' said Doris, who preferred to bring the coffee in almost contemporaneously with the pudding that she might the more quickly clear away afterwards, and had been listening to the conversation, 'called These Foolish Things. Lovely it was. All about the things the lady friend liked, aeroplanes and lipstick and seats for the pictures and a nice cosy evening. They say Mr Strakey wrote it. Funny the way people think things up. You wouldn't never credit that Strakey had the nerve to do it.'

The Rector said he thought it was another gentleman with the same name and then felt he had better leave the subject alone.

'Oh well, it's all the same, Strakey or Strakey,' said Doris. 'Me and Edna's going down to the pictures. You all right?'

Mrs Grantly, who had long ago accepted her peculiar household for what it was worth, which was in service and kind natures a great deal, said she and the Rector were going down to Miss Sowerby's and would lock up when they came in, to which Doris replied Oky Doke and went away. Loud clashings were heard from the kitchen, followed by apparently the Massacre of the Innocents, which the master and mistress of the house correctly interpreted as the washing-up, followed by the putting to bed of all the children of shame. It was still rather early to go to Miss Sowerby, and as it was one of the few fairly warm evenings of that summer they sat in the garden with rugs round their legs to keep the midges off and talked about their family and the delightful discovery of an unsuspected cesspool under the old laundry in the Palace, considered by the Close to be a direct Act of God to get the Bishop and his wife out of Barchester during July, so that one would not have to meet them at garden parties. Then they walked down the High Street to pay their call on Miss Sowerby.

'The Last of England,' said Miss Sowerby who opened the front door herself, standing aside for her guests to pass and waving her hand at the rolled-up carpets and the crates in the hall. 'Also The Last Day in the Old Home. I am going in Mould's car to my sister at Worthing to-morrow and the van will follow on Monday. Come in.'

She took them into the long drawing-room which was looking rather forlorn with some of its furniture gone.

'Mr Adams is buying my best pieces,' said Miss Sowerby. 'My sister has a house full of furniture already, poor stuff, but she never had any taste, and I don't think any good furniture would be happy with her. If you will sit down I will go and get the coffee.'

She went away to the kitchen while the Grantlys sat and looked at the beautiful faded Chinese wall-paper, even more faded where the furniture that Miss Sowerby was taking to Worthing had been, and at the evening light on the garden. But they were not tempted to go out, for they had already had enough of that and the gentlemanly melancholy of the room was not unpleasing. Then Miss Sowerby came back and setting the silver tray upon a table near the front window established herself on a settee before it.

'You come and sit by me,' she said to Mrs Grantly, 'and you take the bergère, Rector. It is one of a set that belonged to my great-grandfather at Chaldicotes. My great-grandmother worked the cushions,' which caused Mrs Grantly to put on her spectacles and examine the muted colours of the tapestry work.

'Not what it used to be,' said Miss Sowerby, to which Mrs Grantly replied that colours, alas, did fade.

'Just as well that some of them do,' said Miss Sowerby. 'Look here,' and she pulled out from under the settee a small foot-stool covered with dark red velvet. 'My grandmother put a cover on this,' said Miss Sowerby, 'so that people wouldn't put their feet on the embroidery. She was always dressing the furniture up to save it. And there the cover stayed till last week when I thought I saw some moths in it and took the cover off. Nailed on with good brass-headed nails it was, so I put press studs on it.'

She unripped the press studs as she spoke and pulled off the cover, disclosing the most hideous, acid, vivid colours that the mind could conceive. The Rector, examining it with horrified admiration, said he could compare it with nothing but the windows in St Mungo's Cathedral at Glasgow, perhaps, he said, the most appalling glass that even Munich in the 'fifties produced.

'And that's your refined civilisation of more than a hundred years ago,' said Miss Sowerby proudly. 'What my great-grandmother's drawing-room must have been I do not like to think. They had fast dyes then and that's about all one can say for them.'

The Grantlys having sufficiently showed their horror, Miss Sowerby put the cover on again and pushed the foot-stool under the table.

'I suppose the wall-paper has faded a great deal too,' said Mrs Grantly.

Without answering Miss Sowerby got up, went to the large Hepplewhite bureau, opened the bottom drawers and extracted from it a roll of paper.

'That is as it was when my great-grandfather brought it back from Canton,' said Miss Sowerby. 'He was a merchant and owned his own ships and made the China voyage several times,' and as she spoke she unrolled it.

'Not very much difference, you see,' said Miss Sowerby. 'Good paper and vegetable colours and wood blocks I suppose.'

So lovely was the paper that Mrs Grantly begged to be allowed to inspect it further, so Miss Sowerby obligingly hung it over a heavy glass firescreen that they might the better admire it while they drank their coffee.

'What I shall miss at Worthing,' said Miss Sowerby, 'is sitting at my window and watching people go by.'

Mrs Grantly asked whether her sister's house was in a garden.

'Oh dear, no,' said Miss Sowerby, 'it is right on the front, but I don't call the objects that walk there *people*. One could never possibly have known them. When I say people, I mean Mrs Goble, or you and the Rector, and look! there are your maids! Going to the cinema I'll be bound. What good-looking girls they are. And very popular. Whenever I see them they are in company.'

Mrs Grantly at once looked out of the window, while her husband had to slew his arm-chair round to get a good view, and both were struck by the evident popularity of Edna and Doris who were the centre of a perambulating group of girls and young men and evidently the magnet which drew them all together. At that moment, by the strange telepathy that makes us know when we are being looked at, Edna became conscious that eyes were upon her, looked about, saw her employers at Miss Sowerby's window and giving Doris a hearty nudge fell into a loud, cheerful, unrefined fit of giggles, in which Doris joined.

The Grantlys, feeling by this time like Peeping Tom, withdrew hurriedly from the public gaze and the cheerful rowdy band went on its way towards the cinema.

'There is an art in looking out,' said Miss Sowerby meditatively. 'My grandmother always had green blinds across the bottom of the window, but my mother did away with them. She was right. If you live in a small town you must contribute your share to its amenities and I am quite certain your maids would feel defrauded if they didn't see Old Miss Sowerby sitting at her window like the Queen of Sheba.'

The Rector courteously deprecated the comparison.

'Well, Jezebel then,' said Miss Sowerby. 'And here is your son Henry as usual. I can almost set my watch by him,' and Miss Sowerby fingered an expensive but unfashionable little watch, engine-turned and enamelled a sickly blue, which was pinned to her black dress with a blue-enamelled true lovers' knot. 'I wonder what he is up to.'

'Nothing particular, I expect,' said Mrs Grantly who as we know was very tolerant of her children and would have been excessively bored if they had tried to give an account of all their doings.

'Well, he is up and down the street every evening as far as the Post Office,' said Miss Sowerby.

'Probably trying to get cigarettes,' said Mr Grantly. 'How thankful I am that I smoke a pipe.'

'You may, if you like,' said Miss Sowerby graciously, upon which the Rector, who didn't want to smoke in the least, confounded himself in apologies.

'What a huge car,' said Mrs Grantly, who was still looking out of the window. 'It's stopping here, Miss Sowerby.'

'Probably Mr Adams,' said Miss Sowerby calmly. 'He can't keep away. I told him he couldn't. "Buy this house," I said, "and it will own you, body and soul." If you will excuse me I will go and open the door.'

The Rector made as if to get up and go to the door, but if Miss Sowerby had been an old-fashioned nurse or governess and the Grantlys her young charges he could not have been more completely trampled on and ignored, as sweeping past him, or somehow managing to give an impression of sweeping although attired in a rather skimpy black dress, she went into the hall.

The Grantlys with unabashed curiosity looked out of the window and saw getting out of the car the large form of the Member for Barchester in a grey suit which just escaped being too loud. A good-looking girl who was obviously his daughter Heather followed him and behind her a young man who might have been any one of Tom Grantly's friends, bearing the mark of the army on him unmistakably. There was a brief talk in the hall and then Miss Sowerby brought her guests into the drawing-room.

'Mr Grantly, our Rector, you have already met, Mr Adams,' said Miss Sowerby. 'Mrs Grantly, this is Mr Adams who has bought the Old Bank House. Miss Adams and—' she paused.

'Pilward. Ted Pilward,' said Mr Adams. 'His father's an old friend of mine and many's the thousand pounds' worth of castings I've done for the brewery.'

'Is it your grey horses that bring the beer?' said Mrs Grantly, who had inherited from her hunting and farming father a real and well-informed interest in horses. 'They are the best dray horses in the county. Are they Suffolks?'

Young Mr Pilward said they were, with a strain of Percheron, he added.

'What can they pull, standing?' said Mrs Grantly, at once at home with Mr Pilward, who replied that their champion dray horse, Pilgarlick, was master of twenty-five hundredweight; but Pilbox and Pilbeam were not far behind him, he added, upon which he and the Rector's wife fell deep into cart-horse talk and young Mr Pilward said how difficult it was to find enough names beginning with Pil, or even Pill, and they mostly had to invent them now.

'And were you with horses during the war?' asked Mrs Grantly.

'So few people were, with this mechanisation,' said Mr Pilward, 'and I had particularly bad luck because I got sent to Iceland where every pony thinks it is a horse.'

'You didn't meet my elder son there, did you?' said Mrs Grantly.

Young Mr Pilward said he might have, but he hadn't quite caught the name. Grantly she said, wife of the Rector.

'Not Tom Grantly?' said Mr Pilward. 'To think of meeting old Tom Grantly's mother. We spent a month up there together and wasted most of our soap ration putting it down the geysers with no result at all. I'd like to see him again,' to which Mrs Grantly replied that Tom was in France but he would, she knew, love to see Mr Pilward as soon as he got back.

'What do you know about this, Heth,' said young Mr Pilward to Heather Adams. 'Mrs Grantly's son was in Iceland with me. This is my fiancée, Mrs Grantly.'

Apart from his use of the dreadful word fiancée (and what we can do about it we really do not know), young Mr Pilward might have been any of Tom's Oxford or Cambridge friends who had been through the war, which pleased Mrs Grantly, for if the right people lived at the Old Bank House it would be more amusing for the Rectory, and though Miss Sowerby was emphatically a right person she was too old and also too badly off to make her house a centre for the young.

'I think you know my friends the Beltons,' said Mrs Grantly, shaking hands with Miss Heather Adams whom she had taken a liking to on sight; perhaps helped to the liking by a consciousness that though Heather was tall, well built and distinctly good-looking, she could not compete with her Eleanor. Though what there was to compete for she had not troubled to consider. 'And are you going to live here?' Mrs Grantly went on. 'I hope you will like it.'

Heather said her father was giving the house they now lived in, an old-fashioned house with a garden near the works, to her as a wedding present and going to make Edgewood his home.

'But I expect we'll be here quite a lot,' she said. 'Dad's not used to having no one about and I don't want him to be lonely. And then Ted and I thought we could leave the children here when we go abroad on business,' all of which was said with the utmost simplicity and a very pleasant manner to an older woman.

Meanwhile the Rector, who in spite of being a father and a clergyman got on very well with the young, had been talking to young Mr Pilward and his opinion of him rose yet further when he found that young Mr Pilward had been at Cambridge before the war and taken his degree in physics and chemistry and whatever goes with them at the other place.

'You were luckier than my Tom,' he said. 'He was at Oxford for a couple of years before he was called up and didn't take his degree. He has gone back to read for Greats – the Classical Tripos I believe you would call it – and now he feels he wants to go on the land.'

'Stiff luck,' said young Mr Pilward, with what was certainly more than a perfunctory expression of good will. 'I must get in touch with him. We might have something in his line.'

'I am afraid he would be quite useless for the brewery,' said the Rector, 'and not much good on the commercial side either.'

'I didn't mean that, sir,' said Ted Pilward. 'But Heather's father is going in for land, you know, and once he gets going you never know where he'll stop.'

The Rector showed his surprise so plainly that Ted Pilward went on, 'He found the vegetables at the works canteen were costing far too much, so he went into the matter with Lucy Marling, I expect you know her people, sir, and he bought a big bit of old Mr Marling's land that needed draining and gave Lucy a free hand, and she's making a splendid job of it, sir. She knows the land inside out and Heather's father keeps an eye on the accounts and I know a bit about fertilisers from my chemistry and it's a kind of family concern now. And I may say the Hogglestock rolling mills and my father's brewery are running the best, most up-to-date, cheapest canteens in Barchester, let alone all England. You ought to see the figures, sir. They'd stagger you.'

The Rector said with perfect truth that he was sure they would and was prepared to continue the conversation, had not Mr Adams and Miss Sowerby overcrowed the whole room by the argument they were having, so that the other talkers were forced down as it were and had to stop.

'Rector, I know you will support me,' said Miss Sowerby, rather unfairly. 'Mr Adams wants to make the second floor into nurseries, which is very reasonable,' said Miss Sowerby with a glance at Heather and Ted revealing unsuspected depths of Gampishness in her, 'and the sooner the better, but I must explain that the east room was *always* the day nursery and if he makes the west room into a day nursery he'll have more trouble with the nurses. Right over the stable yard and chauffeurs and tradesmen about. You will never keep a nurse if you do that, Mr Adams. They'll all get married at once. Every servant that my grandmother had, and my mother too, married from this house. You can't keep them.'

'Well, well, we'll see,' said Mr Adams good-humouredly. 'I like to see people enjoying themselves. As a matter of fact my two girls I'm bringing are both engaged in Hogglestock and nice steady girls. And as for nurses, well, Heth will look after that when the time comes, won't you, girlie?'

Heather laughed and said anyway Dad's housekeeper was so

plain that they had nothing to worry about for the present. And was it true that Miss Sowerby had a lead cistern in the attic with 1688 on it.

'I have,' said Miss Sowerby. 'And what is more,' she added, still trembling from the recent argument, 'I must ask you *not* to use it for geraniums. It has done good and useful work all its life and I will *not* have it made a plaything of. It is still perfectly sound. Sooner than see it turned into Interior Decoration,' said Miss Sowerby with grim determination, 'I will destroy it with my own hands.'

'Well, that you really couldn't,' said Mr Adams kindly. 'Your hands weren't made for rough work.'

'Oh,' said Miss Sowerby, thrusting her garden-worn and garden-grimed hands under his eyes. 'Weren't they?'

'My mistake,' said Mr Adams. 'But I don't like to see a lady's hands look like yours, Miss Sowerby. Klensaway I use for mine and you'd hardly credit the dirt that comes off. I'll have them send you a tin from the works, Miss Sowerby, with my compliments. And as for the tank, you say what you'd like to be done with it and Sam Adams will do it, and I can't say fairer than that.'

'I apologise,' said Miss Sowerby, flushing as she held out her worn gardener's hand. 'I am old and get easily flustered about things I love.'

'It's all forgotten as if it had never been,' said Mr Adams making a kind of rough bow over her hand. 'Now you may say, Why did Sam Adams come here to-night? Well, the answer is he wanted to see you before you left your home and give you his very best wishes for health and happiness at Worthing. And if you want to come and convince yourself that the Old Bank House is being properly looked after and cared for, let me know and I'll send a car to Worthing to fetch you and take you back. And if you feel you never want to see the house again with strangers in it, say the word and Sam Adams will understand. I daresay I'm not good enough for this house,' said Mr Adams, looking round the room with respectful affection, 'but I'm going to do my utmost to treat this house as it has always been treated and as you would wish it to be treated. And what's more,' said Mr Adams, who had now got into his stride and was enjoying himself very much, 'I'll give it everything it wants. I know ladies want powder and lipstick – my Heth does, though she's got a nice complexion of her own – and houses want paint and the best polish and all that in much the same way. You trust me, Miss Sowerby. And now,' he added, 'there's a favour I want to ask you. You did mention some spare rolls of your Chinese paper and that looks like one on the firescreen. I'll give you any price you like for it, unless you'd rather not part with it.'

'I could not possibly accept money,' said Miss Sowerby. 'It is my parting present – to the house. There is enough in the attic to re-paper this room and more.'

At this point most of the party felt they would like to cry and Miss Sowerby said she would make some more coffee. Heather asked if she could help and Miss Sowerby, determined to make her sacrifice a willing and complete one, graciously accepted her offer.

'And when we have had our coffee we must really go,' said Mrs Grantly, 'or Miss Sowerby will be worn out. When do you expect to move in, Mr Adams?'

Mr Adams said it all depended on the contractors, but he had got his works department to tie them up good and tight with a large penalty for every day they overstepped the time mentioned in the estimate.

'I'm not rushing my fences,' he said, and it struck Mrs Grantly afterwards that this was hardly an expression she would have expected from him. 'I'm just having the drains overhauled and necessary repairs done and I mean to come here within four weeks. Time to do the nurseries later, seeing that my Heth isn't getting married till September. I wish Mother could have seen it all,' said Mr Adams, speaking not of his mother but of Heather's, who had died long ago, before prosperity came to her husband. 'She'd have liked the nurseries. Well, well. And now, Mrs Grantly, I'd like to say to you what I said to your husband when I had the pleasure of meeting him here not long ago. If your church wants anything, let me know and it shall be done. I don't want to figure in subscription lists, but me and my Heth we want to take the same pew Miss Sowerby had and we shall come regularly, when we're here. What's your church called, Mrs Grantly?'

Mrs Grantly, suppressing an insane desire to say, 'My child Grild, your child Grild; I to Walp, you to Walp; so so together we go,' said it was called Saint Michael and All Angels and was started about 1473 though much of it was later, and was famous for its four-pinnacled tower and the old weather-vane which bore the date 1625; also for having stood a siege from the Roundheads under the Courcy of the time, and been defended by the Pomfret of the day, and that there were supposed to be bullet-marks on the north porch but she thought probably children.

'I suppose I couldn't go in and see it on my way home,' said Mr Adams. 'I'm a busy man and have to take my pleasure when and as I can. And this would be a pleasure,' he added.

Mrs Grantly said nothing would be easier than for her husband to get the key and show them round while it was still half light, and when they had drunk their coffee they all said good-bye to Miss Sowerby who came out on to the steps to see them go. There was the usual unnecessary argument about who should go in the car, which Heather cut short by saying she and Ted would walk and Daddy could drive Mr and Mrs Grantly to the Rectory to fetch the key.

'Fine old lady, Miss Sowerby,' said Mr Adams. 'Well, that's that. And I hope she'll like Worthing,' and in a few moments they had reached the Rectory where all was quiet, the children of shame peacefully asleep and their mothers at the pictures.

The Rector was never tired of showing his beloved church to people, or walking about in it, or sitting in it alone, and if a new parishioner wanted to see it, all the better. So he got the key and opened the south door and let them in. None of his visitors knew much about architecture, but they neither obtruded their ignorance nor their scraps of knowledge, so the Rector was able to discourse at will and enjoyed it very much. Mr Adams's only criticism was of the brass on the altar, but as his was a technical objection, as from one who knew about metals, the Rector took it in good part.

'Always put something in the box,' said Mr Adams as they went out, and he pushed a piece of paper into the box whose scanty contents did but little to assist repairs to the structure of the church, 'you never know,' which act of charity the Rector took as a rather primitive form of insurance, but was none the less grateful.

'Well, that's that,' said Mr Adams. 'And we must be getting back to Hogglestock. Funny to think we'll be living here, isn't it, girlie? And funnier still,' he added, 'to think you and Ted will be at Hogglestock and your old dad here with Miss Hoggett to keep him in order. I expect I'll have to marry her one of these days,' at which Heather laughed.

He then gave an alarmingly powerful handshake to the Rector and his wife and drove away with his family.

The Grantlys went into the house. From the kitchen quarters the sound of a voice was heard.

'Wireless in the kitchen,' said Mrs Grantly. 'The girls can't be back from the cinema yet. I wonder if Purse has turned it on.'

She went to look and found her son Henry listening to the late news-summary.

'Hullo, mother,' he said. 'I just turned the wireless on.'

'That's all right,' said his mother. 'But why the kitchen wireless? I thought it was the children.'

'Oh, it was something I wanted to listen to,' said Henry, 'and I thought if I put it on in the drawing-room it might disturb you.'

'Well, you know I loathe it,' said his mother, 'but that's no reason for you to go into the kitchen if it's only for the news. What are you listening to?'

'Oh, nothing!' said Henry. 'Only if there's a train derailed, or a mail van burnt or anything, they sometimes tell you. I mean if letters are late there's usually a reason.'

His mother said the letters had come at the usual time that day and that in any case there was now no second post on Saturday and she was going to bed. At the same moment the wireless spat loudly and turned into someone talking gibberish with an overtone of a jazz band. Henry turned it off and got up, looking unaccountably worried.

'Anything wrong, darling?' said his mother, and that he did not at once walk out of the house shows what a very nice young man he was and what a very nice mother Mrs Grantly was.

'No. Nothing. At least, oh nothing,' said Henry. 'Mother, do you think War Office letters ever get lost?'

His mother felt his anxiety but could not quite make out what it was about, so she firmly said that they never did.

'I suppose they might get delayed?' said Henry.

His mother said she supposed they might, and on this very inconclusive state of things they went to bed.

We will not say that Mrs Grantly did not close an eye till her daughter Eleanor returned from her excursion to London, but neither can we say that she went to sleep and forgot all about her. The fact was that like most middle-aged women now she did not sleep very well, partly owing to the strain of the war and far more owing to the grinding depression of the peace and increasing undernourishment, and she knew that if she went to sleep Eleanor's return would wake her, however quiet it was, for a mother's ear never loses the nursery habit of quick waking in the dark hours. So she sat up in bed and wrote some letters and then read for a time, and between half past one and two she heard a car come up the hill and stop outside the gate, then subdued voices and then Eleanor's footstep on the stairs. She turned off her reading-lamp in case Eleanor should see the light under the door and feel that she ought to come in, but much to her pleasure there was a gentle tap at the door, so she turned on the light again and in came Eleanor, looking very handsome and happy.

'It was *heavenly*, mother,' she said as she seated herself on the side of the bed in the way her mother particularly disliked because of making the mattress sag if one did it too often. 'Colin gave me dinner at his club and the play was wonderful. I do think Aubrey Clover is wonderful to write his plays and act in them and Jessica Dean was so lovely and so funny and made me cry dreadfully and then Colin took me to a place called the Wigwam to have some supper and Aubrey Clover and Jessica Dean were there and Oliver Marling and they asked us to their table and we danced and then we all drove down in each other's cars, I mean Aubrey and Jessica were going to Winter Overcotes and Oliver was going to Marling and Colin was bringing me home, so we all kept on getting in and out of Aubrey's and Colin's cars till we got to Winter Overcotes and then Colin brought me home. It was *heavenly*,' and she yawned ferociously.

Mrs Grantly expressed her satisfaction and said now Eleanor had better go to bed.

'Oh, and mother,' said Eleanor, 'Jessica said we must all come to tea at Winter Overcotes to-morrow, I mean to-day, so Colin is going to fetch me after lunch. If only Tom's results were out it would be *perfect*.'

'I'm sure they will be all right,' said Mrs Grantly, which completely deceived her daughter who yawned her head nearly in half, kissed her mother and went away.

The mothers of grown-up children in these days of wrath mostly find, to their own great surprise, that they are not as selfish as they thought they were and that a treat, a pleasure for their young is the only real form of pleasure for themselves. This may partly be because most of them are too tired to enjoy greatly such treats as come their way and find it less fatiguing to enjoy them vicariously; and partly because for most of the young treats are rare and they have to spin their own happiness out of themselves, and their parents admire their cheerful matter-of-fact courage and feel they couldn't do it themselves. But parents do other quite courageous things and probably their reward is that their young rely on them. Being utterly reliable is no inheritance, but it does give one a sense of being in a small way a pillar of society. Mrs Morland's inspired misquotation about one's children expecting one to do things for them all their life may have been sweeping, but there was a good deal of truth in it. And by some twist of the mind the older generation would rather work itself to the bone for its young than see its young work themselves even to the second skin for their elders. Their private reward is, we confusedly think, the knowledge that they stay and earth's foundations stay. Whether the young, the so dear, the so utterly unreliable will in their turn hold the sky suspended to protect the next generation we cannot tell. But if they do not, farewell to faith and welcome State interference and a crushing of all human kindnesses and sacrifices.

Some such thoughts as these, thoughts so nebulous, so inchoate that they fade from sight and reason even as they are apprehended, may have passed through Mrs Grantly's mind before she went to sleep. And when she woke it was with a delightful feeling that something nice had happened; and the niceness was of course that Eleanor had passed such a happy evening in London and had every prospect of a happy afternoon at Winter Overcotes, and during the Early Service she tried to concentrate on gratitude to Heaven for giving Eleanor a treat, but found herself wondering what it would be like when the Adams family sat in the Old Bank House pew where Miss Sowerby was attending her last service in Edgewood.

As Mrs Grantly came out of church she overtook Miss Sowerby in the churchyard and held her hand for a moment, but could not find anything to say.

'Your young people were late last night,' said Miss Sowerby, who Mrs Grantly thought must have been packing well into the small hours of the morning to hear the car. 'I hope dear Eleanor enjoyed herself. Your Edna told me, on her way back from the cinema, for pictures I will not call that entertainment, that she had gone to a play in London with Colin Keith.'

Mrs Grantly said she had had a very happy evening.

'Then here I say good-bye,' said Miss Sowerby, getting into Mould's car which was waiting for her. 'I couldn't take my leave of you in a better place. Bless you all. I believe St Sycamore at Worthing is quite a nice church, but a little High. I daresay people like it. By the way, I *know* Victoria Norton will try to get my Palafox Borealis out of Mr Adams the moment I am gone, so I have told the gardener to bring it to you, if you will accept it. It needs very little care. Cut it down to the root every Christmas, put cinders over it and roll them well in. In 1955 you should have a very fine flower. Good-bye and God bless you.'

Mrs Grantly watched her drive away and went across the churchyard to her home and breakfast, a little sad. But the horror of having to house and be responsible for Palafox Borealis soon drove such weakness away.

'Never mind,' said her husband when she told him about Miss Sowerby's bequest, 'I daresay it will die. I think you had better let the kitchen look after it. That boy Sid has a real gift with plants. It so often goes with a slightly sub-normal mind.'

'Like Lady Norton,' said his wife, which remark was very well received.

6

About three o'clock Colin Keith arrived at the Rectory and having been well brought up he did not sit and sound his horn till Eleanor came out, but rang the bell and asked Doris if Mrs Grantly was in.

'She's in,' said Doris, 'only she's out. In the garden, I mean,' so Colin said he would find her and went round to the side of the Rectory where the whole family except Tom who was still in France were contemplating Palafox Borealis, who had just arrived in a wheelbarrow. Combined greetings took place and Colin said he hoped they had not disturbed Mr and Mrs Grantly last night, or rather this morning.

'Not a bit,' said Mrs Grantly. 'I was reading. What *do* you think of this, Colin?'

'Very, very little,' said Colin. 'In fact I find it highly repugnant. What on earth is it?'

Mrs Grantly explained that it was Miss Sowerby's parting gift and extremely valuable, that is if one liked it, she added. While she was speaking Doris, who had followed Colin to the garden in an artless way because he had spoke so nicely, as she afterwards told Edna, was gazing wide-eyed and open-mouthed at the exotic.

'It's a lovely pot-plant,' she said to the company in general.

'Sid and Glad they was helping the gentleman to take it out of the wheelbarrow and Sid liked it ever so.'

Anyone unacquainted with Doris's vocabulary would have wondered who the gentleman was that trundled wheelbarrows about Edgewood, but Mrs Grantly at once understood what Doris meant and couldn't help smiling as she thought of Miss Sowerby's jobbing gardener. But the words gentleman and lady have lost all value in current use and indeed to describe anyone as a gentleman or a young lady is to cast the gravest doubt on their right to such a description. And why ladies are always young ladies, we cannot say, any more than we can explain why the word gentleman means very little when used by the Ednas and Dorises, whereas young gentleman still means what it has always meant. Brave New English Usage is a strange growth and in many ways alien to the true spirit of England.

'I suppose,' said Mrs Grantly, 'it was really simpler to call everyone citizen.'

'Doubtless,' said Colin, 'but so un-English,' at which Mr and Mrs Grantly laughed and then Mrs Grantly said if Sid would take care of the plant he could have it in the kitchen. Sid, who had been hanging about his mother while the foregoing conversation took place, tugged violently at her hand and said in a hoarse whisper, 'Oy'd loike to have it, Mum. She said Oy could.'

'That's not the way to speak,' said Doris, smacking Sid, though rather as a gesture than in anger, 'don't say she, say Mrs Grantly.'

Sid was heard to mumble something.

'He'll be ever so pleased,' said Doris, interpreting her son, 'and we'll put it in the kitchen window. Say thank you, Sid.'

As it was evident that Sid, whether from principle or shyness, probably the latter, would probably burst before he could release his tongue, Mrs Grantly took pity on him and said he could take the plant to the kitchen yard, which he accordingly did, clasping the pot to his stomach and lurching with a janissary's walk round the corner of the house.

The Rector asked his wife, with some anxiety, if she thought the plant would be safe. Miss Sowerby had, he said, left it with them as a charge. To which his wife replied that if she were a camel that hideous plant would be the last straw and she felt certain Sid would look after it much better than she would. Colin then took himself and Eleanor away from this fascinating scene and drove off with her to Winter Overcotes.

As we all know, the Deans' house at Winter Overcotes had become since the war a centre of amusement and attraction for the youth of Barsetshire and for the not so young. Here every age was catered for, from Sir Edmund Pridham who still at an advanced age kept up all his county activities, to the middle-aged and young married people of the neighbourhood and the many Dean grandchildren and their friends. There was wealth, a spacious house and garden, a generous friendliness, and of late years the added attraction of the youngest daughter Jessica, whose success with Aubrey Clover in his many plays made her not only a star of the London Theatre but a dazzling and attractive star to the county. There had been a time when the county as a whole felt a daughter on the stage to be not wholly desirable, possibly grounding this feeling on the fact that such of their daughters as had Thespian ambitions had never got further than occasional provincial repertory; but Jessica Dean's success had been so dazzling that they had come to accept her as conferring lustre on Barsetshire, though her family was not county. And then in the previous year Jessica's elder sister

Susan, Eleanor Grantly's predecessor as Depot Librarian of the Red Cross Hospital Library, had made a marriage of deep affection with Captain Belton, R.N., whose people were the right sort (the county's expression, not ours, but a truthful one), his mother being a Thorne; and the Deans had been tacitly accepted as belonging (again the county's expression). We may say that the Deans themselves were entirely unconscious of their new status, as they had been of their status as newcomers, for like many large families they made their own circle and owing to their large and varied acquaintance could have dispensed with the county's approval if they had realized such a thing existed.

But happiness is never complete in this world (which makes one wonder about the next) and Mrs Dean, who lived entirely in the world of her family, had just cause for complaint when the Dowager Lady Norton decided after Susan Dean's marriage that she ought to call. This her ladyship had done in her very old Rolls which towered high above all other cars and made everybody sick who rode in the back seat except Lady Norton whose long apprenticeship as Lady-in-Waiting to Royalty had made her immune to everything, choosing as a suitable hour three o'clock on a summer afternoon when Mrs Dean, always the laziest of women, was in a state of coma in a deck chair. Lady Norton's call had been short and she had sat bolt upright all the time, a striking example to her hostess but one from which Mrs Dean had no desire to profit, and had left cards on departing, a piece of ceremony practically unknown to the young Deans most of whom had never possessed cards, or if their mother or mother-in-law, as the case might be, had pressed cards upon them when they married, had never used.

*

'I cannot tell you why it is,' said Mrs Dean on this Sunday afternoon, as she settled herself on her comfortable long garden chair after lunch, 'but I *know* Lady Norton will come again to-day.'

'I must say it will be very forgiving of her if she does,' said her husband, 'seeing that you never returned her call. What makes you think so?'

Mrs Dean said she did not think, she just knew.

'I wish you wouldn't know things, darling,' said her daughter Jessica, who was becomingly attired in a simple and ravishing confection which made anyone who was trying to wear a New Look dress look like nothing at all. 'Why should Lady Norton come?'

Her mother said it was in her bones.

'Well, if she does,' said Jessica, 'Aubrey must talk gardens with her,' for the famous playwright-actor-manager spent most of his week-ends at Winter Overcotes, the one place, he said, where no one asked him silly questions.

'I don't know many flowers,' said Aubrey Clover, 'but I'll do my best. I know Manypeeplia Upsidedownia and Nasticreechia Krawluppia,' but no one present was properly educated so there were no responses, for the present generation only know Edward Lear as someone who wrote limericks, if they know him at all.

'You know everything, darling,' said Jessica.

And then Colin Keith arrived with Eleanor, and then the Freddy Beltons from Harefield and quantities of other Deans and their friends, some of whom played tennis, so that there was a good deal of coming and going, with Jessica always as the centre whether she wished to be or not and Aubrey Clover taking colour from each fresh person, so that no one noticed him much, though he noticed them.

Eleanor, who liked the Deans and was at ease with them,

could not help contrasting this week-end with her week-end at Pomfret Towers; on one side the old life struggling to keep alive and hold its standards high, the ceaseless work for others, the tremendous responsibilities of a position where once had been money and power and now there was so little to give except ceaseless, selfless work for the county, the estate and the tenants, while the future of their very home was insecure. And here wealth without landed responsibilities and as far as could humanly be seen a family well grounded that was increasing and multiplying and thriving. Which was the better she could not say. Perhaps the one was doomed to be succeeded by the other in the whirligig of time. Her sympathies were for Lord and Lady Pomfret gallantly upholding an almost lost cause in the name of Tradition; stinting themselves for the estate and the people who had lived on it for so long and who were not particularly grateful; wondering whether little Lord Mellings would have any inheritance when he grew up; letting Emily and Giles go down into the market-place and fight for their living and their independence. Not very difficult for these last-named young people who seemed to be born with the splendid health and ruthlessness that are one inheritance of an old line; not easy for their elder brother with his *fin de race* sensitiveness and his quick fears. But though Winter Overcotes was everything that Pomfret Towers was not, it had virtues of its own and was far more fitted for survival. Here the head of the family was master in his own business and in his own house, a man who counted for a great deal, who largely through his own energy and perseverance was now in a position to ask from the world what he willed and get it. Here was the large brood of young Deans, with health, intelligence and good looks backed by money, fearing nothing because they had never had cause to be afraid. No one of them except that strange sport, in the language of biology, Jessica the strolling player, of any particular distinction, but all successful and uniting the family forces against all comers.

For the Deans, the future. For the Pomfrets what? Eleanor was not clever enough to give an answer with any certainty, but as she sat among the Deans she felt a sense of ease and well-being as if their very vitality infected her, and glad on the whole that her forebears had not bequeathed to her the burden that fell on Lord Pomfret. Poor Lord Pomfret. And as she thought of him, and the gratitude that had shone from his tired face when he found his way among the accumulation of papers made easier for him, a pang went through her heart, leaving her almost dizzy for a moment.

'What are you laughing at?' said Colin.

'Dickens,' said Eleanor.

'I am all with you there, bless him,' said Colin. 'But why in particular?'

Eleanor could not explain, for suddenly she had seen a comic (in the serious sense of the word) side to her late reflections, realising that as she had arranged Lord Pomfret's papers, so had Florence Dombey worked for little Paul and smoothed the path of learning for his overtasked mind; and as she had imparted fairy tales to Lord Pomfret's children, so had Esther amused and soothed Peepy and his young brothers and sisters. But Colin was waiting for an answer, so in desperation she said everyone was like Dickens if you came to think of it and if they weren't they were too dull to be true.

'And here,' said Colin, 'comes a living proof of your statement. I didn't know the Dreadful Dowager was on calling terms here.'

And as he spoke the Dowager Lady Norton came graciously into the garden, in her usual impressive sables with a flowered toque and a feather boa, at which vision Mrs Dean roused herself and said to her husband, 'Did I ask her?'

'I haven't the faintest idea,' said Mr Dean.

'I am sure you will not look upon this as an intrusion,' said Lady Norton, advancing upon Mrs Dean. 'A very old friend of mine, Mrs Grant, who now lives almost entirely in Sicily, wrote to me the other day and said I must be sure to come and see you again as her son Hilary who married Mrs Brandon's daughter is, she said, a friend of one of your sons. You have such a charming place here.'

Some women, in fact nearly all women, would have been infuriated by Lady Norton's intrusion. But Mrs Dean raising her beautiful eyes to Lady Norton's toque, held out her hand saying 'You must forgive my not getting up. I have a heart. I don't know which of the boys it would be, because they are all such different ages. Do sit down and this is my husband,' after which unwonted effort she resumed her siesta, while Jessica said in low piercing tones that what Lady Norton was after was the variegated lupins. Susan Belton, who had not yet forgotten to be the good useful Dean daughter, felt sorry for Lady Norton, which was pure waste of time, and said she expected it was one of the twins as they had been with the Mediterranean Fleet, to which her brother Robin, who was working on the Martin Leslies' farm at Rushwater, replied that he knew Hilary Grant because Hilary was going in for Grade A milk, of which remark Lady Norton took no notice at all, but to the great joy of the younger Deans put up her glasses and did what Aubrey Clover called quizzing the borders.

'And how did She get here?' said Oliver Marling who had just arrived in a low voice to Jessica.

'Just as you did, my lamb, with petrol and never ask me whose,' said Jessica, kissing Oliver with the easy affection that always wrenched his heart. 'Why haven't you brought Lucy?'

Oliver said she was off somewhere on her own affairs, farm or garden, and had sent her love and would be coming later.

'I heard only yesterday a very interesting piece of news,' said Lady Norton, 'from my dear old friend Hilda Sowerby. She has sold her house in Edgewood to some new people whose name I don't know, very rich, and gone to Worthing. So I felt the least I could do was to drive over and see her. She told me that her Palafox Borealis was doing remarkably well and she expected it to flower in 1955. I am most anxious to see it, for mine is not doing well and I must find out who has bought her house and go and visit them.'

It is almost impossible to describe how little her ladyship's remarks interested the party, all except Eleanor who was certain that her blushes would betray her, for had she not heard with her own ears and seen with her own eyes the Palafox Borealis first cried down and then degraded to the kitchen quarters. She had a horrid feeling that Lady Norton would read her thoughts and would like to have hidden, but there was nowhere to hide as they were sitting on the terrace outside the house.

'You ought to know Aubrey Clover, Lady Norton,' said Mrs Dean, making what was for her an unwonted effort to be a good hostess. 'He knows *all* about flowers. That is he, by Jessica. We are all very fond of him.'

'*The* Aubrey Clover?' said Lady Norton, again using her glasses. 'You must come back to Norton Park with me, Mr Clover, and see my variegated lupins,' to which Aubrey Clover replied that unfortunately lupins always gave him violent hay-fever, but he hoped that some day Lady Norton would come down with him to see his aunt who still had her whole front garden bedded out with red geraniums, marguerites and lobelias.

Lady Norton, who quite understood that actors were not as ordinary people, said how charmingly Victorian.

'That,' said Aubrey Clover, rapidly taking a part in an early Pinero play, 'is a compliment which applies equally to your ladyship,' and bowed slightly from a sitting position.

'I wish I could do that,' said Oliver Marling to Jessica with unfeigned admiration. 'I feel it would suit me. And perhaps a monocle on a wide black ribbon.'

'I will give you one,' said Jessica.

'It would be useless,' said Oliver. 'It would be so precious that I should have to conceal it in my bosom – what an awful word bosom is – and duly draw it out when alone, pressing my lips passionately upon it.'

'Idiot,' said Jessica very fondly, and then a noise which had been approaching resolved itself into Oliver's sister Lucy Marling in company with Mr Adams, both talking at once.

The ranks of the party at once opened to receive them, for Lucy was a valued friend and during the past year Mr Dean and Mr Adams had met a good deal over business and Mr Adams was a welcome visitor at Winter Overcotes. Heather too was liked if not loved, but her absence at college and her engagement had not given her many opportunities of meeting the Deans.

'Lady Norton, I don't think you know Mr Adams,' said Mrs Dean, after which tremendous effort she felt she had justified herself and need not speak again.

'Pleased to meet you, Lady Norton,' said Mr Adams. 'Now, Dean, I know you don't like to talk business in the home, but there's something I'd like to tell you. You know my Heth's getting married in September. Well, I'm going to give the house at

Hogglestock to the young couple. They say the farmer's boot is the best muck and it's the same with the works, and with old Pilward's brewery for that matter. My Heth's going to keep an eye on the rolling mills and young Ted's going to keep an eye on the brewery, and the old fathers are going to sit back a bit. I've many other matters on hand, like for example that market garden Miss Marling is running for our canteen and some oil interests and one thing and another. So I've bought a house in Edgewood, not far from the church, why there is Miss Grantly all the time, I'm sorry I'm sure, how do you do, Miss Grantly – and a grand old gentleman the Rector is, I may say – and I'm going to be a country gentleman. Laugh! if anyone had told Sam Adams forty-five years ago that he was going to be a country gentleman, well he wouldn't have believed them. Not that I was up to much in the way of believing or disbelieving them. A queer little nipper I was. I wish Mother could have seen the house though,' he added thoughtfully, and all who knew him well knew that it was of his wife that he was thinking, who had shared his humble beginnings and left him a widower with a little girl.

The congratulations were very sincere and even Mrs Dean woke up to say that she hoped Mr Adams would ask her to his first party, which he at once engaged himself to do.

'There's only the one thing I'm not happy about,' said Mr Adams meditatively.

'If it's drains, I'm your man,' said Aubrey Clover. 'That is a subject I *do* know something about. If I hadn't somehow found myself on the stage I would have been a sanitary engineer. Will you let me come over one Sunday, Adams, and see the layout?'

'Pleasure,' said Mr Adams, visibly gratified. 'My contractors are starting work almost at once. Name your own day. But it's not that. It's the old lady. Admitted that she did well out of me.

Sam Adams isn't one to haggle if he likes a thing and I believe in paying a fair price for what I want. But when I think of Miss Sowerby having to leave her old home I feel like Hitler,' said Mr Adams.

'Is it you that bought Hilda Sowerby's house?' said Lady Norton.

'That's the one,' said Mr Adams. 'And a cool eight thousand I paid for it.'

'Then you are the man I want,' said Lady Norton.

'Pleased to hear it,' said Mr Adams, 'but I'm not parting with that house, not for double the money, for when you've – well, I'd not say lived as long as I have,' he said with a gallant glance at Lady Norton who was well into her seventieth year, 'but had as much to do with money as I have and known how hard it is to put the first pennies together and make the pounds, you'll know that money isn't what it is, which is pretty well nothing nowadays with this Government, but what it will do. And when you've got what you want no money will buy it from you.'

'Tut, tut,' said old Lady Norton, to the great admiration of her hearers. 'I don't want Hilda Sowerby's house and I haven't the money to buy it if I did. What I want to know is what Hilda has done with her Palafox Borealis. She can't have taken it to Worthing, for she told me there isn't a garden.'

'And what's that?' asked Mr Adams, a question which earned the gratitude of all members of the party who were not horticulturists.

'The Mngangaland Lobengula is its other name,' said Lady Norton. 'Not Matabelensis of course. That is a different genus. Anyone can grow the Septentrionalis, but the Borealis is extremely difficult. I should be most grateful if I could have some of the seeds in due course.'

'Well, it's all Greek to me,' said Mr Adams. 'Do you mean it's something in the garden?'

'I know it,' said Lucy Marling who had been sitting as usual with her legs inelegantly wide apart and her capable brown hands on her knees, 'because I saw it when I took father to London to the Royal Horticultural. It's a great hideous thing with a stalk about two feet high and a knob on top and some things like grey flannel hanging down. The man at the stand said the seeds simply *stink*,' said Lucy with enthusiasm, 'even worse than balsam, but it only seeds every seven years. It was *awful*.'

'Well, there's nothing like that in the garden,' said Mr Adams, 'because I took a good look round. But there were some lovely roses and a nice long border with plenty of colour. My mother never had a garden, but she was as proud as Punch of her window boxes. When I was a boy I used to promise I'd buy her a nice garden when I grew up, but there you are. Well, if I see anything like what you mention, Lady Norton, I'll send it over to you.'

'But are you sure it isn't there?' said Lady Norton, to which Mr Adams replied not if it was like what she said it was and fell into talk with Mr Dean while Lucy listened seriously.

But who can describe Eleanor's feelings when she realised that the rare plant so much coveted by Lady Norton was probably at the moment in the Rectory kitchen window, or in a tub in the back yard. For a moment she thought of telling her ladyship what had happened, and then she reflected that it was no business of hers; but the secret was too weighty to be kept in her own breast, so she told Colin what had happened and he was enchanted and they both laughed a great deal, and then to everyone's great relief Lady Norton said she had to go on to Staple Park and so she went away.

'Was that Lord Norton's mother?' said Mr Adams. 'I know her son. He's on some of my boards and a pompous ass. Well, Miss Marling, I've been telling our host about the market garden and he thinks the figures are A1.'

'You seem to be doing a pretty big job,' said Mr Dean to Lucy. 'My congratulations. Your father must be pleased.'

'I don't know,' said Lucy. 'You see,' she added, with her usual truthfulness, 'vegetables aren't in his line unless you count winter roots for the animals. He jolly well ought to be grateful, considering the price Mr Adams paid for the land though. I'll tell you what, we're going in for poultry this year and pigs the year after, and if we can get father to sell a bit more grazing land we're thinking of a Grade A herd. Of course it's a shame the stuff all goes to Hogglestock, when so many other people need good fresh vegetables, but we couldn't keep our prices down as we do unless we worked in bulk. And pretty big bulk at that,' and she gave a number of figures about tons of potatoes and hundred gross of cabbage that interested Mr Dean, though it didn't much interest anyone else.

'Dear Lucy,' said Jessica to Oliver. 'How interesting she is.'

'Little Liar,' said Oliver. 'What you mean is What a crashing bore.'

'Do I?' said Jessica, turning large starry eyes of childlike wonder on Oliver.

'Don't waste your talents on me,' said Oliver with faint bitterness, but when Jessica rubbed her soft cheek against his coat sleeve he relented and became her slave again, finding the world well lost in her company.

'I say, Mr Adams,' said Lucy, who had been observing with interest her brother and Jessica, 'do you think it's a good thing to be hopelessly in love with someone?' to which Mr Adams replied that she had given him a teaser and he really couldn't say as he had asked Mother (by which Lucy knew he always meant his wife) to marry him the second time they met and she had said Yes on the following Sunday, so he hadn't really had much experience.

'And what do you think, Miss Marling?' he added.

There had been a year in Lucy's life when her young heart thought it cared for Captain Barclay who had married her widowed sister Lettice. How deep the feeling was, or might have been, she did not know, for she had deliberately set herself to bury it for ever and had succeeded. It had not been without some secret tears and grief, but that was long past and her heart had never been touched again. Had it been touched she might have felt more sympathy for Oliver who had never tried to free himself from his captivity, though Jessica had refused his suit and told him that there was only one man in the world that she could marry, but to Lucy it seemed a poor-spirited thing to offer forever a love that was forever refused and this attitude of mind combined with the increased self-confidence that her market-gardening venture with Mr Adams had given her made her slightly contemptuous of her dear Oliver.

'Well,' said Lucy, 'I don't know. If I liked anyone very much and I was a man I'd propose to them. But if they said No I'd take it. I think it's a bit sloppy to go on loving people if they don't love you. I mean *real* loving, not sloppy loving,' though what Miss Lucy Marling thought she meant we cannot say, for her experience of that emotion was not very great and no other had come her way.

Mr Adams looked at her with a kind of benevolent pride, for she was in a way his discovery, his creation. When she had bearded him in his office a year ago to ask his opinion of fertilisers and had broken down into unmanly tears as she spoke of her father's farming difficulties, he had made a quick decision which he had not regretted. He had bought some of Mr Marling's land at a good but not outrageous price and asked Lucy to take charge of it, giving her a free hand and all the backing his wealth and business connections could afford. The results had been even better than his opinion of Lucy had given him reason to hope and his respect and admiration for her had steadily grown. A woman, for one could hardly say a girl, who could handle land like that and produce tons of potatoes and thousands of cabbages and other green stuff and talk confidently of poultry and pigs and Grade A herds, this was the kind of person he could understand and respect, nor did the fact that he had given her a start make him think the less of her. And luckily she and Heather got on very well, each being a thoroughly sensible young woman who appreciated in someone else the gifts or qualities which she had not got. And now his little Heth who was to have been his right hand man was getting married, and though she was some day to have a large interest in Mr Adams's business and had the brain and outlook of a man where business was concerned, she would be Heather Pilward, not Heather Adams, and her husband and family must come before her father. But in Lucy Marling, who was not married and showed no signs of being interested in such a possibility, Mr Adams felt he had backed a winner and one upon whom he could utterly rely. And on the various occasions when their views on the market garden had differed, Mr Adams had to admit that Lucy had usually been right and what was more had not been puffed up about it.

But any further musings on this subject were interrupted by the arrival of Dr Ford, who had been attending a patient at

Lambton and had come on to hear the Deans' news, for he was an inveterate though an honourable collector of gossip.

'Oh, Dr Ford,' said Mrs Dean rousing herself, 'none of us are ill, are we?'

'Not so far as I know,' said Dr Ford, seating himself near her, 'except that everyone in England is ill. I have just been to see Mrs Allen, the Warings' old Nannie who lets lodgings to her ex-babies' families. Nothing wrong with the old lady. But she doesn't get the food she needs. Nobody does.'

'That's right,' said Mr Adams unexpectedly. 'That ration for heavy workers now, I didn't catch your name—'

'Ford,' said that gentleman.

'That ration for heavy workers, Mr Ford, oh Doctor, I beg your pardon, that ration for heavy workers, Dr Ford. Well, I know what I'm talking about with the different businesses I control, and what I say is the extra rations wouldn't fill a hollow tooth. No, nor make one decent meal for a man. I'm doing my best, Dr Ford. Adams, that's my name, Sam Adams and pretty well known hereabouts and elsewhere, and I've got Miss Marling here helping me grow fresh vegetables for my canteen and we're going to go in for hens and pigs and a Grade A herd. But that's only a makeweight if you take my meaning. What my men need is plenty of fat bacon and proper beer and real cheese not this mucked-up, sorry, Mrs Dean, stuff, and good bleeding meat. And when I say bleeding,' said Mr Adams, 'I mean red meat with good blood in it that comes out, well, like a fountain when you put your knife into it, not this grey stuff with water in it. I daresay you'll tell me that we get enough vitamins or vittamins or whatever you call them, but what I say is, Show me a vitamin and I'll believe you.'

'I couldn't,' said Dr Ford. 'It's a catch word, that's all.'

'But,' Mr Adams continued relentlessly, 'it's all so much eyewash. If vittamins did all that good, why do my hands have industrial fatigue and drop things and forget things? Talk of night starvation; it's day starvation they've got, and everyday starvation, too.'

'Quite right,' said Dr Ford, amused and interested. 'I've no particular use for vitamins myself. However They are determined to break us. And when I say us I don't mean professional men like myself or big business men like you, or quiet, hard-working people like all of us here, but the English People. And I daresay They will,' said Dr Ford cheerfully.

A confused but polite clamour then arose from the company assembled which may be disentangled roughly as: Ford was quite right and when some tired civil engineer had passed a faulty specification by a tired contractor and a bridge didn't stand up to its load perhaps They would be sorry (Mr Dean); Jessica was a marvel but if she got any thinner and fluffed her lines and had to have a nervous breakdown he hoped They would be pleased (Aubrey Clover); one got quite enough to eat but it always made one feel too full and she hoped They felt too full too (Mrs Dean, who was almost wide awake in her interest); she would tell one what, one did get enough to eat only it was all the wrong things and no wonder one felt that horrid full feeling and she expected They felt it too and that was probably what made Them so beastly (Lucy Marling); the food in most places was so foul that one really didn't want to eat it (Oliver Marling); if any told him they had found a little restaurant where the food was quite marvellous he simply knew it was a lie and hoped They would have to eat it (Colin Keith); it was scandalous that one had to give up bacon coupons to be allowed to eat one's own pig or give bits of it to friends who weren't so well off and he didn't suppose They had ever seen a pig or scratched its back on a Sunday morning (Robin Dean); where some people got the money from to buy what they did buy on the Black Market she didn't know (Jessica Dean, who frequenting the Wigwam as she did had every opportunity of observing these things).

'I'll tell you what,' said Lucy Marling, riding the whirlwind by the sheer power of her voice, 'there's one thing I can't forgive and that was putting up Their own wages – oh all right, salaries then – the minute They got in and then stopping the Nelson pension. It made me feel so disgraced that I nearly cried. And not giving a penny to the people who won the war for us. It almost made me ashamed of being English, only it would be so *awful* to be French,' she added.

Mr Dean said mildly that the corollary did not appear to him to be inevitable. There were, he added, Rooshians; also Turks and Prooshians.

'Who was it,' said Oliver, 'who said "I hate foreigners and black men begin at Calais"? Whoever it was he had the root of the matter in him.'

'There is one thing that we may thank the French for,' said the quiet voice of Captain Belton, R.N., who had not contributed to this discussion, 'that they did not accept Mr Churchill's offer of equal citizenship during Dunkirk.'

'You're right there,' said Mr Dean. 'Good God, what an offer! One sometimes wonders if Mr Churchill knew they would refuse it.'

'Of course he did, the lamb,' said Jessica. 'He knows everything.'

Eleanor, who had not yet spoken, feeling a little shy of raising her voice among the clamour, said she thought Mr Churchill was a very good artist and his pictures were much the best in the

Academy, which Oliver rather sententiously said was doubtful praise.

'Well,' said Dr Ford, as a kind of chairman closing the discussion, 'I must be getting along. I'm up till two o'clock most mornings now filling in all these new forms. But I won't have a panel. If I had a panel I'd have to empty my consulting room and put benches into it and whitewash the walls once a month and have all the children giving each other mumps and measles and have no time for my hospitals or my own patients and sit up till four in the morning. Talking of hospitals, the Barchester General is having severe pressure put on it by the Ministry of Health to give up two of its wings for out-patients from the County Council Hospital. Where they expect our patients to go, I don't know. It's a rum thing though, they daren't touch the Masonic Hospital. Needs a bit of explaining but I can't explain it.'

'But Dr Ford,' said Mrs Dean, who had been making the most valiant efforts to stay awake, feeling that it was somehow for the good of the country, 'do I have to be a panel patient?'

'Not unless you want to,' said Dr Ford. 'You can go on sending for me as often as you like.'

Mrs Dean looked much relieved.

'I thought the Owl Book said one *had* to be a panel patient,' she said.

'The Owl Book?' said her husband. 'What do you mean, my dear?'

'You know perfectly well,' said Mrs Dean with great dignity, 'that They sent us that little book with pictures of Owls with stethoscopes listening to other Owls breathing.'

'Quite right,' said Mr Adams. 'I had a copy of that pamphlet put into my letterbox, by whom I don't know. Probably by the postman, though why they should have to act as bill distributors for the Government I can't say.'

Lucy said the Post Office seemed to have to do everything and Mrs Margett at the Post Office at Marling said it nearly drove her silly.

'And a sillier piece of Government propaganda I've never seen, though I doubtless shall,' said Mr Adams, ignoring his market-gardener's interruption. 'Why we are supposed to need pictures of Owls to explain a Health Service that the Government are trying on the dog passes me. Like those comic-strip pictures about looking where you're going and taking care on the road.'

Mrs Dean said but surely children needed to take care.

'They may or they mayn't,' said Aubrey Clover, 'but I live in London and use my eyes. Most of the London boroughs have a table of street accidents outside some public building and to quote a celebrated market-gardener, I'll tell you what: less than ten per cent of the accidents are to children. The devil always looks after his own.'

At this remark, unfeeling some may think, but quite fair comment, Mr Adams and Mr Dean so far forgot themselves as to laugh. But Mrs Dean said reproachfully that she knew Aubrey really adored children and no one must listen to him.

'But do I have to have a card or something?' she inquired.

'If you did read the Owl Book as you call it,' said Dr Ford, 'you would know that married women not employed outside the home need not be insured.'

Mrs Dean said she supposed They knew one was safe at home and so didn't need to be insured.

Not so much that, said her husband, as that he had to insure himself and his insurance covered hers.

'Though as a matter of fact I don't know if I'm insured or

not,' he added. 'Miss Perfect at the office does all the Health Insurance stuff and she tells me what I ought to do.'

Eleanor said it seemed a shame that her mother's very nice maids, Edna and Doris, would have to pay insurance just because they weren't married, and everybody knew that they didn't know where their children's fathers were.

Nor who they were, added Colin, who had been told the full and fascinating story of their amiable loves.

Dr Ford unstretched his long legs and said he really must go and he hoped to die before the whole medical profession had been forced into beggary as nonconformists or turned into Owls, and so went away.

After his departure the party gently disintegrated leaving the Deans and the Freddy Beltons who were staying to supper to entertain each other, which indeed they always did, surprising in themselves as Oliver said so many different elements. Oliver and Lucy went back to Marling. Mr Adams said he would go round by Edgewood as he'd like to have a look at his house. Colin and Eleanor did not go very fast and when they got to the Rectory they found Mr Adams's powerful car standing in the drive and heard Mr Adams's powerful voice in the drawing-room, so they went in, and found he was talking to Edna.

'I didn't mean to intrude,' said Mr Adams, 'in fact I hoped to see your father and mother Miss Grantly, but they're still at church. I ought to have remembered that and come back earlier, but now I'm here I'll stay and see them if convenient. This young woman let me in and we got talking and I'm trying to put some sense into her head.'

Eleanor inquired anxiously if anything was wrong.

'That's one I can't answer, but I'll tell you what,' said Mr Adams, who appeared to have contracted this habit of speech permanently from his market-gardener, 'your girl mustn't make teeth a habit.'

'I don't quite understand,' said Eleanor, looking at Colin who was also completely at a loss.

'You tell Miss Grantly your own way,' said Mr Adams to Edna.

'It's about my new teeth, Miss Eleanor,' said Edna.

'Aren't they comfortable?' said Eleanor, for Edna and Doris, who like many country people with otherwise perfect physical health had always had very bad teeth, had recently had complete uppers and unders which they often took out at meals.

'It's not that, Miss Eleanor,' said Doris, 'but it said in the paper we get them free now, so me and Edna's going to have new sets.'

'But why?' said Eleanor, in whose veins ran the thrifty blood of her farming and clerical forebears who had lived well but always in the country phrase put by.

'It seems a waste-like not to, Miss Eleanor, when the Government pays for them,' said Edna. 'Mrs Goble's Sarah she's got a lovely set, you'd hardly know them from the old ones. And me and Doris is going to get glasses too and I promised Purse he should have some. I reckon Doris will look a sight in glasses.'

'You don't need them surely,' said Eleanor. 'You do all your beautiful crochet without them.'

But Edna stuck to her opinion that if you could get a thing for nothing it was sinful waste not to have it, quite irrespective of whether you needed it or not, and as there was nothing to be gained by arguing Eleanor did not try and Edna went back to the kitchen.

'There you are,' said Mr Adams. 'That's what you and I are paying for,' to which Colin replied that one must say in fairness that Edna was paying too.

'A pal of mine who knew about these things,' said Mr Adams,

'tells me They budgeted for eight millions for dentists. More likely to be fifty millions by the look of it. Not much of honest poverty now. Pretty dishonest I call it and I hope I'll pay my own way till I die.'

'I expect we'll have free funerals soon,' said Colin.

'No you won't,' said Mr Adams. 'Undertaking's a trade the Government can't touch. It's about the one trade left that still knows its business. It's a pleasure to watch those fellows at their work. All as correct as a slide rule. And a close trade. You or I couldn't get in for love or money. It beats any trades union, only as far as I know there's never been a strike. It's a rum world.'

Eleanor and Colin would like to have heard a good deal more of this fascinating subject, but the Rector and his wife and Henry came back from church and conversation turned upon the Old Bank House, where Mr Adams said he and his daughter were proposing to have a small house-warming before long and he hoped the Grantlys would all come.

'By the way, Keith,' he said as he rose to go, 'you're an authority on railway law, aren't you? I read your book on Running Powers.'

Colin, immensely flattered, said he did rather specialise in it.

'I'll tell my solicitors to get in touch with you,' said Mr Adams. 'It's about a siding that serves my works and I'm having a bit of a blow-up with the railway about it. They may call themselves British Railways, but the old Barsetshire Line would never have treated me like this.'

Colin was slightly taken aback by Mr Adams's informal manner of approach, but raised no objection and told Mr Adams where his chambers were, adding that he was nearly always at Northbridge at week-ends with his sister Mrs Noel Merton.

'Would you come over for a night, Eleanor?' he said, as Eleanor accompanied him to his car. 'Lydia told me to say she would love to have you and I shall be down for most of the Long Vacation.'

He looked intently at her as he spoke and his look moved her in a way she could not account for.

'Tell Lydia I'd love to come,' she said. 'I don't get my holiday till later, but I can always manage a night.'

'Thank you a thousand times for a most happy day,' said Colin, keeping her hand in his as he spoke. 'Good-bye.'

He drove away and she went back in a dream to the drawing-room, though her dream was so gentle, so quiet, that her parents did not notice it.

7

In due course the Oxford results came out and, to nobody's great surprise, Tom Grantly had a second. His tutor Mr Fanshawe of Paul's wrote to Mr Grantly saying that Tom might have done better but might have done much worse and he thought him peculiarly unfitted for an academical career. As his father had already come to much the same conclusion no bones were broken. Mrs Grantly in her relief and excitement wished to telegraph to Tom, but no one knew where he was, so this was considered waste of money and given up. The Rector, a double first himself in days of more spacious education, would have liked a first, but making allowances for interrupted reading and the difficulty of settling down as a grown-up man and ex-soldier among boys fresh from school or their military service he considered Tom had done well. Mrs Grantly boasted so shamelessly about it that her husband accused her of having an entirely unmathematical mind, incapable of telling the difference between one and two; to which Mrs Grantly replied with dignity that she had read a book by a very celebrated mathematician in one of a series of little books which made people think they knew everything, and when she found the whole of the first chapter was devoted to proving that two and two made four, she was confirmed in her feeling that mathematics were silly, because two and two couldn't be anything else. Henry said jolly good, but was secretly wondering whether his brother having succeeded meant that he wouldn't get his calling-up papers, a feeling which he acknowledged to be superstitious but could not overcome; though whether their arrival would have been expedited by Tom getting a fourth he did not consider. Grace, discussing the matter with Jennifer Gorman, gave it as her opinion that she would rather do an exam like Tom's than that awful School Certificate, because even if you failed at Oxford no one could make you do it again and could Jennifer go to the Barchester Odeon with her on Saturday and see Glamora Tudor in *What Men Desire* with the new male star Hastings Pond, about the love life of Marcus Aurelius. For Miss Pettinger had moved with the times and her boarders were allowed a pretty free hand, which they would have taken in any case.

A few days after the good news Tom came back, sunburned and rather boring about Touraine and even more boring about the different inns and pubs he and his friends had visited. But though his family's congratulations on his second were warmly affectionate, their ill-concealed indifference to his travels and their interest in local affairs soon cured him of travellers' tales and he began to realise the deep truth that no one, broadly speaking, ever wishes to hear what you have been doing.

Two days later his father summoned him to a kind of conference in the study where, affecting a grown-up nonchalance which he did not at all feel, Mr Grantly had said to his elder son, 'And now you have got through your Schools, and I don't see how you could have done better and a good second is not to be despised, have you thought about what you are going to do?' to which his son had answered readily, 'No, father.'

'Well, nor have I,' said the Rector. 'I thought we had better have a talk first,' though he knew in his secret heart that it had been partly a natural desire to postpone difficult things and partly an equally natural feeling that Tom was bound to disapprove any suggestion his father made. After which there was a long silence while the Rector pretended to arrange some papers and Tom examined with apparent interest a copy of the Parish Magazine.

'Well, we must think about it,' said the Rector, to which his son replied Rather and both again became a prey to dumb embarrassment.

'Well, I suppose I must get on with what I'm doing,' said the Rector. 'I have to read a very foolish letter the Bishop proposes to send to the Mothers' Unions, as he has asked my opinion of it. It wouldn't interest you.'

'No, father,' said Tom truthfully. 'Well I'd better see if the lawn needs mowing,' and so escaped through the French window into the garden, where his sister Eleanor, who had got a day off, was cutting dead heads off roses and wondering whether Lord Pomfret had kept his papers in order. Not that it was anything to do with her, but when one had done a good job one liked to feel that other people hadn't undone it.

'Father's just been trying to talk to me about things,' said Tom.

'And then he said you must both talk about it another time, I suppose,' said Eleanor.

Tom said Just about that and it was pretty rotten kicking about doing nothing even if one had got through one's Schools.

'I wouldn't mind so much if I were twenty-two or twenty-three,' he said, 'but it's pretty mortifying at twenty-eight and after being a Major. Not that one expects that to count for anything,' he added gloomily.

Eleanor, at first a little nervously and then warming to her subject, said she had been to Pomfret Towers for a week-end and the agent Roddy Wicklow who was Lady Pomfret's brother couldn't manage everything and Lord Pomfret was being most frightfully overworked because of the estate, and the county on top of the estate, and the House of Lords on top of them both.

'And he's never very fit,' said Eleanor, with a small pang at her heart as she thought of the Earl's tired, patient face, 'and I did help him a bit with some county stuff and he said he didn't know anyone who could help him nor did his agent. So I said What about you and he said to let him know when you were back and I think he will tell Mr Wicklow to see you. I just thought it mightn't be a bad sort of idea.'

She then wished she had not spoken, as we so often do when it is obvious that our best loved prefer to stew in their own juice.

'I must say Lord Pomfret sounds a bit wet,' said Tom after a short silence. 'After all he's a peer and got lots of money and an agent.'

'He's *not*,' said Eleanor indignantly. 'He works frightfully hard and looks *awful*, and they have to live in the servants' wing and sell most of the fruit and vegetables and things. And the children are *darlings*,' she added, suddenly touched by a remembrance of little Lord Mellings and his anxious face and his thin arms round her neck. 'I thought you'd be pleased, Tom,' and she sniffed in a very ungenteel way.

'Sorry,' said Tom, hitting her kindly on the back. 'I didn't mean to be horrid. But things do get one down a bit. Everyone I know's got a job now. And most of them in London,' he added, 'lucky devils.'

Eleanor said of course Pomfret Towers wasn't in London

exactly, but perhaps if Tom could get a job there he could get to London later, upon which her brother told her rather sharply not to be silly and the more one got a job in Barsetshire the less likely one was to get a job in London. And then he repented his contrariness and said one might have a shot at it anyway. Which ungracious remark Eleanor decided to ignore.

'I'll ask Lady Pomfret next time she comes into the office if you could go and see Mr Wicklow,' she said, upon which Tom shied away like an unbroken colt and said it seemed pretty awful to go barging in like that on people one didn't know, so that Eleanor was sorely put to it to keep her temper. But her affection got the better of her pique and she said she was sure Lord Pomfret wouldn't think it was barging, because he was so awfully kind.

'All right,' said Tom, and gave his sister a perfunctory hug with one arm, which she quite understood to mean that he was sorry, at which moment Henry came towards them with a face of deep concern.

'I say,' he said. 'Something awful's happened.'

'Carry on,' said his brother calmly. 'Whatever it is I've seen worse.'

'It's like this,' said Henry. 'A friend of mine that I was at school with wants me to go down to Devonshire for ten days.'

'I've heard worse things than that,' said his unsympathetic brother.

'Shut up, you juggins,' said Henry. 'Don't you see if I go to Devonshire and my papers come while I'm away I shan't be here.'

Eleanor suggested that there was the post, the telephone and also, though it wasn't much use because they always delivered them with the post like an ordinary letter, the telegram; to which Henry objected that (a) they would all forget to forward the letter, (b) they mightn't get through on the telephone and (c) that everyone knew it was just as quick to write as to telegraph now, adding as a rider that there was the most marvellous bathing at Shellacombe. Upon which his elder brother told him not to be a young fool and the War Office would jolly well see to it that he did get the letter and, take it from him, if he went to wherever it was as soon as he got the letter they probably wouldn't be expecting him. So after repeating the argument on both sides in a very boring way it was finally decided that Henry would go to Shellacombe and keep a small suitcase all packed the whole time he was there, just in case he had to leave by the next train. So Henry said he would go down to the Post Office and wire to his host.

'No need to go to the Post Office,' said Tom. 'Send it over the telephone.'

But Henry said he had to go down the High Street anyway and might as well send it there.

'How these kids do worry,' said Tom from his lofty ex-service point of view. 'Let them wait; that's all.'

He and Eleanor then gardened peacefully while Eleanor, very cautiously, put forward a plan that they might lunch together at Barchester on Friday when Tom was going to get his hair cut, which invitation Tom graciously accepted and suggested the White Hart.

'It's pretty awful now,' said Eleanor. 'All sorts of queer people go there and it's difficult to get a table. Even old Burden can't manage it for one, even if he has been head waiter since Queen Victoria's Coronation. You'd better come to the Red Cross Canteen. It's not bad.'

Her brother, who was really very fond of her and knew he had been ungracious, accepted her invitation with the mental proviso that he would have a couple of beers between his barber and his lunch to keep his courage up, and that was the end of their talk for the time being.

Accordingly on Friday Eleanor told her very efficient underling Miss Isabel Dale, whose people lived over at Allington, some kind of cousins of Robin Dale who had married Anne Fielding, that she was going to give her brother lunch at the canteen and would Isabel mind if she had her own lunch a bit late. To which Miss Dale, who was as much of a help to Eleanor as Eleanor had been to Susan Dean, said that was quite all right.

It was just like things that Friday morning happened to be one of the busiest days the office had had for some time. There was a particularly large post to be dealt with, a visit from the police about various small thefts in the cloakroom, two committees and a complete breakdown of the telephone for thirty-five minutes, so that when Tom was announced he found a sister whom he had never seen before, riding the whirlwind and directing the storm.

'About twenty minutes, Tom,' said Eleanor. 'You'll find plenty of books,' and then took no further notice of him, applying herself to the restored telephone and dictating some letters to Miss Dale, while Tom pretended to read a book about thirteenth century stained glass and felt that he was a useless drone, out of his element in all this femininity and resenting his own useless, unemployed condition, so that when Eleanor stood up and said she was ready he was as near the sulks as his very nice nature would allow. Eleanor led him downstairs and through a basement passage to the large old-fashioned kitchen which was now the canteen and as she went in front of Tom she did not see how sulky he was, though she did have a horrid feeling in the back of her neck that there was something wrong and hoped it was only her imagination.

'Good Lord, it's a cafeteria,' said her brother in a displeased voice as Eleanor stopped before a pile of metal trays, took one herself and offered one to him.

'Much the simplest,' said Eleanor. 'Take a plate and a knife and fork and a spoon and fork if you want pudding and a glass. Good-morning, Miss Pildown. Have you something nice for my brother to-day?'

'Well, Miss Grantly, the mutton is just off and so's the stew, but there's some nice spam with salad,' said Miss Pildown who was celebrated for always being cheery. 'And I think we've a few potatoes left. You're late to-day.'

Eleanor cheerfully explained that they had had a very busy morning, feeling all the time Tom's rising resentment at nice spam with salad, while her heart sank. Nor did it rise when the pudding turned out to be stewed dried apricots and custard-powder custard and Tom refused it.

'We find the gentlemen don't fancy sweets as a rule,' said Miss Pildown, adding cheerily that there was some nice cheese.

Tom was heard by Eleanor, though luckily not by Miss Pildown, to say that no cheese was nice now, and accepted a portion with grudging thanks.

'There'll be a table in a minute,' said Miss Pildown. 'We're very full to-day. There you are, Miss Grantly, over by the window,' and Eleanor, thanking her, carried her tray to the far end of the kitchen where a table for four had just been vacated.

'What a bit of luck,' she said, as cheerfully as she could, to which Tom made no answer, for he was by now not only cross but very much ashamed of his crossness and too self-conscious to try to apologise. And though Eleanor was sadly disappointed at the failure of her treat she behaved very well and did her best to talk as if nothing had happened. But it is hard work to pretend to someone who knows you very well and her heart was sinking fast as she realised that she would have no chance of talking to Tom about seeing Roddy Wicklow, when Lady Pomfret's voice said,

'May we come and sit with you, Miss Grantly? I have brought Gillie and there isn't a table left.'

Eleanor got up, as did Tom, even more annoyed by a strange couple coming to the table.

'Of course, Lady Pomfret,' she said. 'And this is my brother Tom.'

'Your sister is our mainstay here, Mr Grantly,' said Lady Pomfret, 'and she was our mainstay when she came to the Towers, wasn't she, Gillie?'

So Tom shook hands with the Pomfrets and his temper began to clear again and he felt ashamed of having given way to it as Lord Pomfret asked him about himself and where he had been in the war with a kind of pleasant diffidence, yet giving the impression that he really wanted to know. Lady Pomfret had at once fallen into Red Cross shop with Eleanor, so the men had to talk to each other and when Lord Pomfret asked some questions about the British Zone in Germany Tom, who had spent some time there, was able to give intelligent answers.

'You must believe me, Mr Grantly,' said Lady Pomfret, 'when I say that we usually have a really good lunch. Your sister must bring you here again. And when next she comes to the Towers she must bring you too. I would like you to meet my brother who is our agent. He was invalided out of the war with a game leg, but he rides and gets about a good deal.'

Before Tom could properly thank her she had risen, saying

that she had a committee and must fly and so went away, leaving her husband to finish his lunch with the Grantlys. Eleanor, well pleased that Tom was getting on well with Lord Pomfret, religiously ate her stewed apricots and custard and thought again how tired Lord Pomfret looked and how good of him it was to be interested in Tom and wondered if anything would come of the talk. Then she looked at the big kitchen clock and saw it was time for her to relieve Miss Dale.

'I'm so sorry, Lord Pomfret,' she said, 'but I'm on duty. Please give my love to the children. Are you coming, Tom?'

'If you will excuse me,' said Lord Pomfret, 'I shall ask your brother to give me a few moments. It may be a good thing for him to see Roddy. Your sister gave me such help Mr Grantly, that I have an almost superstitious feeling about your family. We might discuss some possible plans. Good-bye, Eleanor. If we can do something for your brother,' he added with his pleasant tired smile, 'I shall feel that I have repaid you a little of my debt.'

Eleanor, more confused than she would have thought possible, said some words of thanks and went away, but whatever her feelings, they did not prevent her stopping to ask Miss Pildown if she would be sure to keep something for Miss Dale as it wasn't her fault that she was late, which Miss Pildown cheerfully promised to do. Then she went back to her office where the good Miss Dale had been dealing most efficiently with whatever had to be done, and sent her down to her dinner. But when she was alone she did not find it easy to settle to her work. She was overjoyed that Tom was to go to the Towers, the Pomfrets had been as always most thoughtful for others, most remembering, most kind, but her mind was in a turmoil of thoughts and emotions and she did not understand herself. Lady

Pomfret had called her Eleanor at the Towers, though she always called her Miss Grantly at the office. Lord Pomfret had told her to call him Gillie when he drove her into Barchester, but this she felt quite unable to do. And he had called her Eleanor just now and as good as said that he meant to help Tom because he owed her a debt. What debt could he owe? She had looked through some papers and sorted them. A job any intelligent person could do. She had been able to help Lord Mellings over a difficulty, but any kind-hearted person would have done her best for the little fellow. She did not know that her own name could move her so strangely and felt almost light-headed and more than half-ashamed and when Lady Pomfret unexpectedly came in she wondered, most unreasonably, if it was to tell her not to presume.

'Did I startle you?' said Lady Pomfret smiling. 'I was kept in the office, something that had to be settled, but I am really going now. I am late as it is. I only wanted to remind you to let the Mayor know his letter is being considered. We will arrange a date for you and your brother to come to the Towers. I shall be in again on Monday,' and she went quickly away.

More goodness, more kindness, thought Eleanor and sat dreaming for at least five minutes. Then she gave herself a kind of mental shake and wrote the letter to the Mayor and by the time Miss Dale came back she was her usual competent self again and stayed on late to make up for lost time. When she got home she found Tom bursting to tell her all about his talk with Lord Pomfret and the possibility of an opening on the Pomfret estate, the pros and cons of which he discussed aloud with himself at great length. Of gratitude to his sister for having brought this meeting about there was no word, nor indeed did Eleanor expect any, for she had not arranged anything; fate or chance or whatever one liked to call it had done the arranging. But she did think Tom might have expressed some gratitude to Lord Pomfret.

Meanwhile life went on as usual. The Palafox Borealis flourished in the rich air of the kitchen as it would never have flourished under Lady Norton's old head gardener. At the Old Bank House the drains and the electric light and the gas and the decorating all got in each other's way and accused each other of stealing that bit of seven-eighth inch pipe, or putting that spanner where no one couldn't find it, or leaving that floor-board loose a-purpose so that a chap would break his blinking neck; and the whole was complicated by the sweep who had been summoned a week too soon and took such offence that the foreman had to take him round to the Sowerby Arms for at least an hour. But in spite of all these setbacks, incidental to the refurbishing of any house, the work did go on and whenever there was any serious difficulty Mr Adams found time to come over and deal so faithfully with the trouble-makers that the grumblings subsided and it was universally conceded that he was on the whole a good sport and a man it was a pleasure to work for. And such good progress was made that Mr Adams proposed to sleep in his new house by Bank Holiday week-end and asked the Grantlys to come over and see the house on Bank Holiday Monday and have tea in the garden, an invitation which they accepted with pleasure, and the more willingly as on that Monday there were usually a good many trippers from Barchester and elsewhere who not only visited the church but were apt to trespass into the Rectory garden, belonging as they did to the Brave New World which likes to ignore barriers and leave any green places trampled like a sheep-yard and littered with paper and tins and bottles. And even when they didn't trespass they stood and stared over the hedge so that the Grantlys were driven from the lawn into the kitchen garden.

Once or twice Lucy Marling had come down with Mr Adams to give her professional advice on the vegetable garden which had fallen into neglect under Miss Sowerby, partly through its owner's poverty, partly because she only cared for her flowers. Once Mr Adams had brought her up to the Rectory, where she had got on very well with Tom and had invited him to come over and see the new tractor and the packing sheds on Mr Adams's market garden, where Tom had spent an interesting and instructive afternoon being shown everything and told what by Miss Marling to the fullest extent.

'It's a marvellous place,' he said to his mother when he got back, 'and Lucy runs it like anything. But Lord! what a roaring girl,' which quotation Mrs Grantly did not recognise and reproached her son with want of chivalry, for she had, for absolutely no reason at all, thought that Tom might fall in love with Lucy Marling and so become manager of Mr Adams's market garden. Which shows how silly mothers can be, for Lucy was a good deal older than Tom and it was highly improbable that Mr Adams would make his very efficient manager's future husband a partner in the enterprise. So Tom sulked in a mild way at his mother and went over to the market garden again several times, where Lucy Marling told him all she could in what time she had to spare. All of which so exercised Mrs Grantly that she did not notice how many times Colin Keith happened to be in Edgewood when Eleanor got back from her Red Cross, or if she did notice it she paid no attention to it.

By this time the Barchester High School had broken up and Grace was returned to the bosom of her family and resumed her affection for Colin in an extremely uninhibited manner, hanging on his arm in a way that Colin found very trying though he was too courteous to detach her more than two or three times during one visit.

'I really must apologise for Grace,' Mrs Grantly said to Colin one day when that young lady had gone to the Pomfret Madrigal Red Cross Fête with Jennifer Gorman. 'I do hope you don't mind, Colin.'

Colin said he rather liked it.

'It reminds me of my sister Lydia,' he said, 'when she was about that age and Noel Merton used to come down to Northbridge. Noel used to say that she was so unacquainted with man that her tameness was shocking to him. But he married her in the end.'

'Oh dear! You didn't think I meant—' said Mrs Grantly and then stopped in confusion.

'Not in the least,' said Colin. 'Pray, pray don't think that. Grace is a very good sort of fellow and we get on very well. If it is possible for anyone to look on someone who isn't his sister as a sister, though I don't seem to have made my meaning very clear, I regard Grace in that light, though when she clings to my arm I do sometimes wish she weren't so heavy. But they usually fine down. What I really came for was to bring my sister Lydia's love and she wants to know if Eleanor can come to Northbridge on Wednesday for the night. We will fetch her from the Red Cross and deliver her again next morning.'

To which Mrs Grantly said that Eleanor made her own plans but she felt sure she was free and would love to come and then Grace came in.

'It was a splendid fête,' said Grace, sitting herself on the arm of Colin's chair. 'I spent seven shillings and Jennifer spent ten because it was her birthday last week and while I was waiting for the bus in Barchester Mr Adams came past and there was a traffic hold-up so I flagged him and he drove me home because he was coming to look at his house. I saw Eleanor waiting for the bus but I couldn't get at her because of the queue. I say, Colin, have you read a book called *Northanjer Abbey*!'

'If it is the same as one called *Northanger Abbey*, I have,' said Colin.

'Oh well, Northanger then,' said Grace. 'Is it very awful? We've got to read it in the holidays. I'm going to read John Buchan all over again. I'd like to marry someone like Richard Hannay, only I'd have all the adventures with him, not stay at home with the children. Do you like poetry?'

'One at a time, my girl,' said Colin. '*Northanger Abbey* is unique. I quite agree about Hannay and Mrs Hannay, only I think she's Lady Hannay now. And I like poetry if it's what I call poetry.'

'I've been reading the *Oxford Book of English Verse*,' said Grace. 'It's a bit mixed, but it's very ennobling if that's the word I mean. There's one by someone called Francis Thompson about a child only she's really older than a child and a man going for a walk and they are sort of in love but it says Between the clasp of his hand and hers Lay, felt not, twenty withered years. I thought it was very beautiful and I nearly cried. It was—'

'No, my girl,' said Colin. 'I am *not* thirty-six. Not till September. And I may add I know that poem, and if you think that I know not love from amity I may tell you that I do. And moreover I am *not* your foster-lover. I apologise,' he added, turning to Mrs Grantly, 'for these details, but in view of breach of promise and as I am a lawyer, we had better get everything straight.'

Mrs Grantly who had only just begun to take in the implications of the foregoing conversation looked anxious, but as Colin appeared quite at his ease and Grace was still perched on the arm of his chair leaning heavily over him, she supposed it was all right. And indeed it had to be all right, for she knew, as years ago Mrs Keith had known with her daughter Lydia, that it was quite useless to talk to Grace who was happily unable to see any point of view but her own.

'I say, Eleanor,' said Grace, as her sister came in. 'Why didn't you see me at the Barchester bus stop? I got a lift from old Adams and I shouted at you like anything, but you were too far up the queue.'

'Not old Adams,' said her mother to Grace. 'He can't be more than my age; if he's as old,' but Grace scorned such palterings and showed it by her speaking countenance.

'And now,' said Colin, rising as he spoke so that Grace nearly fell off the arm, 'I must be going. Only I must take an answer to Lydia. Can you come to Northbridge for Wednesday night, Eleanor? You shall be fetched and carried.'

Eleanor said she would love to and accompanied Colin to the door.

'Lydia will be very glad,' said Colin. 'And so shall I, though that is neither here nor there. And what is even more delightful is that Grace won't be with us. She is a fine girl, but overpowering. Good-bye.'

He touched Eleanor's hand and got into his car. Eleanor watched him drive away. He had touched her hand. Not shaken hands for good-bye, merely touched it. There was something about a touch on one's hand that was purely romantic, the moth's kiss. That was a piece of poetry that Grace wouldn't know. And then she laughed at herself and went back to the drawing-room where her mother was alone, straightening the cushions as she always did after visitors had gone.

'I do wish Colin wouldn't encourage Grace,' she said. 'At least, I don't mean encourage, but I wish he could keep her within bounds. I really don't know what people will think if she goes on like that.'

'They won't think, darling,' said Eleanor, feeling much older and wiser than her mother, as we all do in our turn.

On Wednesday afternoon Colin, agreeably to his promise, fetched Eleanor from the Red Cross Hospital Library and drove her out to Northbridge. His sister Lydia was in the garden with her young family who will not however play much part in this story as they were well under Nurse's control and Nurse was not one to stand any nonsense. The two elder, who were engaged in pretending to fish in a small artificial pond, came up to shake hands and Eleanor, admiring their good looks and sturdy forms and cheerful faces, thought with a sudden pang of little Lord Mellings with his anxieties and fears.

'I'm five years old,' said Lavinia Merton introducing herself. 'Harry's only three. And Baby is very silly. He can't talk. Tell me a story.'

'What do we say?' said Nurse.

'Please tell me a story,' said Lavinia, looking up under her long lashes at Eleanor.

'I always said to call your daughter after Lavinia Brandon was a mistake,' said Colin. 'She has inherited every trick of that charming middle-aged flirt.'

Eleanor at once told the story of the Hobyahs, which was an even greater success than it had been at the Towers and had to be repeated three times, after which Nurse said they mustn't bother the young lady any more and whisked them away to bath and bed.

'That's Noel,' said Lydia Merton at the sound of a gate being shut and her husband came in from the home farm, for though he was a K.C. in term time and very well known in London and the legal world, he became a country squire during the Long Vacation and not only enjoyed it very much, but was quite good at it for a Londoner, as his country-bred brother-in-law Colin Keith was always ready to point out to him.

'It's very nice to see you, Eleanor,' said Noel in his deep pleasant voice. 'How are your people?'

Eleanor said her father and mother were very well.

'You might add,' said Colin, 'that your sister Grace is becoming a public menace. Never have I had sheep's eyes thrown so shamelessly at me. Nearly as bad as Lydia used to be.'

'That is highly unchivalrous,' said Eleanor, but Colin did not appear to mind her words. 'Tom is rather worried because he has finished Oxford and he thought he wanted to be a don or a schoolmaster, but now he wants to do something on the land. It is rather worrying.'

'Couldn't we ask Mr Wickham?' said Lydia, referring to the naval ex-officer who had been for some years the Mertons' efficient and trusted agent. 'He's coming to dinner. Let's ask him.'

Colin said this was an excellent idea and he wished he had thought of it first, for the look of gratitude in Eleanor's face was, he felt, too valuable to be wasted on Lydia, fond though he was of her. And then Lydia took Eleanor away to see the baby being bathed and get ready for dinner.

'What a nice girl Eleanor is,' said Noel when the women had gone indoors. 'I hadn't seen her for about a year. And I hear from Lady Pomfret that she is first-rate at the Red Cross. She isn't as good-looking as her mother, though;' which unfeeling and, so Colin considered, untrue remark made him indignantly silent, though his brother-in-law was not aware of the indignation. 'We must see if Wickham can suggest anything for that brother of hers,' at which Colin nearly burst, because if it was anyone's duty to think of Eleanor and do services for her it was his, not Noel's. And as the implications of this sank into his mind he suddenly realised that he would be pleased to shoot anyone, even his dear Lydia's husband, who presumed to do anything for Eleanor, because she was quite different from everyone else and he was the only person who really understood how perfect she was. Not that he was in love. Oh no, not at all. But he felt a strong desire to shelter her from he didn't quite know what, to rescue her from the Red Cross where she was happily doing very good work, to have very long talks with her in comfortable rooms with soft lights and leaping fires, or in summer lanes under green trees with birds singing, all by himself.

It was not the first time that Colin Keith had been a prey to these immortal longings and indeed the county had bestowed him on several eligible ladies, including Mrs Arbuthnot now Mrs Francis Brandon and Susan Dean now Mrs Freddy Belton. But somehow all these goddesses had slipped through his fingers. And now he knew he had found the woman appointed for him from the beginning of time, as indeed one must admit all his other loves had appeared to be, and as he was earning a very good income at the Bar, in addition to his private means, he saw no reason for delay. He would try to find a moment to speak to Eleanor alone. If she loved him, and he thought she might, all would be gas and gaiters. If she didn't he would throw himself into his work, become a judge and sentence people to death. 'Colin Keith, the hanging judge,' people would say, little knowing that every criminal who swung was expiating the folly of a woman who had spurned the judge's love; which beautiful dream was broken in upon by Mr Wickham the agent who came in with a bottle, for Mr Wickham's friends, who were many and of all classes, had a way of testifying their affection in drink which Mr Wickham always shared with his friends.

'Real Kirschwasser,' said Mr Wickham, putting the bottle on the top of a bookcase.

'What's it like?' said Colin.

Mr Wickham said he didn't know, as he hadn't opened it, but the pal who sent it was a pretty good judge, and they might sample it. Not before dinner, said Colin, as far as he was concerned, but after dinner he would be Wickham's man. After which they talked about the Northbridge herd and how the Vicar's wife at Southbridge had found a two-toed fly-gobbler trying to hatch some old and addled eggs belonging to a gold-crested mippet who had deserted them about the beginning of April.

'It takes Effie to find a thing like that,' said Mr Wickham proudly, for he had admired Mrs Crofts when she was Miss Arbuthnot and had even suggested marrying her, though on reflection he could never be grateful enough to her for having refused him, for to have a woman in the house all day, not to speak of when one came home at night ready for a quiet drink and one's slippers, would be more than a man could stand.

'There's something I want to ask you, Wicks,' said Colin, stammering a little; not because he had any delicate feelings about the subject, so much as because the thought of Eleanor induced those feelings and also the appearance of complete idiocy so well described by Catullus and before the war translated freely but not unskilfully by Hilary Grant, who had adored Mrs Brandon before he married her daughter.

'Ask away,' said Mr Wickham. 'I might as well uncork the bottle now,' he added. 'Then I won't have to do it after dinner.'

'You know the Grantlys over at Edgewood,' said Colin, in a light manner calculated to put Mr Wickham off the scent.

'Parson. Great-grandson of the old Archdeacon. Married a good-looking woman from over Gatherum way. Four children. Are there any glasses about?' said Mr Wickham.

'In the dining-room sideboard,' said Colin rather crossly, because he felt he would lose the remarks he had carefully prepared.

Mr Wickham went out and swiftly returned with two glasses in each hand, neatly held head downwards, their stems between his fingers.

'There,' he said. 'Two for us and two over. Carry on. Anything else you want to know about the Grantlys?'

Colin said in a reserved voice that he knew the Grantlys very well and merely wished to know whether Wickham knew them.

'And now you know, so that's all right,' said Mr Wickham, filling two glasses as he spoke. 'Well, here's fun. By Jove, old Travers – man I met at Simonstown in '13, you wouldn't know him – has a pretty taste in drink. Well, here's to him.'

Colin acknowledged the toast by taking a sip of the Kirschwasser which made him choke.

'Swallow it quick,' said Mr Wickham, 'or it'll run out of your mouth. You can't waste stuff like that.'

Colin, extremely ungrateful for this good advice, did swallow it and found that the temporary agony was worth while, for the Kirschwasser was of heart-warming quality.

'Well,' he continued, 'they've got an awfully nice daughter

called Eleanor who works at the Red Cross Library in Barchester and she's staying here for the night and—'

'Just as well you mentioned it,' said Mr Wickham. 'I'll get another glass,' and he hurried into the dining-room and came back with a fifth glass which he put on the table with the others. 'Now we're all set,' he said. 'Carry on.'

'Well, she's got a young brother,' said Colin. 'At least he was in the war and then went to Oxford and has just finished his exams and he wanted to be a schoolmaster, but—'

'Here, your glass is empty,' said Mr Wickham re-filling it. 'Well, here's to schoolmasters. A lousy life but there's no accounting for tastes.'

'But then he found he didn't want to be one,' said Colin, feeling that as a barrister he was presenting his case very badly, 'and—'

'Good luck to him,' said Mr Wickham, draining his own glass for the third or fourth time, though he might as well have been drinking pure water for any effect it had on him.

'And,' Colin went on, determined to say for Eleanor's sake what he had to say, 'he is very keen—'

But at this moment Lydia and Eleanor came in followed by Noel. Introductions were made, and when Eleanor found that Mr Wickham's people had lived for generations over Chaldicotes way she was ready to like him at once and they had a very agreeable conversation about common friends over there till dinner was ready. Colin was not put next to Eleanor, but he was able to look at her and felt more than ever how enchanting she was and what fun it would be if they were married and had dinner parties in London. But there seemed to be no opportunity of speaking to Mr Wickham about Tom, as he wished to do so privately and not in front of Eleanor, in case Mr Wickham was unhelpful and she might be hurt or depressed. So the talk ranged pleasantly over many subjects, including Noel's brilliant defence of somebody or something (for we do not wish to particularise on legal subjects, knowing nothing whatever about them) which was making everyone speak of him as destined before long for very high honours; the success of Colin's long-awaited Keith's *Lemon on Running Powers*; the imminence of Mrs Freddy Belton's first baby; the probability which Noel said, to judge by her appearance when he last saw her seemed to him almost a *fait accompli*; of Mrs Francis Brandon having another baby; Mr Adams buying Miss Sowerby's house at Edgewood which interested Mr Wickham deeply for it was in his country, and other matters all very interesting but highly annoying to Colin who was determined to speak to Mr Wickham himself about Tom before the evening was out and so win Eleanor's favour. To his further annoyance Noel and Mr Wickham lingered over the rest of a bottle of port that Mr Wickham had brought on his last visit and though Colin could have escaped to the drawing-room without anyone being in the least offended or even noticing him, he became a prey to self-consciousness and afraid of going in to the ladies alone; which was most unreasonable in a barrister of his repute.

Meanwhile Lydia and Eleanor had talked very comfortably in the drawing-room about all kinds of things and Lydia, though with no ulterior motive, had praised her dear Colin whom she had always loved best of her family.

'If only he weren't in London all term-time,' she said wistfully, 'and Noel too. You know, Eleanor, I have been rather selfish about that. We could afford to live in London as well as here now, but I do so *hate* London, even with Noel, and it is heaven to have him here when the Courts aren't sitting and for week-ends. And it is heaven to have Colin too.'

Eleanor said she thought Noel and Colin were very lucky and she wanted to live in London almost more than anything in the world.

'Then why don't you?' said Lydia.

Eleanor tried to explain, mentioning her family and her Red Cross work, which excuses Lydia demolished in her usual downright way, saying that there must be Red Cross jobs in London and after all Eleanor could always come down to Edgewood for the week-ends, to which there was really no answer except, Eleanor said, that she didn't feel brave enough to tell her people and the Red Cross that she wanted to go, because she knew they would be awfully nice about it and then she would feel a beast.

'Then you'd better marry someone who lives in London and then you'll have to live there,' said Lydia, merely as a general conclusion and not with anyone particular in mind.

Eleanor laughed and agreed, but not till they had been talking of other things for some time did Colin come into her mind. He lived in London. She liked him very much. He was always extraordinarily nice to her and was one of the people who understood what one said. And then a thought of his look, his voice, the way he sometimes kept her hand longer than was necessary, suddenly pierced her heart with an ache of delight and she heard no more of what Lydia said, though someone called Miss Eleanor Grantly inside whom her new real self was living appeared to be conversing in a perfectly competent and ladylike way.

At last the men came in and again Colin found himself separated from Eleanor by his sister Lydia who wanted to talk to him about the farm, though to do Lydia justice, which we hope we always shall, had she realised what Colin's feelings were she would have at once arranged, with or without diplomacy and probably the latter, to isolate him and Eleanor till she accepted him.

Presently Mr Wickham, who was on excellent terms with most of the Barsetshire landowners and their agents, mentioned Roddy Wicklow, whom he had met at a sale that week.

'He says Pomfret isn't too well,' said Mr Wickham. 'This Government, or whatever you call them, are killing the good landlords. They'd have killed old Marling if Adams hadn't bought that bit of land of his at a good price. They'll kill Pomfret if they aren't careful, in fact that's probably what they want to do, so as to get the death duties and then make the little fellow's trustees sell the Towers for a state laundry and put Lady Pomfret into a villa in Hogglestock.'

Noel said to draw it mild, but Mr Wickham had no intention of doing so and continued,

'He's killing himself over the county and the estate and then he has to go to London which is always bad for him and sit in the House of Lords with people like Aberfordbury.'

'Who is Aberfordbury?' said Lydia, for that peer, formerly Sir Ogilvy Hibberd who had been so signally defeated by old Lord Pomfret in the matter of Pooker's Piece, laboured under the misfortune, common to so many recent creations, of having chosen for his peerage a name which not only meant nothing but which none of his acquaintance could remember and which when they did hear it they could never connect it with its owner.

'Hibberd he was,' said Noel. 'His son didn't get in for East Barsetshire in the last election. And as I was saying, Pomfret sits regularly in the Lords and speaks sometimes, though he hates speaking, because he feels it's his duty. The Party have got their eye on him,' said Noel, who heard a lot of political gossip in London, chiefly from friends in high Opposition circles, 'and I wouldn't be surprised if he were offered the Garter when we get in again.'

'Better say if we get in,' said Mr Wickham.

'I daresay you're right,' said Noel, 'and God help us when and if we do. The Germans knocked most of the City down in '40, but no one has built it again. This lot have pretty well knocked civilisation and decent living and honesty and hope to pieces, but I don't know who is going to build them up. Pomfret would put his last ounce of strength into it, but he couldn't last.'

'Draw it mild,' said Mr Wickham, 'I know Wicklow pretty well – it always strikes me as funny, Wicklow and Wickham, both land agents – and he says if Pomfret had a really good secretary who could do all his letters and correspondence, he would manage all right. He *will* answer everything personally and it doesn't do. And he worries about these County Council meetings, when all he needs is to be properly briefed. Trouble is,' said Mr Wickham reflectively, 'he wasn't brought up to the job. Lived abroad for his health when he was young and never saw the Towers till he was grown up. Old Pomfret hated his father who was next heir like poison, but he liked this fellow, only it was too late then. If he'd spent his holidays at the Towers when he was a kid he'd have taken it all easily.'

'Poor Lord Pomfret,' said Lydia. 'He has such nice children. You stayed there, didn't you, Eleanor?'

Eleanor said she had been there for a week-end and the children were darlings, though she did not mention Lord Mellings and the pony because she thought it would be unfair.

'And I quite agree with Mr Wickham about the secretary,' she added, with no thought of Tom in her mind, only remembering what she had seen at the Towers, 'because there were a whole lot of county papers and Lady Pomfret let me arrange them for him and he seemed really pleased,' said Eleanor with a very becoming kind of shyness. 'I almost wished I could give up the Red Cross and work for him, because he looks so dreadfully tired and is so *very* nice.'

Colin, who had suffered a good deal first by Mr Wickham's interruptions when he was trying to speak about Tom and later by the impossibility of getting Eleanor to himself, suddenly felt an insane wish to jump onto a horse, gallop to the Towers, shoot Lord Pomfret and then fly the country. Possibly all these combined would have served his cause no worse than what he did, which was to say sulkily,

'I haven't much use for people who go about saying they are tired and getting sympathy from people. After all, Lord Pomfret's got a wife,' having uttered which silly words he realised that he had not behaved like a gentleman and wished he were dead.

A deep and not unbecoming flush of surprise and anger covered Eleanor's face and her eyes almost flashed as she said, as nicely as she could for fear of hurting Lydia, that Lord Pomfret didn't ask for sympathy or help, but if one saw a person doing more than his fair share of work and very tired, one naturally tried to help, and then she had to stop because there rose a horrid pricking feeling behind her eyes which made her afraid that she might cry. Noel, who was the first to see that something was wrong, hastily asked Mr Wickham if he could give some advice. Miss Grantly's brother, he said, who had been in the army and then at Oxford was looking for a job connected with the land and could Wickham make any suggestions.

'I will if I can,' said Mr Wickham, who had taken a liking to Eleanor and moreover looked upon the Grantlys as entitled to his protection because they came from over Chaldicotes way.

'If you tell your brother to look me up here one evening, Miss Grantly, any time after six, I'll see what he knows and what I can do for him. Mind you, I can't promise anything, but one often hears about jobs; only you hardly ever hear about the right job and the right man at the same time. Anyway let me vet him,' for which friendly words Eleanor thanked him earnestly, and after some more talk Lydia said they had better go to bed as Eleanor had to be at the office by nine next morning. Mr Wickham repeated his offer of help and Noel said he would keep his ears open, for all of which Eleanor was very grateful. Colin got up and opened the door for the ladies. His sister Lydia kissed him good-night. Eleanor slipped past as she did so, and from the staircase said Good-night, in as friendly a voice as she could manage, though it was not very successful.

Lydia took her to her room, looked round to see everything was comfortable and then kissed her good-night, adding,

'Don't take any notice of Colin. I don't know why he was so rude about Lord Pomfret; it isn't a bit like him. I expect he was worried about something, poor darling,' to which Eleanor could only reply by cheerfully telling a lie and saying she was sure Colin didn't mean it and what a lovely evening it had been and how kind Mr Wickham was, so that her hostess thought perhaps Eleanor had not particularly noticed Colin's outburst; and went to her own room where her husband shortly joined her.

'What the dickens was wrong with Colin?' he asked. 'I have never known him so rude. And about poor Pomfret who is the most conscientious and kind-hearted of creatures. I suppose he is in love again. It always makes him cross. Someone in London probably and we shall hear far too much about it before long. Do you remember how cross and sulky he was when he thought he was in love with Peggy?' for during the summer that Mrs

Arbuthnot was at Southbridge, before she married Francis Brandon, Colin had fallen a victim to her charms and become a great bore to his loving relations.

'Poor Colin,' said Lydia compassionately, and as she brushed her dark shining hair she tried not to remember that Noel too had thought he was in love with Peggy Arbuthnot and turned upon him such a look of quiet deep love as moved Noel beyond words; for he too had been thinking of that summer and wondering whether he could ever make up to Lydia what she had lost during those few months. But he did not speak, in which he was wise, and told himself not for the first time that if Lydia wished for silence she should have it, though it sometimes nearly broke his heart not to make a general confession and be forgiven. But this was his punishment, and his heart and his brain were courageous enough to accept it if Lydia were satisfied.

'Now we'll make the rest of the Kirschwasser look silly,' said Mr Wickham to Colin, 'and then I'll go home. What a nice girl Miss Grantly is. If I were ten years younger and had anything to offer I'd propose to her at once. Well, here's to the man that marries her,' which health Colin felt obliged to drink in case Mr Wickham happened to think that he cared for Eleanor, which of course he now did not.

'And why the dickens did you burst out like that about Pomfret,' said Mr Wickham. 'You really mustn't, you know. He hasn't set the Thames on fire, but he's as good as they make them and so is his wife. Anyone might have thought you were in love with Lady Pomfret and jealous of her husband. Here's all the best to them.'

Colin drank this toast and rather wished the Kirschwasser were poison. What Wickham said was perfectly true. He had not behaved like a gentleman and Eleanor would never look at him again. Mr Wickham, having turned the bottle upside down to extract the last drop, said good-night and walked back to his cottage considering what best he could do for that nice girl's brother, took a couple of fingers of neat whiskey and went to bed to sleep soundly and dreamlessly till his alarm clock woke him at half past six.

Next morning breakfast was early so that Colin might drive Eleanor back according to promise. Neither of them looked forward to the drive. Colin wanted to apologise but was too ashamed and too proud. Eleanor did not want to be shut up with someone who had been so outrageously rude about her friends, but it had to be, so she made conversation from time to time and thought nostalgically of her drive with Lord Pomfret and how he had thanked her for helping him with his papers and said she must call him Gillie. So far she had not succeeded in doing so, even in her thoughts, having if the truth is to be told rather stopped thinking of him in favour of Colin. But now Colin's horridness drove her back to think of her kind, tired, courteous, hardworking host who was rapidly being idealised in her mind and, had Colin known it, all through his fault. As he stopped the car outside the Red Cross Headquarters Eleanor opened the door, got out, slammed it again, said through the window, 'Good-bye Colin. Thanks for driving me,' and was gone before he could speak. Wild thoughts of a Lochinvar abduction ran through his mind, but an angry honking from a car behind made him go on automatically, so he drove back to Northbridge and was so unpleasant for the rest of the day as to leave little doubt in his sister's and brother-in-law's mind that he was deeply attached to Eleanor Grantly.

'He's simply got to marry her,' said Lydia, who always saw things in their simplest terms, 'or the summer will be quite dreadful.'

But instead of marrying her Colin went to friends in Norfolk for a fortnight and peace reigned at Northbridge Manor.

8

Mr Wickham was as good as his word and what is more, Tom went to see him. For as a rule when the young come to one with tales of woe and one moves heaven and earth to get them the right interview, or badgers one's friends to give them a trial, or painfully tidies the spare room to make a temporary home for them, they at once go underground and emerge after several weeks quite unscathed, having landed quite a different job from the one they thought they wanted, or got engaged to the girl they said they wouldn't touch with the end of a barge pole. And always one is taken in and does exactly the same for the next young that comes one's way. Tom however, and we think two years of serious classical reading may have had a good deal to do with it, did not altogether condemn his sister's action in speaking to Mr Wickham, went over to Northbridge for the night and there, in Mr Wickham's comfortable bachelor cottage, was put through his paces and given rum such as does not now reach the pensive public however sad they look. Mr Wickham, reporting to Lydia who rang up Eleanor, had said that Tom had quite a bit of sense for a youngster and if he, Mr Wickham, could hear of anything or do any pushing, he would not be backward in coming forward and what a nice girl his sister was. All of which Lydia faithfully repeated, which made Eleanor have the giggles. Meanwhile, Mr Wickham added, when he met Tom in Barchester on market day, Tom could come over to Northbridge whenever he liked, put up at his cottage and go about the place with him, which Tom was delighted to do. His loving parents were also delighted, for much as they loved their elder son, a large young man with a good brain and no definite prospects can become rather tiresome, and also gave his parents a sense of guilt because they did not know how to push him into jobs; partly because they were not very worldly, partly because they knew that any job found by them would be automatically disapproved and turned down.

Meanwhile the Barchester contractors, spurred on by Mr Adams whose assiduity in suddenly coming down and harrying them was almost equal to Sloppy's when attending Mr Wegg, had almost completed their work. Repairs, painting, plumbing were done more or less, for they are in their nature endless. The drawing-room had been re-hung with the rolls of Chinese paper; and with what pieces were left Mr Adams caused the insides of various cupboards and closets upstairs to be papered, which made a charming contrast to the white walls when they were opened. As for the curtains, Mrs Belton had been invited by Mr Adams to do what she liked, with carte blanche, and as curtains had come off coupons (with the exception of all the thinner materials which might conceivably be made into dresses to cheer the lives of exhausted housewives who didn't want to go New Look because they knew it wouldn't last) she was able to run amuck, taking Heather to London with her for the purpose and returning with the best that Mr Adams's money could buy.

'I can't thank you enough, Mrs Belton,' said Mr Adams, when she came over one Sunday with her elder son and his wife to look at the house. 'If money's needed, Sam Adams has the needful, but he doesn't know what to buy when it's for the Old Bank House. Now any ordinary house, Mrs Belton, I'd know what I wanted and so would my Heth. But with a house like this, a house that's been used to the best and is going to have it, I'm a bit at sea. And so's my Heth. Fack is,' said Mr Adams thoughtfully, 'you can't make a sow's ear into a silk purse all in a day. Not that I've anything to say against pigs and I'm going to have some over at the market garden, but Heth and me we've still got something to learn, and when we want to know the right thing we know where to go,' and Mr Adams made a kind of bow to Mrs Belton which touched her very much.

'Now, Mrs Freddy, you sit down comfortably on the couch,' said Mr Adams, 'and rest a bit, while I show your mother-in-law the nurseries. You can't be too careful these days.'

So Susan laughed and did as she was told, which was quite unnecessary for though, as her brother Charles remarked, her appearance was very ominous, she was in excellent health and spirits.

'I shan't be long, darling,' said Captain Belton and followed his mother upstairs.

Mrs Belton wished, as she had wished more than once, that she could stop Mr Adams calling a sofa a couch, but her regard for him was too sincere to allow her to risk hurting his feelings, so she held her tongue, wondering why such very small things as the name of a piece of furniture should matter. For the fact remains that they do matter and one cannot explain or argue. At least, she said to herself, he had never called the drawing-room the lounge, and then she devoted herself to the tour of inspection and found the house as nearly perfect as need be.

'You do love this house,' she said to Mr Adams as they stood by the future night nursery window, looking into the garden where the herbaceous border was already in the yellows and reds of late summer.

'It's a happy house,' said Mr Adams thoughtfully. 'Now that house I've got at Hogglestock, it's an old house and it's comfortable and it's handsome and it suits my Heth and me and it'll suit Heth and young Ted. But somehow this house is going to suit Sam Adams when he is alone. I'm not much good at putting things into words, Mrs Belton, unless it's a board meeting, or letting someone have a piece of my mind, or saying a few words in Parliament, but it makes me think of a song Mother used to sing to Heth, when Heth was a baby. "I love my mill, it is to me, Like parent, child and wife." I was only a nipper when my parents died, and I lost Mother when Heth was a little thing, and now Heth's leaving me. But the Old Bank House has something in it that's going to make up – and what the dickens do you think you're doing, you fool, that's not the way to lay the top course,' said Mr Adams suddenly at the full blast of his powerful voice to a belated bricklayer who was peacefully defying his union and finishing a low wall. Sentiment vanished and just as well, thought Mrs Belton, for all Mr Adams said seemed to her to be true and made her eyes feel a little misty.

'Blasted fools!' said Mr Adams, 'begging your pardon. That's what workmen are like now. Don't know their job and don't care. A few do. I've got a carpenter working for me here in his own time and there's nothing he isn't master of. Always willing, always handy, does anything from a nice bit of joinery to reglazing a window or unstopping the scullery drain when that damfool plumber had let half a pound of cotton waste go down it. Now we'd better go down and see how Mrs Freddy is.'

Mrs Freddy, whose husband had slipped back to her without being noticed, was extremely well and asked Mr Adams whether his party had expelled him yet.

'You mean what I said before Parliament rose,' said Mr Adams, who was a perpetual embarrassment to His Majesty's Government and known in Opposition Circles as the Barchester White Hope. 'I've made myself by Labour, my own Labour I mean, and I stick to my class, but if anyone tries to push the independent working man out, Sam Adams won't stand for it. You know they are dropping hints about a peerage.'

Mrs Belton said she didn't.

'Well, they can go on dropping,' said Mr Adams. 'A fine fool I'd look in a coronet. As long as Barchester puts me in, and Barchester will go on putting me in,' said Mr Adams, not boasting but as one who knew his power and his place, 'in the Commons I stay. That's where I belong. It wouldn't do Sam Adams no good to be one of those jumped-up peers with a title nobody can remember, like old What's his name, Aberfordbury. Well, suppose we have a look at the garden, that is if Mrs Freddy feels like it.'

Mrs Freddy did feel like it, so they all went into the garden, which was already in apple-pie order with lawns mown, borders clipped and all the conservatories re-glazed and painted. After inspecting everything and particularly admiring the kitchen garden, they were returning to the house when a majestic form approached them down the long gravel walk.

'It's old Lady Norton,' said Mrs Belton. 'What a nuisance,' but these last words were only for Susan's ear. 'I didn't know Mr Adams knew her.'

'I thought I would come over and see what you were making of the garden,' said Lady Norton to Mr Adams, with a nod of patronage to the Beltons.

'I'm much obliged, I'm sure,' said Mr Adams.

Mrs Belton, not at all comfortable, was relieved to see, from one look Mr Adams gave her, that he was as annoyed as she was.

'Very nice,' said Lady Norton, condescending to the herbaceous border with her tortoiseshell eye-glass. 'Dear Hilda Sowerby couldn't put any money into it,' to which Mr Adams made no reply.

'Of course,' continued Lady Norton, 'she never understood Globulosa Multiflora. You must have that all out,' and she pointed with her glass at a large clump of handsome though uninteresting pinky-orange blooms with hairy foliage, while the back of Mr Adams's neck crimsoned with determination not to do so.

'And what have you done with Palafox Borealis?' Lady Norton continued. 'I always told Hilda Sowerby she ought to give it a west exposure.'

'I'm not much of a gardener, Lady Norton,' said Mr Adams with suspicious calm, 'but Miss Sowerby was. And I'm not going to change her border till I see good cause. As a matter of fack she is coming to see it this afternoon. I sent a car to Worthing to fetch her.'

'Poor Hilda, it must be very hard for her,' said Lady Norton. 'I shall have to be going. But I'd like to see Palafox first and I'll send my gardener over later for some seeds.'

What Mr Adams might have said or done we shall never know, for by special intervention of Providence Miss Sowerby, who had been deposited at the Old Bank House by Mr Adams's chauffeur, had come down the long walk and heard her enemy's last words.

'Well, Victoria?' said Miss Sowerby, which simple words caused Lady Norton to look more confused than anyone would have thought possible. And then Miss Sowerby greeted Mr Adams and the Beltons, who were very old acquaintances, and congratulated Mr Adams on the improvement in the grass and the flourishing condition of the herbaceous border, to which Mr Adams replied that it wasn't his doing so much as Messrs Cutbush and Sepal from Barchester, because when he didn't know about a thing he wasn't above getting someone who did.

Lady Norton said Potter and Dibble were the men, but no one took any notice of her.

'Did I hear someone mention Palafox Borealis?' said Miss Sowerby sweetly. 'I have given it to some friends who are taking excellent care of it. And when it flowers in 1955, when I shall probably be dead, they will give the seeds to various people whose names I have put in my will. All keen and successful gardeners.'

Lady Norton said her time was short and she must say goodbye, which no one wished to prevent, and so went away.

'It beats me,' said Mr Adams. 'I've not felt so uncomfortable not since my first boss sacked me for reading his *Journal of Metallurgy* on the sly in my dinner-hour. Now, if you ladies feel like a cup of tea, Miss Hoggett will have it ready.'

So they all went back to the drawing-room and the hideous but devoted housekeeper brought in tea with a service of Chinese porcelain that looked like a first cousin of the wallpaper. Then Miss Sowerby made a tour of the house, shed a few tears, clasped Mr Adams's large hand in both of her gnarled, veined, work-worn hands, though they were sadly cleaner since she had left her garden, and almost blessed him for his care of the house.

'And if your excellent driver does not mind, I shall just go round by the Rectory,' she said, 'to see the dear Rector and Mrs Grantly. They have got Palafox and Victoria Norton will never get a seed of it. But this is a secret. You have a good housekeeper, Mr Adams. Her people have been in the county as long as anyone. But, you know, this house needs a mistress.'

And then the Beltons went back to Harefield and Mr Adams returned to Hogglestock, leaving Miss Hoggett in possession.

Mrs Belton was no gossip, nor were her son and daughter-in-law. Mr Adams after a short reflection on the peculiar ways of some ladies if ladies one could call them, forgot all about the incident. But somehow, whether from Worthing or elsewhere we cannot say, the story of the Dreadful Dowager's defeat at the hands of Miss Sowerby spread all over the county in gardening circles and Lucy Marling, who feared nothing except unhappiness for people she loved, said it was the best thing that had happened in Barsetshire since her father won the Challenge Cup at the Barsetshire Pig-Breeders' Association in the previous summer.

Mr Adams's chauffeur, who was an obliging man and knew a lady when he saw one, had no objection to taking Miss Sowerby round by the Rectory, where she found Mr and Mrs Grantly alone and delighted to see her. The story of Lady Norton's defeat and flight was told and deeply appreciated and Miss Sowerby expressed her complete approval of all Mr Adams had done.

'I've never had any young people of my own,' she said, 'but I imagine one must feel about one's children much as I feel about the Old Bank House. If I had a son or a daughter who was getting married, I think I should feel much the same anxiety as I did about my house. And how are all your young people?'

Mrs Grantly said none of them were going to be married as far as she knew and Eleanor was very busy with the Red Cross and Tom learning something about farming from the Noel Mertons' agent. Harry, she said, was in Devonshire with friends and rang up every evening, charging the call to his parents, to ask whether his calling-up papers had come and Grace was waiting for the results of her School Certificate.

'If I had had girls, I should have had a governess,' said Miss Sowerby. 'Someone like that excellent Miss Bunting who was with the Marquess of Bolton and dear Lady Emily Leslie. I hear from Agnes Graham, who kindly came to see me at Worthing, that Lady Emily is not very well.'

The Grantlys, who did not know Lady Emily intimately but had a great feeling for her, as most people had who came into contact with that irresponsible Spirit of Love, said how sorry they were and not anything serious, they hoped.

'Mostly old age,' said Miss Sowerby. 'I know what it feels like. The world gets further away and one waits with what patience one can. I should like to live to see Palafox flower, but I daresay I shan't. How is it doing?'

The Rector and his wife had known this would come, ever since they allowed the kitchen to take possession of it. Now they would have to confess. It was no good trying to tell lies to Miss Sowerby or to put her off, for in spite of her age she was as determined as ever and quite capable of ransacking the whole garden.

'I hope you won't think we have done wrong, Miss Sowerby,' said Mrs Grantly, 'but my maids, country girls who have a real love for flowers and a natural turn for them, begged to be allowed to look after it.'

'Not a bad idea,' said Miss Sowerby calmly. 'When those sort of people understand plants, it is a kind of genius. They are nearer the soil than we are. Where have they put it?'

'I'm afraid it's in the kitchen,' said Mrs Grantly, feeling that she might as well speak the truth sooner or later.

'Then let us visit it,' said Miss Sowerby. 'Your kitchen faces south-west, if I remember rightly, though I haven't been in it since the year of Queen Victoria's Second Jubilee when some friends of mine took it for August. Will you show me the way?'

The Rector and his wife, feeling rather like beasts being led to the slaughter, accordingly accompanied Miss Sowerby to the kitchen which, as in so many old houses, had all the sunshine while the best rooms faced away from it. In the coldest winter what warmth there was could be found in the kitchen and in summer it was like a Turkish bath, but Edna and Doris were impervious to temperatures, as were the children of shame. The room was large with a heavy wooden built-in dresser right across the back wall; an old coal range which was still used in winter for warmth occupied most of one side wall, while the cooking was done upon a gas range with an alternative of an oil stove for emergencies. The long window with its small panes ran the whole width of the room except for the door into the yard and under part of the window was the sink with its draining boards, so that whenever cooking and washing-up were in progress, the glass was misted with steam. In this favourable atmosphere, upon the wide window ledge, stood Palafox Borealis enjoying the late afternoon sun.

'Miss Sowerby has come to see her plant,' said Mrs Grantly. 'These are the Thatchers from Grumper's End; Edna and Doris.'

'I have heard of you from Mr Miller,' said Miss Sowerby, quite kindly, but not offering to shake hands, an attitude which the Thatchers who had barely emerged from the feudal age appeared to think quite reasonable in a real lady, for the name of Sowerby as we know had been powerful in that part of the world for a very long time.

'Mr Miller's a lovely man,' said Edna. 'He took Jimmy to the hospital when he got appendicitis at the feet.'

'What a peculiar disease,' said the Rector.

'Fête,' said his wife in an aside.

The Rector said Possibly, but it seemed hard to blame Fate for what might happen to anyone, though he still felt it was an unusual complaint and one that one might expect politicians to have, but not the Thatchers.

'And are either of you girls married yet?' said Miss Sowerby.

Mrs Grantly expected her staff to give notice, but evidently the old landed gentry were privileged for both girls giggled and Edna said there wouldn't be much sense getting married now when they'd got all the kids they wanted. Glad, Sid, Stan and Glamora were then brought forward and Sid was despatched to find Purse who was mending Grace's wireless in the pantry.

'My flower is doing very nicely,' said Miss Sowerby with the utmost condescension.

'That's Sid,' said his mother. 'The fuss he makes about it, you'd think it was yuman.'

'In 1955,' said Miss Sowerby to Sid, who had come back with Purse, 'that plant will flower and then there will be some seeds in a green knob at the top. If Mrs Grantly writes to the Secretary of the Royal Horticultural Society, he will probably want to buy the seeds. Don't let him have them under fifty pounds, and mind you keep one for yourself. You are a very good gardener.'

'Please, miss,' said Purse, 'that plant loykes the woyreless. I give him the comic bits, miss.'

'Well, they say plants can be forced by electricity,' said Miss Sowerby, 'and you never know. Perhaps it will flower a little sooner. And don't you let anyone else look after it, Sid.'

'Oy don't,' said Sid. 'If Stan, or Glad, or Glamora, was to touch it, Oy'd biff them,' to which his mother said That was enough and all to run out in the yard and not be a nuisance and what the lady would think she couldn't say and Miss

Sowerby took her departure followed by ill-suppressed giggles from Edna and Doris.

'A couple of nice girls,' said Miss Sowerby.

Mrs Grantly said they were most good-natured and excellent workers, but she sometimes wondered if the Rectory ought to encourage free love, to which Miss Sowerby replied that free love had come to stay and the only sensible thing to do was to take the good the gods provide you and mounting Mr Adams's car went away. Mrs Grantly said to her husband that life in a small country town was almost too much for her, and how incredibly modern Miss Sowerby was in her outlook on things.

'If by things, you mean illegitimate children,' said the Rector, 'I don't think she is particularly modern. The Sowerbys are a very old family, in fact they were Rangers of the Chase for a hundred years or so before it was disforested, and those old families are much less squeamish than we are. If there were plenty of Purses and Sids to keep things going they didn't bother much about their parents' marriage lines, and it seems to me the world is going back to those conditions. I would prefer lawful matrimony myself, but we can't employ Edna and Doris and then cast stones at them. But if the Middle Classes,' said the Rector, 'took to behaving like that I should be seriously concerned.'

'I was wondering,' said Mrs Grantly, 'why Colin Keith hasn't been here lately,' and could not think why her husband laughed.

As we know, the reason Colin Keith had not been at Edgewood of late was because he was in Norfolk and enjoying himself on the whole, though every now and then his heart reminded him that he had disgraced himself in front of Eleanor Grantly: and one's heart does not lightly forgive things like that. And Eleanor thought not infrequently how nice it was when Colin came to

Edgewood two or three times a week, but she had no intention of forgiving him for saying such horrid and untrue things about Lord Pomfret and was much happier without him; and so happy was she that her mother began to wonder if she was going to have influenza.

About a week later Lady Pomfret, partly because she liked Eleanor and appreciated her work at the Red Cross, partly with her husband's paper-laden table in mind, invited Eleanor and Tom to the Towers for lunch and a long afternoon and very kindly included Grace.

'Oh mother, *need* I?' said Grace, when her ladyship's invitation reached her. 'I was going to the Barchester Odeon with Jennifer Gorman. Her mother has let her have a New Style dress and coat. I wish I could.'

Mrs Grantly, mentally envisaging Jennifer's abounding and rather shapeless sixteen-year-old figure, said it didn't suit everyone and it was rather late in the summer to have a new coat. A good deal of irrelevant arguing took place resulting in a draw: Mrs Grantly promising to take Grace to Madame Tomkins, the best Barchester dressmaker, to enquire about a New Look dress and Grace binding herself to go to Pomfret Towers with her brother and sister without any more fuss.

Accordingly on Saturday morning Mrs Grantly, Tom, Eleanor and Grace all went by the early bus into Barchester, where Eleanor disappeared into her office and Tom went off to visit the Deanery where some of the Dean's elder grandchildren were staying, while Mrs Grantly and Grace made their way to Barley Street. Here, in one of the quiet early nineteenth-century houses which had luckily been spared by commerce and the Town Council, lived Madame Tomkins, whose husband, a son of old Tomkins the Cathedral gardener, had deserted her shortly after a romantic war marriage in 1917 and was only heard of vaguely in South Africa and Australia from time to time. Madame Tomkins, a lady of supreme good taste and great firmness of character, had not for one moment repined, but took up her old work of dressmaking, at first in a small way, and gradually became the Arbiter of Taste for the Close, the Town and such of the County as did not go to London. It was Madame Tomkins who had dressed the daughter of Sir Robert Fielding, Chancellor of the Diocese, for her wedding, and at least twenty brides-to-be had gone to her in consequence, though with varying degrees of success.

'For Mees Anne she has chic,' said Madame Tomkins. 'Chien I do not say, but a chic tout ce qu'il y a de plus discret et convenable. Quelle jolie mariée! C'est bien moi qui voudrais habiller le poupon,' for Anne's quiet happy hopes for the early spring were no secret to Madame Tomkins.

To Madame Tomkins Mrs Grantly put her difficulties about a dress for Grace. Madame Tomkins considered the matter, giving it as her opinion that the New Look would not last, that pencil skirts were coming in and that for a jeune fille assez forte, for such was her uncompromising way of describing Grace's untrammelled and coltish figure, something neither too fashionable nor too much behind the fashion was desirable, and she rapidly sketched a design in which a young woman about eight feet high and all out of proportion was wearing a dress which she assured Mrs Grantly would make Grace look more or less presentable.

'But it isn't New Look,' said Grace. 'Jennifer Gorman's new dress has a tight bodice and a long skirt all kind of fluted.'

'Cette Génifère!' said Madame Tomkins in pitying scorn. 'If Mees Grace wishes to resemble Génifère, let her go to Bostock and Plummer,' who were Barchester's old-established drapers and got models down from London when they were just not quite up to date. But, added Madame Tomkins, if Mees Grace wished to look like a lady, let Mrs Grantly trust her, Madame Tomkins, who would neither slumber nor sleep till she had produced the perfect dress. Grace's objections being overruled by Madame Tomkins's loquacity, and the material which Mrs Grantly had brought with her from her hoarded store being more or less approved, measurements were taken and they said good-bye.

As they were going downstairs they passed an open door and out came Canon Joram, the ex-Bishop of Mngangaland, who was Madame Tomkins's lodger, so after friendly greetings they all went down together and walked along Barley Street. Bishop Joram, who liked Mrs Grantly and took an interest in her children, asked after Tom and was delighted to hear that he had a second.

'Excellent, quite excellent,' said the Bishop. 'A first so often unfits a man for everyday things.'

'My husband took one,' said Mrs Grantly smiling.

'Ah then, my dear lady, then it was different,' said Bishop Joram hastily. 'I myself took a first, but in those days the classics counted for something. I shall never forget during the rising in Mngangaland in 1927, fomented of course by the Germans, having to persuade a large number of natives, mostly armed with stolen rifles and poisoned spears, to put off massacring the local whites till next day. I recited, mostly from memory and, I fear, inventing hexameters of my own when I forgot a line, the Sixth Book of the *Aeneid* and you could have heard a pin drop. And when I came to "tu Marcellus eris", the ringleader put his spear down and cried like a child. He thought I was bewitching him. And then of course the whole thing fizzled out. It shows what the classics can do. Ah! I was young then,' said the Bishop. 'And what is Tom going to do?'

Mrs Grantly said he wanted to do something on the land.

'Excellent, excellent,' said the Bishop. 'O fortunatos nimium sua si bona norint. But doubtless Tom is conscious of his good fortune.'

Mrs Grantly said he hadn't exactly got any yet, but several people were being very kind. Mr Wickham, the Mertons' agent, was giving him some practical work and Lord Pomfret's agent was going to see him. 'In fact he and the girls are going over there for lunch,' said Mrs Grantly.

The kind-hearted Bishop Joram was delighted. Then his face clouded. 'Did you notice the rest of the list?' said he.

Mrs Grantly said she had been too excited to read any more and in any case she probably wouldn't have known the names unless they had been friends of Tom's.

'I feel in a way responsible for it,' said Bishop Joram. 'The Head Chief of Mngangaland particularly asked me to keep an eye on his eightieth son, his favourite, while he was at Balliol, and I fear I have been remiss. The wretched lad only just scraped through with a fourth.'

'Was it the usual things?' asked Mrs Grantly, with a vague picture of the Bullingdon, drags, champagne parties, nailing up dons' doors, fighting the Proctor's bulldogs, throwing men into the river and living riotously with barmaids; all of which pleasant recreations have died in the alien air of the Brave New World and with the vast influx of female undergraduates.

'Oh dear no,' said Bishop Joram. 'If only the lad had drunk it would be easy to explain. In fact no man is considered worth anything in Mngangaland till he has drunk so much mnkoko that he is insensible for three days and nights. Mnkoko is of course native millet in fermented palm juice and antelope's entrails and chewed by the Head Chief's wives; quite a powerful drink. But I fear he has sadly degenerated from his forebears. He read nothing but Proust and Sartre and came up to town occasionally to see exhibitions by the Neo-Phallic Group. I shall tell his father that the number four is sacred in England. He has often heard me speak of the Fourth of June,' said the Bishop hopefully, 'as the greatest festival of the year – always of course excepting Christmas and Easter – so perhaps he will believe me.'

Mrs Grantly expressed a hope that he would and as they had come to the end of Barley Street she said good-bye.

'Oh, one piece of news,' said Bishop Joram. 'At last I have a house and shall really be a resident Canon. That beautiful house that Canon Thorne had. I can hardly believe my luck,' on which Mrs Grantly congratulated him with all her heart, for she was fond of the ex-sub-equatorial Bishop, as indeed everyone was except the Palace, which exception was in general estimation but an added tribute to his worth.

Outside the Red Cross Library Lady Pomfret's hard-working car was standing and as Mrs Grantly and Grace came up Lady Pomfret and Eleanor came out of the building and Tom came up the High Street.

'It is very kind of you to spare so many of your family,' said Lady Pomfret, greeting Mrs Grantly. 'I'm afraid we can't drive them back, but Roddy will take them to the bus stop at the Puddingdale Halt,' which care for her guests touched Mrs Grantly who knew how difficult it was in these days to fetch and carry. So she said good-bye to her brood and went to the Women's County Club, which had at last got part of its premises back from Them, much to the pleasure of the real County Club which had grudgingly received its wives, sisters and daughters during the war, and quite right too, for a club is, or was, the one place where men could be by themselves and never feel the need of women, whereas no women's club would run for a day that hadn't a room where men are allowed. Here she had a not very nice lunch and talked to Lady Fielding and then went home by the bus.

While Eleanor sat by Lady Pomfret and talked shop, Tom and Grace sat behind, each a little self-conscious and ready to despise any remark made by the other; a kind of self-consciousness under which we have all suffered when we have to talk to our nearest and dearest in the presence of strangers.

'I say, isn't it ghastly,' said Grace in an audible voice, as the great St Pancras-like bulk of Pomfret Towers reared itself before them at the end of the drive.

'Shut up,' said Tom, hissing the words through his clenched teeth in the style of Victorian novelette villains.

'Isn't the Towers ghastly,' said Lady Pomfret, half turning her head to the back seat. 'Gillie's old great-great-uncle, Lady Emily's grandfather, built it after he had seen the Great Exhibition,' which was not strictly accurate, for Pomfret Towers was not erected till the early '70s.

'There,' said Grace under her breath to Tom, so that when the car stopped at the West Wing and they got out, Tom was in the sulks.

Lady Pomfret took them to the Home Farm where an old groom was helping the Honourable Giles to get off his pony, with the rest of the nursery looking on. The children flung themselves on Eleanor with shrieks of joy, demanding the Hobyahs.

'Shall I take Pillicock in, my lady?' said the old groom. 'I dessay his lordship won't want to ride now.'

Eleanor looked quickly at Lord Mellings, who said with a good imitation of an off-hand manner, 'Just once round, Wheeler,' and came up to the pony. Wheeler helped him to mount. Pillicock, who had the wisdom that only a good children's pony has, walked once round the yard, broke into a very gentle trot and after the second round stopped quietly in front of Wheeler; so quietly that Lord Mellings, though with an anxious face, got off quite creditably by himself and then sped back to Eleanor.

'I say,' said Grace, suddenly losing her shyness. 'Could I ride that pony, Lady Pomfret?'

Lady Pomfret said certainly, provided Wheeler didn't mind and Wheeler appeared not to mind, so Grace hoisted herself astride Pillicock in a highly ungraceful way and cantered round the big yard, while Nanny said she never did.

'The young lady'd do nicely on the mare, my lady,' said Wheeler, jerking his head towards the stables, and Lady Pomfret laughed and said Grace must come and try her some day and they all went back towards the house and lunch. As they walked, a small hand was pushed into Eleanor's and Lord Mellings said, 'Pillicock likes *me* to ride him. He said Giles wants him to go too fast. Did you see me get off by myself?'

'I did,' said Eleanor, feeling absurdly elated by this small triumph of her small friend. 'You did it very nicely,' and then Emily and Giles demanded the Hobyahs even more loudly than before, and by the time the big black dog had jumped out of the bag and was eating the Hobyahs all three were shrieking with excitement and Nurse said That was quite enough and what would Miss Grantly think of them.

Lord Pomfret then came in and was pleased to see Eleanor and welcomed her brother and sister, and he was soon followed by Roddy Wicklow and his pretty, dark, quiet, adoring wife who finding Grace to be a dog-lover told her all about the puppies that her children were walking and how one of the hounds had been lost in an earth for twenty-four hours, and altogether it was a pleasant meal and Eleanor would have been very happy had not poor Tom, suddenly overcome by shyness, become so lumpish, not to say oafish, that she could have cried with vexation. For of all the social mortifications to see one's relations doing themselves no credit is one of the worst, especially if one happens to be very fond of them. She thought she saw Lord Pomfret, once or twice, look at Tom with faint disapproval or surprise, and would willingly have got under the table, crawled out of the door and walked home.

'Your brother's a bit nervy, isn't he?' said Roddy Wicklow in his quiet voice.

Eleanor said, keeping her tears of mortification back, that she was afraid he was. But not usually, she added.

'Lots of 'em are like that,' said Roddy. 'In the war, I suppose?'

Eleanor said Yes, for the last two years of the war and a lot of peace-time.

'They've all got it coming to them sooner or later,' said Roddy. 'I was a bit knocked to pieces myself, but I had Alice,' and he looked towards his quiet gentle wife. 'Don't worry, Miss Grantly. I'm going to take your brother round the place after lunch if he'd like to ride.'

Bursting with gratitude, Eleanor said that they all loved riding, but couldn't afford horses, and Tom would simply adore a ride, and after this she was able to talk at her ease with Lord Pomfret, who said what a success the pony Pillicock had been, and how Mellings was really getting over his fear of riding.

'And it is mostly your doing,' he said. 'In fact he has so much more confidence that Roddy is thinking of getting another pony for Giles and letting Ludovic ride Pillicock. Giles can sit anything – like Sally,' and he looked towards his wife with the ceaseless love and wonder that he felt, though Eleanor, thinking only of his first words, did not notice this.

Soon after lunch Wheeler brought the horses round and Roddy and Tom went off together. Grace finding that the nursery party were going to pick raspberries asked if she could go with them, and Mrs Roddy went back to her own nursery.

'I must do those W.I. papers,' said Lady Pomfret to her husband. 'Take Eleanor for a walk, darling. If you go by the obelisk you'll probably meet Roddy. He was going to take Tom round by Starveacres Hatches and Hamaker's Spinney.'

'Don't work too hard,' said Lord Pomfret. 'Shall we go, Eleanor?'

The Pomfret property is still very large, in spite of sales to meet death duties, sales to meet taxation, land practically confiscated for housing schemes or approved schools, and a man may ride for most of a day in it if he wishes to see all the farms and go over the shooting land. The road or rather the rough track which Lord Pomfret took led them downhill to a long valley which curved gently away at each end. On the steep slope behind were beeches rising to meet the sky. On the other side of the rich green valley where cows were grazing the ground sloped upwards again on a gentle rise, the beech and wild cherry interspersed with conifers. Drives for the guns were cut here and there, fern-carpeted, and at the end of one of them, outlined against the sky, was the obelisk, erected in about 1760.

'Would you care to go up and see it?' said Lord Pomfret. 'It's not really very far.'

But Eleanor, looking at him quickly, felt that he was offering more than he ought. On horseback she would have said Yes. But on foot No. So she said perhaps it was rather far, and thought a look of relief passed over her host's face.

'In that case,' he said, 'we might go back along the valley and call at Wheeler's Farm. He's the uncle of Wheeler that you saw at the stables and another uncle was the family chimney sweep for years. In fact half the Pomfret population is Wheelers or Wheelers by marriage.'

'It's mostly Gobles our way,' said Eleanor. 'And of course it used to be Sowerbys when Chaldicotes belonged to them.'

'My uncle used to talk about the Sowerbys,' said Lord Pomfret, alluding to his predecessor in the title. 'I think old Miss Sowerby was a flame of his once. Did someone tell me she had left Edgewood?'

Eleanor said she had sold her house to Mr Adams from Hogglestock.

'I see a good deal of him one way and another,' said Lord Pomfret. 'On committees down here and sometimes in town while Parliament is sitting. We differ about politics, but I have a great respect for his honesty. If we have got to go,' by which we think Lord Pomfret meant the class to which by long descent and breeding he belonged rather than a political party, 'we might have worse successors than the Adamses. They are English and loyal to England and ready to carry on English tradition. But I hope I'll be dead by then,' he added rather illogically; and Eleanor found nothing to say.

By now they were approaching Wheeler's Farm where from a house of incredible Morlandesqueness, shaded in the best tradition by a sycamore in its heavy black late summer leafage, a thread of blue smoke was rising from a chimney.

'Early English water-colour,' said Eleanor reverently.

'I think that whenever I come here,' said Lord Pomfret, 'and sometimes I think I'll hire a labourer in a smock and a female labourer in a spotless gown with muslin fichu and four or five curly-headed, rosy-cheeked rascals with chubby limbs, and a spinning-wheel, and dress up in my great-great-grandfather's high-collared coat and buckskin breeches and chuck the female labourer under the chin,' at which Eleanor, not to be outdone, said she would put on a muslin gown and black sandals and a broad-brimmed straw hat with blue ribbons and take a likeness of the landlord with his faithful tenantry and have it reproduced in a Book of Beauty, and in elaborating this eighteenth century scene they laughed a good deal. And when they got up to the farm, which was really little more than a large cottage, they laughed even more, for there was old Wheeler, in a moleskin waistcoat and very shabby leggings, leaning over a ramshackle sty where several pigs were pretending to be Morlands.

'As it was in the beginning, still is in some lucky places, and alas, never shall be again,' said Lord Pomfret, more to himself than Eleanor. 'Well, Wheeler. What are the partridges going to do this year?'

Wheeler, touching a shapeless old hat, said he did hear on the wireless last night that the prospex for September were good. But if his lordship were to ask him, he said, he'd say that no one could say for certain, and some of those young devils from Hogglestock had been about last Saturday night and he wished there were man-traps, like his old grandad said his father told him about. Lord Pomfret looked worried.

'You can't do anything unless you catch them red-handed,' he said. 'And if you did you'd need a bodyguard and no jury would convict them. They'll steal anything to sell it in the Black Market. Have you seen Mr Wicklow, Wheeler?'

Wheeler said he'd seed Mr Wicklow and another gentleman ride past not twenty minutes ago. Going Hamaker way they was and the young gentleman was making his horse jump over them trees that had been felled.

'Well, look out for the poachers,' said Lord Pomfret and walked on, hoping inwardly that Eleanor's brother had not broken the horse's knees, and presently they came up with the horsemen who had dismounted and were examining the bank of a wide stream, and Lord Pomfret fell into a discussion about otters with Roddy Wicklow and Tom who seemed to know a good deal about them, so that his sister marvelled at his knowledge, for one is apt to forget that people whom one has known all their lives have sides that are unexplored by their relations.

'It is curious,' said Lord Pomfret, as he and Eleanor walked back, leaving the horsemen to their own devices, 'that when poor devils who never got enough to eat and had large families stole a partridge or a rabbit they could be jailed or transported. And now blackguards who only steal to sell on the Black Market can't be touched. It pays to be dishonest now.'

'But not *really*, does it,' said Eleanor, not wishing to preach but feeling that somehow the Ten Commandments were still true.

'"There's a great text in Galatians,"' said Lord Pomfret half to himself, which words meant nothing, we regret to say, to Eleanor though Mrs Robin Dale would doubtless have recognised them as a line from one of her almost favourite poets, Robert Browning, 'God is not mocked.'

'I suppose it is true,' said Eleanor.

'I think it has been proved,' said Lord Pomfret, again more to himself than to her. 'And now,' he continued, in a quite different voice, 'we must be getting back, or Nurse will be offended. We are expected to be punctual at Saturday tea because the children come down.' And they walked briskly along the woodland path that finally brought them out into the rough track and so up the hill to the Towers, where they found tea just beginning and Miss Merriman and Clarissa over from Holdings.

'Merry says Cousin Emily is staying in bed for a few days,' said Lady Pomfret to her husband. 'Nothing much, but the doctor thought it would be a good plan.'

The look of anxiety which the afternoon's walk had dissipated came back to Lord Pomfret's face and Eleanor's heart stabbed her at the sight, which was unreasonable and yet in a way pleasurable, for she felt (quite wrongly) that only she in that party really understood his feelings. Whereas if anyone understood his feelings, which it is practically impossible for any of us, even the most loving and beloved to do, it was certainly not Eleanor, nor even Sally, but Miss Merriman, the sleepless guardian of the doomed class that she had loved and protected all her life.

'Hobyahs,' said Lady Emily Foster with her mouth far too full, hastily adding Please, which nearly made the cake come out of her mouth.

'Too, too disgusting,' said Clarissa, firmly wiping her young cousin's mouth. 'I say, Grace, you're Grace, aren't you, you know Jennifer Gorman, don't you?'

Grace said she did and Jennifer had a New Look dress and coat.

'I think she's too, too awkward,' said Clarissa, in a most affected grown-up way. 'I used to go to dancing class with her; and her curtsey, my dear!'

At these words, unkind and even a little ill-bred as they were, for Clarissa in spite of her worldly air was still in what is so truly called the difficult age, a great light suddenly broke on Grace.

Madame Tomkins had lit the candle, Clarissa had fanned the flame. It is mortifying to have to admit that any parent is ever right, but Grace felt that her mother's want of enthusiasm for Jennifer was perhaps not misplaced, and she sat silent for quite two minutes reflecting on life till Roddy Wicklow and Tom came in, to whom Clarissa at once attached herself in an artless way. Not by hanging on his arm as Grace did to Colin, but by the subtler method of drawing him into a private conversation with a view to impressing him, though whether she quite succeeded is doubtful.

'And what are you doing?' she said, as an aunt might ask a nephew.

Mostly lounging around and suffering, said Tom, amused to see that Clarissa did not take the quotation. And looking for a job on the land, he added.

'I must ask Gillie about one,' said Clarissa in a grown-up way, to which Tom replied by thanking her very much and saying that he had been out all afternoon with Roddy Wicklow who had been very nice to him, at which moment Lord Pomfret asked Tom how he had got on and what he thought of Starveacres Hatches.

'It's an awfully jolly place, but the ground's a bit chalky, isn't it,' said Tom, wondering if one could say Sir to a lord, as to say My lord sounded what that little Clarissa would call too, too eighteenth century.

'That's the trouble whenever you get near the downs,' said Lord Pomfret. 'Old Marling had a lot of trouble with that bit of his on the Barchester side till he sold it to Adams.'

'Oh, do you know Mr Adams?' said Tom. 'He's bought Miss Sowerby's house where we live, I mean in Edgewood,' said Tom, feeling the English language almost too much for him. 'He's spending an awful lot of money on it and he's going to have a party.'

Lord Pomfret gave his usual courteous attention to his guest's remarks, but Eleanor couldn't help feeling that he wasn't interested in Mr Adams except as a public man and her hopes for Tom went down again, a seesaw business of which she was heartily tired, though longing for him to be a success.

'By the way,' said Roddy Wicklow to his brother-in-law and employer, 'I heard a rum thing. Adams has been poking about, or paying someone else to poke about for him, among the old title deeds of that bit of land and they find it was called Adamsfield about two hundred years ago. He's as pleased as Punch and going to use the name for the market garden. And by Jove, Gillie, Lucy Marling has got the land into good condition. I wish I had her here,' at which words, which Eleanor felt to be the final destruction of Tom's hopes, her heart sank again. And then Roddy took Tom away to show him some of Lord Pomfret's ever increasing files of papers and Lord Pomfret followed them, so her heart rose again and when the children clamoured for more stories she told them the story of the Cat and the Mouse and Titty-mouse and Tatty-mouse, and after the fashion of children the more horrible and terrifying the story the more they enjoyed it, and Giles pounced upon Emily so often, saying 'And I'll eat you good body, good body,' that Lady Pomfret had to tell him to stop and Emily not to scream so loud.

'It isn't all *exactly* true, is it?' said Lord Mellings, coming close to Eleanor, his little face in its anxiety so like his father's, and Eleanor hastened to assure him that it was only an invention to amuse small children.

'Like Emily and Giles,' said Lord Mellings loftily and Eleanor said Yes, wondering what on earth one could tell children if one was to be sure of not frightening them, for she remembered when she was small enjoying nothing more than tales of robbers and bogeys and the Massacre of St Bartholomew, while she had screamed the whole household out of bed three nights running because of a simple tale of a girl whose mother had died and bequeathed her a mirror, and seeing her own face so like her mother's in the glass she had believed her mother lived there and watched over her.

'You never know what will frighten them and what won't,' she said aside to Miss Merriman, who said that when David Leslie was seven he wouldn't go into the library because there was a Gainsborough portrait of one of his forebears and no one could understand it till years afterwards when he told his mother that the drapery of the cloak made a face which he dreamt about.

'We do our best for them,' said Lady Pomfret who had overheard, 'and so often it turns out to be the worst.'

'I ought to be getting back to Lady Emily,' said Miss Merriman. 'I'll go and find Lord Pomfret and say good-bye,' and she went away to the estate room, while Eleanor and Lady Pomfret and the girls played noughts and crosses with the children and Lord Mellings won his game three times running and flushed with pleasure.

'You didn't help me, did you?' he asked Eleanor anxiously and Eleanor was able to say quite truthfully that he had really won it himself.

After an absence of about twenty minutes Miss Merriman came back and the men with her.

'Give our love to Cousin Emily and Agnes,' said Lady Pomfret, 'and I shall get over to Holdings next week.'

'Do,' said Miss Merriman, her eyes meeting Lady Pomfret's and we suppose some message passed between them for Lady

Pomfret looked disturbed. And then Miss Merriman took leave of the rest of the party and carried Clarissa away.

'Come to Holdings one Sunday,' said Clarissa to Tom as she left the room in Miss Merriman's wake, 'and bring your sisters,' at which Grace nearly burst with indignation and even Eleanor had to admit to herself that she was slightly mortified. And then Roddy said he would take them to the Puddingdale bus stop, so more good-byes were said. Eleanor longed to ask if Tom had given satisfaction but was too shy and the good-byes had to be said quickly, as there was not much time.

'I enjoyed the walk so much,' said Lord Pomfret. 'You must come again soon.'

Nurse then appeared and swept the children off to bed and Lord Pomfret sat down in a large comfortable chair and smiled at his wife. Gillie had been overdoing it again, thought Lady Pomfret, with an unreasonable spurt of annoyance against Eleanor, and then told herself not to be silly for it was she who had suggested the walk. So she sat down near her husband and picked up her tapestry work.

'Can't you *ever* rest, Sally?' said Lord Pomfret, and any complaint was so unusual from him that his wife was quite taken aback and sat silent, her hand with the needle in it raised.

'Sorry, old girl,' said Lord Pomfret, smiling at her and as she came to life again she smiled back.

'Hard day?' she said.

'A very nice day,' said Lord Pomfret. 'Wheeler says the poachers or rather the Black Market gang, are out again. I really don't know what we can do. I took Eleanor round by the valley and the farm and the copse.'

And that was twice too far was what his wife wanted to say, but she refrained and asked how Tom Grantly had got on.

'Roddy will tell you,' said Lord Pomfret. 'He seems to have the hang of the actual out of door work and Roddy says he would shape very well indeed outside. But when he tried him on the estate room—' and Lord Pomfret looked thoroughly depressed.

'Not a success?' said Lady Pomfret, the old ache at her heart; an ache which had lain there sometimes quiet, sometimes awake, ever since she had first met and loved young Mr Foster in his uncle Lord Pomfret's house.

Lord Pomfret shook his head.

'He can't read maps and doesn't know the first thing about committees,' said Lord Pomfret. 'I haven't time to teach him, nor has Roddy. I'm very sorry, my dear. If only Merry were here,' he added.

'I know,' said Lady Pomfret. 'Well, we'll manage something, even if I have to do it myself. I will *not* have you killing yourself, Gillie. I wish the horrible title had never been invented, or that your selfish old father hadn't died. If he were Earl we could have had some fun. My poor Gillie.' And my poor little Ludovic she thought, but did not say it, for her husband had trouble enough without thinking of his little heir's future.

'Well, there's one thing, I've always got you, Sally,' said Lord Pomfret, looking at his wife with the deep affection that she could sometimes hardly bear, so little did she feel worthy of it. But doubtless her husband felt the same about her.

Roddy Wicklow decanted the three Grantlys at the bus stop just as the bus came round the corner, so that there was scant time for good-byes and all Eleanor's plans of having a few grown-up sisterly words with Roddy had to be given up. In the noisy rackety bus conversation was impossible, and again in the bus from Barchester to Edgewood there were too many people who knew them. They got out of the bus at the Post Office and walked up the High Street. As they passed the Old Bank House, where a car was waiting, Mr Adams came out with Lucy Marling, so they all stopped to talk.

'My head market-gardener has been giving the kitchen garden the once over,' said Mr Adams, looking proudly at Lucy. 'She's going to tell me what cabbages and onions and so forth to buy. You ought to see the job she's doing at Adamsfield. This young man,' he added to Lucy, nodding at Tom, 'wants to do a useful job on the land. You're going to Pomfret Towers, I believe,' to which Tom gave a mumbling reply to the effect that one never quite knew what one was going to do.

'I'll tell you what,' said Lucy, towering over Tom as she stood on the doorstep, 'when you come over to Adamsfield next week I want to talk about a tractor,' and she gave a long, and to the Grantlys a rather boring disquisition about a machine which seemed to plough, sow, reap and mow all by itself and practically pay the wages and taxes as well.

'You do the way Miss Marling says and you won't go far wrong,' said Mr Adams. 'Well, good-bye Miss Marling and I'll see you again on Monday. Marling Hall,' he added to the chauffeur and Lucy was taken away while the Grantlys walked home.

As soon as Mrs Grantly saw her elder son she knew that the day had not been successful. With a sickening feeling at her heart she decided, very courageously we think, not to put off the moment of reckoning any longer than she could help, and followed her son to his bedroom

'Well, darling?' she said, when to her great surprise Tom, instead of saying he wished he were dead, or mumbling something about wishing people wouldn't ask questions, looked out of the window and said, 'No good, mother. Roddy Wicklow was awfully decent and went round the place and I thought things were all right. But then he took me to the estate room and I just mucked everything up.'

Mrs Grantly, without protesting against this language, said she was sure it would be all right, though she knew perfectly well that she didn't believe what she said.

'Well, Wicklow said I would learn the out of doors easily and I remembered a lot of things Mr Wickham had told me,' said Tom, still looking out of the window. 'But he said I would need to go to some place or other and learn the office side if I wanted to take it seriously. Mother, I *can't* go to school again. I've been back to Oxford and I love Oxford but it was *ghastly* to be a schoolboy again. I'm sorry, but I'm a damned fool.'

This was not the way to speak to his mother, but Mrs Grantly felt such gratitude to heaven for allowing her firstborn to speak so clearly to her that the manner of speaking did not matter. That Tom had wished to go back to Oxford and read for Greek; that he should have found that neither the enclosed life nor the work he was doing were what he wanted; that after choosing a country life on the land he should find he had once more to go to school and loathe the thought of going to school with all his heart; all this was sad and worrying enough. But even more worrying to his mother would have been that he should enclose himself in his own miseries (and how great the miseries of the young can be only they know) and eat his heart out, not to speak of the attitude of sulks and aloofness which would have gone with them. He *was* a damned fool, said Mrs Grantly to herself. But however a damned, or triple or quadruple fool, he was her child and she was going to stand by him; if he would let her.

'Well, what do you think we had better do?' she said, not yet knowing what else to say.

'I don't know, mother,' said Tom, apparently addressing the garden. 'I'll go over to Adamsfield again and see what Lucy Marling says. But I simply *can't* go and learn things in a school, or a college or whatever they like to call themselves again. After all I'm twenty-seven.'

And how young, how young his mother thought. But it would not do to say this to Tom. And she must think of her husband, who happened to be Tom's father.

'I'm perfectly sure it will be all right,' she said firmly, though entirely without any inner conviction. 'I'll tell father that you are going to Adamsfield for a bit. Supper will be ready in a few minutes.'

Tom remained at the window, his back turned to the room, till his mother had gone, and even then he did not move, in a vague unreasoning hope that by keeping quite still he would escape from life and its burdens. But youth is hungry and when he heard the gong he reluctantly turned from the window and went downstairs, where his mother and Eleanor exerted themselves to such effect, helped by Grace's uninteresting chatter about how she was going over to Holdings to see Clarissa, that everyone felt as if a thunderstorm were brewing.

9

The interest taken in the Old Bank House by a great part of Barsetshire was really a tribute to Mr Adams's character. When Mrs Belton remembered the uncouth barbarian in a thick Teddy Bear coat of orange-brown hue, a huge woolly scarf, a vivid check cap pulled well down on his head and leather gloves with fur backs like a bear's paws who had come to her door late on a winter evening to see his daughter Heather after she had fallen through the ice into the lake by her own wilfulness and been put to bed in Mrs Belton's house, she could hardly believe that the Mr Adams of Old Bank House was the same man. What he owed to Mrs Belton few people knew, though he never forgot it. And as his daughter Heather grew out of the fat flapper stage into a very intelligent and not unattractive young woman, doing brilliantly at Cambridge, engaged to a most suitable young man, so had Mr Adams gradually shed some of his more alarming mannerisms, got into Parliament, become richer and used his riches well, sat as an equal with people like Sir Edmund Pridham and Sir Robert Fielding on committees and boards and was now consolidating his position in the county by coming to live at Edgewood. Whether he had set out to do this we do not know, and if he had not met Mrs Belton he might have stayed at Hogglestock, contented with his extremely golden mean. But in knowing her he had apprehended other sides of life and was now in a fair way to being accepted among the best of Barsetshire as a man whose word, as he far too often said, was as good as his bond, who loved his native county and was willing to work for it with all his power.

When the plan of having a housewarming for the Old Bank House had first been suggested, Mr Adams had put his ears back, showed the whites of his eyes, and dug his hoofs well in. But Heather's natural wish to have a party and Mrs Belton's persuasion had brought him round, a day was fixed and invitations sent. Nearly everyone accepted, some from curiosity, a great number from a real and warm feeling for their M.P., whatever his politics. Lady Norton, who had not been invited, said she wondered that poor Hilda Sowerby's father did not turn in his grave to see the Old Bank House in such hands, but her very dull daughter-in-law with whom she was staying said old Mr Sowerby had been cremated, which put a stop to further speculation.

'Here is the invitation to Mr Adams's housewarming,' said Mrs Marling to her husband at breakfast. 'Saturday week, four till seven. Lucy says the garden will be perfect.'

Mr Marling, in his most Old English Squire manner, said he didn't know what the world was coming to and if Tom Sowerby had been alive he would have never sold the house.

'He'd have had to, father,' said his daughter Lucy in a dutiful bellow. 'He was Head over Ears in Debt.'

'All right, all right, I'm not deaf. No need to shout,' said Mr Marling, which caused his daughter Lucy to say quite audibly, Yes you are, having said which she felt ashamed of herself.

Oliver Marling said he believed the garden was very beautiful and he looked forward to going; perhaps knowing that the Deans had already received their invitation and hoping that

Jessica might be there. For the Cockspur Theatre had shut for a fortnight as it usually did in August, much to the annoyance of all the other theatres who could not afford such a luxury.

'The garden's all right,' said Lucy. 'Herbaceous border and all that. But the kitchen garden wants a lot of pulling together. I'll have to see about it when I can spare time from Adamsfield.'

'Adamsfield? Never heard of it,' said Mr Marling.

'Yes, you have, father,' said Lucy in a benevolent bellow. 'You remember when Mr Adams got that man from London to look up the records and they found your land over Barchester way used to be called Adamsfield.'

'I never heard it,' said Mr Marling. 'Nor did my father, nor my grandfather. They'd have told me if they had. All these new-fangled names. It's enough to make one stop taking in *The Times*.'

His wife said it wasn't *The Times*'s fault, but there was something about that article on the right hand middle page that was in two columns only not coming down to the bottom that made it quite impossible to read it; quite impossible to read the article, she meant, and it would be very nice to see Mr Adams's new house. For Mrs Marling, though not much interested in Mr Adams personally, was prepared to approve all he did because he had bought a piece of her husband's land and was giving Lucy the kind of job she liked. Sometimes, it is true, she wished Lucy were not working for what she still thought of as an outsider, but when she saw her unmarried daughter busy and contented as she had not been since the year when her elder sister Lettice married Captain Barclay and went to Yorkshire, she felt she could bless Mr Adams and would bless him were he twice the outsider he was. 'Outsider?' her husband had said when she once spoke of Mr Adams as one, 'outsider? He's no gentleman, my dear, but he knows exactly what he is and there's no nonsense about him. We'd be in the workhouse if he hadn't bought that piece of land; Adamsfield he calls it, stupid name, my old father never called it Adamsfield. And he gives Lucy her head with fertilisers and what not. I couldn't afford it. You know that as well as I do, my dear.'

To all of which Mrs Marling agreed, but secretly wished Lucy would think less of fertilisers and tractors and potato spinners and meet some nice men. But where were they? Lucy's contemporaries were now married men with growing families. There were several younger men, like Charles Belton, but to them she must seem an aunt rather than an eligible girl. There were older men available like Sir Edmund Pridham, but this kind of marriage Mrs Marling could not think of for her daughter. There would not be much money for Lucy when she and her husband were dead and what would Lucy do? Have a small cottage and go on gardening till she was too old for the work? The prospect so depressed Mrs Marling that a few bitter tears came to her eyes. Then she checked them, for crying was a luxury she could not afford, and tried not to think of it. But the thought and the anxiety remained.

At Arcot House the invitation to Mr Adams's party gave great pleasure and was enthusiastically accepted by everybody. Mrs Freddy Belton, who still thought of herself as Susan Dean, was now living with her husband on the second floor of his parents' house, pending a house of her own, and expressed her determination to go to the party even if the baby was born in Miss Sowerby's herbaceous border. So her mother-in-law asked Dr Perry's advice and Dr Perry said as the baby wasn't due for at least three weeks he thought the outing would do her good and cheer her up.

'I don't need cheering up really,' said Susan Belton, who lived in a state of calm happiness that deeply touched her husband's heart, 'because it's all heaven. But I must say it would be fun to see Mr Adams and Heather at home. Do let's go, Mrs Belton,' for she had not yet found any other name for her mother-in-law and as they were very fond of each other this did quite well.

Mr Dean at Winter Overcotes announced to his family assembled that he was certainly going and hoped his wife would come too, as he understood from Lucy Marling that there was a beautiful Chinese-Chippendale sofa in the drawing-room and she could go to sleep to her heart's content. At which Mrs Dean opened her beautiful ox-eyes (and if the Greeks found this a suitable epithet for a handsome woman, who are we to differ from them) and said with great dignity that she never slept in the day time, at which such of her family as were present gently hooted.

From Harefield there were also coming Mr and Mrs Sydney Carton; Mrs Carton having been Miss Sparling the Headmistress of the Hosiers' Girls' Foundation School; also her successor Miss Holly, who was rather like the Plum-pudding Flea but a brilliant mathematician and excellent commonsensical Headmistress. In the kindness of his heart Mr Adams had thought of inviting Dr Morgan who had attended Heather after she fell into the lake at Harefield, but Heather said if Dad was going to ask that ghastly psychoanalytic woman she would shut herself up in her bedroom, and then kissed her father very affectionately.

'All right, girlie,' said Mr Adams. 'I didn't take to her much myself, so we'll cross her off. It's your party.'

'It's S. and H. Adams's party,' said Heather.

'Well, that's what we used to think,' said her father musingly. 'You were going to be my little partner, weren't you, Heth? But now you've found another partner and your old Dad will have to get on as best he can. It's going to be T. and H. Pilward now, isn't it?'

His voice was entirely cheerful and his face unruffled, but Heather felt a sudden pang of compassion for the father she was leaving. It is very rare for a young creature in love to think of the empty place her marriage will make and it had certainly not occurred to Heather. Now it came upon her like an electric shock that her father would be alone in the Old Bank House, alone in the London flat, alone wherever his home might be, and the prospect frightened her and made her feel guilty.

'Don't you worry, girlie,' said her father. 'It says in the Bible that we've got to leave our father and mother when we marry; not that I left mine, because Dad was dead falling under a lorry when he wasn't sober and when I married Mother my mother was dead too,' which might have puzzled an outsider, but was quite clear to Heather who had heard her mother called by that name ever since she could remember. 'I've got a nice house and Miss Hoggett to look after me and enough business on my hands to keep me busy for the next hundred years, not to speak of wasting my time in Parliament,' to which his daughter, wisely side-tracking the emotional issue, said that her father mustn't talk nonsense and if all the M.P.s were like him England wouldn't be in such a mess.

'Well now, you listen to me, Heth,' said Mr Adams. 'We've talked business before many a time and many's the time you've given your old Dad good advice, the way Mother used to do though she hadn't your education. You know what I'm settling on you, Heth. And you know as well as I do that if They nationalise steel it'll make a big difference to me. And,' said Mr Adams thoughtfully, 'my men know it's going to make a big difference to them and their hearts won't be in it the way they were. But they've got to earn their wages and that's that. But as far as your money can be made safe, and that,' said Adams grimly, 'is pretty well impossible with the party I belong to in power, it *is* safe. And you can't fool with it, nor can Ted. And if we did lose everything, Heth, and I wouldn't be surprised if we did one way or another, you've got a good education and brains and so's Ted, and you'll do all right. I wonder They don't nationalise ants,' said Mr Adams reflectively. 'There's a whole lot of them down by the flagged path, walking about like the Tubes at the rush hour. Whether they copy us or we copy them I don't know, but it's a nasty sight either way. Well, girlie, it's up to you and Ted to make good now, and don't you worry about your old Dad. I've heard the men at the works call me an old devil sometimes, and the devil looks after his own.'

All of which did not depress Heather unduly, for though she loved her father very much she had his independence and had always told herself that she would not depend on his money, having the happy, as yet untouched confidence of the young that their elders may have been stupid or unlucky, but for them all will go well. And how much their elders wish this for them, only their elders know.

The Saturday of Mr Adams's party was obliging enough to be warm; as warm that is to say as any day was in that unkind summer and that is not saying much. For as Madame Tomkins observed to Lady Fielding who had come in about having her last year's summer dress lengthened, her old customers who had managed to get two dresses every summer through the war and even the peace, whether by cutting up curtains, or having a dress they had decided to throw away made over for the third time, or by material brought back at vast expense and heavy customs duty from France and Italy and other ruined and bankrupt countries where life ran easily and shops were full of goods they were allowed to sell, were now having one dress if indeed they had even one.

'It is this dog of a climate,' said Madame Tomkins, who still dropped into French in moments of emotion, in spite of her fluent and execrable English, 'where one morfondres oneself. My clients do not command but an only dress. If it made good weather, they of them would command at least two, even with this Government. Doubtless it is the will of the good God, but that one there does not comprehend that which passes itself here below. Enfin—' and Madame Tomkins shrugged her Gallic shoulders.

Had we the pen of Sir Walter Scott, or that of James and Horace Smith when masquerading in his name, we would catalogue the approach of Barsetshire to Edgewood in proper style. But as we have not, we will refrain. Heather and Miss Hoggett the housekeeper had done most of the arranging and Messrs. Scatcherd and Tozer the Barchester caterers supplied the tea, coffee, ices such as they were, sandwiches and cakes. Mr Tozer himself had come over to superintend and was being entertained by Miss Hoggett in the housekeeper's room.

'Now Miss Rose Birkett's wedding at Southbridge School, just before that Hitler began creating,' said Mr Tozer, 'that *was* a wedding. Champagne, I believe you. Eight dozen, or maybe ten dozen,' to which Miss Hoggett replied that this was a garden party and not a wedding.

'Admitted,' said Mr Tozer, 'and I must say the garden looks very nice with Our Tables and Our Tea-Urns. I remember at Miss Rose's wedding,' continued Mr Tozer, 'a quite shocking occurrence. Our Firm had been co-opted by the territorial camp at Plumstead to assist with their catering and owing to the breakages in the mess there was quite a hiatus about small tumblers for the lemonade. Plenty of large wineglasses we had, but of course lemonade should *never* be drunk except from small tumblers,' said Mr Tozer with a slight shudder.

Miss Hoggett said that was as might be, which so froze Mr Tozer that he had nothing to say, and as Miss Hoggett was obviously determined not to help him he found himself in a very uncomfortable position until deliverance came in the person of Mr Adams's extremely competent secretary, Miss Pickthorn, who wanted to ask Miss Hoggett about tea for the chauffeurs, if any, so that Mr Tozer was able to escape.

'It seems funny, miss, me being here,' said the faithful Miss Hoggett, who approved of Miss Pickthorn because she was a real help to Mr Adams. 'I've lived in Hogglestock all my life and so did all my people as long as anyone can remember, and now I'm to live in Edgewood among foreigners. I daresay I'll get used to it, but it seems a bit strange not to know everyone. I sometimes wish I was staying on at Hogglestock with Miss Heather, but all things considered my duty lies here. I hope I'll be buried in Hogglestock though,' to which Miss Pickthorn replied, though quite kindly, that she was sure Mr Adams would have no objection, which roused Miss Hoggett from her depression and she went off to Heather's bedroom which was to be used for any coats or parcels that the ladies wished to get rid of, for although it was a garden party and the guests were coming in what good clothes they had, there is hardly ever an occasion when one is not festooned with parcels and the women of England are likely to become permanently lop-sided owing to the eternal shopping-basket.

Mr Adams and his daughter had been exercised on the subject of flowers for the house. Anything that money could buy was within Mr Adams's reach, but he knew that there were still a great many things that money could not buy, 'and if you and your old Dad and Miss Hoggett were to arrange the flowers it would be like the cemetery on a Sunday afternoon,' he said, 'and I don't like to ask Mrs Belton. She's busy enough as it is,' and then it was that he was inspired to suggest Clarissa Graham. As our reader may or may not remember (and we must admit that there are a great many things we don't remember ourselves) Lady Graham's second daughter had broken away from her family background and wanted to study engineering draughtsmanship, to which end she got Mrs Belton to introduce her to Mr Adams at Anne Fielding's wedding. Mr Adams, amused by this well-bred, pretty, precocious child, had passed her on to his daughter Heather then at college with a mathematical scholarship, and when Clarissa went to college, also with a mathematical scholarship, Heather had befriended her, and the two girls had remained friends though they did not often meet.

'Good idea, Dad,' said Heather approvingly. 'I'll ring her up.'

'Now wait a moment, girlie,' said her father. 'You and Clarissa are friends and you've been to her father's house and she's not been here yet, though of course it stands to reason that she couldn't till the house was fit to come to,' said Mr Adams reflectively. 'And it seems to me the civil thing to do is to ask her father and mother too, especially seeing as how we met Lady Graham at Lady Fielding's the day little Anne was married. They needn't come if they don't want to and no bones broken.'

An invitation was accordingly sent to General Sir Robert Graham, K.C.B. and Lady Graham and Miss Clarissa Graham. Lady Graham at once accepted for herself and her daughter, having a mild curiosity to see the Old Bank House which she had known in former years, and regretted that Sir Robert Graham would be unable to come. For, though this she did not put in her letter, her husband hardly ever got down from Town till late on Saturday and cordially disliked anyone he had never met before.

The protocol being settled, Heather asked Clarissa if she would come over by the bus and arrange the flowers, which Clarissa did, enjoying rapturously the delphiniums, lupins, gladiolus, roses and every flower of magnificence that the Barchester nursery gardens could produce. She and Heather had previously spent a day in Barchester buying pots and vases in the second-hand shops with no expense spared and the result under Clarissa's clever, elegant fingers was very beautiful.

Meanwhile Mr Adams was walking about his garden with his old friend Mrs Belton, whom he had asked to come a little earlier than the other guests and help Heather and himself to do the honours, a request which had touched her very much.

'I couldn't come before the others by myself,' she said, 'because we've only enough petrol for one car, so we all squashed into Freddy's, which is a bit bigger than ours, but my husband and my young people have gone up to see the Grantlys first. How nice Heather is looking,' which was not idle praise, for Heather's looks had improved out of all knowledge since Mrs Belton had first known her as a spotty-faced plum-pudding of a schoolgirl.

'She's a good girl,' said Mr Adams, 'and she owes a great great deal to you, Mrs Belton, and she doesn't forget. Nor does Sam Adams,' he added. 'And how is Mrs Freddy?'

Mrs Belton said very well, and the doctor said about the third week in August but Wheeler, the old ex-nurse and present parlour-maid, said it would be September the first and twins, to which Mr Adams replied thoughtfully that to look at Mrs Freddy it might be triplets, but there was no offence in his words and Mrs Belton laughed and said she rather agreed.

'A partridge pair, my old mother used to say,' said Mr Adams. 'Funny how these things come back to you. Life's a rum affair, Mrs Belton, and I'll tell you a queer thing. I've been in the metal industry one way and another all my life and I've worked hard and I've had some luck and some good friends, and I've got some pretty big business interests outside the works. But as I get older I'm turning to the land. My mother's people were labourers and when she married and came to Hogglestock she pined without a bit of land, not even a back yard where we lived. She had window boxes, poor soul, that was all. I suppose I take after her side. I've bought this house and a big garden and I've got Adamsfield, and sometimes I feel I'm doing more good work with the greenstuff I'm raising, or I should say Miss Marling's raising, than with all my furnaces and rolling mills and shops. I wouldn't be a bit surprised if I turned myself into a limited company and let them do the worrying and lying awake at night and grew a few turnips myself.'

Mrs Belton, interested, but not taking him too seriously, said turnips were a good thing and her husband had lost money steadily over his farm ever since she married him, though not nearly as much, she was thankful to say, as Mr Marling had lost.

'Well, he's all right now, till the Government take his capital away,' said Mr Adams. 'I paid him a good price for Adamsfield.'

'And my husband got a good price for our land on the Southbridge Road and we do not forget that,' said Mrs Belton, for it was largely owing to a word from Mr Adams to the Secretary of the Barsetshire War Agriculture Committee after Freddy Belton had picked Heather out of the lake that Mr Belton's land had not been requisitioned for crops (for which indeed it was quite unsuitable) and he had been able to sell it to the Hosiers' Girls' Foundation School trustees for building a new school. 'And that's how we all live, selling our children's inheritance a bit at a time,' to which Mr Adams replied that if she was thinking of Freddy and Charles, he was quite sure they would rather see their parents live in such comfort as the present condition of things allowed than come in for land themselves; which talk made Mrs Belton feel partly depressed and partly, though she could not explain why to herself, hopeful.

And now the guests began to arrive, among the first being the Grantlys with the rest of the Beltons. Inside the house every door was wide open so that guests might pry, admire, criticise and see all that was to be seen. Mrs Grantly, who had not been inside the Old Bank House since Miss Sowerby's going, was overcome with admiration for the beauty of the rooms, so long tarnished and obscured by poverty. The long drawing-room newly hung with the Chinese paper, the Chinese-Chippendale sofa conscious of its elegance, the curtains of pre-war silk whose price only Mrs Belton and Mr Adams knew, the gilded mirrors, its sole ornament two or three immense Chinese vases with flowers rising from them like a flower-piece; the dining-room with its silver-striped paper and severe mahogany with some good silver and crystal; the noble staircase newly painted and carpeted; the library behind the dining-room where the Sowerby books which Miss Sowerby had consented to sell with the house had been lovingly cared for, their fine calf bindings shining like dull gold upon the white shelves with golden headings; the cool stone hall leading to the large glass door through which the green lawn and the brilliant herbaceous border could be seen; all these looked so noble, so full of contentment and repose, that Mrs Grantly exclaimed aloud at their beauty.

'I've tried to do my best by it,' said Mr Adams seriously. 'But it's really Mrs Belton's doing,' at which Mrs Belton protested and Heather said it was six of one and half a dozen of the other and Dad knew more about furniture than he would admit, and there was a slight but friendly squabble which Mr Adams ended by inviting Mrs Grantly to come and see the first floor before anyone else came. This she was delighted to do and went upstairs with Mr Adams and Mrs Belton while the younger people went into the garden.

'Here's my bedroom,' said Mr Adams, who had chosen a small room, probably once a dressing-room, overlooking the street. 'Bachelor's quarters as you might say, but they suit me. And a bathroom off it. And the other side of the bathroom my spare bedroom. And when I think of Sam Adams having a spare bedroom,' said Mr Adams, standing in the door which led from the bathroom to the spare room, 'I hardly know myself. Four rooms we had when I was a kid and thought we were kings. Two downstairs and two up. Four of us slept in one room and mother and dad in the other.'

'I never knew you had brothers or sisters,' said Mrs Belton. 'Where are they now?'

'That,' said Mr Adams, 'I couldn't exactly say. They all died when they were kids and I was a miserable shaver myself, though you wouldn't think it to look at me. I daresay Dad being run over when he was drunk and my poor old mother dying soon afterwards put me on my mettle. Anyway I wouldn't die and what's more I don't intend to yet. Come in,' and he stood aside to let his guests pass into the best bedroom which Mrs Grantly had occasionally seen in Miss Sowerby's time with an old-fashioned brass bedstead and good but sadly shabby mid-Victorian furniture. We do not intend to describe the room, nor any more of the house, and will content ourselves by saying that both ladies were consumed with equal quantities of unbounded admiration and sheer envy, so simple, so handsome were the room and its furnishings. Mrs Belton, recovering herself first, asked Mr Adams how he had dared to ask her help, knowing how busy she was, when he was capable of making a room like that for himself.

'I don't know,' said Mr Adams, looking both pleased and slightly embarrassed. 'I thought the room ought to be like this, so I made up my mind it should, and when Sam Adams sets his mind to a job he usually does that job. It's like what I thought it ought to be, that's all.'

'And who will be your first guest?' said Mrs Grantly.

'That I don't rightly know,' said Mr Adams. 'My Heth will have a say in that as long as she's here, and that won't be very long now as the wedding is fixed for October. Her room and Ted's are at the back and very nice rooms too with a bathroom, and the nurseries are upstairs, but I'm leaving Heth to do what she likes about them and so long as the young Pilwards are happy their old grandfather will be happy too,' said Mr Adams, looking prophetically into the future. 'Just have a look at Heth's room.'

He led them to a large room at the back of the house with a view over the garden to the little stream and away beyond it to some rising ground. Here Miss Hoggett was seated by the window knitting and when the guests came in she rose and came forward.

'This is Miss Hoggett, my housekeeper,' said Mr Adams. 'She was with me at Hogglestock. I daresay Mrs Belton and Mrs Grantly would like to look round.'

Mrs Belton, who had once met Miss Hoggett at Hogglestock, had a few words with her, admiring the house in its new beauty.

'Yes, it's a fine house, madam,' said Miss Hoggett. 'Mr Adams he was saying that he'd lived hard as a boy and worked all his life to get a house like this and I'm sure he deserves it. We lived pretty hard too when I was young in Hogglestock. It wasn't a big place then like it is now. I remember my father saying when he was a boy it was only a village and a poor miserable one at that. His father was a brick-maker and they were a very poor, rough lot.'

'I'm sure I've heard your name,' said Mrs Grantly. 'My husband is the Rector here, as you probably know, and I'm certain I've heard him mention the name Hoggett when he was talking about his grandmother.'

'I couldn't say, madam, I'm sure,' said Miss Hoggett. 'Of course Grantly's a very respected name in these parts, but I'm sure my old father never mentioned it over our way. But I'm very pleased to have met you, madam, because I'm a churchwoman,' which words she accompanied by a slightly defiant look at her employer.

'Miss Hoggett doesn't hold with chapel,' said Mr Adams. 'But as I told you, Mrs Grantly, ever since the Reverend Enoch Arden talked so much nonsense, and dangerous nonsense I call it, about Jack being as good as his master or better, me and my Heth we've been church. And if your church needs anything, you've only got to say the word and Sam Adams will put his hand in his pocket.' This sudden incursion into religious differences amused Mrs Belton but slightly alarmed Mrs Grantly, who after seeing the glories of the Old Bank House was beginning to feel that Mr Adams's wealth and his wish to befriend the church might sometimes be a little difficult to deal with. But luckily at that moment the admirable Miss Pickthorn came upstairs to say that the Cartons and Mr Oriel with Miss Holly, the Headmistress of the Hosiers' Girls' Foundation School, had just arrived and Sir Robert and Lady Fielding with Bishop Joram were getting out of their car, so the whole company went hastily downstairs leaving Miss Hoggett to herself.

On the stone terrace behind the house Heather had been receiving guests during her father's temporary absence and was at the moment greeting affectionately Mr and Mrs Sydney Carton; for Mrs Carton when Miss Sparling and Headmistress of the Hosiers' Girls' Foundation School had helped Heather through the most spotted, clumsy, self-conscious and rebellious period of her difficult years and it was largely owing to her that Heather had taken up the study of mathematics under Miss Holly and done so well at college. Mrs Carton, who had not seen her ex-pupil for a long time, was delighted to see the big, good-looking, self-possessed girl who was partly of her making, made most friendly enquiries about her plans and was pleased to hear that the wedding was to be soon.

'And is the wedding to be here?' she asked.

'No,' said Heather. 'It's a beautiful church and Mr and Mrs Grantly are so kind, but we're only newcomers here, Miss Sparling. Oh, I mean Mrs Carton,' she added, crimsoning.

'I'm quite used to it,' said Mrs Carton. 'Miss Holly called me Miss Sparling only the other day. Will it be at the Cathedral then?'

Heather said no, just at the Hogglestock parish church.

'You see,' she added, 'they all know me at the works and Mr Pilward's people at the brewery all know Ted, so it would be a shame not to have the wedding there. Daddy's giving them a day's holiday on full pay.'

'And if any of them turn up the day afterwards I'll be surprised,' said Mr Adams, who had overheard his daughter's last words. 'If beer was the price it used to be, or the quality,' said Mr Adams regretting the past, 'they'd be dead drunk in the gutter by the evening. That's the way my Dad got run over and killed. But even with the miserable stuff we get now and the price a working man has to pay, we won't get more than half of them back next day, lazy blighters. Never mind, they're a good lot, take them all round and we've never had a real strike yet, because I know who's boss and they know it too. But if the Government take over my business they'll find they've bitten off more than they can chew,' said Mr Adams thoughtfully. 'And if my men strike it'll be no good the Government coming squealing to me.'

But at this moment the Fieldings who with Bishop Joram had been waiting to greet their host came forward and the Cartons passed on with Mr Oriel in their wake, who was a little disappointed because, as so often happened to him, he had been crowded aside before he could speak to his hostess whom he last remembered as Audrey in the school performance of *As You Like It*, needing at that time no aids in the way of make-up, so extremely oafish, flumpy and ungracious she was.

'Well, Lady Fielding,' said Mr Adams. 'I never thought when I was at Miss Anne's wedding last year, Mrs Dale I should say though Heth and me always think of her as Anne, that I'd be having you and Sir Robert here before my Heth's wedding. October it's to be, at Hogglestock, and I hope you will come.'

'Of course we shall,' said Lady Fielding. 'And I have brought a little present for Heather. I left it in the hall. It is a small water-colour drawing by Girtin of Hogglestock in 1795, which I thought might interest her. Though when I say Hogglestock, there is only a group of poor-looking cottages among the fields, and the little church.'

Mr Adams, who was really overcome by Lady Fielding's thought of Heather, said things were a bit changed since then, but he daresaid his housekeeper Miss Hoggett would remember the cottages as her father had lived there and was a brick-maker.

'And what about Miss Anne?' he said. 'It won't be like a party if she doesn't come,' and was glad to hear that she and her husband were coming from Southbridge, and then a great surge of Marlings and Deans with Aubrey Clover came onto the terrace and everyone moved out onto the lawn.

It was not to be a large party, perhaps forty people, all of whom had known Mr Adams for some time and most of whom knew each other, and as they sat or stood about on the grass and admired the herbaceous border some of them felt that for a while they were in the land of lost content. These were the older people. As for the younger ones, though most of them had done valiant work during the peace they had not known even the comparative ease of life as it was between the wars, and to them the world they lived in was normal. The older generation knew that never would they see glad confident morning again, but they had had their day. The people for whom Mrs Belton, as she looked at the party, felt most sorry were the girls and the men who were between the old and the young. People like Lucy Marling and her brother Oliver who were working valiantly for a world which had very little to give them. And looking at her daughter-in-law's quiet steadfast happiness, she felt a pang of joy that her dear Susan had escaped from the work she did so well and was shaping a new life. Not but what Eleanor Grantly was doing remarkably well in Susan's place, for Lady Pomfret had told Mrs Belton more than once what a blessing it was that Eleanor had been able to take on Susan's work or she really didn't know what they would have done.

Mr Marling, who appeared to be under the impression that the Old Bank House was his ancestral property, reft from him by the revolution as represented by Mr Adams, had come prepared not to enjoy himself. In vain had his wife told him that Mr Adams had really done Miss Sowerby a good turn by buying the house at a very good price and putting it into good repair, in vain had his daughter bellowed to him that he never liked that bit of land he had sold to Mr Adams as all it did was to eat up money, in vain had his son Oliver tried mild reasoning. Mr Marling was determined to enjoy himself in his own way and arrived looking, as Oliver irreverently said, rather like Highland Cattle at Bay.

'Well, Adams,' said Mr Marling as he shook hands. 'You've done yourself very well here. I remember the house when old Sowerby lived here. His uncle ruined himself gambling and what happened to him I don't know. Place has been going to rack and ruin ever since. Well, well, that's what all the old houses are coming to. A pretty penny it must have cost you first and last,' said Mr Marling, who had looked into the rooms as he came through the hall and was now eyeing the garden rather malevolently.

This being a subject after Mr Adams's own heart, he gave Mr Marling a very interesting account of some of the prices of repairing and furnishing and curiously enough Mr Marling instead of being angry and envious (though envy was not in his nature for all his grumblings) was deeply interested and gave himself the pleasure of telling Mr Adams where he could have got various bits of work done more cheaply; all of which Mr Adams took in very good part.

'Hullo, Mr Adams,' said Lucy Marling who had for the last two minutes been apostrophising her respected parent under her breath rather in the fashion of old Mr Smallweed. 'Oh, bother, I've split my glove. I knew I would if mother made me wear them. I'll tell you what, I've got the name of a man who's A1 on cowsheds. Sylvia Leslie told me and he's worked for her and Martin at Rushwater. He's coming over to see me on Tuesday about them.'

'Well, we'll talk about them when you've seen him, young lady,' said Mr Adams, good-humouredly moving her along.

'I do admire the way you handle Lucy,' said her mother. 'She has been too much for me ever since she was born.'

'Well, I've had some experience, as you might say,' said Mr Adams. 'I've been handling men all my life and I have to handle all my accountants and clerks and sekertaries and most of them are women; like Miss Pickthorn,' said Mr Adams as an afterthought, in case, we suppose, Mrs Marling did not know what a woman was. 'And take them by and large they're all right. Your girl, Mrs Marling, is one in a hundred. Her and me see eye to eye in most things about Adamsfield. I back her and she goes ahead. You know we're going in for a grade A herd and pigs. A friend of mine that's in the County Council passed me the word and I've bought a good bit more land along the river. It'll annoy old Budge, he wanted it for his gas works,' said Mr Adams, alluding to Councillor Budge who had done such good work in handling the *Barchester Chronicle* and the *Barchester Free Press* during the General Election. 'But Miss Marling said that land was what she wanted for cows, so Sam Adams saw to it that she got it. And it seems a pity, come to think of it,' said Mr Adams, 'to spoil a nice bit of pastureland along the river with coke heaps and gasometers. There's room for them round my way, and though I was born and bred in Hogglestock it's so ugly that you couldn't make it worse.'

Mrs Marling who had been wishing, as many of Mr Adams's friends did, that fond as they were of him they would sometimes be grateful if he did not do so much of his thinking aloud, then escaped to the lawn, leaving her host to deal with the Crawleys who had just arrived, and fell into a nest of comfortable county gossip where we will leave her.

'I see mamma is quite safe for the next hour,' said Oliver, who had almost unconsciously gravitated to the Dean party, 'and my papa is well away with Mr Oriel about the Bishop,' for the Vicar of Harefield, a mild, elderly scholar, could become like St Augustine and St Jerome rolled into one where his pastoral superior was concerned.

'The Bishop is so *dreadful*,' said Mrs Dean. 'Is there anywhere I could sit?' she continued looking about her with her large sleepy eyes.

'Oh dear, mother has an exposition of sleep come upon her,' said Jessica Dean, ravishingly smart but yet subdued so that she might not depress the younger ladies of Barsetshire, for she managed to keep a kind and thoughtful heart for others among all the work and excitement of her stage life. Or rather, as she had once explained to Oliver, not kindness, but a sense of what was good theatre; for to turn up at a country garden party consisting mostly of old friends in what Paris was wearing would throw the scene out altogether.

'What I like about you is the way you know your Shakespeare,' said Oliver, remembering how she had quoted from *As You Like It* against herself the first time he met her. 'I am sure we can find something for you, Mrs Dean.'

As the mariner cast by Poseidon's wrath upon a rock, seagirt and inhospitable, casts his eyes now hither now thither vainly seeking a couch where haply slumber may ope for him the ivory gate and shew him his spouse imploring the gods ah! most vainly for his safe return, while his little ones draw the mimic sword or, unknowing their father's fate, weave a chaplet for the sister of Io whose full udder gives them many a milky repast, so, in a way, did Oliver look for somewhere for Mrs Dean to sit and as there were a number of deck chairs on the lawn (also provided by Messrs. Scatcherd and Tozer), several of which were not occupied, it seemed not unreasonable to expect that she would use one of them.

'Here is a nice one,' he said, 'with a little cushion thing to fit your neck fastened to it.'

'I couldn't,' said Mrs Dean, looking to heaven with her cow-like eyes. 'That bar across the front gets under one's knees in the wrong place and those chairs never stand properly.'

'We must do *something* about it,' said Jessica, who had come to look upon her mother almost as an adored, slightly mentally defective child. 'Do you think you could ask Heather if we could have a cushion, Oliver?'

'When you ask me to do something for you it almost gives me hope,' said Oliver. 'How you do understand making use of people. But I'll go.'

'Wait,' said Mrs Dean. 'I did see, on the right-hand side as we came in, a very nice sofa in the drawing-room. I am sure Mr Adams wouldn't mind my sitting on it.'

As Mrs Dean had not only the beautiful, sad, meaningless eyes of a cow, but also a full measure of that animal's placid obstinacy, Jessica and Oliver looked at each other despairingly.

'You do it, darling,' said Jessica to Aubrey Clover, who was looking so like someone at a garden party that very few of the guests had recognised the famous actor-manager-playwright who was among them.

'Selfish. That's what you are,' said Aubrey Clover without heat. 'And maîtresse femme, what's more. You'll be like Lady Norton when you're old. You bring your mother along and I'll see about the sofa.'

Accordingly Mrs Dean, supported by Oliver and Jessica, moved with her heavy indolent grace towards the house while

Aubrey Clover went ahead, having some difficulty in making progress against the outcoming tide of guests.

'I am so sorry to interrupt you,' he said to Mr Adams who was having rather heavy going with Mrs Tebben from Worsted, 'but might I speak to you for a moment.'

These words, said with an art that made Mr Adams almost wonder if a writ was out against him, or a corpse had been found in the electric washing machine, caused him to interrupt Mrs Tebben's flow of conversation and turn aside to Aubrey Clover, whom he had met more than once at the Deans'.

'Anything wrong?' he said.

'Nothing,' said Aubrey Clover. 'Mrs Dean doesn't like deck-chairs and nothing will serve her but to use your Chippendale sofa in the drawing-room. Would you object?'

'She's a wonder, that lady,' said Mr Adams, almost admiringly. 'The way I've seen her take a nap at Winter Overcotes beats the band. This is Liberty Hall to-day and anyone can go to sleep anywhere they like.'

'Well, here is Lady Macbeth,' said Aubrey Clover rather disrespectfully as Mrs Dean came forward leaning on Oliver's arm in a sleep-walking condition, her daughter Jessica dutifully following with various impedimenta.

'Oh, Mr Adams,' said Mrs Dean. 'I hear you have a sofa. *Might* I rest for a little?' to which Mr Adams replied with great gallantry by offering her his arm and squiring her across the terrace, through the hall and into the drawing-room.

'That's the sofa,' said Mr Adams, pointing to the handsome Chinese-Chippendale creature which stood at right angles to the fine fireplace with its austere delicacy of carving and its pale golden marble, only where the fire-grate would be in winter was a great spreading sheaf of flowers. 'And I may say, Mrs Dean, that the sofa is good enough for you and you are just right for the sofa.'

Mrs Dean, apparently disregarding this tribute, sank down upon the pale golden brocade cushions and looked at her host with gratitude in her great liquid eyes.

'So kind,' she murmured. 'I shall just sit here and no one will take any notice of me,' with which words she somehow wafted her respected legs onto the sofa and lay back. Aubrey Clover, a silent well-trained servant now, took one of her wraps from Jessica, a Spanish shawl of pale gold embroidered with flowers and birds in brilliant colours, and laid it over her feet.

'It beats cock-fighting,' said Mr Adams respectfully. 'You couldn't hardly credit anyone could do it. Well, I must go back to the garden or my little Heth will be reading the Riot Act. You'll find drinks in the dining-room, Clover,' with which hospitable words he went back to the garden.

There was no reason why anyone should stay with Mrs Dean. Nor was there any real reason why Oliver Marling should come to look for Jessica, except that he followed his secret heart; and we may say that although he thought it secret it was really on his sleeve for daws, in the shape of the whole county, to peck at. But the daws were as a whole kindly creatures and while amused by his pursuit of Jessica had found nothing unfriendly to say. We do not of course count Lady Norton, who told Mrs Crawley at the Annual Meeting of the Barchester Conservative Association's Ladies' Branch, that she heard that young Marling, who after all came of good family, was making quite a fool of himself over that actress-daughter of the Deans'; to which Mrs Crawley replied that her husband was practically in love with her himself and the Bishop would give his gaiters to meet her only he daren't because of his wife, to which Lady Norton took exception being a devoted adherent of the Palace, and Lady Pomfret, the President, had to ring her bell and recall the entranced meeting to the subject in hand.

'If,' said Aubrey Clover, 'Dr Mesmer is needed to recall the subject from her trance, pray let me know. Otherwise I am going; not to have a drink, but to cultivate Mrs Tebben and see life.'

So saying he looked at Jessica and then looked at Oliver and went back to the garden.

To Oliver, who had lived so long with such small crumbs to feed him, to be alone with Jessica was balm from heaven. And as he was fastidious about his surroundings to be alone with her in this large quiet beautiful room, the westering sun shining through its windows, everything a glow of pale incandescent gold and old ivory, a pleasant murmur of voices from the garden and a Sleeping Beauty for chaperone, was peace and healing to his spirit. Jessica moved to the west end of the room and sat down on a little settee against the wall and Oliver followed her.

'The back of the sofa is as lovely as the front,' said Jessica, looking at it. 'And as mamma will probably sleep till we take her home it will be very nice to rest here. Come and sit with me.'

'Thank you. I will stand,' said Oliver. 'Or walk about,' which he accordingly did, looking earnestly at the one or two good pictures and the elegant pieces of furniture that Mr Adams and Mrs Belton had acquired. Jessica, sitting quiet and relaxed as she had taught herself to do, looked at him with a curious kind of loving compassion till he turned and met her eyes.

'Well?' he said.

'Quite well,' said Jessica. 'Have we no cheers?' at which echo of Mr Pinero's ever enchanting play Oliver smiled and sat down beside her.

'You know quite well by now and you have known it for a long time,' said Oliver, 'that it is all I can do not to put my arms round you and kiss you to death, so I think it very unfair to invite me to sit by you.'

'That's why I do it. Because I know you won't. I mean,' said Jessica, 'because you are a gentleman.'

'Devil,' said Oliver. 'But I am a broken-spirited fool and take what you give me.'

'I can give you about ten minutes,' said Jessica, 'and then I must go back to the party or I shall be compromised,' with which words she favoured him with Mrs Carvel's famous wink.

'If you would like to be compromised, I am the man for your money,' said Oliver hopefully, but Jessica made no answer, only looking at him in a way that he could not understand, a mingling of affection and pity he felt, and did not want either. A heart's love he would consider, but not the Treue Schwesterliebe which some depressing lady had offered to a depressed knight in a loathed German poetry book of his schoolboy days. So he very gently took Jessica's hand. She did not withdraw it and he sat with its warmth in his own, but did not press it for fear this rare bird should take wing.

'This close-compassioned, inarticulate hour,' he said half aloud and more to himself than to Jessica.

'That's not you. Who is it?' said Jessica.

'A Victorian called Mr Rossetti, my ignorant child,' said Oliver.

'When I am old and toothless,' said Jessica, 'I shall give Poetry Readings, and you must choose the poems for me because I have never had time to read.'

'I'd do more than that for you,' said Oliver, and then took a breath as though he were going to say something, but gently let the breath go away again without speaking.

'No, no; don't,' said Jessica.

'I will, or shall, whichever is the more correct,' said Oliver. 'And what's more I am going to now, while your mother is here to chaperone you. Out upon it, I have loved, one whole year together. Oh blast! Must one *always* be affected? Kindly tell your hand to stay where it is. I want it. For the last time, Jessica, will you marry me. On your own terms. On any terms you like. I shan't shoot myself if you won't, but I shall want to.'

'Darling, darling Oliver, I can't,' said Jessica, letting her hand remain, passive, in his.

'You mean you won't,' said Oliver.

'I couldn't if I wanted to. Aubrey and I were married on Thursday,' she said. 'I meant to tell you.'

It appeared to Oliver that the room rocked and the sunlit air became black, but he remained very quiet.

'I told you from the beginning he was the only person I could ever marry,' said Jessica.

'You did,' said Oliver, looking attentively at her hand and thinking how slim and beautifully boned it was. 'You played perfectly fair,' and as he spoke, a hundred lines of English poetry all upon the everlasting theme of true love cast away ran through his head and he cursed himself again for being affected and second-hand.

'It suits us both better in many ways,' said Jessica, 'except for income tax of course. Otherwise it means very little. You will come and go just as you always have, my dear, and we will go to the Wigwam and dance and Aubrey will read you his plays before anyone else hears them.'

'I offered you any terms you liked; your own terms,' said Oliver, 'but I didn't think they would be as hard as these.'

'Not hard, my lamb,' said Jessica. 'Remember I am a rogue and vagabond and the Theatre is my master. As mamma is still asleep I think we might leave her and go back to the garden. Come.'

She rose with an easy grace born partly of herself partly of long training and Oliver, still holding her hand, rose with her.

'You may,' said Jessica, answering his thoughts and he held her to him for a moment, very carefully, only letting her hair brush against his cheek as he bent his head. Lucy who had been upstairs to talk to Miss Hoggett who was a friend of hers came down the stairs and saw through the open drawing-room door her brother and Jessica. She thought that Jessica had at last promised to marry Oliver and felt her heart throb violently at the double thought of her dear brother's happiness and her own loneliness. But hating and despising any display of feeling, she determined to keep Oliver's secret until he told it to her himself and slipped round the bottom of the staircase and so out into the garden, hoping no one would notice anything special about her, as indeed they did not, for as we expect our friends to look what they usually look like, there needs to be a good deal of difference in them for it to strike us.

In the garden, Mr Adams was playing the host very well and enjoying his own party, the only drawback being Mrs Tebben, who having been once baulked of her prey was all the more eager to pounce on him again and tell him about her son Richard. And just as he had got comfortably into talk with Dr Crawley and Sir Robert Fielding and Bishop Joram, with no women to bother them, Mrs Tebben bore down upon them, wearing a flowered cotton dress of no particular period and stockings that were getting rather spiral, shoes known to shoemakers as sensible and to most of us giving a strong impression of bunions, and a floppy hat of coarse straw with a wreath of poppies round it, while in one hand she held what is, or used to be known as a Dorothy bag, which for the benefit of our male reader, and any readers too young to know what we describe, is a horrid kind of pouch, preferably of some home-woven material, with ribbon run round it a couple of inches below the top; which ribbon being pulled tight produces a shape rather like a large turnip with its top cut short, all very horrid.

'And here I am,' said Mrs Tebben, 'to finish our talk about Richard,' for her only son Richard, formerly in Mr Dean's employ, was now one of Mr Adams's men and though a selfish and not very agreeable young man had done extremely well on the commercial side and had been very useful in Sweden, where he had married a Swedish wife.

On hearing this Sir Robert Fielding very basely escaped, but the Dean and the Canon with great courage stood their ground, feeling that the Church should show a united front.

'My husband and I had a most delightful holiday with them in June,' said Mrs Tebben, whose face was gleaming with heat and the excitement of a party. 'My daughter-in-law, who was Petrea Krogsbrog – you have heard of her father of course – is one of my very best friends. I was always determined,' said Mrs Tebben, 'that when dear Richard married my relationship with his wife should be a very beautiful one.'

'She's a very fine-looking young woman,' said Mr Adams. 'I met her at the Deans' last year. A bit on the heavy side.'

'Oh, not if you know her,' said Mrs Tebben. 'She's like a great big loving animal, a wonderful primitive creature like those great old Sagas. Whenever I see her I think of Burnt Njal.'

On hearing this her audience could think of no reply. Mr Adams did not know what she was talking about, as indeed there was no reason why he should. Dr Crawley, who knew and respected Mr Tebben as an authority on the literature of

Scandinavia and Iceland, wished he had the courage to say to Mr Tebben's wife 'Peace, woman,' as tradition had it that Mr Grantly's maternal great-grandfather had said to Mrs Proudie, wife of the bishop of the time.

'It is a curious thing,' said Bishop Joram, 'how these stories repeat themselves all over the world. In Mngangaland there is a folk-myth which has many points of similarity with Burnt Njal, except of course that everyone is black and Njal's prototype has forty wives while Gunnar's has twenty-seven, and the bull's hide is represented by a lion's skin. These things make us wonder,' and then, having caught sight of Lady Graham, he excused himself and hastened, a willing moth, to immolate himself before her soft radiance, while the Dean, taking advantage of Mrs Tebben's rapture over a large contemptuous tabby cat who had just appeared, escaped to Mr Oriel to discuss the dreadful goings-on at Hallbury where old Dr Dale's successor as Rector of St Hall Friars was said to be doing most outlandish things and celebrating the canonisation of St Ælla, the possible patron of the church, in a positively Romish way.

To several of those present it was a surprise, one might almost say a shock, to see Lady Graham at the Old Bank House, for Mr Adams had never come into the Leslie circle nor was he known to General Sir Robert Graham, K.C.B., and Heather's friendship with Clarissa was not known to many people. But everyone was pleased as Lady Graham, concealing as usual her extreme toughness under an exquisite and fragile exterior, came into the garden where she was greeted with dignified courtesy by her host and with frank pleasure by Heather.

'I think your house is quite beautiful,' said Lady Graham to Heather. 'I do wish mamma could see it for she used to come here when she was a girl, but she doesn't feel up to long drives now.

My youngest girl Edith made a poem about it.' She paused with what in anyone less beautiful and composed might have been described as an expectant simper, so Heather very obligingly asked her what the poem was.

'It was quite short, only two lines,' said Lady Graham.

'That, my dear Lady Graham, is quite in order,' said Bishop Joram, who having got himself into Agnes's orbit found it quite impossible to tear himself away, nor did he wish to. 'An elegiac couplet is perhaps one of the best ways of expressing a sentiment. The literature of Rome abounds in them, and scholars throughout the ages have used the form.'

Like Gray, said Lady Graham, much gratified.

'He did write Latin verses,' said Bishop Joram. 'In fact no man of education and breeding in the eighteenth century could omit this duty. But I do not know of any particularly outstanding couplet.'

'I was thinking,' said Lady Graham, 'of the elegy about the country churchyard, though why it was Stoke Poges I have never known,' with which fine confusion of terms Bishop Joram found himself unable to cope and begged to hear Edith's poem.

'It is quite short, you know,' said Lady Graham.

"'The car for darling Gran doth stay,
But she will not go out to-day.'"

A hum of appreciation rose from her audience, though less for the poem than for the reciter.

'There was another one,' said Clarissa, who much admired her young sister's gifts, being unable to rhyme herself. 'It said,

"The car is waiting at the door,
But darling Gran will drive no more."'

There was for a moment a dead silence. All those who had heard the lines were devoted admirers of Lady Emily Leslie, and Edith's artless verse struck chill to their hearts. Not one of them but had seen with grief the change that the last year had brought to that entrancing, wilful, maddening spirit of love. That wind-blown rainbow fountain was ebbing; the winds were stilled, the sparkling waters and the rainbow spray were gently returning to the earth.

The silence was long enough to make Clarissa realise what she had said and her pretty face crimsoned slowly and tears came to her eyes when most luckily the Pomfrets were announced and created a small stir as their presence, like Agnes's, surprised a good many people. Mr Adams, as we know, had seen a good deal of Lord Pomfret on committees and when Parliament was sitting, and had met Lady Pomfret on various public occasions, but it had not occurred to him to invite them, for though fully conscious of his own position in the county he remained very modest about himself as a person, and the party was to consist entirely of his or Heather's friends. But meeting Lord Pomfret at a County Council committee he had happened to mention his housewarming party and Lord Pomfret in his quiet diffident way had made it clear that he and his wife would like to come if Mr Adams liked to ask them.

'My wife has so little time now,' he said apologetically, 'and we don't get to know our new neighbours much. But if you will do us the honour of asking us, we should like it very much. My young cousin Clarissa talks a great deal of your daughter and as the young people are friends I hope their elders will be friends too.'

One cannot but feel flattered if an Earl, and what is more the Lord Lieutenant of the County, invites himself and his wife to tea, and if Mr Adams's heart swelled slightly within his bosom, why so would ours. Being a shrewd man who had seen a good deal of human nature in his time, the smooth as well as the rough, he could not help wondering whether politics lay behind Lord Pomfret's words, which doubt he had propounded to Miss Lucy Marling while in breeches and a very dirty old pullover she was at work in the market garden, to which Miss Marling had replied Rot, and if Gillie wanted a treat he ought to have one because he worked like twenty men and got no thanks for it, after uttering which words she made a horrible girring noise with the tractor and went away like the Transit of Venus only not quite so. We do not know all that was in Lord Pomfret's mind, for he was of a reticent nature except to his wife and to his cousin Lady Emily Leslie, but if he with others of His Majesty's Opposition looked upon Mr Adams as a man to be cultivated, there seems to us to be no reason why he should not have taken a step in that direction, though what may come of it we cannot say. One thing we feel is certain; if Mr Adams at some future time decides that his political views have changed, it will not be because he sees a reward: office, a title, a salary. It will be because his faith in one cause has been betrayed, which will give him no pleasure at all.

'I know what you want,' said Mr Adams to Lord Pomfret, feeling a kind of protecting pity for him, 'you don't want to stand about with a lot of people, you want to sit down and have a nice quiet chat with someone you know,' which acute diagnosis of his feelings made Lord Pomfret laugh and his wife seeing him laugh felt that she could relax her vigilance for a time.

'Now, here's Lady Graham,' said Mr Adams, 'and here's Mrs Freddy Belton. If you sit with them you'll be all right. And this is my sekertary Miss Pickthorn. Miss Pickthorn, I don't want

Lord Pomfret to be worried. He's going to have a talk with Lady Graham. And now if you'll excuse me I must go and talk to my guests. I see Mrs Morland has just arrived.'

'Is that the Mrs Morland who writes the thrillers?' said Lord Pomfret.

'That's right,' said Mr Adams. 'And very good they are. I don't read fiction much myself nor thrillers neither; my works give me all the thrills I need like when some damn fool messed up my last big casting and as for fiction what goes on in the costing department you wouldn't hardly credit. But that book of hers where the hero put a steel chain round his waist and gets picked up by the overhead electric magnet and rescues the heroine from the villain when he's disguised as the fireman of the works light railway, well, there I said is a woman that can write.'

'I would very much like to meet her if it isn't a trouble,' said Lord Pomfret. 'I have often read her books in bed at night and find them very helpful. Well Agnes, how nice to see you. And how is Mrs Freddy?' he said to Susan, for Mrs Belton was a cousin of the late Lord Pomfret's countess and Susan had been adopted as one of the family by the Towers.

'Mrs Freddy is very well, thank you,' said Susan, who with excellent health, a devoted husband, a loving mother-in-law and for the moment no domestic worries, was waiting for her first-born in a kind of placid dream. 'You know about Jessica?'

Lord Pomfret said he certainly did and no one could help knowing about her and an enchanting minx she was.

'Oh, I don't mean *that*,' said Susan, dismissing the Cockspur, 'I mean did you know she's married?'

At these words Lady Graham, who had been placidly thinking of her gifted and remarkable children and had for the moment forgotten her anxiety for her mother, came to with a start and said May was such a nice month for a baby with the summer before it. Lord Pomfret looked bewildered.

'It's not a baby, Lady Graham,' said Susan. 'She married Aubrey Clover last Thursday. We all supposed she would. He's very nice and one hardly knows he is there. Mother is pleased because he makes such a perfect son-in-law. I don't know,' she added, looking away.

Lord Pomfret didn't quite know either. He had been to the Cockspur once or twice and not enjoyed it particularly though admitting Jessica's brilliance and charm; but the stage wasn't much in his line.

'Sally, my dear,' he called to his wife who was near, 'did you know that Mrs Freddy's sister Jessica had married Aubrey Clover?'

'Good gracious, no,' said Lady Pomfret. 'Is he here to-day?'

Susan said he was talking to Mrs Morland by the tubs of agapanthus, but at that moment Mr Adams took Mrs Morland in charge and brought her over to Lord Pomfret who got up and said what a pleasure it was to meet her and how much he had enjoyed her books.

'We all do,' said Lady Graham. 'I read one aloud to darling mamma but I never could remember where I left off, so mamma painted a bookmarker which I lost. *So* annoying.'

'I often can't remember myself where I have got to,' said Mrs Morland, rescuing a large hairpin just before it fell down the front of her dress. 'I mean when I start again next day, I mean where I left off the day before, I simply cannot *think* why I wrote what I wrote yesterday. It all seems rather silly, or else quite different from what I expected and I have to sit and *sit* till something starts and I force myself with *great* agony to begin to write. And even then I often don't know why I wrote it next day,' said the gifted authoress, self-analysis not being her strong point. But Lord Pomfret, who knew no author except his cousin Hermione Rivers of whom he saw as little as family decency would permit, was fascinated by Mrs Morland's picture of the artist at work and consulted her in great good faith as to how he ought to begin if he wanted, as he did, to make a little book out of some old letters exchanged during the Risorgimento between the Pomfrets and their Italian cousins the Strelsas.

'I don't know,' said Mrs Morland, pushing her hat backwards in a kind of distracted sympathy. 'If it's letters the writing is mostly done already. I suppose you have them typed and see that the dates are right. And you might put something in about how silly we are to encourage foreigners, I mean Mazzini using the British Museum Reading Room *free*, just like Karl Marx, and then they all turn round and bite us. Look how we let the Mixo-Lydian refugees be here in the war and what do we get for it? They say we are devils and Tony has to work seventeen hours a day and all his week-ends about their dreadful boundaries. I cannot *think*,' said Mrs Morland, readjusting her hat, 'why foreigners always want boundaries. I suppose it comes of not knowing geography, because if you know where the Edge is, well there it is.'

During this interesting literary conversation Mr Adams had come back with Aubrey Clover to whom he gave a kind of mass introduction and went away to his other guests. Lady Graham greeted him with the approval she felt for anyone who got married and said she was sure his mother would be pleased.

Aubrey Clover said she died last winter.

'Oh dear, I *am* so sorry,' said Lady Graham, thinking of her own beloved mother and of the shadow that was over Holdings. 'It is very sad that one can't have another mother. But perhaps that is why you got married,' she added.

'Not at all,' said Aubrey Clover. 'It just seemed simpler in various ways.'

'I expect you love children,' said Lady Graham whose existence had been bounded from the year after her marriage to the present day by her adored offspring. 'They do keep one young.'

'You are a living proof of that,' said Aubrey Clover. 'Do tell me about yours,' and he at once became the child-lover who has never had a child of his own, giving his heart to dream-children, whimsical, sad beneath the clown's mask, Charles Lamb up to date, while Agnes expatiated on the keen wish for soldiering of James, the fine cow-mindedness of Emmy, the brains of Clarissa, the goodness of John, Robert's wonderful sense of words and Edith's poetic talent, during which monologue Aubrey Clover became by sheer stage genius each child in turn with its peculiar idiosyncrasy.

> 'And in the course of one revolving moon
> Was chymist, fiddler, statesman and buffoon,'

said Mrs Morland suddenly.

'God bless you, Mrs Morland,' said Aubrey Clover. 'You are the only person who has ever understood me. May I tell you all about myself?'

'People usually do,' said Mrs Morland, 'and then they think I have used them for someone in a book, and I can't explain to them that they are so dull that no book would take them.'

'Ah, we artists!' said Aubrey Clover suddenly becoming the Yellow Book incarnate so that Mrs Morland expected to see a green carnation in his buttonhole and told him so, after which they got on extremely well and Aubrey Clover promised to let her go all over the Cockspur Theatre so that she could use it for the scene of her next book where Madama Koska was to take into her dressmaking establishment a young girl of surpassing beauty and talent whose stage career had been ruined by a jealous rival who told the actor-manager that she was secretly married; whereas the young girl of surpassing beauty really loved the actor-manager with consuming love and everything was to come right in the end and Madame Koska was to dress the new play.

'And will you tell me what things like flats and O.P. are,' said Mrs Morland. 'I know O.P. means Old Prices, because of the Rejected Addresses.'

'Lord! I didn't know anyone read them now,' said Aubrey Clover, to which Mrs Morland, putting on her spectacles for no reason at all, said nobody did but she had been brought up on them and intended to die on them. Also on the Poetry of the Anti-Jacobin, she said, of which Aubrey Clover happened to be a devotee.

Lady Pomfret, perhaps a little out of it among so much literature, said she was afraid they must be going. Miss Pickthorn, who had been standing by, extricated Mr Adams from a political discussion with Sir Robert Fielding so that he might accompany his guests to their car, and Heather came too.

Almost like Royalty, and as simply as Royalty, the Pomfrets managed to say a word to nearly everyone as they left the garden. At the terrace steps Eleanor Grantly was talking to Charles Belton and as Lord Pomfret came up she moved towards him.

'Eleanor!' said Lord Pomfret. 'Why didn't I see you before?'

'I was here,' said Eleanor, trying not to imply a reproach, yet not sorry to make him feel a little in the wrong.

'You must forgive me,' said Lord Pomfret with his usual gentle courtesy, and in the words of the Arabian Nights Eleanor's heart was contracted and for a moment she felt almost dizzy. That Lord Pomfret so hard-working, so kind, so tired should ask her, Eleanor Grantly, to forgive him, was too much. Their eyes met and Eleanor's fell before Lord Pomfret's who was thinking as he always did how wonderful it was to have Sally and be able to go home with her and have a peaceful evening.

'Well, it's been a pleasure to see you here,' said Mr Adams as he took the Pomfrets through the hall, 'and I wish Mother, that's Mrs Adams as was Heth's mother, were here to see you too. I'd like you to have a look at the drawing-room before you go,' and he stood aside to let his guests admire through the open door the gracious, sunlit room where Mrs Dean reclined upon the Chinese-Chippendale sofa in her usual semi-conscious condition.

'Is she ill?' said Lady Pomfret. 'Hadn't we better call someone?'

A tall, thin, not quite young man who had been looking out of the window with his back to the room turned and said, 'It's only Mrs Dean. She always goes to sleep but it doesn't mean anything.'

'I didn't know you were here, Oliver,' said Lady Pomfret. 'I had a talk with your mother in the garden. Lucy looks very well.'

'So she does,' said Mr Adams. 'Miss Marling manages my market garden, Adamsfield that's its name, and an A1 manager she is. Well, it's been a pleasure to see you, Lady Pomfret and my little Heth here she feels the same.'

Lady Pomfret thanked her host and said he must bring Miss Adams to lunch at the Towers one day and then took her husband away. And though Lady Pomfret did not forget her promise to Mr Adams, making a special note of it in her engagement book she was glad the day's duties were over and so was her husband. Now they could be with the children and have their home quietly to themselves for a few hours, and as for Eleanor Grantly neither of them gave her another thought except when Lady Pomfret said she had left in the office a letter that needed answering and would ring Eleanor up about it.

'Nice girl that,' said Lord Pomfret, 'but you have spoilt me for nice girls. Sally, Sally, what *would* I do without you!' to which Lady Pomfret, who rarely joked, said Marry the Dreadful Dowager and Lord Mellings was so much amused by their laughter that he laughed too.

After the irruption of the Pomfrets Oliver felt he must pull himself together, for sooner or later he must go into the garden and be an ordinary person, though he still felt that he was in a nightmare and could not wake up. Again someone looked in at the door; this time Mr Dean in search of his wife.

'You here, Oliver?' he said, looking at his wife's peaceful repose. 'I never knew a woman who slept so easily. Wake up, my dear. We must go home.'

'I *am* awake,' said Mrs Dean with great dignity and closing her eyes went to sleep again.

'Will you find Aubrey or Jessica,' said Mr Dean to Oliver. 'She pays more attention to them. You know about Jessica I suppose.'

Oliver said he did. In fact Jessica had told him and he was delighted.

'I must say it's more than I am,' said Mr Dean, 'though I daresay I'm wrong. How Jessica came to be an actress I don't know. There's no trace of talent on either side. I've nothing against Aubrey. He's a good fellow and the whole family like him. And if he hasn't any family in particular, no more have I. We're both self-made. But I did hope my little Jessica would marry among our friends. Well, there it is. I had an idea that you and she—'

'She told me a year ago I had no chance,' said Oliver. 'She has played perfectly fair.'

'I'm sorry,' said Mr Dean and as there was nothing to be said silence fell upon the room.

'I heard you all the time,' said Mrs Dean, opening her beautiful eyes, 'and then when you stopped talking I woke up,' at which her husband laughed and even Oliver could not help being amused. He went into the garden where the guests were beginning to say good-bye and found Aubrey Clover deep in literary conversation with Mrs Morland again.

'I'm so sorry to interrupt,' said Oliver to Mrs Morland, 'but Mrs Dean has an unusually ferocious paroxysm of going to sleep. Could you come and help, Aubrey? Mr Dean seems to think you are the only person who can get her off the sofa. And my congratulations and a thousand good wishes for you both.'

For once, and for the first and only time since Oliver had known him, Aubrey Clover stood as himself with no defences and Oliver though very wretched could not feel anger or jealousy. On an impulse he put his hand out and Aubrey Clover took it.

'I should have realised when I married Jessica that I had made myself responsible for her mother,' said Aubrey Clover. 'Out Goes She,' and with this quotation, the title of one of his most amusing plays, he hastened towards the house, a bridegroom tenderly solicitous for the health of his wife's adored mother.

'Damn him; but I can't help liking him,' said Oliver aloud to himself.

The party, which had been reinforced by Robin Dale and his wife from Southbridge and young Mr Pilward with his father, had enjoyed itself very much, which means that everyone had talked to the people he or she knew best about the same things they talked about every day, which is on the whole the most restful kind of party. Those who remained all came towards the house together and there was a good deal of polite noise in the hall while leave was being taken. In spite of his stunned condition Oliver noticed with amusement that Lady Graham was holding the farewell reception and that Heather appeared to be quite willing for her to do so. Oliver's parents had gone some time ago and he was waiting for his sister Lucy who had the market garden car. Then Lady Graham with Clarissa went away and Mr Tozer and his assistants began to fold the tables and pack the china and glass.

'It's been a marvellous party,' said Lucy Marling to Heather as they stood on the terrace watching the guests disperse. 'I've not enjoyed myself so much since I went ten times on the round-about at our Red Cross Fête last year. I wish it wasn't over.'

'Why don't you and Oliver stop to supper and finish up the cakes,' said Heather.

'I wish I could,' said Lucy, 'but I've got a Young Conservative thing at eight o'clock. I say, Heather, will you tell Oliver I'm in the stable yard starting up the Adamsfield van. She's a bit sticky on starting and once I get her going I don't want to stop again, so he'd better come too.'

So Heather obligingly went to find Oliver and Lucy strode to the stable yard where the market garden van was waiting and had to make so much noise with the machinery (for if we tried to say exactly what knobs or handles she pressed or turned or trod on, we should but expose our ignorance) that she did not hear her brother Oliver's approach.

'In trouble again?' said Oliver.

'What do you think?' said Lucy. 'I'll have to get her taken down unless Ed can fix it,' for Ed Pollett who worked on Mr

Marling's estate though far below the normal as far as intellect was concerned had a genius for cars and any kind of machinery. 'Get in before she stops again. Oh, blast!', for even as she spoke the engine stopped roaring. 'I know,' she added, bundling herself out of the van. 'Petrol. I've got some in the back. I meant to fill her up and forgot. All right, I can do it.'

While she emptied her can into the tank Oliver stood watching her, wondering if one could force oneself to live in the present; not remembering the past nor hoping for the future. His sister Lucy put the can back in the van, straightened herself and then, suddenly remembering what she had seen in the drawing-room said to Oliver, 'I say. I was coming down the stairs when you and Jessica were in the drawing-room. I wasn't looking but I couldn't help seeing you because the door was open. Was it—' and she paused, inexpert in matters of love and not quite knowing how to put what she wanted to say.

'As a matter of fact,' said Oliver, speaking in what he hoped was a perfectly natural voice, though to his sister Lucy it was a voice she had never heard before, 'I was congratulating Jessica. She and Aubrey Clover were married on Wednesday; no, Thursday it was.'

To his horror his sister Lucy's face crimsoned until he thought she might burst and she sat down on the running board and burst into tears.

'I say, Lucy, don't,' said Oliver, who had never seen his manly sister so moved. 'It's quite all right. Aubrey's a thoroughly good sort of fellow and they both think of nothing but the Theatre.'

'It's not that,' said Lucy thickly, with a kind of despairing bellow. 'But I thought you – oh, well you know what I mean,' and her tears flowed fast and unbecomingly.

'If you mean you thought I was in love with her, I was. And

I am. And I always shall be,' said Oliver, half of him knowing that some day the pain would lessen, the other half feeling that his dear Lucy wouldn't understand this.

'No you won't,' said Lucy, blowing her nose violently and polishing her whole face with her handkerchief to dispel her weakness. 'One doesn't. Oh, Oliver!'

Something in her words reached Oliver's heart through all his own grief and his mind went back to the year when Tom Barclay had been much at Marling Hall and had finally married his widowed sister Lettice Watson. Small things he had forgotten came back to him and he saw, drawing together, parts of a puzzle which he had hardly suspected.

'My poor Lucy,' he said.

'No I'm not,' said Lucy rather fiercely. 'It's much, much worse for you, because you're a man,' which Oliver realised to be an unconscious indictment of his own sex for making heavier weather of their troubles than women do.

'Well, that's that,' said Oliver. 'Come on, Lucy, or the Young Conservatives will go to the Communist Whist Drive at Marling Halt.'

'Oh, all right,' said Lucy and got into the car again and they drove back to Marling almost without speaking.

'Well, thank goodness there's Adamsfield,' said Lucy when she had put the car away and was walking back to the house with Oliver. 'And if we can get going with our cowsheds and pigs we'll make a good job of it.'

'Adams and Marling Limited,' said Oliver, amused by his sister's use of the word we.

'One might,' said Lucy quite seriously. 'It's a big job, but I like it.'

'Good,' said Oliver.

*

Meanwhile the Grantlys had lingered in the hall to admire Lady Fielding's present to Heather, as beautiful an example of Girtin's genius as one would wish to see. Miss Pickthorn said Hogglestock had changed since then, hadn't it.

'I say, daddy, we ought to let Miss Hoggett see it,' said Heather, as the housekeeper came downstairs. 'Look Miss Hoggett, this is what Hogglestock was like in 1795,' to which Miss Hoggett replied that it was very nice and she had left everything nice and tidy upstairs, and was there anything more she could do.

'Well,' said Mr Adams. 'Tozer's men have cleared up their stuff and now we'd better finish clearing up ours or we won't get home before midnight. All these cigarette ends and things, Miss Hoggett, and if you'd tidy the drawing-room. And we'll take the best of the flowers back with us.'

Mrs Grantly said if she and Eleanor could help they would be delighted, but Mr Adams would not hear of his guests putting themselves out.

'When one has given a party and then looks at the result,' said the Rector, whose hospitable house had given many parties under war conditions, 'one wonders why one ever began. Still things get tidied in the end. It's dogged as does it, as my grandmother used to say.'

'That's funny, sir,' said Miss Hoggett. 'My old grandfather always said the same and he said his father said it before him. They were all from Hogglestock, sir, like me.'

'My grandmother lived at Hogglestock when she was young,' said the Rector. 'From what she used to tell us when we were children Hogglestock must have been almost as lovely as it is in the Girtin. I daresay it's a Hogglestock saying.'

'Excuse me, sir, but might I ask your grandmother's name?' said Miss Hoggett.

'Mrs Henry Grantly,' said the Rector. 'Her father Mr Crawley was curate at Hogglestock I believe before he went to Barchester.'

'There now, sir,' said Miss Hoggett. 'I've heard grandfather say Mr Crawley was very good to his father. Grandfather would have been proud to know you, sir, and I'm sure I am, if I may say so. Well, well, I'd better get on with the drawing-room.'

So the Grantlys said good-bye and went home. As they got to the Rectory the telephone was ringing. Eleanor went to answer it, with an unreasonable hope that it might be Lord Pomfret, though why he should ring up she did not stop to think.

'Well?' said her father when she came back.

'Only Henry,' said Eleanor, half cross half laughing, 'about his papers. And he'd reversed the charge as usual.'

The Rector said it would be cheaper and less wearing if Henry came home and then Grace who had been to play tennis at the Brandons', despising garden parties as unmanly, reported that Colin Keith was there and sent his love to everyone and would ring up. And later in the evening Colin did ring up and Eleanor answered the telephone again hoping in an entirely foolish way that it might be Lord Pomfret asking her to come and help him with his papers.

'It's only Colin,' she said when she came back. 'He says Lydia is letting him have a water-party on Saturday and can we come. Henry will be back then.'

Her mother asked who exactly 'we' included.

'Oh everybody,' said Eleanor, 'and row up to Parsley Island and have a picnic.'

'Goody, goody,' said Grace. 'I'll take my bathing things.'

Mr and Mrs Grantly with one voice contracted out of the party which to them would mean discomfort in every form; by sunburn and midges and smells if it were hot and the river low, by cold and damp and probably wet feet if it were chill and the river running high, and in any case, though they did not say so for fear the words might be repeated, boredom: for though they liked the Noel Mertons very much they were not of their generation and had not enough in common to last them through a picnic party.

'You'll come, Tom,' said Eleanor.

Tom said he was going to Adamsfield on Monday to see Lucy Marling and if she needed him on Saturday he felt he couldn't let her down, at which piece of pompousness his sister Grace openly jeered and was pursued through the French window by Tom till her shrieks died away in the kitchen garden.

10

It was about a year now since Lucy Marling had called upon Mr Adams at the works to ask his advice about fertilizers; for among his many subsidiary interests Mr Adams had a controlling share in Holman's Phospho-Manuro which by some was considered a much better product than Washington's Vimphos, or Corbett's Bono-Vitasang, and by others to be far less valuable. As all these were made by Mr Adams's friend Mr Holman who was like Cerberus three gentlemen in one, there was perhaps not much to choose, but as Mr Holman truly said competition was good for trade and if this Government were out to stop competition he thought he would retire and offered Mr Adams half his shares at 73; and a week later Mr Adams bought seventy-five per cent of his shares at 64½, which really proves nothing except that Mr Adams was the better business man of the two.

There had been no formal arrangement between Mr Adams and Miss Marling. Lucy had a free hand to order what she wanted and do as she liked and at first used to lie awake for quite ten minutes at night wondering if she could make a success of the job. But her real knowledge of farming, her willingness to learn anything from anyone who had something to teach, her habits of hard work, her way of getting on with all other workers from Mr Adams's head accountant to the labourers who did the harvest work and the gypsies who came in season to do with careless sullen skill their own special jobs, and her bull-dog pertinacity in wearing officials down and not being worn down herself, had shown remarkable results. Within the year she was supplying all the vegetables, green and root, for the huge Hogglestock canteen with an overflow to Amalgamated Vedge the chain-greengrocers. And now, as we know, she was planning for cows and pigs. Her family did not see much of her, though as her conversation was increasingly monotonous they did not mind and were secretly very proud of their younger daughter.

'Well Lucy, what are you doin' to-day?' said her father on the Monday morning after Mr Adams's party.

Lucy said she was going to see that man from Winter Overcotes about cowsheds and Emmy Graham was coming from Rushwater to help.

Mr Marling said ploughshares weren't what they used to be.

'Nor are you,' said his daughter Lucy sotto voce and then raising her voice to its usual powerful pitch she said it was COWSHEDS.

'All right, all right, I heard you,' said Mr Marling. 'No one knows how to make a proper cowshed now. That man used to be good, can't remember his name, over at Winter Overcotes. Foxy man with a red moustache. I don't know what the world's coming to.'

'I told you I had a man from Winter Overcotes, father,' said Lucy in a loud patient voice. 'Spadger he's called.'

'Well, if you take my advice you'll have Spadger,' said Mr Marling, hitting on a perfectly new idea. 'I've not got anything much to do to-day. I'll come over to Adamsfield – damn silly name, it was never Adamsfield in my time – with you and give you a hand. If I remember Spadger he needs some handling,' and he got up and went slowly out of the room.

'Awful old man,' said Lucy dispassionately to the empty breakfast-room and then her brother Oliver in his London clothes came in and said he was off and would be down on Friday night.

'Are you Wigwamming as usual?' said Lucy and then went red in the face, for she had temporarily forgotten Jessica's marriage.

'Yes,' said Oliver. 'Tuesday night. Don't let Papa fall into the chaff-cutter,' and so went away to Marling Halt and caught the London express at Barchester.

Had Lucy been a really undutiful daughter, or even an ordinary daughter who resented her parents, it would have been the easiest thing in the world for her to give her respected parent the slip and get away by herself. But she was a very honourable and gentlemanly creature, so when she was ready she ran her father to earth in the home field where he was playing Tarquin, only instead of cutting the heads off the weeds he much more sensibly dug them up with a special long-handled tool to which he was much attached, and bundling him into her hard-working little car took him off to Adamsfield.

It was, we feel, a very good thing that Mr Adams got in ahead of Mr Pilward of Pilward's Entire in the matter of buying Mr Marling's ground. Not only did he, we think, treat Mr Marling more generously than Mr Pilward would have done, but a piece of pastoral country remained unspoiled. The land was just high enough above the river to be very rarely flooded and had borne good crops and good grass in its time till the war and Mr Marling's lack of ready money had impoverished it, but it was rapidly picking up again. Beyond it, further up the river, were several large fields and here the ground was lower and a stream ran meandering through it. In early summer the fields had been soft green, with yellow iris and blue forget-me-nots along the rushy stream and meadow sweet under the hedges. Now all was flowerless and rather dull under an August sky, but it was evident to anyone with a farmer's eye that cows would do well there.

Lucy stopped the car in front of a gate, got out, opened the gate, got back into the car, drove the car through the gate, got out and shut the gate and then drove fifty yards or so to a little group of buildings, rather ramshackle but showing signs of being repaired, beyond which rows of vegetables of every kind then in season muttoned into the infinite as Verlaine so beautifully puts it.

'Here we are, father,' she said and helped her father to lower himself out of the car, for which kindly action he was more than ungrateful.

'Nice little place this used to be,' he said, looking at the cottage and barn and sheds. 'Old Nandy used to live here. You never knew him.'

His daughter said she knew that horrid old Nandy who lived down near the railway at Marling Halt, but her father was speaking of old Nandy's father and like most elderly people liked to despise the younger generation for not having known people who died before they were born.

'Old Nandy's people had lived here as long as my people had been at Marling,' said Mr Marling. 'Shockin' farmer old Nandy was. Never did a hand's turn about the place and always comin' on my father for repairs. Cowsheds a perfect disgrace. When he died his son didn't want the place and my father took it back and pensioned him. All very well for my old governor to pension people,' said Mr Marling in an aggrieved voice, 'with the income tax what it was then. He might have thought of me.'

'I always wondered what old Nandy lived on,' said Lucy, who was so inured to her father's grumbling that she hardly heard it. 'Awful, dirty old man he is.'

And even as she spoke from round the corner of one of the dilapidated farm buildings came Mr Nandy himself, a very old gentleman who affected the Newgate frill of an older generation, his wicked face seamed with the dirt and wrinkles of a long disgraceful life.

'Mornin', Nandy,' said Mr Marling. 'What are you doin' down here?'

'That Ed Pollett he's down here doing a job of work for Miss Lucy,' said old Mr Nandy, 'and I come too. The Hop Pole don't open till twelve. If I had my rights I'd be a-living here like my old Dad, and a nasty old piece he was,' said old Mr Nandy embarking upon the quest for time forgotten. 'Lived with his housekeeper he did, but she wasn't no more his housekeeper than I am. I've always kept clear of women. Pick your pockets, that's what they do. Old Nandy he's never gone with women. Beer, that's what he goes for. Beer and baccy.'

'Well, you'd better go to the Hop Pole and get some,' said Mr Marling, taking a handful of change out of his pocket and choosing half a crown.

'No, father,' said Lucy. 'He doesn't need it.'

'That's right,' said old Mr Nandy. 'I'm a gentleman, I am; got my bit of money put away where those gormed Government folks won't find it. Miss Lucy, she's a sharp one. But the Russians are the sharpest,' said old Mr Nandy provocatively. 'If I was in Russia I'd be a commissionaire.'

'If you were in Russia you'd be doing some work instead of spending all your time at the Hop Pole,' said Lucy. 'Where's Ed?'

Old Mr Nandy, whose ancestors had probably been bullied for

their own good by Marlings for several hundred years, far from resenting Lucy's peremptory manner sat down on a low crumbling brick wall, pulled out his filthy old pipe, lit it with horrible suckings and wheezings and said Miss Lucy was a one-er, which effort made him cough in a revolting way and spit quite horribly.

'Ed! Ed, where are you?' said Lucy in her most powerful bellow.

From the barn Ed Pollett appeared, a kindly creature, distinctly half-witted, but with a genius for cars and machinery of any kind. He and his wife Millie, who was also slightly subnormal and as good-looking as she was amiable, had a large family of good-looking children, one born before, the second just after their parents' official wedding, and all the rest most honourably in wedlock though faster than anyone would have thought humanly possible. Without Ed, Marling Hall could hardly have kept going. He was general utility in the garage and with the tractor, mended everything from a main fuse to the electric iron the housemaid left on all night, put washers on taps, repaired the cook's sewing machine, understood the electric incubator as no one had ever done, and represented the one link of a dying civilisation with the mechanised world.

'The tractor's O.K., miss,' said Ed, pulling his forelock, an archaism which his employers cherished. 'She's going a treat now. And Miss Emmy she's down looking at the sheds, miss. Ed's going to look at her Ford van, she isn't running sweet enough.'

'Right,' said Lucy. 'You stay here, father. I shan't be long.'

'Wait a minute, wait a minute,' said her father, hoisting himself up. 'Why do you young people always want to hurry. You can't hurry nature.'

Lucy undutifully said aloud to herself that she supposed her father's second name was nature and then, being a well-disposed young woman, helped him to get himself onto his legs.

'And there's Mr Spadger from Winter Overcotes, miss,' said Ed. 'Miss Emmy she told him to come and see the sheds, miss.'

'COME ON FATHER,' said Lucy, adding under her breath, 'if you must' and she strode across the squalid yard to the further side where the old cowsheds were. Here Emmy Graham, Lady Graham's elder daughter who lived at Rushwater with her cousins the Martin Leslies and was supposed to be more cow-minded than anyone in the county, in shirt and breeches, her cropped brown hair in curls about her handsome weatherbeaten face, was in deep converse with an elderly man in a greasy shapeless felt hat and a very dirty mackintosh, which were Mr Spadger's uniform summer and winter alike.

'Hullo,' said Emmy.

'Hullo. Hullo, Mr Spadger,' said Lucy, nearly tearing that gentleman's hand out by the roots in the warmth of her greeting. 'This is my father,' she added as Mr Marling came up, leaning rather obtrusively on his stick. 'He would come,' she added aside to Emmy, 'and he doesn't get much fun.'

'Oh, he's all right,' said Emmy, with the large tolerance we all have for other people's relations. 'He's like Macpherson. They're a bit of a nuisance, but you must give them their head. Macpherson's supposed to be retired and go to his niece in Dunbar, but he doesn't.'

'I wouldn't, if I had his house,' said Lucy, for the old Rushwater agent had what had become through long use a kind of life tenancy of a charming small Regency house on the Rushwater estate. 'I say, Mr Spadger. What do you think about those sheds?'

'If I was to take a piece of chalk and chalk up a large O on the wall, Miss Marling, that would be what I think,' said Mr Spadger.

'That's all right,' said Lucy. 'I thought so too, but as it's Mr Adams's land and his money I wanted to make sure.'

'Here, you're not the Spadger I knew at Winter Overcotes,' said Mr Marling, saluting Mr Spadger not without suspicion. 'Red moustache he had.'

'So did I, sir,' said Mr Spadger. 'And I remember you, sir, with a brown one. That was when you were putting up the new cow-sheds up at the Hall, sir.'

'Well, well, we're none of us as young as we were,' said Mr Marling, putting out his hand which Mr Spadger shook with respect. 'This daughter of mine runs everything now. Family all right, eh?'

'As far as I know, sir,' said Mr Spadger. 'I buried my wife five years ago come turnip-hoeing, and we never had any family.'

'Bad thing; bad thing,' said Mr Marling, very skilfully covering his retreat by this equivocal remark. 'Well now, Spadger, we've got to put our heads together about these sheds.'

At this quite maddening piece of interference on the part of her father Lucy would willingly have shaken her fist under his nose, when a lucky diversion was caused by Tom Grantly who had bicycled over from Edgewood and owing to the bumpy nature of the yard nearly fell off at Emmy Graham's feet.

'I say, I hope I'm not late,' he said to Lucy, adding anxiously 'I didn't want to let you down.'

'Who's that?' said Mr Marling. 'That your man, Spadger?'

'It's Tom Grantly, father,' said Lucy. 'You know his father. He's the clergyman at Edgewood. He's awfully interested in cows.'

'Nice bit of glebe there,' said Mr Marling. 'How many cows has your father got on it?'

'I'm awfully sorry, sir,' said Tom, rather overpowered by Mr Marling, 'but my father hasn't any cows.'

'Lucy said he had,' said Mr Marling.

'Oh bother father,' said Lucy to Emmy and then raising her

voice she said, 'It's Tom that's interested in cows. He's keen on farming so I told him he could come over and look. This is Emmy Graham,' she said to Tom. 'She can tell you *everything* about cows. And Mr Spadger from Winter Overcotes has come to see about cowsheds and this is Ed, he can do anything, and that's old Nandy who can't do anything at all. Well now, Mr Spadger, I'm doing this job for Mr Adams and it's his money, so it's up to me to see he doesn't pay too much.'

A personally conducted tour of the farm buildings then took place under the benevolent and despotic leadership of Miss Lucy Marling, with a view to seeing whether any of them were worth salvaging from a cow's point of view. When it was purely a question of cows Lucy was ready to bow to Emmy Graham's superior knowledge and after a thorough inspection both Emmy and Mr Spadger gave it as their opinion that the old buildings were quite impossible.

'Well, that's that,' said Lucy. 'It's a pity we can't use them, but there it is.'

'That barn, miss,' said Mr Spadger. 'You could make a nice job of that. It wouldn't do for cows, but there's lots of uses for a barn. The walls are pretty firm and the roof's not too bad.'

'You'd need a permit, wouldn't you?' said Tom, wishing to attract Lucy's favourable attention by showing intelligent zeal.

Lucy, Emmy and Mr Spadger exchanged glances expressive of patient resignation.

'Of course if you *want* trouble you go asking for permits,' said Emmy.

'There's a nice lot of tiles lying about here,' said Mr Spadger in an abstracted way, 'and some timber in them old cowsheds that would come in quite handy.'

'I'll tell you what,' said Lucy to Tom Grantly. 'There's always a way of getting things done if you give your mind to it. If we put in for permits we'd be here till the General Election and longer,' at which words Tom felt that even going to an agricultural college would be better than being hectored by Lucy, and looked longingly towards his bicycle.

'She's three-speed gear, isn't she, sir?' said Ed's slow voice at his elbow. 'She's a daisy, sir, but her chain wants tightening up a bit.'

'I know,' said Tom. 'It came off three times as I was coming over.'

'Ed'll fix it for you, sir,' said that gentleman. 'You didn't ought to oil her so heavy, sir,' he added accusingly, so that Tom again felt very small and miserable.

'Right,' said Lucy in answer to some remark of Emmy's. 'We'll go down the field now and show Spadger where we thought the new sheds might go. Oh bother, I'd better ask father if he wants to come I suppose,' but her heroic self-sacrifice was rewarded by Mr Marling saying he would stay where he was and talk to Ed, so Mr Spadger and the two ladies, followed by Tom, walked down the field to the site proposed by Lucy and sanctioned by Emmy for the sheds which were to shelter the grade A herd. To the position and aspect of the ground Mr Spadger raised several objections, but these were only part of the proper ritual doubtless with the intention of propitiating Them (by which we refer in this context to unseen powers and not to His Majesty's present Government), and after what seemed to Tom a rather meaningless rambling round the subject Mr Spadger gave the whole project his approval.

'Now here you *do* have to get a permit,' said Emmy to Tom in what he felt to be a rather threatening way.

Tom said he supposed it would take ages, at which remark Emmy and Lucy exchanged pitying glances and Mr Spadger opened his mouth to speak and then shut it again.

'I'll tell you what,' said Lucy. 'You know who all the land belongs to.'

Tom said Mr Adams.

'Well, there you are,' said Lucy, though to Tom it seemed he was exactly where he was before, and none the wiser. 'Hullo, here's the boss. He'll talk to you, Mr Spadger,' and as she spoke Mr Adams came across the field towards them, looking remarkably like a prosperous farmer. Both girls fell upon him with a torrent of talk to which Mr Adams listened patiently for a moment and then turned to Mr Spadger.

'Now, young ladies,' he said. 'You talk so much I can't hear myself think. Well, Spadger, what's the verdict.'

Mr Spadger, who had been writing in a very small dirty book with a pencil stump about two inches long, said the old farm buildings weren't fit to put humans in, let alone cows, except that old barn and she'd be a tidy job if he, Mr Spadger, got onto her with some of them tiles and some timber out of the shed.

'Then you'd better put the barn in order,' said Mr Adams. 'We'll find a use for it all right, at least my manager will,' he added, looking towards Lucy. 'And what about the new sheds?'

Mr Spadger referring to his note-book, said it was a nice bit of land and a nice aspect and a place it would be a pleasure to put cowsheds on, and the water wouldn't have so far to come as at the old buildings.

'If Miss Graham and Miss Marling say it's all right and you say it's all right,' said Mr Adams, 'it *is* all right. You get down to your specifications, Spadger, and find out what permits we need and I'll see that we get them.'

'There's one thing, sir,' said Mr Spadger. 'Was there anything special you wanted the barn for? While I'm doing it I daresay I could find some bits of wood and put up a partition or anything you needed.'

'Well now, there you *have* got me,' said Mr Adams. 'Any suggestions, Miss Marling, or Miss Graham?' but for the moment neither of the girls had any plan to offer.

'Excuse me, sir,' said Tom to Mr Adams, 'but wouldn't it make a good place for sorting the vegetables and packing them? I mean I don't know how Lucy does it, but I thought if the vegetables came in at one end one might have long tables, or a conveyor belt or something and grade them.'

There was dead silence and Tom began to wish he were dead too.

'There's some sense in that,' said Emmy Graham, and so broken was Tom's spirit that he thought she was using the word 'that' in reference to himself and felt he probably deserved it.

'I wish I'd thought of it myself,' said Lucy, 'but I didn't.'

Mr Spadger said he'd never believed that college (by which we think he meant school) education did a chap any good, but if young Mr Grantly had a few more ideas like that he'd take it all back.

'I'll tell you what,' said Lucy to her employer. 'Spadger can bring the water up here and we'll have a big sink or a hose or something and clean the vedge up a bit before they go to the canteen. We've had a lot of trouble lately getting the girls in the kitchen to clean the carrots and potatoes and things and if we can get a man on the job we'll deliver them ready for cooking.'

'Very nice, very nice, young lady,' said Mr Adams, 'but don't run before you walk. We'll have to get Spadger here to go into this. Well, I've got to be getting back to the office. I'll pay my respects to your father, Miss Marling, and then I'm off,' so the whole party walked back to where Mr Marling was sitting on a stone watching Ed tighten the chain of Tom's bicycle and exchanging with him from time to time a few words in the slow Barsetshire speech which Mr Marling had learnt as a child among the men on the place and never forgotten, while not far away old Mr Nandy was smoking his disgusting old pipe and waiting till it was time for him to go to the Hop Pole.

What Mr Marling thought in his heart of Mr Adams we cannot be sure. He had known slightly the wealthy manufacturer as he was before he burst upon county circles through Mrs Belton, for he and Mr Adams had sat on the bench together, but the Mr Adams he had known then was a very different man from the Mr Adams who was Mrs Belton's friend, M.P. for Barchester and Miss Lucy Marling's employer. His dependability, his self-reliance, his integrity, his justice, the balance of brain and heart had probably been there all the time, but his manner of speech and dress had hidden many of his better qualities from the world. Under Mrs Belton's influence, though she would have been the first to disclaim it, he had seen a more gracious side of life and made part of it his own; as also had his daughter Heather, and the county was unconsciously accepting him as part of itself. It says a great deal for Mr Marling that he respected even if we cannot say liked Mr Adams as much as he did, for he was under a deep obligation to Mr Adams for buying his land at a moment when money was badly needed, and it is a commonplace that benefits received bite quite as nigh as benefits forgot. And Mr Adams in his turn had exercised considerable patience with the old squire whom he had helped, though the bargain had also been advantageous to himself, and did not forget that for Mr Marling it might seem a come-down to have his daughter working for Mr Adams; a delicacy of perception which came partly from Mrs Belton's unconscious influence, partly from his own very good sense.

'Well, Squire,' said Mr Adams, who had affected this style of address recently and was amused to see that Mr Marling rather relished it. 'Miss Marling has settled it all for us and we're to build cowsheds down the three-acre.'

This remark put Mr Marling into a difficult position. He had said from time to time that if he were putting up new cowsheds the three-acre was the place, but of course he was out of date and nobody would listen to him. Now his daughter, with Agnes Graham's girl and Spadger had made the same decision themselves. The question was, should he say That is exactly what I told you and not be listened to or believed, or should he show independence by going back on his own words and decrying the site.

'Well, Squire,' said Mr Adams, 'these young ladies and Mr Spadger have hit on the same bit of ground you did, so we're all agreed,' which spiked Mr Marling's guns and rather annoyed him, so contrary is human nature. 'I don't know much about land yet, but it's a pretty bit with the stream and the elders.'

'Alders,' said Emmy.

'Alders,' said Mr Adams good-humouredly, 'and that old cottage.'

'Ar,' said old Nandy, coming forward and knocking out his disgusting pipe on his dirty, horny hand. 'My grandfather's father lived there. He was an old sinner he was. Seven children he had and never married. They didn't call it the three-acre then.'

'What did they call it?' said Lucy, who liked to get to the bottom of things.

'Call it?' said old Mr Nandy. 'Same as it was always called till the gentlefolks come along with their three-acre. Adamsfield it was. My old grandfather he said to me, "That bit of land and that cottage that's Adamsfield. And for why? Because my grandfather he was Adam Nandy, and don't you forget it," he said. And he gave me a good thrashing to remember it by and remember it I do. Three-acre they says, great gormed fools. I'm off to the Hop Pole,' and with a final revolting and malevolent access of coughing and spitting the nasty old man hobbled away.

'Mr Nandy he didn't ought to speak like that, he didn't,' said Ed. 'Millie, she'd give Ol and Cassie a good smacking if they said gorm.'

'Well, I'm gormed myself,' said Mr Marling, but without heat. 'To think I've lived here all my life and never knew about old Nandy's grandfather's grandfather. They're a long-lived family. That must take us back two hundred years or more. Well, Adams,' he said, heaving himself up, 'you've won your case. Adamsfield it was and Adamsfield it will be. And if my land has a good master I shan't be sorry. But whether you'll be master with these two young women on the job I don't know. You drivin' me back, Lucy?'

'I'll take you home, Squire, if you've no objection,' said Mr Adams. 'These young ladies will be wanting to have a word with Spadger and Marling's on my way.'

Mr Marling, in very good humour over Nandy's contribution to local history even if it put Mr Adams in the right, accepted the offer and Mr Adams after unobtrusively helping him into his car drove him away.

'Now father's gone we can get on a bit,' said Lucy undutifully. 'I'll tell you what, Emmy, Tom Grantly wants to go on the land so I said to come over here and I'd tell him about the farming part and the market garden, but there's a lot I don't know about cows. You'd better let him come to Rushwater.'

'Right,' said Emmy, eyeing Tom in a way that made him feel that if he were even a two-headed calf he would have more claim on her interest. 'Come next week and I'll show you round.'

Grateful, but rather terrified of this cow-minded Amazon, Tom said he would love to come, only he was going to a water-picnic at Northfield.

'Well, cela n'empêche pas,' said Emmy, who from long conversations with her grandmother Lady Emily Leslie's maid Conque spoke French almost without thinking. 'I'm going too. How do you get there?'

The usual confusion of advice about buses then arose till Tom managed to break in and explain that he had a bicycle.

'That's all right then,' said Emmy. 'You come back to Rushwater with me and on Sunday we'll have a good day with the cows. I say, Lucy, Rushwater Churchill nearly got old Herdman yesterday. I've never seen him lose his temper before. It was the flies, I expect, horrible big gadflies, and he got Herdman into a corner of the stall, silly old fool. I've told him forty times he'd do it once too often.'

'What happened?' said Tom, not quite sure if the silly old fool was the cowman or the bull.

'I gave him a great almighty bang across his nose,' said Emmy, illustrating her action with a piece of wood, 'and he won't do it again, nor will Herdman. Not when I'm there. Come over soon, Lucy.'

Mr Spadger also took his leave and Tom was left alone with Lucy.

'What can I do to help?' he asked.

'Well, what can you *do*?' said Lucy and then put Tom through a gruelling examination on crops and vegetables, after which he felt as if he had been boiled, mangled and pegged out to dry.

'I've an awful lot to learn,' he said.

'If you know that, you know something,' said Lucy. 'You're not so bad. And you know more about onions than I do,' at which praise Tom felt more elated than he had felt since he got news of his second in Greats. 'We're shorthanded here and I can't get a good labourer at the moment. I'll tell you what. If you can come over every day anyway till the end of August, I'll take you at standard wages. You can have Saturday midday till Monday morning off if you're going to Rushwater for the week-end, otherwise you work as long as I need you, which will be as long as I'm working myself. Can you drive a tractor?'

'I have,' said Tom. 'Is yours a Quickset Combination?'

'I say, you haven't worked the Quickset?' said Lucy. 'I've been trying to get one for Mr Adams since March.'

Tom said he had done some ploughing for a friend of his in the Christmas vacation and he believed the friend was going to Canada and wanted to sell the machine.

'Come into the office,' said Lucy and took Tom into the farmhouse where in the least dilapidated room there was a large writing-table with a telephone on it.

'Only temporary,' said Lucy. 'We're going to rebuild this and have a proper office. Get on to your friend. I'll speak to him when you've got through.'

Tom, feeling that he was in a dream, indeed almost a nightmare if Lucy were not so real and so fiercely benevolent, lifted the receiver and asked for a trunk number. By good luck the friend was in. Lucy then took command of the telephone while Tom stood amazed at her efficient certainty.

'That's settled then,' she said after a short discussion. 'My letter to confirm our talk will be posted to-day. And of course Mr Grantly will get ten per cent commission from you on the sale.'

'I say, Lucy,' said Tom in an agonised whisper, 'I can't sting old Donald for commission.'

'I've done that. All you have to do is to take it,' said Lucy, and then in a very business-like way typed a letter.

'There,' she said. 'I'll post it on the way home. You'd better come back to lunch with me. You won't mind my mother, will you? Father won't be in.'

Tom said he had a mother of his own and rather liked parents on the whole, so they got into Lucy's hard-working little car and drove back to Marling Hall where Mrs Marling who was very good at families knew all about the Grantlys and made Tom feel quite at home. As soon as lunch was over Lucy said they must get back to Adamsfield.

'Come up to lunch whenever you like,' said Mrs Marling to Tom. 'I'm so glad you are working with Lucy for a bit. She does far too much. I would very much like to see your mother again, but it is so difficult to get about. There are four of you, aren't there?'

Tom told her the names and ages of his sisters and young brother, adding, not without modest pride, that he was twenty-eight. It seemed to him that a very faint shadow of disapproval passed across Mrs Marling's face, but she said good-bye in a very friendly way and he forgot all about it.

When he and Lucy had gone Mrs Marling cleared away the lunch things and left them in the pantry and then went from the old servants' wing where the dining-room had been for greater convenience since early in the war to the main building, part of which, including her sitting-room, was in use. Here she settled herself at her desk and went on with the work lunch and a guest had interrupted: all kinds of letters, papers, forms, to do with useful work in the village and the western part of the county. But she found it difficult to take up the threads of her correspondence again, for her thoughts wandered to her younger children. She had heard of Jessica Dean's marriage and though Oliver had spoken quite easily about it she knew, with the sixth sense that mothers often wish they had not got, that he had felt it deeply. And Lucy, so valiant, so reliable, so affectionate at heart. She was pretty sure that Lucy had once given her heart, but to whom she did not know and probably never would. And as the years passed she saw no sign of fresh love springing and sometimes wished Lucy were less capable, less reliable, less of a good companion to men, for no softer emotion ever seemed to touch her. There was not going to be much money for Lucy when her parents were dead. What prospect was there for her? Perhaps she and Oliver would live together not unhappily. But this was not what she wanted for her youngest child who was so constantly and uncomplainingly bearing the burden of the estate. To manage a market garden for Mr Adams was all very well but no inheritance. She sat musing, not very happily, till she heard the stable clock strike three.

'Pull yourself together, my good woman,' she said aloud to herself. 'It's no good imagining things about Tom Grantly. He is a nice boy and I like his people, but he is much too young for Lucy. Oh, well.' And she resolutely set herself to her letters.

Tom Grantly was not afraid of work. He had won a scholarship for Paul's by hard work as a schoolboy. He had done his utmost in the army and emerged as a Major, vain title now. He had worked hard at Oxford and got a very creditable degree. But never in his life had he met, to use his own inelegant expression, such a glutton for work as Miss Lucy Marling, and was hard put to it to keep up with her, not to speak of being told what almost more often than he could bear. But he was a sensible young man and fully realised how much he could learn from Lucy and what a clog his half-trained efforts must be on her activities and the two got on very well together during the week.

'Time for you to knock off,' said Lucy as the distant noontide chimes of Barchester came floating down the river on Saturday afternoon. 'I'm knocking off too. Stick your bike on the back of the car, it's full of vedge inside, and I'll take you as far as the Northbridge Road.'

So Tom tied his bicycle to the luggage carrier and they drove as far as Melicent Halt where the railway runs through a cutting under the road.

'I'll give you a hand with those,' said Tom, for Lucy was wrestling with a case of tomatoes which had been crammed into the car and wouldn't come out. 'Where do you want them?'

'Platform,' said Lucy, striding ahead with a sack of lettuces.

Melicent Halt was too small for a station-master and was managed by a ticket-clerk who was also the porter and a very nice man; as was not his predecessor Bill Morple who had been promoted to Winter Overcotes Junction and there stolen Mr Beedle the station-master's joy and pride, the Silver Challenge Cup given for the best kept station on the line, won by Winter Overcotes for three years in succession and so a permanent possession of the station. The Cup had been restored mysteriously, some said by a repentant Bill Morple though this was never made clear, and to the great pleasure of all men of good will Bill Morple had since got seven years for robbing a post office with some friends and half killing the postmaster.

'Hoy!' said Lucy at the top of her powerful voice.

'Good afternoon, miss,' said the ticket-clerk coming out of his little office where a nice coal fire burnt all the year round. 'Anything we can do for you?'

'Only these,' said Lucy, pointing to the sack of lettuces, and the large case of tomatoes. 'Amalgamated Vedge want them in a hurry and I'm too busy to take them in the van. Can you send them off by passenger train and they'll send a man up to Barchester Central to collect. This is Mr Grantly. He's helping me at Adamsfield. He comes from Edgewood.'

The ticket-clerk acknowledged Tom's presence courteously, for he was a good railway servant, but with a certain reserve as to a foreigner who still has to prove his worth.

'He was with the Barsetshires,' said Lucy, 'and now he wants to farm.'

'Well now, miss,' said the ticket-porter, 'that's what you might call quite a squinstance. There's a friend of mine in the ticket-office at this very moment and his son was in the Barsetshires. I'm sure Mr Beedle would be ever so pleased to meet the gentleman.'

'Is that the station-master from Winter Overcotes?' said Lucy, who had an encyclopaedic knowledge of county names, only surpassed, so the cognoscenti said, by Sir Edmund Pridham, who had had at least forty years' advantage of her.

'He's retired now, miss,' said the ticket-porter. 'I'll bring him to speak to you, miss.'

He hurried into the ticket-office and came out with a tall, kindly-faced elderly man very neatly dressed.

'This is Mr Beedle, miss,' said the ticket-porter.

'I'll tell you what, I've heard about you from Mrs Winter,' said Lucy, 'the one that was Leslie Waring.'

'I'm proud to meet any friend of Miss Waring's, miss,' said Mr Beedle, withdrawing his slightly mutilated hand from Lucy's powerful grip. 'Sir Harry and Lady Waring are highly respected friends of mine, if I may say so, and Miss Leslie too. It was on the low level at Our Station Miss Leslie got engaged to Colonel Winter as he was then.'

'And your son was a prisoner of war,' said Lucy. 'After Dunkirk.'

'That's right, miss,' said Mr Beedle. 'And thank God, he came back to us safe and sound. But he doesn't seem to settle down, miss.'

'Wouldn't the railway take him?' said Lucy, knowing that the railways, and more particularly the Best Line in the World, were in some cases an almost friendly affair, son following father from generation to generation.

'I'd have wished it, miss,' said Mr Beedle. 'And one or two of Our Directors that travel on the Winter Overcotes line said they'd put in a good word for him. But when the time came he didn't seem to fancy it. "No, mum," he said to Mrs Beedle, "my heart's in the land," he said. Mrs Beedle and I we talked it over and we agreed Henry must have his own way. "We don't know what our Henry's done, nor yet what he's seen, Beedle," that's what Mrs Beedle said to me, "and we haven't got the right to interfere." And Mrs Beedle was right, miss, as she always is, because the railways aren't what they were. British Railways may be all very well, but when a man's taken a pride in the Line he serves it fair breaks his heart to be lumped in with a lot of other lines that go to Manchester or Norfolk or where not,' said Mr Beedle with the patriot's contempt for lines that knew no better than to serve strange northern and eastern gods instead of turning their faces to the kindly west. 'I can tell you, miss, I was glad to retire and that's a thing I never thought to live to say. Our Directors spoke to me very kindly, miss, and gave me a gold watch, but we are all out of the railways now. It's a cruel bit of work.'

While he was finishing his elegy on the great lines of England a bell had been ringing violently.

'You had ought to be attending to your call,' said Mr Beedle to the ticket-clerk.

'It's only Joe Packer at Southbridge,' said the ticket-clerk. 'The local ought to be along any moment. When I don't answer Joe knows it's O.K.'

'It's only Joe Packer at Southbridge,' said a sturdy young man, with the indefinable air of having been in the army, coming out of the ticket-office. 'She'll be a few minutes behind time.'

'There; you did had ought to have been attending to your call,' said Mr Beedle to the ticket-clerk. 'This is my son, miss.'

'Hullo,' said Lucy, surprising Henry Beedle very much by the violence of her handshake. 'This is Mr Grantly. He was in the Barsetshires.'

Dunkirk and five years as a prisoner of war are a very different form of war service from two years including D-Day, but the bond of the regiment remains strong and Tom at once got into talk with young Beedle and they found acquaintances in common, notably the regimental ne'er-do-well, George Bunce, who could cheat at cards better than any man in the division.

'I'm just starting on farming,' said Tom. 'What's your line?'

'You've drawn the lucky ticket, sir,' said Henry Beedle. 'Mum and Dad were a bit against it and they wanted me to go into the railways, sir, but I'd got kind of keen on the land if you know what I mean, sir.'

Tom asked if he was on a farm before the war.

'No, sir, it was when I was a prisoner of war, sir,' said Henry Beedle. 'It was a camp out somewhere in the country and we worked in the fields. Vegetables mostly, sir; cabbages and potatoes and mangolds and all sorts. If I could get among the cabbages again I'd feel fine. Peas and beans and all that sort are all very well for the summer,' said Henry, his eyes lighting with the enthusiast's gleam, 'but cabbages and sprouts and roots are the goods. And onions, sir. Fritz wasn't too bad and I learnt a lot about red cabbage. It was the officers I was sorry for, miss. There was a lot of gentlemen would have loaded cabbages or laid the onions with the best of us, but officers mayn't work. It don't seem fair to me, miss. There were us boys out in the fields and the officers in the camp all day, poor devils, I beg your pardon, sir. If you know of a job, sir, I'd be glad if you'd pass me the word.'

'Just wait a minute,' said Tom, turning towards Lucy. 'I say, Lucy, you said you wanted another man at Adamsfield. Young Beedle's a cabbage expert and wants a job.'

A distant hoot announced the approach of the local.

'Hold her a minute,' said Lucy to the ticket-clerk. 'I'll tell you what, Mr Beedle,' she said to the ex-station-master. 'Tell your boy to come and see me at Adamsfield, you know, the new market garden I'm running, anyone will tell you. I can give him all the work he wants. If it's too far to come every day he can have a room at the farm only he'll have to do for himself.'

'That's O.K., miss,' said young Beedle. 'A Prisoner of War Camp teaches you to keep the place neat. Shall I come on Monday, miss?'

'Now, Henry, you let your dad speak,' said Mr Beedle. 'I'm sure Mrs Beedle and myself are very grateful, miss, and Henry's a good lad and he'll do his best. I did think he'd work for Our Line and perhaps be station-master at Winter Overcotes some day, but the lad's right, miss. This naturalisation if that's what they call it has taken the heart out of the railways. They won't find it so easy to get men now, miss, and the men they won't be the sort we used to get. I'm very much obliged, miss, I'm sure. And so will Mrs Beedle be.'

The ticket-clerk who had been holding the driver of the local in parley said 'O.K., George' and the local puffed heavily away, carrying the Adamsfield lettuces and tomatoes with, or rather inside her. Tom got onto his bicycle and rode off towards Northbridge, the ticket-clerk with Mr Beedle and Lucy's new employee went back to the ticket-office and Lucy drove home alone. Her parents were out on various duties, so she lunched alone and then gardened alone till dinner-time. At dinner her father was more wilfully deaf than usual and her mother's mind upon the Women's Institute and after dinner she gardened again till dusk. Oliver was not coming down that week-end. A huge lop-sided moon hung in a detached way in the evening sky looking rather frightening, as moons are apt to do, alone save for one star shining. In fact everything seemed pretty well alone that evening, thought Lucy, in what for her was a rare flight of fancy, and for a moment she felt sorry for herself, a feeling to which she never gave any encouragement at all. But in spite of all her efforts at discouragement her eyes smarted and having thick gardening gloves on she could not be bothered to blow her nose and sniffed loudly. The telephone rang insistently from the house.

'Bother,' said Lucy. 'Oh, well.'

She laid her tools and gloves neatly on the ground and went indoors.

'Adams speaking,' said the telephone. 'Miss Marling in? Oh, it's you, Miss Marling. I thought you'd like to know it's all right about those permits. I've seen a pal and got him on the job.'

'Splendid!' said Lucy. 'It's all right, I suppose,' she added.

'As right as rain,' said Mr Adams. 'My pal's in touch with all the right departments.'

'I meant – I mean, I suppose,' said Lucy, fumbling for the words she wanted, not wishing to say them, but anxious in her complete honesty to be sure that Mr Adams knew what he was doing, 'I suppose it's all right. I mean—'

And then she stopped, partly because she could not find the words that would explain her anxiety that Mr Adams should not do anything in the least doubtful, partly because she felt she had no right to question him.

There was a silence which lasted long enough for Lucy to wonder whether the line had been disconnected. Then Mr Adams spoke in a voice which sounded to Lucy infinitely remote.

'Everything's quite O.K. and above board,' said the voice of Mr Adams, 'so you needn't worry.'

'Oh, I *am* glad,' said Lucy, 'and I've found a good man for Adamsfield, an ex-prisoner of war and—'

But a girring noise told her that she was no longer connected so she went back to the garden and cleaned her tools and put them away. And as she worked she thought of Mr Adams and the permits and a very horrid feeling began to creep into her mind. A feeling that Mr Adams thought she suspected him of unfair means in getting a permit.

'But I didn't!' said Lucy aloud, indignantly. 'I only meant was he quite sure it was all right, because one has to be so awfully careful or people say you are cheating.' And as she locked the tool-house door and walked back towards the house an increasing feeling of misery and of having something hitting her inside till she felt almost sick, made her stop dead.

'Well, I've done it,' said the Manager of Adamsfield. 'Oh *don't*, Turk,' for her large dog, who was exhaustingly faithful and affectionate and an increasing nuisance to everyone, came bounding at her, evidently moon-struck and expecting a wild game. 'Turk, I *have* been a fool. Why on earth can't one say what one wants to say without saying what one doesn't want to say?' But what is said cannot be unsaid and Lucy went through the week-end with a heavy heart and suddenly feeling very sick for no reason, all of which she kept to herself, in which she was probably wise, for to reserved natures an outpouring is strong poison. To such natures the beautiful words 'Get it off your chest' are useless, for the small temporary relief is at once followed by increased unhappiness.

'Anything wrong, Daddy?' said Heather Adams to her father who had been out of the room answering the telephone.

'Nothing, girlie,' said Mr Adams. 'Just a spot of business. Don't you worry, Heth. Your old Dad's old enough to look after himself,' but he was preoccupied and Heather felt uneasy.

'Dad,' she said.

'Well, girlie?' said her father, emerging from the *Financial Times*.

'It's not anything about Ted, is it?' said Heather, for though she was a very sensible girl and a mathematician she was human; and if a shadow of misfortune or unhappiness is in the air, we naturally feel it is directed against our own dear self, or those most dear to us.

'Of course it isn't Ted, you silly girl,' said her father. 'You go and ring him up.'

Heather said she had nothing particular to say to him.

'You never have,' said her father, 'but you say it all the same. My telephone bill's twice what it was before you got engaged. Run along and get it over.'

Heather laughed and almost blushed and went away to speak to Ted Pilward, which took quite twenty minutes, though neither party had anything of any value to say. Her father read the *Financial Times* for a little and then folded it neatly and put it on a table.

'I'm wrong,' said Mr Adams aloud to himself. 'She wouldn't

hint a thing like that. If she wanted to know anything she'd ask straight out. I'm a fool. And an elderly fool,' he added, looking at himself in a mirror with considerable disfavour. 'I'm a fool to think a lot of things I do think. I wonder what Mrs Belton would say.' But Mrs Belton was in Scotland with her daughter Mrs Admiral Hornby and the grandchildren, and Mr Adams had no guide except his own heart and common sense; which we may add was probably more useful to him than any advice.

'She's the best stainless steel,' he said, and the words roused an echo in his mind. They were the words he had said, or thought, about Mrs Gresham at Hallbury, the summer when he had made the Fieldings' acquaintance. He could not help laughing at himself and with the laughter his anxiety died. He would go over to Adamsfield on Monday and clear up this silly muddle; so when Heather came back she found her father quite himself, though whether after twenty minutes' conversation with young Mr Pilward she was in a state to notice whether anybody was themself or not, we would not like to say.

11

The water-party planned by Lydia and her brother Colin had by now swollen to a rather unmanageable size but, as Lydia said, most of the people who were coming hated going in boats so she supposed it would be all right. This conversation took place in the garden where Lydia and Colin were sitting on the stone edge of the pond watching Miss Lavinia Keith and Master Harry Keith who were adventuring in a small rubber boat, the gift of their uncle Colin. As it was a warm day they were in bathing things and looked extremely agreeable.

'There's the Grantlys,' said Lydia, 'that's four, and Everard and Kate and the children makes ten and the Birketts are coming but they don't count and the Brandons but they don't count either and Charles Belton and some of the Grahams.'

'That makes at least twenty,' said Colin.

'But most of them won't want to go on the river,' said Lydia. 'We'd better have the punt and the boats. There's the coracle too if anyone feels brave enough.'

'I don't,' said Colin. 'Do you remember the picnic on Parsley Island the summer I was a schoolmaster and Tony Morland and that boy Swan were camping? I saw Tony the other day in town. He has a very nice wife and a baby and still has the inscrutable face he used to put on for master-baiting, young devil. I wonder what Swan is doing now. He used to bait Philip Winter by looking at him through some very hideous new-fangled spectacles. Lord! how long ago it all seems.'

'Well, it is fairly long,' said Lydia. 'Twelve years. What *does* happen to time, Colin?'

'L'amour fait passer le temps, Le temps fait passer l'amour,' said Colin sententiously, 'though as a matter of fact the blasted Germans killed six years for us, spurlos versenkt, and the dear Russians are doing their best to kill time now. Not to speak of Them,' he added. 'I suppose They consider that time was made for slaves, and slaves is what we pretty well are. Never mind, I'll be a judge some day and say nasty things to everyone in a wig. No, Harry, don't,' for Master Merton was standing up and shouting at the top of his voice and in imminent danger of overbalancing himself, the boat and his sister.

Master Merton, intoxicated by a life on the ocean wave, paid no attention to his uncle and shouted more loudly than ever. He then sat down suddenly and threw a handful of water at his sister Lavinia who began to scream.

'I suppose I'll have to go in and kill Harry,' said Colin. 'But I'll have to take my shoes off first and roll my trousers up.'

Luckily before he could take these violent measures Nurse, who had been holding a watching brief in the background beside Miss Kate Merton's perambulator, came forward and said to stop that nonsense at once and would Mr Colin pull the boat to the edge as it was time to get ready for lunch. Accordingly Colin with a boat hook which was kept for the purpose caught the boat and brought it to the steps.

'Say thank you to Uncle Colin and come along and get clean,' said Nurse. A dripping Lavinia threw her arms round one of his grey flannel legs and rubbed her face against it.

'Really, sir, I don't know what makes Lavinia so forward,' said Nurse, outraged. 'Come along, Lavinia.'

Colin said it was all right and Lavinia always hugged his legs.

'Really! A gentleman's legs!' said Nurse and withdrew her young charges just in time not to hear Colin and Lydia laughing at the implications, the more terrifying for being so vague, conveyed in Nurse's remonstrance.

'I thought,' said Colin, as the tumult and the shouting died away, 'I'd take Eleanor in the coracle. Paddling is rather conducive. I wonder whether I dare punt it. I haven't tried for ages. The coracle's tricky if you don't know it.'

'I can't punt it up and down the river now,' said Lydia. 'It's funny how you get afraid of things you usen't to be afraid of, like the coracle and walking on high walls and going very fast downhill on a bicycle. I suppose it's a kind of thing that happens to you so that you won't be so likely to get killed and worry about the children.'

'I always said you weren't a clear thinker, my girl,' said Colin, 'but I think I see what you mean.'

'I am a *very* clear thinker,' said Lydia. 'Noel says I have the clearest mind he knows. But thinking is quite different from talking. You have everything quite clear in your head and then it's like those ginger-beer bottles one used to get with a glass ball in them and everything gets all choked up as it comes out. What I said was if you get killed by doing something you needn't do you couldn't ever be happy again when you were dead, in case the children were being neglected or anything.

'Never mind,' said Colin, patting her hand affectionately. 'You won't get killed and if you do I'll see that Noel marries Lavinia Brandon. And let me remind you, if it's any comfort, how many things there are that one used to be afraid of and now one isn't afraid in the least,' at which wise words Lydia cheered up and said she used to be terrified of old Lady Norton and now she only felt Poor old thing.

'I wish the Dreadful Dowager could hear you say that,' said Colin. 'Well, lunch. And I'll take the small boat.'

'And Eleanor,' said Lydia, who liked to get her facts in order.

'Yes, Eleanor,' said Colin. His sister Lydia, who knew him very well and loved him dearly, looked at him.

'Yes,' said Colin. 'I don't know anything yet. I am afraid I rather fear my fate too much. And have a sneaking conviction that my deserts are small. And I am honestly quite terrified of the idea of putting anything to the touch. And also convinced that far from winning I shall probably lose it all. Lunch!'

Lydia put her arm through his in a hugging way, but said nothing, for she could see no reason why her brother Colin should not win anything he wanted and they went back to the house.

The first to arrive were of course Lydia's sister Kate Carter with her husband Everard Carter, Headmaster of Southbridge School, and their three children, who were at once wafted away to the nursery only to be heard of as voices off. The Birketts from Worsted followed hard upon them and Charles Belton from the Priory School at Beliers. As Mr Birkett was Everard Carter's immediate predecessor and Charles Belton's Headmaster was an old assistant master of Southbridge and Colin as we know taught for a term there, the gentlemen were able to have a delightful conversation about school shop and take no interest in the proposed water-party at all, while the two wives talked with Lydia about their children and in the Birketts' case grandchildren and of course, inevitably, food rationing and food in general.

'The really important thing,' said Kate Carter earnestly, 'is for everything to go on being rationed.'

Mrs Birkett said the minute things were unrationed they vanished, but she still thought de-rationing, if that was the right word, would be very nice because one wouldn't have not to lose one's ration book; which will be quite clear to all our readers who have lost one and had to go through the formalities of getting a new one.

'But I cannot think,' she said, 'why S.P.Q.R. We are not the ancient Romans.'

'What do you mean?' said Lydia.

'You only have to read your ration book,' said Mrs Birkett. 'Page ten and eleven. It says S P Q R again and again along the bottom. It says it on some other pages, too, only they've got the letters rather muddled.'

'It *can't* be,' said Lydia. 'I'll look in my book. Yes, you are perfectly right. Noel,' she said appealing to her husband who had just come down from London. 'What *do* you think S P Q R means in the ration book?'

'Some Pretty Queer Rations, I should think,' said Noel kissing his wife, and after a friendly greeting to his sister-in-law Kate and Mrs Birkett he was at once drawn by an irresistible attraction to the schoolmasters' camp.

'Well, I suppose that is it,' said Kate Carter. 'It all seems very peculiar. But so long as They don't stop rationing it doesn't matter.'

'Why this insistence on a peculiarly irritating form of control, my love?' said her husband, who loved her so much that he would even stop talking with other men for the pleasure of exchanging a word with her. 'Especially as we all know that people who like to pay can get what they want.'

'Because,' said Kate, with the certainty of a really good Headmaster's Wife, 'if They do take it off next year it will only be because of a General Election in 1950.'

'Out of the mouths of babes and sucklings,' said Mr Birkett. 'You ought to write for the Sunday papers, Kate,' which led to a general discussion of our Sunday Press during which it transpired that the eminently respectable citizens there assembled all read the most lurid and scaremongering organs on Sunday, although on weekdays they only read organs of the highest respectability, in the middle of which discussion Tom Grantly came in looking rather hot from his bicycle ride and was shortly followed by Eleanor, Henry and Grace who had come by bus.

Although the Grantly family had known the Keiths fairly well they had never been intimate and Eleanor felt slightly shy on coming into what was almost a family party and even shyer when Colin singled her out and as it were recommended her to his sister Lydia. But any slight feeling of being out of it melted at once before Lydia's welcome, even if Eleanor felt the welcome was more for Colin's friend than for the friend herself; in which we think she exaggerated, for though Lydia was always disposed to like each fresh flame of her dear Colin, she was very ready to like Eleanor for herself, having heard from various sources of the excellent work she was doing for the Red Cross Hospital Libraries. We need hardly say that within two minutes Tom Grantly and Charles Belton had discovered that they had not met each other in several places during the war and fell deep into old army shop. To Grace it appeared that everyone except Charles was very old, so she attached herself to her brother Tom and took stock of the company in silence.

'I expect you are just going soldiering,' said Mrs Birkett to

Henry, who was looking as if he might bolt through the French window at any moment.

Not for nothing had Mrs Birkett been known as Ma Birky to many generations of Southbridgians and within three minutes Henry was confiding all his thoughts to her and his fear that the army were going to forget to call him up. The same old story, thought Mrs Birkett, remembering the summer of 1939 and how the senior boys had feared the war would not wait till they got there and the less senior had nearly gone mad until she and her husband and Everard Carter had given them their word of honour that the war would go on till they were old enough for it. And once more, although for the moment war did not loom so imminently, the generous youth of England must be stayed with promises and comforted with reassurances.

A simultaneous irruption of the Brandons from Pomfret Madrigal and Emmy Graham with her sister Clarissa made the party complete, and Colin said the boats were waiting and no one need go who didn't want to. He himself, he said, was neither a grown-up nor a youth movement but was going to sacrifice himself for the pleasure of others and would everybody who felt like it come down to the boats.

Francis Brandon said if there was a forlorn hope the house of Brandon would always be found in the foremost ranks.

'And Peggy?' said Colin, who had for a brief period fallen a victim to the charming widow Peggy Arbuthnot, though this was now quite old history.

Francis said that not content with having brought one more unfortunate into this vale of tears, she was proposing to do it again and he thought death by drowning was not indicated.

'You oughtn't to say things like that, Francis,' said his mother, now mostly known as Grandmamma and bearing the honour very charmingly.

'If I didn't say it, my dear mamma,' said Francis, 'everyone would be thinking it, so it comes to exactly the same thing. Peggy goes about like a galleon in full sail if you so much as look at her.'

'That, Francis,' said his mother with great dignity, 'is quite enough.'

'King Charles the Second said it, mamma, not I,' said Francis, 'and he knew. Are you coming, Lydia?'

But Lydia preferred to stay on dry land, so the younger people followed Colin into the garden and left their elders in peace.

'We thought not a picnic after all,' said Colin to Eleanor. 'All very fine for Grace and Emmy and Clarissa and such young fry, but tea out of a thermos in a rocking boat or a damp punt is not my idea of happiness. We'll go up as far as Parsley Island and come back to Northbridge for tea. Are you sea-sick?'

Only if it was oil, said Eleanor, which made her sick at once, but never in a sailing boat or a rowing boat.

'It isn't exactly either that I propose,' said Colin. 'It is a collapsible dinghy, rather like a coracle of the ancient Britons. You can paddle it, but it's much more fun to punt it. It's rather a Northbridge speciality.'

'I say, do let me punt it,' said Grace, who after the unashamed and rather boring habit of youth had again attached herself to Colin and was weighing heavily on his arm.

'Certainly not,' said Colin. 'You can go in a nice boat with Henry and Francis, and you can steer if you like. And now if you will let me get at my pocket I'll unlock the boathouse,' with which firm words he extricated himself from Grace's Laocoön grip and taking a key from his pocket opened the landward door of the boat shed.

'I say, isn't it ripping,' said Emmy to Tom, and indeed it was a pretty and romantic sight to look through the open door into the boat shed where the sunlight was mirrored in a thousand dancing lights from the water and beyond the cool green cavern the river flowed in its leisurely course from Barchester towards the sea.

'Our generation ought to stand together,' said Colin aside to Francis, contemplating with an elderly eye the mob of youth under his charge. 'Do you mind taking the small boat with Henry and letting Grace steer. Her brother Henry will ask you, as an old soldier, at least forty times whether the War Office has forgotten about him.'

Francis said he sighed as a father and obeyed as a friend.

'Don't boast like that,' said Colin. 'Peggy only married you because I am well known as not a marrying man. If I had any children they would be much older than yours,' to which Francis replied rather coarsely that as far as his second child was concerned it would be difficult to be much younger as it was still minus; and then turning his facile charm upon Grace he asked her if she would steer for him, to which that easily inflamed young woman replied by walking into the boat so firmly that it nearly sank by the stern.

'Shall I row in front of you or behind you, sir?' said Henry.

'You mean stroke or bow,' said his sister Grace contemptuously.

'You go behind me,' said Francis and they took their places, 'and you'd better ship your sculls till we are well out,' he added, as Henry poked one scull into the side of the boat shed and nearly knocked himself over. 'And may Heaven reward you for what you have wished on me,' he added as he got the boat out past Colin.

The larger boat was more easily manned for Tom had rowed without distinction at Oxford and Charles at his public school, while Emmy and Clarissa had handled boats on the Rising since their childhood and could at least be trusted not to do anything silly.

'And now the coracle,' said Colin to Eleanor. 'You are sure it won't alarm you?' and he gave her his hand as she stepped securely into the little rocking boat. He laid a punt pole along the coracle, asked Eleanor to see that it didn't fall overboard, and taking a paddle got in himself.

'The river's a bit winding here for the punting,' he said as he paddled up-stream in the wake of the other boats. 'When we get above Parsley Island we can go full out for half a mile.'

'Don't hurry,' said Eleanor, meaning nothing by her words except that she was enjoying the water and the sun and friendly company, so Colin paddled gently among the rushes and past the ferry where old Bunce the ferryman was working in his garden and touched his cap to Colin.

'How's Effie?' Colin called across the water.

'Hooring about as usual,' said old Bunce. 'Why the Almighty gave me a daughter like that I don't know, Mr Colin. She's going with a chap from Hogglestock now and I don't hold with foreigners. I gave her a beating last Sunday night she won't forget and she gave me nearly as good as she got. She's her father's daughter, whatever her mother says,' and cackling in a very unpleasant way old Bunce resumed his digging.

'Local colour,' said Colin, 'for which I will not apologise. But his son is a fine cowman.'

Eleanor said there was no need to apologise because it was just as bad at Edgewood with Edna and Doris, only they were very good daughters, and had she told Colin about the awful day when the Bishop was holding a confirmation at Edgewood and he would go into the kitchen.

'Excuse my interrupting, but why?' said Colin.

'Father said he thought the Bishopess had ordered him to,' said Eleanor, 'because she wanted to know if we were hoarding food.'

'Excuse my interrupting again,' said Colin, 'but it is well known by anyone who has stayed at the Palace that there isn't any food to hoard. Nor any drink either,' he added, which made Eleanor laugh.

'Well anyway she poked about,' Eleanor continued, 'and found out the children hadn't any fathers.'

'Parthenogenesis,' said Colin, and apologised for the decent obscenity of a learned language.

'Idiot!' said Eleanor. 'And she gave Edna and Doris a kind of sermon and Mother was terrified because she thought they might give notice, and then Doris said the Bishop ought to be ashamed of himself not having any children him with his apron and all and Edna said something awfully rude about Sarah because she reads the Bible quite a lot and the Bishopess was furious.'

'Annals of the Parish,' said Colin, not expecting Eleanor to take him up, but having spent all her life in a house full of books she was well educated and smiled at him, which made him almost catch a crab with his paddle.

'I went to Aubrey Clover's new play,' said Colin after a short silence. 'Jessica is more divine than ever. And I went to the Wigwam afterwards and saw them all there. I mean her and Aubrey and Oliver Marling. I'm willing to bet twopence that Aubrey will make a play out of that triangle. When will you come up and see it with me?'

Eleanor said any time and she was getting a week's holiday quite soon, so Colin said she had better spend it with her aunt in London and they would have a week of guilty splendour and do a play every night, an invitation which Eleanor accepted with enthusiasm.

'I sometimes think I'll die if I don't get away from Edgewood,' she said. 'I mean I adore it, but it's rather depressing to think of Red Crossing every day by the bus. Of course I do love the work,' she added, not wishing Colin to think ill of the Red Cross, 'but – oh, well, I don't know. Lady Pomfret did say something about them needing someone in London and would I like to go.'

'Do go,' said Colin, who was now paddling just enough to keep the coracle from being carried downstream. 'We could have such fun.'

'It would be heaven,' said Eleanor and then looked confused: but it might have been the sun in her eyes.

'There is another job that you might consider,' said Colin, who somehow found his breathing rather impeded.

'Really? What is it?' said Eleanor, conscious that her voice was speaking but that she, Eleanor Grantly, was not there.

'A kind of hostess job,' said Colin. 'Entertaining for an eligible though not quite young barrister who is fairly well off. I don't know if I make myself clear?'

'Oughtn't we to go a bit faster,' said Eleanor. 'They'll be waiting for us.'

Colin might have taken this for a rebuff, but their glances crossed and Eleanor's face made him feel safe; so safe that he would willingly have kissed her except that the balance of the coracle made all movement inside it a matter of fine adjustment.

'As fast as you like,' he said. 'I'll use the pole. We're in the straight here,' and unshipping it he stood up and made the coracle rush so fast through the water that the river was disturbed, a long wake of ripples that were almost waves broadened behind them, and with each stroke the prow of the coracle dipped almost to the water's level. He thought he had never seen anything so handsome, so noble, as Eleanor's face, happily disturbed by his words and exulting in the swift motion of the little boat. And Eleanor in her turn thought nothing more romantic than Colin wielding the pole in rhythmic sweeps, his body bending and balancing as a skilled rider's bends and balances with his horse, had ever been seen. Of course they were both wrong; Eleanor was as nice-looking, well-bred a young woman as one could wish and Colin a very favourable specimen of a not so young man with brains and some skill in punting, and that was all. But luckily the illusion is there and those of us who are lucky carry it down the years with us and remain young.

'Parsley Island,' said Colin, checking the onrush of the boat and turning it gently into a small inlet. He held the boat steady by grasping a low branch and gave Eleanor his hand to help her out and felt it respond to his touch. Then he landed and tied the coracle to a post.

'I think,' said Eleanor, 'that noise must be the others. I can hear Grace.'

'And I can hear Emmy giving Tom instructions about cows,' said Colin. 'This way,' and he held aside some branches to let Eleanor pass. The island was not large and a winding path led through a small thicket to the brink of what looked like a small disused gravel or sand pit in which the rest of the party were sitting or standing.

'Last time I was here was in 1936,' said Colin, half to himself, 'when Swan and Morland were camping. It was the year Kate and Everard got engaged. Well, well, it all makes me feel very old.'

While he was thinking aloud he became conscious of a presence hovering about him which was Henry. Any brother of Eleanor's was welcome to Colin in his present state of mind, so he asked Henry if he had had a good time. Henry said it had been awfully nice and wasn't Colin a lawyer. Colin said he was.

'But not a solicitor,' he added. 'Only a barrister. If you want to make a will I can tell you a good man in Barchester.'

'It's not that,' said Henry. 'I was only wondering if people promised to do a thing and broke their promise, at least not exactly broke it but kept you waiting for ages and you thought they'd forgotten you, could you get a lawyer to hurry them up?'

Colin said it would depend largely on the various circumstances involved.

'It's the War Office,' said Henry, looking appealingly at Colin. 'I've been waiting for my papers for ages. Couldn't I do something to hurry them up?'

In an ordinary way Colin who was pleasantly selfish, as any successful bachelor who is a good deal sought after may well be, would have hedged and somehow got rid of this persistent boy. But Henry was Eleanor's brother, and if by supreme luck he was also going to be Colin's brother-in-law it was Colin's duty to care for him. So he said he didn't know much about the working of these things, but he would ask a friend in the War Office and see if he could get any information.

'Thanks most awfully, Colin,' said Henry, his face suddenly brightening as he smiled with Eleanor's smile, and Colin thought what a very nice boy he was. He could not monopolise Eleanor all afternoon and she seemed to be quite happy with Francis Brandon, so he looked round for entertainment and caught Charles Belton's eye which seemed to be appealing to him for help. Why Charles should need help when he had Grace Grantly and Clarissa Graham with him, Colin could not understand, but men must stick together so he strolled over to them.

'I say, Charles,' Grace was saying, 'you simply must come to the Barchester Odeon next Saturday. It's Glamora Tudor and Croke Hosskiss in *Love and Lust*. I saw the pre-view bits of it on the screen last week. Croke Hosskiss is a kind of crook that likes torturing people and when he finds a girl that really *enjoys* being tortured he thinks it's dull and goes away. Only really she didn't like being tortured a bit and only did it to please him so she throws herself off the top of the Empire State Building and leaves a letter to tell him and he takes the elevator up to the top to stop her so when he sees it's too late he jumps over too and there's a close-up of them. It's AWFUL.'

Charles, looking extremely embarrassed, said he was going to Holdings that Saturday and Clarissa's pretty face showed an equal amount of boredom and scorn.

'You could easily go to Holdings another time,' said Grace. 'Jennifer Gorman is coming too.'

'A Quite Dreadful girl,' said Clarissa, with such an air of remote hauteur that Colin hardly knew whether to laugh at her or smack her, though of course he could do neither. It was now quite clear that the young ladies were behaving like Polly and Lucy over Macheath, but the parallel did not hold, for Charles was far from taking it easily and would obviously have preferred both dear charmers to be away until they had recovered their tempers. The kindest thing Colin could do for Charles was to rescue him and make no bones about it, so he asked Grace if she would like to come back with him in the coracle which at once restored her good humour. As they walked away he heard Clarissa say to Charles,

'Of course, my dear, if you don't want to come to Holdings, you needn't. Too, too promise-breaking, of course,' and was pleased to hear Charles saying quite firmly that he had said he was coming to Holdings and come he would and if Clarissa was going to cry she could have his handkerchief, and Clarissa fawned like a spaniel upon him.

'Treat 'em rough,' said Colin to himself. Not that Eleanor needed treating rough. Blast Grace, why must she and Clarissa drag him into their silly quarrels so that he could not take Eleanor back to Northbridge and make her say the words she had not yet said. And when they reached the bank the coracle was gone.

'You don't mind us having it, do you?' said the voice of Tom across the water. 'Emmy's telling me about contagious abortion. She thinks there's a case near Rushwater so she's just going over the ground with me in case we see it. Carry on, Emmy.'

Colin was on the whole pleased not to have a prolonged tête-a-tête with Grace, for he was too old for bread-and-butter misses, or perhaps not old enough, so he took a place in the large boat with Henry and Francis while Charles and Clarissa took the small boat and the whole party embarked on the return journey.

Meanwhile the elder half of the party had been quietly enjoying itself at Northbridge Manor. The Birketts and Carters could never exhaust the subject of Southbridge School. Peggy Brandon had spent a whole term in Southbridge when she was Mrs Arbuthnot before she married Francis Brandon, and was deeply interested in School affairs. Noel and Mrs Brandon indulged, as they usually did, in a mock sentimental vein and as both were accomplished parlour flirters they enjoyed themselves very much.

'Dear me,' said Mrs Brandon, looking with frank admiration at her hands, still very pretty and soft in spite of war and peace, 'it is about a thousand years since you and Lydia came to Stories for your honeymoon.'

'Eight, to be exact,' said Noel. 'And not much of a honeymoon as I had to go to France next day. But how like you it was to think of lending it.'

'I didn't really lend it at all,' said Mrs Brandon. 'I simply had to go to London to get some clothes for Delia.'

'You never think of yourself,' said Noel, looking her in the eyes with all the sentiment he could muster, at which Mrs Brandon began to laugh and Noel laughed too. And Lydia, who was not talking very specially to anyone, looked at Noel with great affection and felt glad he had Mrs Brandon to laugh with, for she had felt for a long time that Noel could laugh with other people more easily than with her. Her mind suddenly went back to a day during the war when she and Noel were billeted on the Warings at Beliers Priory and Noel was working at the local Hush-Hush camp with Philip Winter. They had lunched at the Sheep's Head and Leslie Waring who was now Mrs Philip Winter was with them. Philip had asked her which of the party had, in her opinion, a sense of humour. Lydia had at once said that if he meant her she didn't think she had a sense of humour; not, she explained, like Philip's or Noel's, but said she quite often laughed at things inside when it didn't seem polite to laugh at them outside. Probably she did not remember this conversation as clearly as we do, but the gist of it came back to her and she told herself that she could never be amusing like Mrs Brandon, or Peggy, or Jessica Dean, or Noel's friends in London. And then, for her nature was not only generous but very honest and given to facing things as they came, she told herself that none of these charmers could give Noel the love and security that she gave and that she would trust Noel to the end of the world; even as far as Pomfret Madrigal or the Cockspur Theatre. And as she was never a great talker her silent meditation was not noticed for some time till Mrs Birkett, who as an ex-Headmaster's wife had been accustomed to keeping an eye on people, considering them mostly we think as parents in esse or posse who must be humoured but not indulged, drew Lydia into the Southbridge talk and asked if she had read Miss Hampton's last book.

'What is it?' said Lydia, who was not a novel reader.

Mr Birkett, basely deserting Noel with whom he was having a depressing talk about the probable Nationalisation of the National Trust, said it was a powerful study of agricultural life under present conditions entitled *Ways be Foul*, embodying what Miss Hampton and Miss Best had seen while on a fortnight's tour in a caravan through the Morgan ap Kerrig country.

'They had the usual party when it was published,' said Everard Carter, also drawn against his finer feelings by the lodestone of Miss Hampton's name into the conversation. 'Twelve bottles of gin and six of whiskey I counted with my own eyes, not to speak of beer. The Red Lion was dry for about a week afterwards.'

'It was a very hospitable party,' said his kind wife. 'It began at Adelina and then Mr Feeder took the ones that couldn't get in to Louisa and when they were too full Mr Traill had some at Maria. Everyone enjoyed it so much.'

'And Feeder's mother at Editha had the overflow,' said Everard Carter. 'She is a remarkable woman. She goes to Belgium with three old family servants every year and gives them each the full amount of money They let one take. Then she sends them to the cinema at Ostend, gives them a night in bed and pushes them back to England and spends four people's money. It seems quite logical.'

'She brought me back some red fillet steak last time she went,' said Kate. 'When I saw it I nearly cried. Do you know it was *red* and had *blood* in it and one could *chew* it,' at which beautiful words there was such a silence as greeted the Holy Grail appearing athwart a sunbeam.

> 'Tough meat and grey gravy,
> God help the British Navy,'

said a cheerful voice and in walked the Mertons' agent Mr Wickham, who had been out bird-spying with Peggy Brandon's sister-in-law Mrs Crofts, wife of the vicar of Southbridge. 'Your sister-in-law is in fine fettle, Mrs Francis,' he said, sitting down by Peggy Brandon. 'We've been all over the Great Hump and Lord! how that woman can walk! She nearly killed me, but we did see a Spottletoe in Copsen Spinney. Have you any tea, Mrs Merton?'

Lydia, accustomed to Mr Wickham's ways, looked at Noel who went away and came back with beer and glasses on a tray. He was followed by the deeply disapproving old parlourmaid Palmer with tea-things and then the noise of the returning water-party was heard and the room was full of people and talk and the gentle clashing of tea-cups, while Lydia poured out for everyone and Colin and Noel made themselves useful, and then the noise of talk abated as the younger members fell upon the scones and honey and the home-made cake.

'There are forty feeding like one,' said Mrs Brandon suddenly.

'My dear mamma, you mustn't say things like that,' said Francis. 'It's very unlucky. The one who gets up first will burst.'

'It is Poetry,' said Mrs Brandon with majesty. 'Somebody wrote it. I have seen it in a book somewhere.'

'Wordsworth,' said Mr Wickham. 'Not that I read him myself, but it was in the crossword on Saturday and I couldn't do it and if you wait till Monday you lose interest, so I rang up Mrs Robin Dale and she told me. Lord! how that young woman can quote. Well, here's to her,' and he drank his beer and refilled his glass. 'Your sister-in-law Effie Crofts has been going it, Mrs Francis. Up to town for two nights and going to Aubrey Clover's play; and her husband with her,' he continued, as if this added a high light to the debauch. 'Well, here's to little Jessica. Why she married Clover I don't know but good luck to them both. Clover was with the Little Ships and good luck to him for it,' each of which wishes he accompanied by a ceremonial drink.

As most of those present knew Jessica Dean and a good many knew Aubrey Clover an animated discussion took place about what Noel called the Amazing Marriage, though Mr Wickham maintained it was what he had always expected.

'I adore little Jessica,' he said, 'but a day and a night of her would put me right off my drive. Too much verve and all that. I'm a bit vervy myself and we'd throw tea-pots at each other. Now Aubrey's a nice quiet fellow. Here's luck to him.'

The voice of Henry Grantly, strangled with emotion and stuttering with chivalry, was understood to say that Jessica Dean was roughly speaking the quintessence of beauty and a jolly good sort and if anyone thought she wasn't he only wished his calling-up papers had come and he'd shoot them. After thus taking up the gauntlet for beauty in distress he went bright red and filled his mouth with bun and honey. We regret to have to state that Charles Belton, Francis Brandon and Colin Keith, all of whom knew Jessica quite well, and had a good deal of respect for her as well as admiring her gifts as an actress and liking her as a person, took it upon themselves to warn Henry against Sirens, a warning which he took very ill but was too embarrassed to speak again.

'Of course,' said Clarissa, now the complete blasée woman of the world, 'what is too, too dreadful is Oliver, poor fish.'

'That's not the way to talk about him, even if he is your cousin,' said Charles Belton. 'You girls will hit below the belt.'

'Too, too Sporting Club, my dear,' said Clarissa, but her affectation passed unnoticed in the talk that burst out.

As Mrs Brandon said later, someone ought to have given Clarissa half a crown for her indiscretion, because then everyone else felt they could be indiscreet. The whole county had watched Oliver adoring Jessica for the past year and if everyone had contributed a penny for each mention of his or Jessica's name for a Marling Relief Fund, Oliver would have been well enough off to have to pay more taxes than he could afford in the following year. Everyone talked at once. The voices of the females became more and more like peacocks. The men had a kind of We could an if we would conversation among themselves, though in no way discreditable to Jessica. Henry ate and sulked, imagining a happier world in which, in his new uniform, he would kill Aubrey Clover, cut out all the older men and take Jessica to some unsuspected isle in far-off seas. Mrs Birkett obtained a momentary hearing on the grounds of knowing Miss Hampton who knew Aubrey Clover's mother who had died last year, but she did not try to press her advantage, for all she really knew was that the late Mrs Lover, which was Aubrey Clover's real name, had been the widow of a bank manager and had never seen her son act because she wasn't much interested in the theatre. Grace said wouldn't it make a marvellous film if Aubrey Clover died of a fit on a first night or something and Jessica married Oliver Marling.

'If I was Jessica and Aubrey Clover died, I'd marry you, Colin,' she added, at which her sister Eleanor almost blushed with shame at her young sister's forwardness, but Colin smiled at her so understandingly that her heart rose on wings, fluttered and sank again to rest, while Emmy was moved to say if she married an actor she'd feel an awful fool.

'Well, he'll just have to be that word however you pronounce it,' said Grace, 'and carry her fan and things, like Croke Hosskiss did for Glamora Tudor in *The Ladies' Man*, all about Casanova and things.'

'What word?' said Francis Brandon hopefully. 'I know a good many, but this one may be new to me.'

Grace said she didn't know if it was chiss-something or kiss-something.

'As in the Elgin marbles the Greek g or gamma is always hard,' said Mr Birkett, but none of the younger people took any notice, being uneducated.

'Cicisbeo,' said Mrs Brandon suddenly. 'And I know *why* I know that,' she added apologetically, 'it is because of my dreadful cousin-in-law Felicia Grant, Delia's mother-in-law, who will live in Calabria and expects people here to kiss her hand.'

This lucid explanation was very well received and Oliver was by popular acclamation given honorary rank as Cicisbeo after which the party, having eaten itself almost to a standstill, was fairly quiet till Lavinia Merton, portly but attractive in a bathing suit, looked shyly in at the window. Her mother told her to come in and say how do you do. Lavinia assumed a coquettish air.

'Now then, do as mother says, Lavinia,' said Nurse, materialising behind her with Miss Angela Carter, upon which Lavinia came into the dining-room and pressed her stout form affectionately against her uncle Colin's left leg.

'That's not the way to behave,' said Nurse perfunctorily. 'They've all had a nice tea, madam, and we're going to sail boats in the pond.'

'Can you manage them all?' said Kate Carter, for her four and Lydia's three seemed rather a handful. 'Shall I come and help?'

'Thank you, madam, I'm sure,' said Nurse, 'but Nanny Twicker had tea with us and has taken the younger children to the pond. She quite understands them,' said Nurse graciously though Mrs Twicker the gardener's wife had been nurse to Kate and her brothers and Lydia and was still capable of controlling any number of children by sheer Nanny-power. 'I'm sure if you and any of the ladies and gentlemen like to come we'll be very pleased, won't we, Angela?' she said to Miss Carter, who suddenly realising that she was six years old and no longer a child left Nurse and singling out Henry as a suitable object for her attentions stood by him and made eyes.

'Hullo,' said Henry. 'Who are you?'

'Angela Carter,' said that young lady. 'Who are you?'

'I'm Henry and I'm going to be a soldier,' said Henry.

'And sword people and blood them?' said Miss Carter.

'Rather,' said Henry. 'And bomb them and squash them,' at which point Nurse, outraged by this forward behaviour, called her to come along to the pond. Miss Angela Carter who had a very strong character took Henry's hand and before he knew where he was he had joined the nursery party at the pond, and Lydia suggested that they should all go out. Emmy, who had previously taken Tom on a refresher course on the Northbridge Home Farm, said she would have to go back to Rushwater as Herdman was still a bit shaky since Rushwater Churchill tried to gore him in the stall and she might be needed and Tom was coming with her to see the cows, so she and Tom collected their bicycles and rode away. The Birketts who lived at some distance also took their leave and the rest of the party sauntered, if we may use so demoded a word, to the pond, where Nanny Twicker was in charge of the nursery party.

'This pond,' said Colin to Eleanor, 'has seen many peculiar sights. My sister Lydia wearing a kind of sack with holes in it for her arms and legs and bright red with sunburn, one of the Crawley girls the same and three boys from Southbridge School cleaning out the pond with brooms was one.'

'I can't imagine Mrs Merton like that,' said Eleanor.

'Nor can I now,' said Colin, looking affectionately at his tall, handsome, quiet sister.

'How pretty this is,' said Eleanor, standing by the little balustrade at the lower end of the pond. Here there was a sluice gate through which the stream that fed the pond trickled to a lower level and widened into a deep pool fringed with wild mint and grasses. In the clear water above the sandy bottom some minnows were flirting about.

'This is also the scene of a dramatic episode,' said Colin. 'Philip Winter who runs the Priory School now was engaged to Rose Birkett who was perfectly lovely but as silly as they make them and I am thankful to say she lost her temper once too often and pulled off the engagement ring and threw it at Philip, and Lydia saw him drop it into the pool.'

'So it was lost for ever,' said Eleanor.

'As a matter of fact it wasn't,' said Colin. 'We found it long afterwards when the pool was cleaned out and Lydia gave it back to Philip and Philip asked Lydia to keep it for Leslie Winter that he was in love with and then he and Leslie somehow got engaged with it at Winter Overcotes station, so it came in useful after all.'

'How romantic,' said Eleanor, looking at the pool where the minnows swirled among the green weeds.

'If I happened to have an engagement ring on me,' said Colin, who had been far less embarrassed when addressing uninterested jurors or a deaf judge; and then he stopped dead.

'If you had?' said Eleanor.

'I wouldn't throw it into the pool,' said Colin and Eleanor's eyes met his and then she looked down, away, anywhere and he felt as if all his breath had gone.

'*Do* come and swim, Colin,' said the voice of what might be his future sister-in-law and Grace hooked herself on to his unresponsive arm and hung heavily on it. Eleanor looked at him, smiled and moved away. 'Charles and Clarissa won't, so *do*,' said Grace.

Colin said as patiently as he could that he didn't feel much like swimming and then Eleanor said they must go or they would miss the bus. Among the good-byes there was no chance to get Eleanor to himself. For a moment outside the house he got her to himself and said he would not forget that they were to meet in town.

'I'd love it,' said Eleanor, looking up at him in a way that nearly destroyed his balance so beautiful did it seem, 'so long as Lord Pomfret doesn't need me. I might be helping him with some papers. Good-bye Colin.

She pressed his hand warmly and went away with Grace and Henry. Colin thought of moving after them and escorting them to the bus, but that girl Grace was bound to come plaguing him and Henry would plague him too about the War Office. Better to bite on the bullet. Lord Pomfret indeed. If Eleanor preferred Lord Pomfret to Colin Keith, let her. His good sense told him that as Lady Pomfret's second-in-command at the Red Cross Eleanor must naturally see something of the Pomfrets. But when love was waiting for her it was unreasonable to speak of arranging papers. Just like women to feel that their work mattered when there were things far more important; things like love.

Then the Carters went away with all their children. Charles Belton and Clarissa had gone on their bicycles and the family were alone, for Mr Wickham was so often in and out that no one noticed him. Colin walked down to the river to be moody and misunderstood and also to make sure that the boathouse was locked and all safe for the night, for the increasing lawlessness of the rising generation means that nothing is safe from thieving and there is little redress when crime is soft-heartedly and soft-headedly described as split personality.

'I'd split their personalities for them if I caught them pinching the boat cushions,' said Colin aloud to himself, glad to vent his feelings on something or somebody, and then took himself for a walk along the river the better to practise upon himself some refinement of self-torment.

The children had now gone indoors and Nanny Twicker had gone back to her cottage. Noel and his Lydia tidied garden chairs and when everything was orderly they walked down to the pond and stood looking at the pool.

'How awful it was when Rose threw Philip's ring at him,' said Lydia, 'and he dropped it into the pool. I couldn't have thrown mine in because we were engaged and married all in one breath.'

'I must admit I never thought of a ring,' said Noel. 'I only thought of you.'

Lydia rubbed her head against his shoulder in companionable silence.

'Peggy looks very well,' she said presently.

'She does,' said Noel. 'And she is as enchanting as ever. But not for me.'

'Don't, don't,' said Lydia.

'I will,' said Noel. 'Only this once. You asked me if she hurt me. She did. But she didn't mean to and it was my conceit that was hurt, not me. I can't ask you how much you were hurt and I won't, because I can never love you enough to express how much I love you, which isn't in the least what I mean and what the use of an expensive career as a barrister is I don't know if one cannot make oneself clear in the home, in spite of which one last remark I wish to make, one last explanation I wish to offer which is that you are and always have been everything and Peggy, except that I like the hussy, absolutely nothing.'

Then he stopped, wondering if he had said too much or too little. His Lydia laid her head on his shoulder as she had done on the day he came to Northbridge after her father's death; only then it was for a moment and he had released her lest this bird might take flight. Now it was tried and steadfast love. They stood in silence and he could hear the Barchester bells coming down the river.

'What *should* we do without Dickens?' said Lydia.

12

After the noise and the chatter at Northbridge Tom found it very pleasant to bicycle along the country roads with Emmy, sitting at her feet as well as one can do when bicycling, and absorbing cow-lore, which would, he hoped, be useful at Adamsfield. For in his present frame of mind he felt that sooner than go back to school once more in any form he would be a kitten and cry Mew, or in other words be a day-labourer and hoe turnips under Lucy Marling's kind if domineering rule.

'You know Lucy is going to do pigs too,' said Tom, as they turned off from the main road towards Rushwater.

'We aren't much good at pigs,' said Emmy. 'I'm pretty keen on them myself. Father's man Goble nearly won a prize with Holdings Goliath at the Barsetshire Pig-Breeders' Association's Show last year, but Rushwater doesn't seem to do so well. We're going to do nicely with our sheep up on the downs, and if we had first-class pigs it would be a good show, but Macpherson, that's the old agent, isn't pig-minded so we'll have to wait. Pigs and cows and sheep; that's my idea,' said Emmy with the face of one who follows the Gleam.

'Suovetaurilia,' said Tom, more to himself than to Emmy.

'This way,' said Emmy, suddenly turning her bicycle's head and cutting across him so sharply that only by a series of skilful wobbles did he keep his balance. 'What was that you were saying about?'

'Sorry,' said Tom. 'It was only what the ancient Romans used to say. They were rather like you.'

'I did do Latin when I was young,' said Emmy, from the height of her twenty-odd years, 'but I don't see how they could *talk* it. You'd have to think quite differently. If it's French you don't have to think at all, you just say it.'

'I wish I did,' said Tom. 'But I don't suppose the Romans had to think. Latin probably seemed quite natural to them.'

'Well, what did that mean, anyway?' said Emmy. 'There's Rushwater,' and she poked her face towards the unbeautiful beloved home of the Leslies.

'It meant just what you said,' said Tom. 'Pigs and cows and sheep; only the Romans said Pigs and sheep and cows.'

Emmy said tolerantly that they always put the words the wrong way round in their sentences and so dismissed the Romans for good, which Tom quite unreasonably found a very reasonable attitude. Emmy, pushing ahead of Tom, led him round the house to the stable yard where cats and pigeons were sunning themselves and a noise of horses moving could be heard.

'Stick your bike in the harness-room,' said Emmy, 'and I'll take you round. We don't have supper till eight in the summer, so we've plenty of time.'

Tom looked round and fell in love with Rushwater at sight. He was not the first and will not be the last, we hope. What exactly the secret of Rushwater was it is difficult to say. The best one can say of the house, built in a kind of red-brick Gothic by the present owner's great-great-grandfather, is that it might have been worse than it was and that the rooms were large and comfortable. It lay in what David Leslie disrespectfully called a frog-hole with rising ground behind it, beech crowned, beyond which lay the open downs. The gardens were bounded by the little Rushmere brook and bordered by woods and fields. Nothing unusual. Not a house for *Country Life*. But an eternal home, which is perhaps what houses are for. For many years Lady Emily Leslie had warmed and transfigured Rushwater by the radiant love in her nature, making it a home to all who came and informing every room, every path, every lawn and flower with her own fascinating, exasperating personality. Since the early days of the war Lady Emily had lived with her daughter Agnes Graham. There her husband had died and then her grandson Martin had come back from the war and settled at Rushwater, his property since his grandfather's death. Lady Emily at first had paid frequent visits, but as petrol was cut down and age came upon her she was not able to visit her beloved home often, yet her spirit was in Rushwater and though Martin and his golden wife Sylvia were endlessly busy looking after the place and the people and the animals, the house never lost its feeling of leisure, of time resting, not time flying. Even Emmy's ceaseless and violent activity fell into a kind of rhythm, whirled round in earth's diurnal course with cows and pigs and sheep.

'We've not got much in the stables,' said Emmy. 'Martin rides a lot because he got a queer leg in Italy and Sylvia that's his wife rides too. I have the pony if I want him, or anybody's horse that they aren't using. Do you ride?'

'Rather,' said Tom.

'That's all right,' said Emmy. 'We might have a ride to-morrow. Come on and I'll show you Rushwater Churchill.'

They walked through the gardens to the farm and found the cowman doing something with a wheelbarrow in the yard.

'That's Herdman,' said Emmy. 'He knows everything about

cows, but I'm better on bulls. Hullo, Herdman. How's Churchill? Mr Grantly's come to see him.'

'Evening, sir,' said Herdman. 'He's got the devil in him that bull. Went for me in his own stall he did, sir. But he's a fine bull, whatever Miss Emmy says.'

'I don't say anything,' said Emmy, 'except how silly you were to let him have a go at you. He won't try it on me.'

'Old Churchill he knows a lady when he sees one,' said Herdman, chuckling at his own wit. 'Here he is, sir.'

The upper half of Rushwater Churchill's front door was open. Tom looked over the lower half. At first the gloom obscured his vision, then as his eyes became used to the half light he saw the immense bulk of the young champion bull towering like the great San Philip and heard him blowing through his nostrils like Etna and moving as Etna may have moved when Enceladus turned.

'*What* a fellow,' he said reverently.

'Isn't he?' said Emmy, much gratified. 'He knows me,' she added, as a new recruit might say of a Colonel who had remembered his face.

'Do you think he would know me?' said Tom.

'Now, Miss Emmy, you're not going to let that young gentleman go too near him,' said Herdman. 'You know the way he went for me. You're a devil, that's what you are,' he added, looking at the bull with affectionate pride.

'I think you'd better not go too near, it might worry him,' said Emmy who, as Tom noticed with amusement, seemed more concerned for the bull's feelings than for his visitor's safety.

'I'll talk to him,' said Tom, and he leant against the bull's half front door and began to speak. Neither Emmy nor Herdman knew what he was saying. Nor do we, except with a crib. The bull stopped his restless trampling and came a little nearer and turned one wicked, intelligent eye upon Tom. When Tom had finished the bull made a noise like a railway accident in the middle of an air-raid and returned to his champing and stamping.

'Gosh!' said Emmy.

'I'll lay you got that from the gypsies, sir,' said Herdman, who was obviously now quite ready to make a carpet of himself for Tom if necessary.

'It's a kind of Romany,' said Tom.

'I say, do you *know* Romany?' said Emmy.

'Not really Romany,' said Tom. 'Only Roman. I told him a story out of Virgil about a bull having a fight with another bull over a heifer.'

'Ah, that's what got his lordship,' said old Herdman chuckling. 'We've not found a heifer for him yet, sir, but Lord Pomfret's man he told me—'

But Emmy said good-night to Herdman in a firm voice and took Tom away.

'I say,' she said, as soon as the wooden door of the kitchen garden was shut behind them. 'I never knew Latin was like that. There must be something in it.'

'There is,' said Tom. 'I can't account for it. My tutor at Oxford, Mr Fanshawe, said he had been to Australia once to give some lectures and he read Virgil aloud for half an hour in the Town Hall, Melbourne or Sydney or somewhere, without any translation and it made such a nice noise that they lapped it up. You know, Emmy, that's what's so rotten. I do love Latin and Greek frightfully, but I don't want to be a schoolmaster or a don; and I do love farming most frightfully but everyone says I'd have to go to an Agricultural College to learn things properly and accounts and how to get round the Government and things, and I think I'd *die* if I had to go back to school again. It was pretty difficult going back to Oxford after you'd been a Major and could cut people's heads off, but to go to another college would be plain hell.'

Emmy, as we know, had during the war gone straight from the schoolroom to the farm owing to her inherited love of the land and animals and the need for help at Rushwater, and had helped her cousin Martin to run his property. When he married Sylvia Halliday, herself a farming squire's daughter, he and his wife had asked Emmy to stay with them which she had gladly and happily done and somehow though none of them had been to any school of agriculture, their brains and their wish to make the best of Rushwater and their willingness to learn anything that would help the place had conquered most of the difficulties. Nor must we forget old Mr Macpherson the agent who had no training except working on a Scotch estate under a good factor in his youth, and so had accumulated knowledge of men and beasts and earth and trees and all that appertains to the land and had never stopped learning. But this was probably the first time that Emmy had met anyone who talked as Tom had been talking and though it was not in her to understand anyone who was diffident about his own capabilities her kind heart was touched by Tom's confidence and she sympathised loudly with him in his wish never to be a schoolboy again.

'The awful thing is,' said Tom, encouraged by her interest to speak more openly than he had ever done before, 'that father's so awfully decent. I mean he practically said I could do what I liked as long as I made a do of it, so I jolly well must make a do of it. If only he'd say he'd cut off my allowance,' said Tom, 'or cut up rough somehow, it would be easier. But he's so damnably decent that I'd feel a heel if I let him down. You know, Emmy, it would be much easier if one's people would throw their weight about a bit and tell one to do things instead of asking one what one wants to do.'

'I know what you mean,' said Emmy. 'At least I think I do,' she added diffidently, for the finer shades were not as a rule apparent to her. 'Clarissa's like that.'

'Clarissa?' said Tom. 'But she's as cocksure as a bantam,' which comparison moved Emmy, whose sense of humour was not as a rule very acute, to friendly laughter.

'She is on top,' said Emmy, 'but not inside. She says just what you do, that if mother and father would say Don't, or even Do, it would be much easier. It's like people in shops saying Would you like to go to the next counter instead of Next counter. I suppose we'd better wash.'

She took him into the house and upstairs to a bedroom with darned white dimity curtains and bedcover and a faded paper of large roses with sprawling foliage.

'If you hear a noise next door it's Eleanor,' she said.

'Who?' said Tom, for he naturally thought of his sister.

'Sylvia's baby,' said Emmy. 'She's going to have another one in March. I think it's a good idea, because then she'll have two,' by which product of her powerful mind Tom was much struck.

When he came downstairs he found Emmy telling Martin and Sylvia Leslie about his classical interlude with Rushwater Churchill and wished she wouldn't, for it now struck him as a piece of rather affected showing off, but as they listened with polite and unaffected want of interest he felt himself slipping comfortably into the background again and listened to the professional talk between Emmy and Martin and Sylvia until a chance word made Martin realise that Tom had seen active service abroad, after which their talk became entirely reminiscent and the ladies had no need to exert themselves or make conversation for their guest. So long did their army talk go on that Sylvia had to drive them out of the dining-room to let Deanna from the village clear the things away, and the talk continued on the terrace in the warm late twilight. Presently Emmy after several body-rending yawns said she would go to bed and Sylvia soon followed her.

'Come and see the office,' said Martin, a little unsteady as he got up, for sitting long in one position always made his lame leg stiff. 'It's nothing much, but Sylvia keeps it very tidy,' and he took Tom to where, in one of the many rooms of the old servants' quarters, he had made the estate office and showed him plans and maps and neatly filed forms and documents.

'It reminds me so much of the army that I feel quite homesick sometimes,' said Martin. 'It's all very simple really; and most of it quite unnecessary,' he added not without bitterness. 'I'm all right because the army got one into the way of using forms and Sylvia has a genius for them. But how the small farmer manages I don't know, poor devil.'

'When my mother has forms she can't understand she takes them to wherever they came from in Barchester,' said Tom, 'and makes the people there do it for her,' which appeared to give Martin a very high opinion of Mrs Grantly.

'I know Emmy wants to take you round the cowsheds tomorrow morning,' said Martin, 'and after church we might ride over and have a talk with our old agent, and in the afternoon we are going to Holdings where Emmy's mother lives and want to take you too. They've got an excellent bailiff who might help you. By the way, do you know exactly what it is you want to do?'

Until Martin, resting his game leg on an office chair, asked him this plain question, Tom had never considered it. The malaise of the world, affecting the youth of the world in many different ways, does not help them to see or steer their course. All he could do was to tell Martin, haltingly and childishly as he had told Emmy, how he had wanted to read for Greats at Oxford and then loathed the idea of being a schoolmaster or a don, and how he longed to farm but couldn't stand the idea of an agricultural college, and how awful it was that his father was so kind.

'I sympathise with you about the teaching and about the agricultural college,' said Martin. 'As far as parents go I can hardly remember my father. He was killed in 1918, and my mother has lived in America for years with her second husband. But it was all much easier for me because I knew this place would come to me if I wasn't killed in the war, so I had to take it on. But I'm not sure if I could have kept going without Sylvia.'

Tom felt this was all very interesting but not very helpful and said it must be very nice to have a wife; a useful one he meant.

'Well, there's plenty of time for that,' said Martin, looking kindly down from his thirty-odd years on Tom's twenty-eight. 'Don't be too down-hearted. We'll go and see Macpherson tomorrow and hear what he has to say. Don't be alarmed if you hear a great clumping noise in the night. My cousin Emmy feels any night ill-spent in which she hasn't assisted at the birth or death of something in the cowsheds and always puts on her hobnailed boots to do it.'

He got up and stood for a minute to get his leg used to its new position. The garden, fields and hills were enchanted by the light of a mist-haloed golden moon and there was no sound. It made Tom think of some poetry only he couldn't quite remember what it was. Martin said, with the nearest approach to peevishness that he ever allowed himself, that a moon like that meant rain and he hoped the hay was in and never felt happy about the second cutting and then took his guest indoors.

Tom slept deeply and dreamlessly, nor did he hear Emmy's hob-nailed boots which were really only a family joke, born of the night when Martin Leslie and Sylvia Halliday had played the part of Lucina in the cowshed while Emmy slept, which romantic episode had made them get engaged by breakfast-time. Martin had been right. The moon had changed the weather and a soft warm rain was steadily falling. Emmy showed some annoyance at the weather, but on hearing from Martin that the hay had all been got in she cheered up and said it wasn't the vicar's fault, because she had particularly asked him not to pray for rain last Sunday and he hadn't.

'Mr oh bother I always forget, Canon Bostock is awfully nice,' said Emmy. 'He plays squash with me, because Martin can't because of his leg. And he mends bicycle tyres quicker than anyone I know.'

For some reason that we cannot explain Tom found Emmy's eulogy of the vicar in poor taste and wished they were not going to church. But go they did and Tom tried, as we all do in our way, to attend to the service and not think about squash and bicycles and also tried to make a kind of prayer that everything (though he was unable to explain precisely what things) should come right (though he could not think of any suggestions as to what kind of rightness he meant). And if anyone says that this was nearly what Tony Morland used to call superstitious, we can only say that it was also rather like faith, which has often to be a pretty blind virtue till it vanishes into sight. After the service they sheltered in the porch till the vicar came out and

Martin pointed out to Tom the Leslie burying-place, surrounded by spiky railings but those railings so overgrown by a sweetbriar hedge that they were hardly visible.

'Gran had this hedge planted years ago,' said Martin. 'I always take her some sweetbriar when I go to Holdings.'

'When Gran came over for her birthday party last year,' said Emmy, 'that idiot Herdman brought Rushwater Churchill up the lane to call on her. Martin nearly had a fit, because he'd told Herdman it would be too much for Gran to walk to the cowsheds. But Gran loved seeing him. I wish she could see him now. He's about a ton bigger and heavier.'

'I wish she could too,' said Martin. Tom thought he was going to say something more, but nothing more was said.

Canon Bostock then came out and on hearing that Tom was the son of Mr Grantly at Edgewood shook his hand warmly.

'I shall never forget,' said the vicar, 'how beautifully, if I may use the word with all reverence, your father took the funeral service for old Canon Thorne. Without putting anything into words he somehow managed to convey what we all, and when I say all, I mean all men of goodwill and by men I of course mean women, in the larger sense I mean,' said Canon Bostock, torn between his loathing of the Bishop as broadly speaking a priest of Baal and his very proper respect for the episcopate, 'what we all, I say, feel about the Palace. In a jocular way I alluded to him afterwards, when talking with the Dean, as St Grantly Chrysostom, and Dr Crawley was amused.'

Tom was able to cap this instructive anecdote by telling Canon Bostock about the cesspool under the Palace basement and how the Bishop and Bishopess had to go away for a month, which judgment so impressed the vicar that he preached on the following Sunday a sermon on the abomination of desolation with a reference, whose meaning was not quite clear to his audience nor to himself, to the fishpools of Heshbon.

'And how is Lady Emily?' he asked.

Martin said much the same and they were going to see her that afternoon and Canon Bostock sent messages to her and then, greatly daring, to Lady Graham who always had a very upsetting effect upon him.

Martin, who walked as little as possible when his leg was tired, had ordered the horses to be brought round and while Sylvia and Emmy paid the consecrated Sunday visit to the farm he and Tom rode over to see the old agent Mr Macpherson in his pleasant little Regency house or cottage orné with very improbable stucco battlements and a small Gothic porch. Mr Macpherson was in a chair on the verandah looking over his lawn to the Rushmere Brook and away to the distant hills, now veiled by the persistent gentle rain. An elderly kind of groom-factotum came out and took the horses.

'Well, Macpherson, how are you?' said Martin. 'This is Tom Grantly. You remember his father the Rector of Edgewood.'

'You'll excuse me not getting up,' said Mr Macpherson shaking Tom by the hand. 'The grasshopper is a sore burden to me at times. I mind your father very well. He married over Gatherum way but I do not remember the lady's name.'

Tom told him and Mr Macpherson nodded approvingly.

'A good farmer your mother's father was,' he said. 'When I first came here, fifty years ago, it was said that his bread was all his own from the sowing to the reaping, from the reaping to the threshing, from the threshing to the grinding and from the grinding to the baking. But it's no use to speak of bread to-day. The poor misguided creatures, blind mouths as Milton calls them, that are growing up to-day have never seen nor tasted good wheaten bread, nor the good barley bread we had in Dunbar when I was a boy. Well, well, it's time I was away to Dunbar to lay my bones with my forebears.'

'Macpherson is an old impostor,' said Martin. 'He has been threatening to retire ever since I came back from the war, but here he still is, eating the bread of idleness,' and he looked very affectionately at the old agent.

'The bread of affliction,' said Mr Macpherson, 'for the Lord is chastening me in a way that leaves me no doubt of his love. Fifty years I have been here,' he went on, speaking half to Tom half to himself. 'I came to Rushwater when I was thirty, and a cocked-up youngster I was then. Her ladyship was the same age. We have grown older together, but she is no longer at Rushwater. How is her ladyship?' he asked Martin.

Fairly well, Martin said, but not so well as she had been last year and Agnes had said she thought the drive to Rushwater might be too tiring for her mother, so he and Sylvia were taking Tom over to Holdings in the afternoon.

'And now, Macpherson,' he said, 'I want you to talk to Tom and what's more make him talk to you. He has been a soldier and a scholar and he wants to be a farmer. See what sense you can make out of it and if we can help him,' and then he got onto his horse and went to see some old friends in the cottages down the valley.

After half an hour or so he came back and sat down with the other men on the verandah.

'Old Mrs Poulter's pretty bad,' he said. 'Dr Ford wants her to go to the Barchester General, but she says she wishes to die in her own bed. I rather agree with her.'

'So do I,' said Mr Macpherson, 'like the old body who prayed the Lord to take her on a Saturday night with the kitchen weel redd up. Ah well. Her daughter-in-law will give a hand. Lily's a good girl and Ted's earning good money. And now about the lad, Martin.'

'Well?' said Martin, who knew by Macpherson's use of the word lad that Tom had passed muster.

'He has the root of the matter in him,' said Mr Macpherson. 'He is young and opinionated, and forbye too easily cast down as many of these young soldiers have every right to be, poor weans. But he is not his grandfather's grandson for nothing. To be frank, I doubt that he will ever understand cows as Emmy does, but the creature has glimmerings of sense about crops and as good a notion of ingans as need be,' said the old agent who always went back to the Doric when moved. To Tom this seemed damnably faint praise, but Martin who knew Mr Macpherson's ways seemed to find it quite satisfactory, and thanking the agent for his help said they must be getting back to lunch.

'Give my respectful regards to her ladyship,' said Mr Macpherson. 'We came here together and we've won through together and in God's good time we shall meet together. And tell your good wife, Rushwater, that it's over long since she came to see me.'

Martin promised to tell Sylvia and the two men mounted and rode away.

'What an astounding old fellow,' said Tom. 'It's like Scott come to life.'

'It's partly deliberate,' said Martin, 'and partly that when he is excited he gets more Scotch. It's the first time he has called me Rushwater.'

'I expected him to get up on a bank like Meg Merrilees and say, "Ride your ways, Laird of Rushwater, ride your ways, Martin

Leslie,"' said Tom, and Martin looked at him approvingly, for a man who knows his Scott is not to be despised and though Martin's domestic bliss was unalloyed he sometimes went so far as to wish that his womenfolk were better read.

At lunch Martin delivered Macpherson's message and Sylvia said she knew she had been neglectful during the last few weeks and would go and see him at tea-time if Martin didn't particularly want her to go to Holdings. Martin said that broadly speaking he always wanted her to go anywhere that he went, but he agreed that it would be a kind deed to go to tea with Macpherson and Agnes would quite understand. So presently he and Emmy and Tom drove through the fine misty rain to Little Misfit. Here they found Lady Graham in the room known as the Saloon which had long windows onto the terrace, and was used as a general meeting ground during the summer with young people coming and going and Agnes Graham brooding with what her brother David had lovingly called her divine idiocy over her children and their friends. There they found also Lucy Marling who had come over to lunch in the Ford van with a young pig that Sir Robert Graham had bought from Mr Marling. Lucy, though not quite in her usual spirits, was pleased to see Tom and asked him how he had got on at Rushwater.

'He's not bad,' said Emmy who, as Mrs Siddon the old housekeeper at Rushwater frequently said, was never backward in coming forward. 'He said some Latin to Rushwater Churchill and Macpherson says he is awfully good on onions.'

Regarded as a testimonial Emmy's contribution left something to be desired, but Lucy, understanding between the lines, was pleased to hear so good a report of her pupil.

'Well, I've got to be getting back,' said Lucy. 'I'll see you to-morrow, Tom. Oh, and I'll ring Mr Adams up about the Quickset Combination. Your friend rang up to say he was driving it down himself and Mr Adams will like to see it.'

'It's no good ringing him up till the end of next week,' said Clarissa.

'Why?' said Lucy, not willing to believe her cousin's unexpected news.

'I was talking to Heather last night,' said Clarissa, who in a very becoming check apron was putting some touches of gold on the frame of an old mirror, 'and she said her father had gone to London. Some business, I don't know what, and wouldn't be back till Friday or Saturday. I'm going to give Heather this looking-glass for a wedding present. Merry and I found it in that secondhand shop in Barley Street. It had a bit of the gilding knocked off so I'm mending it.'

Lucy was standing with her back to one of the long windows so her face was in a slight shadow and nobody noticed her look of anxiety, or alarm, one could not tell which.

'What a bore,' she said, in her usual manner. 'Never mind. You can help me with your friend, Tom. Good-bye, Agnes. Can I go and say Good-bye to cousin Emily?'

'I think she is resting,' said Agnes. 'And she usually sleeps in the afternoon now. I'll give her your love when she wakes up. Come again soon.'

So Lucy said Good-bye and went away, busying her mind with work that must be done, for work she must and as hard as she could, sooner than think.

'And now tell me all about yourself,' said Lady Graham to Tom. 'Are you going to be a farmer? Darling papa loved the farm. He used to go round the fields poking at things with a stick,' at which description of a gentleman farmer her nephew

Martin laughed in an irreverent way and said he would take Tom Grantly to see the pigs.

'Yes do, Martin darling,' said Agnes. 'You will find the boys somewhere about and Edith and Charles Belton. Emmy can stay and talk to me and Clarissa. But where is Sylvia? She isn't here.'

'Bless your heart, sweet chuck,' said Martin, 'have you only just noticed that? She is being a proper Squire's Lady and visiting the sick.'

'*Not* whooping cough,' said Agnes with mild firmness. 'You must not let her visit whooping cough. If darling Eleanor caught it she would be so unhappy. When darling Clarissa had whooping cough she was sick every twenty minutes for three nights running. And in Sylvia's condition you never know what harm it might do.'

'It certainly would be very alarming to have a baby whooping inside one as if one had swallowed an alarm clock,' said Martin, which caused his Aunt Agnes to look at him with mild interest and Emmy to utter what we can only call a guffaw, while Clarissa quietly gilding her mirror, managed to put into her elegant fingers an alarming expression of scorn and distaste. 'But it's quite all right, my dear aunt. She has gone to tea with Macpherson. He is getting very old and I think he is lonely. He was talking about Gran and how he came to Rushwater when she was just married. They are the same age.'

'How very peculiar,' said Agnes.

'Not really,' said Martin. 'When you think of all the millions of people in the world lots of them must be the same age as each other.'

'Dodo Bingham's cousin whose name I have forgotten, the one who wanted to know of a nice pension in Munich the summer Mary was staying with us and Dodo's letter was blown away in the garden, was exactly the same age as I am,' said Agnes. 'At least he was several years younger but our birthdays were on the same day I am almost certain. Or if it wasn't the same day it ended with the same number because I distinctly remember thinking how curious it was that I was the twenty-seventh of June and he was the seventh or the seventeenth, I've forgotten which, of another month. And then Rose Bingham married David which was so nice.'

'You are the most valuable woman I know,' said Martin, kissing his aunt Agnes affectionately. 'So, as I was saying, Sylvia has gone to cheer Macpherson up. He sent all kinds of messages to you.'

'Dear Macpherson,' said Agnes, thinking of her happy youth at Rushwater, and she sighed.

'My pensive public, wherefore look you sad?' said Martin, though he knew the words would be wasted on his aunt. 'Nothing wrong is there? Tell me if there is and I will help you.'

'You dear boy, nothing,' said Agnes. 'Only I get a little sad sometimes when mamma is so tired. She never used to be tired. But she will love to see you after tea.'

So Martin, with a nameless cloud of anxiety over him, took Tom down to the Home Farm where they found the other young people and had a delightful talk with Goble the bailiff and took no notice of the small, soft rain. Agnes went on with her tapestry work, Clarissa, her insolent pretty head a little on one side, touched up the gilding of the mirror, while Emmy entertained them with bulletins from the cowsheds. Presently Miss Merriman came in and was warmly greeted by Emmy.

'Lady Emily is asleep,' said Miss Merriman in answer to a look from Agnes, 'and she is looking forward very much to seeing Martin after tea.'

'Oh, I say, isn't Gran going to have tea with us?' said Emmy.

'I think not,' said Lady Graham. 'Darling Gran gets rather tired when there are many people talking at once. She will want to see you, Emmy, before you go.'

'She has given us all presents,' said Clarissa, eyeing her work professionally and taking another brushful of gold paint. 'She gave me her brooch with the Pomfret crest on it and she gave Edith a huge book to write poetry in and a golden pencil.'

Emmy expressed a desire to see the brooch, so Clarissa took off her apron and showed the brooch, heavily set with precious stones.

'It belonged to Aunt Agnes,' said Lady Graham, 'darling mamma's sister who died a long time ago. I was called after her. She had a little dog called Carlo. That horrid Guido Strelsa who was one of the Italian cousins gave it to her and it died of overeating,' after which interesting addition to the annals of the family her ladyship went on with her tapestry and thinking of nothing in particular.

'And she gave all the boys a book that belonged to great-grandpapa,' said Clarissa, as she wiped her brushes and put them away. 'James had Byron's poems and John had young Mr Tennyson's poems 1830 and Robert had the Ronsard poem that great-grandpapa translated in a special binding. I wish Gran wouldn't give us things.'

Miss Merriman asked why.

'I like her to have them better than us,' said Clarissa and went to the window and looked out upon the warm misty rain through which the farmyard party could now be seen approaching. Miss Merriman made no comment, for she thought she understood Clarissa's meaning; a protest against Lady Emily relinquishing anything, because everything she possessed was so permeated by her own spirit that it could only be happy with its owner and might pine in stranger hands. Then she blamed herself for foolish fancies and began to clear the big table, for when there was a large party it was easier to have tea in the Saloon where everyone could be seated.

Then the rest of the party came in and Emmy's brothers threw themselves upon her with enquiries about Rushwater and the animals and plans for coming over and clearing the kitchen-garden pond as they had done last year. Charles Belton went over to Clarissa who was tracing with her elegant forefinger the course of a raindrop slowly meandering down the outside of the window.

'I have done all the pig-talk I know,' said Charles. 'Those two,' he added, looking towards Martin and Tom, 'will go on till all is blue. What a pretty bauble you have.'

Clarissa looked down at her brooch and fingered it.

'Gran gave it to me,' she said. 'I do wish people wouldn't give one things.'

'You ungrateful sparrow,' said Charles. 'I'd be jolly glad if anyone gave me a brooch like that.'

'And what would you do with it?' said Clarissa, looking intently at the raindrop which had now englobed another drop and changed its course.

'Hock it,' said Charles. 'I could do with some cash and I bet it's all real.'

'My dear boy, your army language appals me,' said Clarissa.

'That's all right,' said Charles cheerfully. 'No, I won't hock it, or pop it if you like the expression better. I'd give it to you.'

'Why?' said Clarissa, casting a sheep's eye at him quite deliberately and provocatively.

'Because you like it,' said Charles. 'And don't tell me you don't like it, because all girls like pretty things.'

'But it's just because I do like it that I don't want it,' said Clarissa impatiently. 'I want Gran to have *everything*. Not to give things away. Men are so *stupid*.'

'Temper, temper, my girl,' said Charles. 'Remember what Shakespeare said.'

'What did he say?' said Clarissa, turning from the window as the raindrop came to its end, in a corner of the pane.

'He said some very pertinent things about man's ingratitude,' said Charles. 'By which of course he also meant woman's.'

'How too, too schoolmaster,' said Clarissa, but without heat and then Lady Graham called them all to tea.

How Lady Graham managed to make such good Sunday teas was a common subject of discussion among her friends. The answer was partly in her cook who believed, as she said, in filling young stomachs and if we can't give the young ladies and gentlemen a proper tea, your ladyship, and beat the Government and with ten ration books too, we did ought to be ashamed of ourselves, and partly in the generous and continued kindness of friends in America.

'Which I do think,' said Agnes to Martin, 'is *most* peculiar.'

'Why peculiar, Aunt Agnes?' said Martin, who found his aunt's mental processes an endless source of innocent entertainment.

'Well, anybody could send one parcel,' said Agnes, her usually unruffled brow bent in analytical thought, 'but not everyone could send the same parcel twice.'

Martin said he supposed they couldn't, if it was the same parcel, as if it had been sent it had been sent.

'Don't try to confuse me,' said Agnes with a dove's dignity. 'You know perfectly well what I mean. If I knew someone was being persecuted by their Government I should certainly be very sorry for them and I would send them a food parcel. But I don't think I would do it again. But my friends in the United States and Robert's friends simply go on sending us parcels, which is quite *dreadful*.'

'Why dreadful, my dear aunt?' said Martin.

'If you thought for one moment,' said Agnes severely, 'you would understand. It is so difficult to make one's letters sound as grateful as one is and when I get another parcel from America I nearly cry because everything one writes must sound so silly when it gets across the Atlantic. And if only I could explain how really grateful we are and how wretched we are at not being able to do anything to show it, I should feel much happier.'

Much as Martin loved his aunt Agnes he had never yet known her feel anything acutely unless it was connected with her adored family and this proof of sensibility seemed to him very touching.

'Why not get Edith to write a poem to them?' he said. 'Edith,' he called down the table. 'Poetess forward, please. Your mother wants a poem to thank her American friends for remembering her not once but again, and again, and again.'

'And again and again and again,' said John and Robert Graham in chorus.

'I must have my book and my pencil,' said Edith, who was rather above herself owing to her grandmother's gifts. She got down from her chair and fetched the book and the pencil from a drawer in one of the cabinets.

'Showing off,' said John.

'I can't hear what you say any more than if you hadn't spoken,' said Edith, without looking up from the book in which she was scribbling violently.

'Did you get a good talk with Goble about the pigs?' said Emmy across the table to Tom.

'I did indeed,' said Tom. 'In fact he offered to come over to Adamsfield and give me some hints about the new styes.'

'That's all right so long as Pucken doesn't mind,' said Emmy, for Pucken was Mr Marling's pigman and might resent an outsider giving advice so near Marling and to Miss Lucy Marling.

'He seems to know Pucken quite well and has a very good opinion of him,' said Tom. 'In fact I believe the whole thing is an excuse for Goble and Pucken to have a day out together. But I'll ask Lucy.'

'I have made the poem,' said Edith, shutting her book with a bang.

'Well, open the book you silly and tell it us,' said her brother John.

'You don't need books to say poetry from, only to write it in,' said Edith witheringly. 'The poem says,

"You sent to us a lot of food
Which we did find so very good.
And when again you sent us more
Our thanks to you again did soar.
And every time you send us food again
To you our thanks we'll write in joyous strain."

The last two lines are longer than the others,' she added. 'That's on purpose, but really it was because I couldn't get all the words in.'

This ode or effusion was very well received. Edith put her book and pencil away and applied herself again to her tea.

'We shall have to go soon,' said Martin, looking at his watch. 'Emmy wants to be back by six. I can't remember why. Cows probably. Shall I go and see Gran, Aunt Agnes?'

Agnes asked Miss Merriman if she would see whether the Lady Emily had finished her tea and was ready for visitors. 'Though she would love to see you always, Martin,' she added as Miss Merriman left the room. 'You are one of the most precious people in her heart, because of your father, dear boy.'

'I wish I'd known him, but I couldn't,' said Martin, whose father had been killed so many years ago in France.

'My dear boy,' said Agnes compassionately. 'But you have your darling little Eleanor and there will be another baby next year,' and Martin couldn't help laughing at his aunt's infallible specific for melancholy, and then Miss Merriman came back and said Conque had taken Lady Emily's tea away and she was ready to have a talk with Martin.

Lady Emily now spent much of her time on the big sofa in the drawing-room, which was partly the reason why Agnes used the Saloon for family gatherings that summer, and here Martin found her lying against a pile of cushions. He thought she looked as beautiful as ever though very frail, her keen loving hawk's eyes dark in her white face, her thin exquisitely curved mouth breaking into a brilliant smile of welcome to the only child of her first-born who had left her more than thirty long years ago.

'My darling Martin,' she said, holding out a thin, jewel-laden hand in welcome.

Martin kissed the hand and sat down by his grandmother.

'How are you, Gran?' he said.

'They say I am remarkably fit for my age,' said Lady Emily, flashing a smile of amused tolerance at Martin. 'But I miss your father so much. More every day, I think.'

'Poor Gran,' said Martin, realising very well that when Lady Emily spoke of his father she was now thinking of his grandfather, for past and present and the different generations were often as one in her mind, especially when she was tired. 'Sylvia sent you her love and will come over next week. She has gone to see Macpherson who hasn't been very well.'

'Poor Macpherson,' said Lady Emily. 'He came the year I was married and we are the same age. He will be tired too. If ever I die, Martin, it will only be of tiredness,' and she lay quiet for a while, looking at Martin with loving eyes, while he told her small bits of news about Rushwater and how well Rushwater Churchill was doing.

'Henry will be delighted,' said Lady Emily, who often spoke of her husband as if he were alive.

'I have brought you some sweetbriar from the churchyard, Gran,' said Martin, laying a little branch on the shawl that covered her.

'Oh sweet, sweet,' said Lady Emily. 'Your grandfather did not want me to plant sweetbriar round the family grave, Martin, but I am glad I did. Only the actions of the just, Smell sweet and blossom in the dust. He was the most just man I ever knew, except papa.'

Now, thought Martin, darling Gran had got the generations right again, so he told her what news he had of the Pomfrets, to which she listened with great interest.

'I am an old woman and a useless one,' she said, with her enchanting smile, 'and I don't suppose I shall see the Towers again in this life. The doctor very stupidly says the motor would be too much for me, so I humour him. But I *would* like to see papa again,' she added a little wistfully, and Martin did not know whether she wished to see the sixth Earl of Pomfret, dead so many years ago, at the Towers or in another world. 'And how is your leg?' said Lady Emily with one of her quick changes of thought.

Martin said not too good, but the electric treatment was helping him and Sylvia was wonderful.

'Dear boy,' said Lady Emily. 'You and I are not so good at walking as we were. I used to walk with your father, Martin, when he was a boy. At first I went too quickly for him. Then he caught me up and soon he could out-walk everyone, even the gillies when we went north for the shooting. And here I am, an old woman on a sofa and you hirpling with your lame foot as Macpherson used to say.'

They sat in silence for a while and then Martin said he must go.

'Wait one moment,' said Lady Emily, holding his hand in her own, 'I am coming.'

A pang went through Martin's heart as he felt the slight, frail bones in his grandmother's hand, and he waited quietly.

'You have walked so far and so fast,' said Lady Emily, with a ghost of her old mischievous smile, 'but here I am at last, my darling.'

Martin remained perfectly still. There was no sound but the soft warm rain outside the window. Then he laid his grandmother's hand very gently upon her shawl and got up, painfully, and taking his stick went to find Miss Merriman.

13

We cannot say that the whole county mourned Lady Emily Leslie. The war and the increasing unease and oppression of the peace had loosened many ties. The face of Barchester was changing, not always for the better; old friendships were submerged in the common woe. Had Lady Emily been able to remain at Rushwater the house would still have been the commonplace setting glorified by that iridescent, opal-changing, diamond-sparkling fountain, that wind-blown spirit. But her husband's death and her life at Holdings had withdrawn her into a small though very faithful circle and Barsetshire sometimes forgot whether she was still alive. What was mortal of her was laid by her husband's side in Rushwater churchyard while the soft warm rain came steadily down and the heavy air was scented with sweetbriar, and after the service the family and close friends walked back to Rushwater. Mr Macpherson had insisted upon coming against the advice of everyone, including his doctor. Martin, whose leg was more than usually painful with the weather and the shock which one does not feel till long after the blow has been bravely met, walked beside the old agent.

'The end of an old song,' said Mr Macpherson. 'You ought to be resting with your leg up, Martin. An old lamiter like myself can hobble about, but it grieves me to see you. If your grandmother were here she would make a fine to-do about it.'

'Dear Gran,' said Martin. 'She would probably hold up the whole funeral to get a cushion from the vestry for me and would certainly have tried to conduct the service, bless her. Do you remember the concert in the racquet court the year I was seventeen and we had the dance, and how Gran stopped Gudgeon in the middle of his song to ask about grandfather's shoes that needed mending?'

'If I were to begin to remember all her ladyship's intromissions,' said Mr Macpherson, 'I would be talking till midnight. Do you mind when her ladyship took up enamel work and had the furnace put in the service-room so that the footmen couldn't get past and your grandfather got up from the luncheon-table and ordered the car and drove straight to London and went on a cruise to Norway?'

Martin said he had never heard about it before.

'Of course you haven't,' said Mr Macpherson. 'You weren't born. It was your father who was a little boy then. The older you get the more a thousand years are like an evening gone and a fine muddle you get into. The young laugh at us old ones, but they will come to it themselves. And talking of young people, that young Grantly has the makings of a farmer in him. With a lad like that at Rushwater and Emmy with the animals you could take things more easily. The Rural District Council isn't enough for a Leslie. You ought to be on the County Council, like your grandfather before you.'

'But Tom isn't coming to Rushwater,' said Martin. 'At least not so far as I know. Emmy could tell you probably. He's her find,' and then he joined Lord and Lady Pomfret and they all went into Rushwater House.

To those who had been at the family gathering the year before it was like an echo of past time. Tea was laid on a round table in the big drawing-room. Clarissa, her pretty insolent face pale with crying, had with Charles Belton's help cut great branches from the laurels and the beeches and disposed them about the room and on the table a great bowl of sweetbriar. Agnes, in mournful beauty, her large dark eyes so like her mother's but with a softer radiance, having looked after everyone's comfort handed the hostess-ship to Sylvia and Emmy and took Lord Pomfret to a sofa where they could talk.

'I feel I haven't really a right to be here,' he said. 'I only came into the family sideways, as it were. If Mellings hadn't been killed in India my father wouldn't have become the heir and then I would have been plain Gillie Foster, and perhaps less of a burden to myself and others.'

'Poor Gillie,' said Agnes. 'But you mustn't sin your mercies, as Macpherson says. You have Sally and such darling children. Mellings is just like you and Emily is so like grandpapa and Giles is exactly like Sally.'

'If Emily is going to be like Uncle Giles,' said Lord Pomfret, alluding to the seventh Earl, Lady Emily's brother, his predecessor, 'she will bully us all into our graves. What an old tyrant Uncle Giles was. But I got very fond of him and so did Sally.'

'Darling mamma was so fond of Sally,' said Agnes. 'And Sally was always so sweet and understanding with mamma. mamma said you were the best Pomfret, except of course grandpapa, that there had been.'

Lord Pomfret's tired face flushed a little with pleasure at this praise.

'Aunt Emily could never see anything but the best in people,' he said. 'It made one feel one had to live up to it.'

'You do, dear Gillie,' said Agnes.

'I suppose I try,' said Lord Pomfret. 'But one always feels one ought to have tried harder. I wish a thousand times that poor Mellings had not been killed. Then I wouldn't have to be an Earl and a Lord Lieutenant and sit in the Lords, and I would have time to see Sally and the children. And Sally works ten times harder than I do, bless her.'

'My poor Gillie,' said Agnes, quite forgetting her own grief in her sympathy with her cousin. 'I can only think of one other person who works harder and better than you do and as unselfishly.'

'Who is it?' said Lord Pomfret, possibly a little piqued.

'His Majesty, of course,' said Agnes. 'And he came into it sideways too.'

'I'm sorry,' said Lord Pomfret. 'I ought to have thought of that.'

'When I think of how hard he has worked for us and all the quite *dreadful* things he has to do like listening to speeches or having people to dinner or having to be interested in dull things,' said Agnes, 'it makes me cry. And I am afraid I am crying a little now,' she added, dabbing her eyes with a handkerchief almost as soft as her own cheek, 'only it is partly about darling mamma. We do miss her so dreadfully and Robert says he does so wish he had seen more of her, but you know he can never get down except at week-ends and even then it is usually Saturday night and he has to go up on Sunday night or Monday morning early. And he is so unhappy that he could not be here to-day. Bring Sally and the children to see me soon, dear Gillie,' and she got up, for her guests must not be neglected.

'Tired, darling?' said Lady Pomfret, whose watchful eye had

been on her husband. 'Talking to darling Agnes is a little like being drowned in a butt of Malmsey sometimes.'

'She was being very sweet,' said Lord Pomfret smiling, 'and also a little reproving. In fact she gave me a lesson I deserved.'

Lady Pomfret asked what it was. Her husband said it was only a joke, and Agnes was an angel and they must be going.

'Where is Merry?' said Lady Pomfret. 'I haven't seen her since we came out of church.'

Sylvia, who heard her, said she thought Miss Merriman was answering the telephone and how sad it was that David couldn't be there, but he and Rose were in America with the children. Then Miss Merriman came in looking as calm and efficient as ever; as calm as she had looked the day after Gillie Foster the Earl of Pomfret's heir had proposed to Sally Wicklow the agent's sister.

'Come and see us soon, Merry,' said Lord Pomfret and passed on.

'Come and help him when you are ready,' said Lady Pomfret.

'I haven't forgotten,' said Miss Merriman, and then Lady Pomfret took her husband away and as they drove, not to the Towers but to some place where Lord Pomfret had another duty to fulfil, he said in his own mind that Agnes had spoken the truth and when he was tired and wished he could be an ordinary person he would remember the Majesty of England, who was giving up far more, working far harder, and always put his people before himself.

'I say,' said Emmy to Lucy Marling, 'do you remember how Gran made a speech at lunch when we had the party last year and everything fell out of her bag onto the floor, and Merry and Clarissa had to grabble round the table.'

'And the awful mess she made with her scone and her tea in the slop-basin,' said Lucy, beginning to laugh.

'And the way she dropped her bag and her stick and her scarves in church,' said Emmy, laughing too.

'I'll tell you what,' said Lucy. 'This isn't a sad party. I mean it is awfully sad about Cousin Emily, but when one thinks of her one has to laugh. I don't mean horridly, but when you like a thing frightfully it makes you laugh at remembering it sometimes.'

'You've hit the bullseye,' said Emmy, and whether she thought this expression was connected with Rushwater Churchill we cannot say. 'Everyone has to laugh about Gran and she'd have laughed herself,' and Emmy spoke very truly, for it was as if Lady Emily's spirit at its most gay, loving and irresponsible were upon the guests who, notwithstanding their sense of poignant loss, remembered her in happiness.

'It's the other way round sometimes,' said Oliver Marling, 'and just when you think you are happy you remember something you'd rather not remember and then you stop laughing.'

'That's quite true,' said Emmy seriously. 'When Bluebell dropped a dead calf I was awfully sorry and then I forgot about it, but there was something about a calf in the First Lesson or the Second Lesson I don't remember which, but anyway it was either golden or fatted and it made me think of Bluebell and I cried so much I couldn't sing the Benedictus.'

Oliver said gravely it must in that case have been fatted and he quite understood what Emmy meant. Emmy was much uplifted by this tribute having always admired her cousin Oliver as an intellectual and went away to talk to Mr Macpherson about cows, her simple panacea for all ills. For though very unlike her elegant adorable mother physically, she had something of the same one-track mind, only in Agnes's case it was her children. Oliver stood a little apart by the huge branch of magnolia which

Charles and Clarissa had put in a great blue and white Chinese vase. Its burnished dark green leaves among which shone a few ostentatiously creamy opulent swooningly-scented flowers partly screened him from the room and he thought again of what he had said: how whenever he thought he had conquered himself something reminded him of Jessica and made the old wound bleed again.

'Self-pitier,' he said scornfully, half aloud, and wished he could hate Jessica; or even forget her. But neither was possible nor, he had to admit, would he really wish to lose this pain, to stop pressing the dagger to his heart, and he envied Lucy and her absorption in her work at Adamsfield. But how little we know of our nearest and dearest.

Lucy had found Clarissa and expressed her admiration of the flowers.

'It was half Charles,' said Clarissa. 'He isn't afraid of gardeners and took whatever I wanted. Poulter was too too livid about the magnolia, but I had to have it. And he got the sweetbriar for me. Darling Gran had some sweetbriar from grandpapa's grave when she died, so I thought she would like some here to-day. Do you remember how Gran got her scarf entangled in the sweetbriar in the churchyard last year? She did get more entangled than anyone I know,' and at the thought Clarissa could not help laughing, though in a very loving way.

'Have you heard if Mr Adams is back?' said Lucy. 'Every time I ring up he isn't there and we've got to settle with Spadger about the bricks for the pigstyes.'

Clarissa said Heather had rung up to ask if she would arrange the flowers for her wedding and she thought Heather had said her father would be in London longer than he expected. Lucy said in an offhand way that it didn't matter and went to say good-bye to Agnes. Oliver had described her own feelings more accurately than she liked, but being a courageous young woman she tried to look her own feelings in the face. She had been extremely stupid when Mr Adams rang her up about the permits and it was now quite evident that as she had feared he was offended, hurt, whatever one liked to say. And now he was in London and time was passing and every day she woke to a dull ache somewhere inside her which on inspection turned out to be fear that Mr Adams had misunderstood her question and thought she was hinting at some dishonesty on his part. Daily did she tell herself not to be an idiot and not to worry, but oneself can be very deaf to good advice and Lucy's self took no notice at all. Oh well, there were plenty of things to be done at Adamsfield and one could work till late in the evening, though even with summer time the August evenings were not long enough for her. Oh, well.

The party had now mostly dispersed. Agnes had gone to the housekeeper's room to talk to Mrs Siddon and praise her for the tea. Sylvia had gone upstairs to draw comfort from Miss Eleanor Leslie. Emmy and Macpherson were talking cows. Martin and his uncle John Leslie were discussing the memorial tablet which Lady Emily's children wished to dedicate to her.

In the housekeeper's room Agnes found Mrs Siddon showing her family photograph albums to Conque, Lady Emily's faithful and highly incompetent French maid, who was so blotched and swollen with tears that she could hardly see.

'I was just showing Miss Conk the last photo of her ladyship with Our Miss Eleanor,' said Mrs Siddon.

'I haven't seen that one,' said Agnes sitting down. 'Darling mamma, how she loved all the babies. Do you remember, Siddy, when darling Clarissa was a baby how mamma painted pictures in all the corners of the nursery so that if she was put in a corner for being naughty she would not feel dull.'

'Yes indeed, my lady,' said Mrs Siddon. 'And then Master John put moustaches and beards on all the pictures and Nurse was going to smack him, but I said, "If you want to punish Master John, Nurse, leave it to me,"' upon which she paused dramatically.

'How dreadful,' said Agnes, entirely unmoved. 'So what did you do?'

'"Master John," I said, "I asked you to have tea in My Room if Nurse said yes. But there is no tea for naughty boys who spoil their granny's beautiful pictures."'

'Ce pauvre John,' said Conque. 'Enfin, il faut que les enfants s'amusent, et miladi qui aimait tant ce pauvre John! Il y a des gens qui n'ont pas de cœur.'

'So what happened?' asked Agnes, secure in the knowledge that Siddon had not understood Conque's words, but only too certain that she had guessed their sense.

'Master John took Master Robert's india-rubber and rubbed all the beards and moustaches off, my lady,' said Siddon.

Agnes said that was very nice.

'Unfortunately, my lady,' Siddon continued, 'Master Robert saw Master John using his india-rubber and Flew At Him, so that there was quite a quarrel. So then Nurse said if they both said they were sorry she would pass it over, and both the young gentlemen came to tea in My Room.'

Agnes said how nice it must have been.

'I had made some of my little cakes like dominoes, my lady,' said Siddon, 'with white icing and chocolate spots, and the young gentlemen played a game before they ate them.'

Conque muttered something in which the word sale figured prominently but Agnes deliberately did not hear her.

'You used to make those cakes for David and me, Siddy,' said Agnes.

'Fancy your remembering, my lady,' said Siddon, much affected. 'It's all very different now, though little Miss Eleanor is as sweet as an angel. If only Mr David could have been here to-day, my lady. It was so lovely in church and I remembered the old days when you were all small, my lady.'

'And how naughty we were and how we teased poor Conque. Didn't we, Conque?' said Agnes, turning to her mother's maid.

'Pour taquiner je ne dis pas,' said Conque. 'Mais Monsieur David etait tellement gentil. Même quand il a mis des grenouilles dans ma cuvette je n'ai pu que rire, tant il etait gentil. On lui donnerait le bon Dieu sans confession celui là. Et dire qu'il n'a pu revoir miladi avant sa mort,' with which words she began to cry as if she had not cried before.

'I would know that voice anywhere,' said David Leslie opening the door. 'Agnes, my darling. Good old Siddy. Cheer up, Conque,' and he embraced each of the ladies heartily.

'David darling,' said Agnes, clinging to him as if she could never let him go. 'Oh David I have wanted you so much. We all wanted you so much.'

'I didn't get your cable in time,' said David. 'Rose and I were in the Far West, motoring with friends. I flew back at once and now I'm too late. Tell me about mamma.'

'You come in the kitchen with me, Miss Conk,' said Siddon, 'and I'll make you some of that nasty camomile stuff.'

'Bless you, Siddy,' said David, as the tear-beslobbered Conque withdrew, saying something about la tisane calming her nerves. 'And a nice cup of tea for me like an angel, Siddy. Tell me about mamma, Agnes.'

'There's nothing really to tell,' said Agnes, her lovely eyes misty for a moment. 'Darling Martin was with her. He had brought some sweetbriar from papa's grave. She was a little confused about people at the end, you know, and Martin thinks she thought he was his father come back again and she just lay quite still. Poor darling mamma. You look dreadfully tired, darling.'

'I am,' said David. 'Oh good kind Siddy,' he said as Mrs Siddon came in with tea on a tray. 'Bless you, Siddy. Now go and give Conque her cat-lap. Flying this way you arrive practically before you start, all most confusing. And I'm sure however much time you save by flying you leave your stomach and your brain behind; they can't keep up with aeroplanes. That's why people at peace conferences and what not are so silly. Rose sent you a thousand loves. mamma loved Rose.'

'Darling mamma loved everybody,' said Agnes.

'That is her epitaph,' said David. 'And what love it was,' and while David drank his tea they talked of the past and their mother's ways and found themselves laughing.

'That is mamma all over,' said David. 'I know she is watching us laugh and thinking what mischief she can do next, like the time when she painted doves, or fishes, or hares, I can't remember which on my looking-glass to welcome me home and I had to shave in John's room for weeks.'

'If you are rested, I know Macpherson would like to see you,' said Agnes. 'He has got very old. And Merry will want to see you too. I must tell her you are here.'

'She knows,' said David. 'I rang her up from Winter Overcotes aerodrome. Good old Gerry Coverdale lent me his racing car. But I couldn't get here in time.'

'Darling mamma couldn't have seen you even if you had

got here in time for the service,' said Agnes, and David felt admiringly, as he had so often felt, that his sister Agnes in spite of her delusive appearance of elegant helplessness had more commonsense than the rest of her generation put together. 'Will you come to Holdings, David? Or are you going to stay at Rushwater?', but David, elusive as ever in spite of being a respectable married man, said he thought he would go back to London unless he was urgently needed because he meant to fly back to Rose next day. So Agnes and he went to the kitchen where Conque embraced David and cried more than ever if that were possible, while Mrs Siddon looked on with reserved disapproval.

'Ne vous en faites pas, ma pauvre Conque,' said David. 'Je parie que maman vous a légué quelque chose.'

'Ah mais non, Monsieur David,' said Conque, 'ce n'est pas pour un legs que je pleure, c'est pour miladi, et quoi qu'en dise le révérend père Ossquince,' Conque added, with firm though impeded utterance, 'miladi était un ange du bon Dieu.'

'Well, I'm sure Father Hoskins never said she wasn't,' said David, already bored. 'Rose sent you her love, Siddy, and so did the children. I must fly,' and he embraced both the ladies and went away with Agnes to the drawing-room, where John and Martin and John's nice dull wife Mary and Martin's golden Sylvia welcomed him with open arms and offered him beds everywhere; but David had already almost exhausted the pleasure of seeing Rushwater and explained how he must get to London so that he could fly back to Rose in America next day. And if the truth were known he felt that Rushwater would unman him if he stayed much longer. For many years now Rushwater had not been his home, but last year when he and Rose had come to the great Leslie Reunion Lady Emily had been for one day the chatelaine of Rushwater again and David had almost captured the illusion of permanence. Now he felt like one who treads alone some banquet hall deserted and could almost have cried for his mother. Home was no more home to him. His home now was wherever Rose was and Rose was with Martin's mother and her American husband and he must rejoin her as quickly as racing cars and aeroplanes would let him. He would have slipped away at once had not Agnes gently insisted upon his going to talk to Macpherson. He was shocked by the change in the old agent, though he did not say so, and for once did not face a situation with his usual facile charm, for he felt that Macpherson might die at any moment to express his devotion to Lady Emily and also felt, which was even more alarming, that Macpherson was probably deaf.

'I'm glad to see you, David,' said the old agent, 'and you need not shout for my hearing is still very good. So you have come.'

There was not, we think, any shadow of reproach intended, but David felt a prick of conscience. True he could not have known that his mother would leave them silently, invisibly, but there had been a thousand occasions when he might have come to see her, or written, or telephoned, and they rose up in his heart making him feel small and guilty. And to be told by Macpherson how much his mother had loved him and what his visits had meant to her was not balm to his mind. Probably we all feel small and guilty in the same way about someone whom we have loved but for whose pleasure we have not always taken pains. One thing is certain; that these people have never complained, nor have they felt any slight, for our happiness is their life.

'I can see you are ettling to be gone, David,' said Mr Macpherson personifying abstract justice in David's eyes. 'Give my love to Mrs David. She's a fine woman. Your father, honest man, would have liked her,' and the old man retired into his memories, one of which, and at the moment a very lively one, was of old Mr Leslie describing David as bone selfish. With many affectionate farewells David went away in Gerry Coverdale's racing car and the waters of Rushwater family life closed over his head.

Only the immediate family remained. Agnes took the opportunity of having a talk with her elder brother John, comparing their families and laughing over things said or done by their mother in old days.

'What about Merry?' said John. 'Will she stay on at Holdings?'

'I don't quite know,' said Agnes. 'mamma left her something and she has a sister whom she might live with. She has mentioned that sometimes. But I don't think she would be happy with one of her own people. She needs to be caring for someone. She helped Cousin Edith for years in London and Italy and at the Towers and then she helped me with mamma.'

'I expect she could help you now,' said John.

'I don't know,' said Agnes. 'I am very fond of her, but that's not the same as always having her in the house. Of course she was a great deal with darling mamma. She and Conque really were like a little private household for mamma,' and tired by the long day and her grief Agnes let a few tears fall.

'Cheer up,' said her brother John putting an affectionate arm round her.

'I do,' said Agnes. 'And you know mamma left Conque a hundred pounds a year for her life. With that and her economies that she is always boasting about she ought to be quite comfortable. I expect she will go and live with Mrs Baker at Folkestone.'

'Good Lord! old Baker isn't still alive, is she?' said John, for

Mrs Baker had been housekeeper at Rushwater before Mrs Siddon and celebrated for her bad temper.

'Indeed she is,' said Agnes, 'and Conque still goes there every year for her holiday and they have frightful quarrels.'

'And what about you, Agnes?' said John. 'We haven't talked about that.'

'Me?' said Agnes, to whom it had never occurred, wrapped up as she was in her family and ceaselessly thinking of them and working for them, that she was a person to be considered at all, 'Of course I shall miss darling mamma quite dreadfully. But Robert will be retiring presently which seems so ridiculous and as the Government are nationalising everything he won't have any directorships and we shall have to go carefully till his Aunt Florence dies, when he will be quite well off. So Robert will be much more at Holdings I hope and there are the children. They are *so* good, John. Clarissa is the only one I worry about sometimes. She is so clever and she did love darling mamma so much.'

'I don't follow your reasoning, but I am sure you are right,' said John. 'Don't worry about Clarissa, she is as tough as mamma was. So are you,' he added thoughtfully, 'and thank God for it. We must all keep alive in this horrible new world if it's only to try to help our young.'

'I know,' said Agnes. 'But the worst of it is they don't want to be helped. Darling mamma was so sweet about that. She never minded being helped even when she was so frail and she laughed about herself to the end. We must go now, John dear.'

The young Leslies and Grahams were rounded up. Only Clarissa was not to be found and Charles Belton said he would go and look for her. Ever since she had stumbled over the rope of the tea-tent at the combined Conservative Rally and Barsetshire Pig-Breeders' Association the year before and he had comforted her by conversation about a pig-club at the Priory School where he was a master, he had felt a certain responsibility for her. She was a kind of cousin of the Beltons and Charles felt strongly that cousins should stick together. He also rather enjoyed dealing with her fits of temper, having acquired a good technique in the army, and no one would have been surprised if he had beaten her with a horsewhip after the fashion of heroes in novels who wish to make ladies love them; some of her relations even going so far as to wish that he would. Poor Clarissa. So pretty, so clever, so worldly on one side; so young, so insecure on the other. But Charles who took things much as they came also took Clarissa as she came, affectionately but firmly, and Clarissa usually ended by licking the hand that held the whip, like a true woman.

Charles had seen Clarissa fleeing from her own unhappiness when her father's pig did not win the first prize. Now she had probably fled from her own unhappiness again and he had a pretty shrewd guess where he would find her. So he went upstairs to where, in what had been one of the second-best bedrooms, facing south with large windows and a faded Chinese wall-paper of crooked bamboos and huge sprawling peonies, Miss Eleanor Leslie aged nearly a year and a half was sitting in a tall chair, wearing a blue flannel dressing-gown and blue slippers, a feeder tied round her neck, enjoying a light supper of milk and rusks. By her sat her mother and opposite her was her cousin Clarissa, thimble on finger, peacefully darning a small tear in one of Miss Eleanor Leslie's frocks. The picture was so charming that Charles paused in the doorway. The ladies had not heard the door open, for Miss Eleanor Leslie had laid down her rusk and was drinking her milk with a vulgar gobbling noise, grasping the mug with determined though unsteady hands.

'Hullo,' said Charles.

Miss Eleanor Leslie jerked her head away from the mug, caught sight of Charles, stretched out her short fat arms and said, 'Adder.'

'I'm not,' said Charles.

'She means Daddy,' said Sylvia proudly.

'It may be clever of her to think I'm a man, but if she thinks I'm Martin, she must be half-witted,' said Charles.

On hearing these words Miss Eleanor Leslie was overcome by shyness, or rather simulated shyness with the most abandoned effrontery, rolling her eyes and holding her feeder before her face for the complete conquest of Charles, who took the wind out of her sails by kissing the eminently kissable back of her neck.

'Come on, Clarissa,' he said. 'Your mother's going.'

The look of peace fell from Clarissa's face and she folded her work neatly and got up without a word.

'Come again soon,' said Sylvia. 'Say good-bye to Clarissa, Eleanor.'

'Good-bye, baby,' said Clarissa, kissing her small cousin's milky face. 'Good-bye, Sylvia and thanks *awfully*.'

A second appeal to say good-bye produced nothing more than the word 'Adder' from Miss Eleanor Leslie.

'I wouldn't be your father for six pennyworth of halfpence, you ridiculous object,' said Charles.

'Jobbick,' said Miss Eleanor Leslie.

'What a *clever* girl to say Object,' said Sylvia. 'Good-bye, Charles. I'll try to come over and see the Priory School pigs next term. Now baby, eat up your rusk.'

The life of the nursery flowed back into its normal course while Charles and Clarissa went downstairs.

'I wish I could stay with Eleanor,' said Clarissa. 'It feels so safe.'

Charles said after all Holdings was quite safe.

'I suppose it is,' said Clarissa in a flat voice. 'But Gran isn't there. Oh, Charles.'

'Steady,' said Charles.

'I don't know if I can,' said Clarissa, pausing at the foot of the stairs where Gudgeon the old butler had been wont to beat his gong.

'Of course you can,' said Charles. 'I wouldn't cry if I were you. There isn't really time and your mother wants to get home. She must be very tired. Don't be selfish, my girl.'

Conflicting emotions raged in Clarissa's bosom. Half of her wanted to burst into tears. The other and better half reminded her that her mother needed her help and Gran would have wanted her to give it; Gran who never failed anyone. After a short tussle the better half won.

'All right,' she said. 'Thanks awfully.'

'Good girl,' said Charles approvingly and they joined Agnes in the drawing-room where Clarissa said quietly that she had been watching Eleanor have her supper and was sorry she had been so long. Miss Merriman was waiting, Conque was ready in the car, and they drove home in silence.

By now Mrs Siddon had cleared the tea away, Emmy had got into breeches and gone down to the farm and only Martin and Mr Macpherson remained in the great drawing-room. Martin noticed with concern how tired the old agent looked.

'I'll drive you back, Macpherson,' he said.

Mr Macpherson said he had his own car.

'I daresay you have,' said Martin, 'but you're going in mine. I'll tell Poulter to bring yours up later.'

'I have been a servant of this house for fifty years,' said the agent, 'and it would ill become me to contradict the laird now. You're a good lad, Martin.'

The soft rain had gradually ceased and the country was bathed in a golden mist of rain-charged evening sunlight. Martin opened the gate of the agent's garden and walked up to the cottage with him, to be sure that his housekeeper was at hand.

'And what will you do with the cottage when I'm dead?' said Mr Macpherson. 'It's too good for an agent as I have often told you. The next man had better have one of those new houses in the village. This should be kept for the family.'

Martin said first Mr Macpherson was not going to die and second he didn't want another agent.

'I shall die when I choose,' said Mr Macpherson rather crossly, 'or rather,' he added, 'in the Lord's good time, though whiles I think he has forgotten about me. Emmy had better have my house. You and Mrs Martin will be filling the big house with children and Emmy should have a house of her own. You must have someone to help you, Martin. Your leg won't thank you if you overwork it. Take an old man's advice who loves Rushwater and all in it as if it were his own. Tell your good lady what I said; she has some sense in her,' with which faint praise Mr Macpherson went into his house and shut the door.

Martin drove home through the golden mist and put the car away, thinking of what Macpherson had said. It was no use kicking against the pricks. His leg would probably be a trouble for the rest of his life and for Sylvia's sake and the sake of Rushwater he must spare himself when and as he could. Still he would not think about an agent while old Macpherson could get about.

Dinner was very quiet, for even Sylvia had felt the strain of the long day. When we say quiet, we must be understood to mean that Martin and Sylvia did not speak much, for Emmy held forth not only in the dining-room but afterwards in the little sitting-room at the top of her powerful voice on the cowsheds to be built by Mr Spadger for Mr Adams, a subject in which neither Martin nor Sylvia took a great deal of interest, so that when they went to bed, very early, Sylvia agreed that fond as she was of Emmy there was something to be said for Mr Macpherson's suggestion.

14

Much has been written and said about the relations between people and houses. Some of our friends live in hideous houses, not to speak of Emperor's Gate or Observatory Gardens which are the cordons bleus of hideousness, and yet so inform these graceless tenements with their own personality that after their death we think of them as palaces of delight. So had old Lady Pomfret lived in the Towers, that frightful memorial of St Pancras railway station; so had Lady Emily lived in the uncompromising plainness of Rushwater. Others have inherited or acquired houses famous for their beauty and managed to make them feel like an unfriendly Scotch Hydro; a notable example being the Dowager Lady Norton whose mere existence had turned Norton Hall, that perfect example of mid-eighteenth century architecture, built by Wood and altered by the Adam brothers who were also responsible for the fine plasterwork and the exquisite door-handles and finger-plates and key-holes, into a place of dullness and depression. Again there are houses which always get the better of their owners whether rich, poor, intelligent or stupid. Only beautiful houses can do this. It is perhaps rash to make so sweeping a statement, but we believe that for one ugly house that degrades the owner to its own level there will be found twenty beautiful, or handsome, or elegant houses that have exercised a good influence on everyone who has lived in them. And so it was with the Old Bank House which in extremes of wealth and poverty had always kept the upper hand of its tenants. To Miss Sowerby it had resigned itself meekly, knowing that although she could not afford to spend a penny on it, she would dust and polish and love as long as her strength lasted. When it saw Mr Adams approaching it may have felt some apprehension, but it was too well-bred to show it and when it had heard and witnessed Mr Adams's interview with Miss Sowerby it took him under its wing.

We will not say that the house makes the man; but it is an undoubted fact that given the right man, or woman, people will value that man or woman far more in the beautiful house than in its ugly sister; expertae crede, but I have forgotten my Latin, as Miss Harriette Wilson once wrote. Mr Adams, without any fuss and with no further demonstration than a small garden party of people who all happened for various reasons to be his personal friends, was accepted by most of the county. As for the Dowager Lady Norton, to be disliked by her was almost a passport to society, and the Omniums and Hartletops stood apart, looking to London rather than Barchester. Upon this citizenship Lord and Lady Pomfret's visit had perhaps put the seal; but the Pomfrets would certainly not have come if they had not felt a liking and a certain respect for Mr Adams.

'So on the whole I think we are extraordinarily lucky,' said Mr Grantly to his wife. 'The Old Bank House will be cared for and if only Adams doesn't insist on giving me a complete set of altar plate in chromium steel, or an electric heater for the font, I think we may feel quite happy.'

'And I really think Heather Adams may be good for Grace,' said Mrs Grantly. 'The municipal golf course with Heather sounds extraordinarily dull to me, but it is so much better than the Barchester Odeon with Jennifer Gorman,' and then they went on to speak about Eleanor and whether it would be a good thing for her to work in London.

'Why London, I can't think,' said Mrs Grantly, 'unless it is my Aunt Patience coming out. She loathed the country and became Head Almoner at St Sinecure's when Head Almoners were just People and didn't have to do exams.'

The Rector said he remembered being terrified of her Aunt Patience at a dinner party at the Deanery years ago.

'Everyone was terrified,' said Mrs Grantly, with the curious family feeling that makes us boast about Uncle Tom who added an extra nought and an extra y to a cheque for eight pounds and only escaped prosecution by dying of what used to be known as Russian Influenza, or Aunt Jean who killed seven companions and left all her money to Queen Victoria, 'but no one would be frightened of Eleanor. Well, if she wants to go, go she will, and apparently Lady Pomfret thinks London wants her. But what will Lady Pomfret do without her?'

'Just do without her, my dear,' said the Rector. 'It is extraordinary how well one does without people even when they are indispensable. If Eleanor goes to London and Tom really does go to learn farming and Henry is in the army, there will only be Grace.'

'And she will be at Barchester for another year,' said Mrs Grantly, 'and then go to Oxford or Cambridge I suppose, which must be so dull.'

'And then,' said the Rector, looking with faith into the future, 'we shall be alone for large portions of the year,' and this he said with no regret, but rather with a beautiful and religious anticipation of heavenly joys to come.

'I must say it will be extraordinarily nice in many ways,' said his wife. 'I do love them all, but sometimes they are an exhaustion to the spirit.'

'And then we needn't ever have the wireless on again,' said her husband, pursuing his dream of a New Jerusalem

'Some people don't know their luck,' said Mrs Grantly. 'Look at birds. Every year their children go to London or the colonies and every year they have some more. I suppose it is the triumph of hope over experience,' but her husband said it was just want of brains and one only had to look at a bird's face, especially a mother bird's, to see how silly they were.

Unaware of her parents' heartless conversation, Eleanor was having lunch at the White Hart with Colin Keith while her secretary took her place at the office.

'Crême Barchester,' said Eleanor who was studying the menu. 'That's out of a tin with some powdered milk in it. Boiled cod and parsley sauce.'

'The fish under the present Government,' said Colin, 'makes me think of the nursery rhyme,

> "Will you have it hot,
> Will you have it cold,
> Will you have it in a pot nine days old."

Let's give it a miss.'

'All right,' said Eleanor. 'Then there's Hamburg steak which is all the leftovers mixed up with lots of bread, and venison, which is just old goat.'

Or horse, said Colin, but Eleanor said horse was for London and that was why she wanted to go there. Colin asked her if it was really settled.

'Not quite,' said Eleanor. 'In fact it's rather mortifying because Isabel Dale could quite well take my place here, but I don't think I'm as good as the other girl who is up for the London job.'

'I could give you a much better job in London,' said Colin. 'I won't say what, because it would sound conceited after what I've just said and in any case you know perfectly well what I mean.'

'I thought I would be here for ages when I got Susan Belton's job,' said Eleanor, not answering Colin.

'Good girl, Susan,' said Colin. 'I nearly proposed to her the year before last.'

'Why?' said Eleanor; not rudely, but surprised, or even to her own great surprise almost affronted that Colin whom she had no intention of marrying should have dared to think of someone else two years ago.

'The usual reason,' said Colin. 'How incredibly revolting that so-called Hamburger is. I suppose it's the Government fat. I wanted to marry her.'

To Eleanor this appeared to be unparalleled effrontery. How dare Colin tell her about girls that he had wanted to marry. When they had gone up the river in the coracle she had thought he was the kind of person one would not mind knowing better, even a great deal better. Now he was calmly speaking of girls he had wished to marry, which caused her to say in a not very agreeable way, 'Why didn't you, then?'

'She turned me down before I really got to the point,' said Colin cheerfully. 'I rather gathered that she thought me a laggard in love and a dastard in war, though heaven knows I was in the army right from the word Go. Also I had been having tender, but bless your heart most innocent amatory persiflage with Peggy Brandon who was Peggy Arbuthnot then. I loved as never man did love who hadn't got a bean, And my heart, my heart was breaking for the love of Susan Dean. Though as a matter of fact I have quite a number of beans. And that, to refer to the original subject of our talk, is why I am asking you to consider my proposal.'

'Your proposal?' said Eleanor, turning scarlet.

'Why not?' said Colin. 'I proposed a delightful and well-paid job to you as hostess-housekeeper to a successful barrister. Who dares propose more is probably not speaking the truth. I repeat it. At least, please take it as repeated. And stop pushing that revolting piece of Hamburger about the plate and look at me.'

We do not attempt to pretend that Eleanor was not enjoying herself extremely. To be pursued is far more attractive than to be the pursuer and also puts one in a stronger position. When she put her fork down and looked at Colin she saw in his face that he was romantically speaking at her feet and all might have been well and saved them a good deal of unnecessary unhappiness had not the devil entered into Eleanor and caused her to say that the job sounded exactly what she wanted, but there was always Lord Pomfret to consider and if he needed help with his papers she had promised to give it.

'Bill please, Burden,' said Colin to the old waiter who was whisking imaginary crumbs off the rather grey and darned tablecloths with a napkin. Burden produced the bill which he had been waiting to give Colin for some time, for his feet were aching and they were the last guests.

'Right,' said Colin, giving the old waiter a handsome tip. 'Will you excuse me if I rush off. I have to see Keith and Merton,' for the two families were still represented in the well-known Barchester firm of solicitors, though Noel Merton and Colin Keith had chosen the higher branch of the legal profession. Why higher, we do not know.

'Oh, of course,' said Eleanor, whose pot of milk was lying in shards in a puddle.

So Colin went off to see Keith and Merton and there met his and Lydia's elder brother Robert Keith and they talked about some family investments, while Eleanor went back to the office with the delightful conviction that she had wrecked her whole life and could never be anything but a careerist. But as a callus grows over a wound or a broken bone to protect it, so did Eleanor try to cover her self-inflicted wound with the thought of helping Lord Pomfret and perhaps giving him the understanding which, in spite of liking Lady Pomfret very much, she sometimes felt he needed. Unfortunately there was no one to tell her what we know, namely how extremely wrong she was. So she took her broken heart back to the office and behaved as if nothing had happened, so that her secretary when she went home said to her mother that Eleanor Grantly looked as if she were going to have flu and she did hope it wouldn't go through the office, and Mrs Grantly said to her husband after supper that if Eleanor went on looking like that she would send for Dr Ford and it was all Eleanor's own fault for not taking her holiday in June when Lady Pomfret had offered it. And Mr Grantly said to his wife that children were such a trial from their birth to whatever age they happened to be that he had a good mind to get a nomination to St Aella's Home for Stiff-necked Clergy, now under the direction of the former Vicar of Southbridge, and end his days in peace.

Lady Pomfret also noticed that her Depot Librarian looked run down and as she was rather tired herself she did what all good women do and quite unnecessarily asked Eleanor to come to lunch at the Towers on Sunday, thinking the outing would please her and also we are glad to say, for it is very seldom that we have found Lady Pomfret doing anything for her own benefit, that Eleanor might help her with the children, for Nannie had grudgingly consented to take Sunday afternoon off.

'I suppose,' said Lady Pomfret to her husband, 'that we are very lucky to have a faithful nurse who won't have holidays but we have to pay for it,' to which her husband, who would have enjoyed the funny side of life if he ever had time, said they were just as bad themselves and he was going to have on their tomb-stone Were Your Public Activities Really Necessary, at which his wife smiled dutifully and thought inside herself that there was no answer to that question.

'You know, Sally,' said Lord Pomfret, 'the real answer to that is No. If I fell down dead to-morrow the House of Lords and the County Council and the Lord Lieutenancy and the Towers would all go on, and if you fell down dead the Red Cross would go on and everything else. The Towers would be rather different of course, but nobody's death stops things suddenly. It would take the Black Death on a large scale to do that.'

Lady Pomfret said not even the Black Death, because even then England did go on.

'Pray God she will now,' said Lord Pomfret, who in spite of his natural shyness was one of the rare people who can say a prayer aloud without any self-consciousness. 'Is anyone else coming to-day?'

'Agnes if she can and Merry and Clarissa, I hope,' said Lady Pomfret, and then Eleanor came in by the side door having walked from the bus stop and Nannie brought the children in and consigned them to their parents, evidently expecting the worst results.

'How are you, Nannie?' said Eleanor.

'I don't complain, miss,' said Nannie, which was an appalling lie. 'I'm glad you've come, miss. Ludovic, have you got your clean pocket-handkerchief Nannie gave you?'

Lord Mellings felt in his knickerbocker pockets and shook his head.

'Well really, I don't know what Miss Grantly will think, I'm sure,' said Nannie.

'I've got *my* handkerchief,' said Giles in a virtuous voice and plunging a hand into each pocket he pulled out, as from a conjurer's hat, a succession of revolting handkerchiefs, each greyer than the last. 'You can have one, Ludo,' he added kindly.

'That's enough, Giles,' said Nannie. 'Where did you get those from?'

'From the laundry,' said Giles. 'It's no good having clean handkerchiefs because they always get dirty, so I got some dirty ones.'

'They won't get clean, silly,' said Emily, at which the grown-ups were ill-advised enough to laugh. Nannie did not reprove them, for she knew that grown-up people are beyond help or prayer. She took Giles's horrible handkerchiefs with one hand, gave him her own clean handkerchief with the other and went away, rigid with disapproval.

> '"The Wolf has gone to Devonsheer
> And won't be back for seven year,"'

said Emily. 'Story please, Eleanor.'

'Lunch please,' said Lord Pomfret which witticism was a great success with his family who were all as good as gold during the meal except when Emily tried, very unfairly, to take all the browned part off the mashed potatoes, and Giles blew into his father's beer to make a bird's nest, as he said, and sent froth all over the table, and Lord Mellings tried to drink out of the wrong side of his glass and nearly choked.

After lunch Eleanor volunteered to take the children for a walk, which was just what Lady Pomfret had hoped she would do. How exhausting a walk with three delightful, intelligent, active children can be, only their mothers and elder relations know. What with Emily hanging heavily on one arm and Giles on the other, hopping most of the time, Lord Mellings having a stone (whether real or imaginary Eleanor never knew) in his shoe every five minutes and having to have his shoelaces done up again for him, Giles wanting to go by the farm while Lord Mellings wanted to go by the stream, the older children demanding different stories while Giles told a long and very discursive story about a frog aloud to himself, Eleanor had seldom found an hour and a half so slow and so heavy and was very glad to see Lord Pomfret and Roddy Wicklow riding along the lane. Both these gentlemen very good-naturedly got off their horses and gave rides to Emily and Giles.

'Uncle Roddy,' said Lord Mellings presently.

'Well, old chap?' said Roddy.

'Does your horse like walking slowly?' said Lord Mellings.

Roddy said he didn't think the horse had any particular objection.

'Then I'll give him a treat,' said Lord Mellings. 'I'll let him walk, very very slowly.'

'Right, old fellow,' said Roddy. 'Come off, Giles, it's Ludo's turn now,' and he lifted Giles down and put Lord Mellings up.

'I think your horse would like you to hold him, Uncle Roddy,' said Lord Mellings, 'just in case I made him too fast and spoiled his treat,' so Roddy held the reins and kept the horse at a gentle pace.

'Ludovic is getting much braver,' said Eleanor to Lord Pomfret, who was leading his horse with Emily perched solidly on it.

'You were such a help to him,' said Lord Pomfret. 'He really began to pick up courage then. How is your brother getting on?'

Eleanor, who in her foolish innocence did not realise that it was one of Lord Pomfret's self-made, self-imposed duties to remember not only all the names and faces that came into his life but everything connected with them as far as he could, gave her host a long and highly uninteresting account of Tom's experiences at Adamsfield and how he had been to Rushwater to see cows with Emmy Graham.

'We were dreadfully sorry about Lady Emily,' she said. 'I don't think father and mother really knew her much, but everybody seemed to be so fond of her.'

'When people like Lady Emily die,' said Lord Pomfret, speaking his thoughts aloud, 'it is not only their loss that hits one, but there is the feeling that one is now in the front line. You won't know what that means for a long time, I hope,' he added kindly; so kindly that Eleanor was emboldened to ask if she could do anything to help him.

'Lady Pomfret did say something about a good job for me with the London Red Cross,' said Eleanor, 'but if I could do anything for *you* I'd much rather stay here. I mean to sort your papers, or absolutely *anything*.'

'Giles! Stop that at once!' said Lord Pomfret in a voice Eleanor had never heard. 'Hold the horse, Eleanor,' and he ran forward to Giles who had found a large branch of dead thorn-tree and had already given Roddy's horse a blow on the hindquarters. Luckily his arm was not strong enough to do much harm, but the horse had started. Roddy's hold on the reins was firm and Lord Mellings kept his seat.

'I only wanted to see if Uncle Roddy's horse would go faster,' said Giles in an aggrieved voice.

'If ever you hit a horse again I shall stop your riding,' said Lord Pomfret.

'And I'll wallop you,' said his Uncle Roddy. 'Come on, Ludo.'

'Silly boy!' said Emily contemptuously from her seat of vantage on her father's horse.

'I am sorry,' said Lord Pomfret coming back. 'Down you come, Emily. That's the end of rides now. If you will excuse us, Eleanor, we will go on,' and he and Roddy trotted away.

The rest of the walk was enlivened by a squabble between Emily and Giles during which Emily called her brother a simple Simon and he called her a bold-faced jig which Eleanor, being well-read, recognised as a quotation from a nursery rhyme; and by Lord Mellings boasting in a most conceited way of his own courage, so that Eleanor was heartily glad to be back at the Towers. Here to her surprise they were met by Nannie.

'I thought you were out for the afternoon, Nannie,' said Eleanor.

'I was, miss,' said Nurse, 'but when I got as far as the bridge I saw his lordship and Mr Wicklow riding down the lane and I said to myself there'd be trouble, so I came back. What did you do, Giles?'

'Nothing,' said Giles, looking at the landscape.

'Gentlemen don't tell fibs,' said Nannie.

'Giles isn't a gentleman,' said Emily, 'he's a common boy.'

'That's quite enough, Emily,' said Nannie. 'Come along now and get washed for tea.'

'Uncle Roddy's horse reared like anything when Giles hit him,' said Lord Mellings, 'but I kept on. Giles wouldn't have kept on.'

'I don't want to hear about horses or *anything*,' said Nannie, with fine nursery want of logic, 'and what Miss Grantly will think, I don't know. Now along you go,' and she herded her charges towards the nursery.

In the sitting-room Eleanor found Lady Pomfret with Miss Merriman and Clarissa and stopped short, wondering whether she was wanted.

'Mother sent you lots of love,' Clarissa was saying to Lady Pomfret. 'She did want to come, but father came down for the week-end and she was sure you wouldn't mind.'

'Of course I don't,' said Lady Pomfret. 'Come in, Eleanor. Miss Merriman you do know.'

'And we met, I think, at Mr Adams's garden party,' said Clarissa, with such grownupness as nearly made them all laugh, and then Lord Pomfret came in and they all had tea. They had barely finished when the children burst in, clamouring for their father and each demanding a different treat: Lord Mellings to pick raspberries, Lady Emily to climb the mulberry tree and the Honourable Giles to ride his pony very fast up and down the drive.

'We can't do them all,' said Lord Pomfret, 'so we will let Clarissa choose.'

'Fishing in the frog-pool,' said Clarissa promptly. 'Gran used to fish in the frog-pool when she lived here and she caught a minnow in a jam-jar and kept it in the nursery till it died.'

'Which is the frog-pool?' said Lord Pomfret.

'*Really!* Cousin Gillie,' said Clarissa. 'Don't you know?' But Lord Pomfret didn't, nor did his wife.

'Don't you know Mint River, or Blackbeetle Gate, or Marble Path?' said Clarissa, and not one of the party, grownup or child, had ever heard of them.

'Then I'll show you,' said Clarissa. 'We shall need some bread and some jam-jars, Cousin Sally. Could we, do you think?'

Lady Pomfret said there were some clean jam-jars in the kitchen waiting for bottling and Clarissa could take two.

'Come on, Ludovic,' said Clarissa. 'Please, Cousin Sally, will you all go to the kitchen garden and then Ludo and I will show you the way.'

The grown-ups looked on each other questioningly, but it was all a mystery to them, so they did as they were told and walked across the Italian garden and so by the green walks to the kitchen garden, where Clarissa and Lord Mellings were waiting, each carrying two jars. On the far side of the garden the ground sloped to a little stream almost overgrown by reeds and grasses, yellow with wild iris in early summer, blue with forget-me-nots. Clarissa led her party to the gate.

'This is Blackbeetle Gate,' she said. 'It is called Blackbeetle Gate because there was a dead blackbeetle here and a lot of ants eating it. Come on, Ludo.'

'The stream is higher,' said Lord Pomfret, 'since the rain.'

'It isn't a stream,' said Clarissa, 'it's Mint River,' and as they followed her along the bank of the rivulet, crushing the scented wild mint as they went, the reason for the name was obvious. Presently a clump of alder and willow blocked the path and it had to make a detour to get back to the stream which a few yards further on widened to a shallow, sandy-bottomed pool from whose depths the spring came stirring through the sand. Beyond the pool was a kind of rough stone grotto built against the little rise in the ground from below which the waters flowed.

'This is Frog-pool,' said Clarissa. 'That was Marble Path where we had to go round the trees.'

'I thought I knew the place pretty well,' said Lord Pomfret, 'but I never heard the name. I wonder if Uncle Giles's father meant to face the grotto with marble. It was the sort of thing he would have done. He always had Italian workmen about so old Hoare used to tell me when he was in a good temper, which wasn't often,' for Mr Hoare was old Lord Pomfret's agent and almost as old and ferocious as his master and not well-disposed towards young Mr Foster as the present Lord Pomfret then was.

Clarissa, who had been waiting with marked impatience for Lord Pomfret to come to the end of what he was saying, now saw her chance.

'Not that sort of marble,' she said in a patient voice. 'It was because Gran found a marble in the path; one of those ones with hundreds of coloured whirligigs inside them.'

'What do you mean?' said Lord Pomfret.

'Gran found a marble in the path,' said Clarissa patiently, as one who humours an idiot. 'She and old Uncle Giles when he was a little boy and Aunt Agnes that died invented all the names. Uncle Giles invented Blackbeetle Gate and Aunt Agnes invented Mint River and Gran invented Marble Path. We often used to talk about it,' she added, looking away into the past. 'She gave it to me,' and taking a handkerchief from her pocket Clarissa undid a knotted corner and showed them a marble with swirling spirals of many colours.

'And now,' she said, 'we'll fish in the frog-pond. Come on, Ludovic. Put some crumbs on the water and then when the minnows come up to eat them, catch one in a jam-jar. You said two, Cousin Sally, but I brought four. I hope it doesn't matter, but I thought we had better have one each.'

She sprinkled the bread and her three young cousins knelt on the edge of the little pool with her, ready to dip their jars. It all seemed very pleasant and amusing to Eleanor who rather wished she were young enough to do the same and was watching the minnows swirling upwards towards the crumbs so intently that she did not notice Miss Merriman walking hurriedly away. But the Pomfrets noticed her. Lord Pomfret looked at his wife and said, 'Had I better go?' She nodded and he went quickly after Miss Merriman, who had just passed the alder-clump at the other end of Marble Path.

'Merry,' he said, in his usual gentle voice.

Miss Merriman turned and Lord Pomfret took her in his arms.

'It's all right, Merry,' he said. 'I know, I know.'

'It was the marble,' said Miss Merriman, fighting against King Lear's *hysterica passio*, 'Lady Emily had it in a little box on her writing table. It suddenly made me think of her, of what we have lost. I am sorry, Lord Pomfret.'

'Poor Merry,' said Lord Pomfret compassionately. 'What you want is a good cry. We all need it. There can't ever be anyone like Cousin Emily again. But no need for me to tell you that. You know it better than I do.'

But Miss Merriman was not going to have a good cry, for it was part of her self-made unwritten code that one did not cry. One's duty in this world was to take care of the people who needed one. Old Lady Pomfret had needed her for many years. Lady Emily had needed her. Now she was not needed, for though Agnes had affectionately and seriously begged her to stay at Holdings, Agnes for all her sweetness and gentleness was perfectly capable of looking after herself, and Miss Merriman felt that if she were not needed by the class she had spent so much of her life in protecting and sheltering, there was little reason for her to be in the world at all.

'I don't want to bother you, Merry,' said Lord Pomfret with great courage, for Merry's tears had made him acutely unhappy and also for no reason at all had given him a feeling of guilt, 'but may I talk to you about something else for a moment? I think Sally did speak to you about it last year at Rushwater, when Martin had the party for Cousin Emily's birthday. We do need you at the Towers, Merry. Sally said perhaps you would come back here when Cousin Emily didn't need you. She doesn't need any of us now. I wish to goodness she did. Could you bear to come here? It's not very comfortable now, but we do our best and if you knew what muddles I get into in the estate room you would be almost sorry for me. And Sally is doing far more than she ought, but someone has to do it.'

Miss Merriman was now, except for a slight pinkness about the eyes, her own quiet, competent, undemonstrative self.

'I shall be glad to do anything I can for you and Lady Pomfret,' she said. 'Whenever you like.'

'Whenever you and Agnes like,' said Lord Pomfret. 'Bless you, Merry. I feel I could almost tackle the Bishop now. How pleased Sally will be. And so will old Wheeler. He's past work now but he said to me the other day that if Miss Merriman came back to the Towers he would clean her bedroom chimney himself as none of them young fellows knew what a proper job of work was like.'

'I must go and see Wheeler,' said Miss Merriman. 'Does his own chimney still catch fire in the winter?'

'With unfailing regularity,' said Lord Pomfret. 'He holds with the gentry having their chimneys swept because it supports chimney sweepers, but he doesn't hold with it for himself because it stands to reason a good bundle of flaming newspaper clears the flues as soon as spit in your eye. I believe he'd put a goose up the chimney if it weren't that there aren't any. All his were stolen by Black Marketers in a car just before Michaelmas last year and he won't start again.'

Most of Lord Pomfret's friends would have been surprised to hear him talking in so very unserious a way and indeed it was but seldom that he let himself go to such an extent, but Merry needed helping. Whether Miss Merriman knew what was in his mind we cannot say, but we think that she was so ashamed by her late outburst that for the moment she could not think at all and was thankful for any kind of help, an article which she hardly ever recognised or accepted.

'I had an idea that Miss Grantly might be of some use to you,' said Miss Merriman.

'Eleanor? Good gracious, no,' said Lord Pomfret. 'She is a nice girl and splendid with the children and Sally finds her most useful in the office, but it would drive us both mad to have her living here. And in any case I understand she is taking some job in London. Something to do with the Red Cross I think. No, Merry. You are the only person that would fit in here. Let's see if they have caught any minnows.'

The minnow-fishing had been very successful. At least not from the point of view of catching any, but we believe that the true fisherman finds a catch, except for the very legitimate purpose of boasting, an almost unnecessary adjunct to the pleasure of the game. And by the frog-pool there was pleasure in plenty. Clarissa had caught and lost again one minnow and the front of her dress was soaked. Lord Mellings had caught three, boasted horribly about them, and then let them go in an access of humanitarianism. Lady Emily and the Honourable Giles had lost interest and were indulging in that ever delightful and romantic pastime of making harbours and canals at the edge of the pool and were damp and mud-spattered from head to foot. Lady Pomfret and Eleanor were talking about the Hospital Libraries and how nice it was for Tom to be working with Lucy Marling and studying cows at Rushwater, and as Lord Pomfret and Miss Merriman debouched from Marble Path they thought they had seldom beheld a more charming English scene of rural life.

'Good gracious,' said Eleanor suddenly. 'I ought to go or I'll miss the Barchester bus and then I'll miss the Edgewood bus too. They don't run so many on Sunday, just to help.'

'They wouldn't,' said Lady Pomfret. 'They don't care for anyone's comfort, let alone Their people who come off even worse than we do.'

Miss Merriman said in her pleasant quiet voice that she had the Holdings car and could drop Miss Grantly at the bus stop in Barchester if that would help, which Eleanor gratefully accepted.

Lady Pomfret then summoned her flock to come home and after the regulation protest of 'Oh, *need* we, mother?' they left their aquatic and paludian diversions.

'What are you going to do with your minnow?' Lady Emily Foster asked Clarissa.

'Send it home again,' said Clarissa, emptying her jam-jar into the pond.

'I thought you were going to eat it,' said the Honourable Giles in an aggrieved voice.

'"Yin, twa, three,
My mither caught a flea.
She roastit it and toastit it
And had it to her tea,"'

said Lord Mellings.

'Where on earth did you learn that?' said his father.

'Angus told it me when we were in Scotland,' said Lord

Mellings. 'And when I told it to Aunt Catriona she laughed like anything,' for Lady Ellangowan, who had not married Admiral Hornby R.N. when he was only a Captain, was one of the many Pomfret connections and very loyal to her family for the shooting season.

Lord Pomfret laughed and said he must tell Ellangowan to look after his keepers, and they retraced their steps by Marble Path, Mint River and Blackbeetle Gate, through the kitchen garden, along the green walks, in and out of the low box hedges of the Italian garden to the house.

'You needn't go for a quarter of an hour,' said Lady Pomfret to Miss Merriman. 'Let's sit on the terrace. Gillie, where are those old photographs of your Aunt Edith that we found in the housekeeper's room? I want to show them to Merry.'

Lord Pomfret thought they were in one of the drawers of his wife's writing table and they went indoors to look. The children had gone up to the nursery and Miss Merriman was talking to Clarissa. Eleanor did not wish to appear to be listening, so she sat down on a chair outside the sitting-room window.

'Here it is,' said Lord Pomfret's voice. 'I knew it was somewhere. By the way, Sally, it's all right about Merry, bless her. She will come whenever it suits you and Agnes.'

'Thank God,' said Lady Pomfret with real fervour. 'I was afraid she mightn't want to. I could have asked Eleanor to stopgap, but it might have been difficult.'

'It might,' said Lord Pomfret's quiet, tired voice. 'I have a horrid feeling, Sally, that I appear romantic to her, which is a great pity, because I like her.'

'I thought so too,' said Lady Pomfret's voice. 'Why people fall for you I cannot imagine. If they knew you as well as I do I could understand it.'

'It's because I look as if I didn't have enough to eat and am of an interesting pallor,' said Lord Pomfret. 'Still, now Merry can come we needn't worry.'

And that, thought Eleanor, frozen to her chair with shame and mortification, was that. Then good manners bade her move quickly lest her hosts should guess she had been near the window and be embarrassed, so she walked along the terrace and looked over the Italian garden which might as well have been the drop scene at a pantomime for all the reality it had to her. Hot with shame and cold with misery she did not know which way to turn, her whole mind being for the moment concentrated on keeping her involuntary eavesdropping a secret. Which led her to the unpleasant fact that it had not been wholly involuntary. If one hears oneself being discussed honour bids one flee to the farthest pole or, failing a pole, to knock over a chair, or cough, or do something to show that one is there. She had not been honourable and her punishment had been swift and we think undeserved. Now, if she did really like Lord Pomfret, was the time to prove it by holding her peace; the galling part being that no one would ever know how noble she had been. It did not occur to her at the moment that her silence would also have the advantage that no one could know how silly she had been, neither did she think for one moment that either of her hosts would betray her foolish secret of which she was so heartily ashamed. And in this she was of course right, for not only were the Pomfrets much too kind to say anything about it, but the whole thing was of so little importance that they had already forgotten all about it and were laughing with Miss Merriman over photographs of a shooting party at the Towers in the early nineties with His Royal Highness in an Inverness cape smoking a huge cigar, two Royal Princesses suitably attired for following the guns in long tweed skirts, feather boas and high-perched toques, the late Lord Pomfret looking like a low-class keeper, his sister Lady Agnes in a long mackintosh buttoned all the way down with her pug in her arms and his younger sister Lady Emily managing to look enchanting in spite of any fashion.

'There was something about jackets that buttoned right up to one's throat that made men look incredible cads,' said Lord Pomfret. 'Where are you, Eleanor? Come and look at Uncle Giles.'

Eleanor came in by the french window, looked at the group, and said Lord Pomfret looked exactly like Lord Welter.

'Welter?' said Lord Pomfret. 'Is he one of those new peers?'

Lady Pomfret said he couldn't be with a simple name like that.

'Ravenshoe,' said Eleanor, to explain.

But the name was unknown to her hearers who turned the page to look at little Lord Mellings, he whose death on the North-West Frontier had eventually brought the title to Gillie Foster, sitting in a donkey-cart driven by his nurse who wore a tight-waisted jacket with puffed sleeves, a straw boater and a veil which was screwed round and tucked in under her chin.

'Come and see the rest another day,' said Lord Pomfret. 'You ought to be going now.'

Good-byes were said and Miss Merriman took Clarissa and Eleanor on board and drove away. At the bus stop near Barley Street she pulled up. Eleanor got out, thanked her and said good-bye to Clarissa. The car sped away and she took her place in the queue for the Edgewood bus, already far too long. In its own good time, which was twelve minutes late, the bus came up. After a good deal of pushing and a certain amount of cheating four passengers were taken on board and the rest left stranded.

The queue then all talked at once, saying they had been there first; what things were coming to when people shoved in front at the last moment I really don't know; foreigners, that's what it was; I'll have something to say to that conductor next time I'm on his bus; it's all the Minister of Transport whoever he is; might as well be in Russia; look at those Russians the way they won't let those poor women come to their husbands I'd tell old Staylin what I thought of him if I was them; well, if jam does go off points I'll tell you for why, because They've got more jam than They know what to do with and not first quality neither you mark my word; and you mark *my* word what They put in your pocket with the one hand as the saying is They take out with the other and you'll find syrup will go up on points. With all of which comments and many more Eleanor would have at any other time agreed heartily, but just now felt too unhappy to care and would not even have minded being offered tinned pilchards. It was a choice between going to the Deanery, asking for hospitality, and coming back for the next bus with a good chance of not getting a place, or staying where she was in case a rumour of a relief bus turned out to be true. Both alternatives seemed to her highly repugnant.

At this moment Lydia's elder brother Robert Keith, of whom we do not know very much because although a very successful solicitor and very nice he was so dull, and had been made even duller by his nice wife, sister to the Fairweathers who had married Rose and Geraldine Birkett, formerly Head Girl, or to put it in Miss Pettinger's own beautiful words, Girl of Honour of Barchester High School and still a keen hockey player. And in company with Robert Keith was his younger brother Colin for whom Robert felt, apart from his strong brotherly affection, the mingled envy and contempt which any good provincial solicitor may be allowed to feel for a brother provincial who has done very well at the bar.

'Hullo,' said Colin, forgetting that he had forsworn Eleanor for ever only three days previously. 'You know Eleanor Grantly, Robert.'

Robert said he knew her father at the County Club and hoped he was well.

'Very well, thank you,' said Eleanor, 'I'm waiting for the Edgewood bus.'

'You've missed it, I'm afraid,' said Robert Keith.

'I know I have,' said Eleanor. 'At least I didn't miss it, but I couldn't get on. They say a relief may be coming.'

One may have forsworn a lady's company three days previously, but if one finds her in distress three days later, the merest common politeness dictates an offer of help.

'I've got my car,' said Colin, 'and as for petrol, never ask me whose. I'll run you back.'

'Oh, thank you awfully,' said Eleanor. 'Oh, will you have enough to get home yourself?'

Colin with sad lack of chivalry said he wouldn't have offered if he hadn't.

The evening seemed much more agreeable than five minutes ago. If one had been rather silly about Lord Pomfret, well everyone was bound to be silly about something and in its own good time one's subconscious self, or whatever it was, would put layers of mother of pearl over the grit, leaving one with a rather beautiful and romantic memory instead of just feeling ashamed and mortified. Eleanor's parents were quite pleased to see Colin and asked him to stay to supper.

'I may tell you,' said Mrs Grantly, 'that it isn't spam and bread and marge and ration cheese, because Edna and Doris don't hold with cold meals for themselves or their children. As far as I know, only I seldom do because Edna never cooks what she says she is going to cook, it is a kind of hot-pot of chicken. Or do I mean hotch-potch?' she added, looking to Colin as a lawyer.

Colin said it was hotch potch in law and was one of the things that made legal phraseology so like nursery rhymes.

Mr Grantly said this point was new to him and interesting. Would Colin explain.

Had Mr Grantly, said Colin, got a Mother Goose.

'Of course we have,' said Eleanor. 'What do you take us for?'

'Fine upholders of our best literary traditions,' said Colin. 'But you never know. Mrs Brandon, whom I adore, has never possessed one and must be classed, I regret to say, as illiterate.'

Eleanor took a copy of Mother Goose from a bookshelf and gave it to Colin who fingered the pages expertly.

'This is quite a good example,' he said and read aloud in a reverent voice,

> '"As I went through my houter, touter,
> Houter, touter, verly;
> I see one Mr Higmagige
> Come over the hill of Parley,
>
> But if I had my early, verly,
> Carly, verly, verly;
> I would have bine met with Higmagige
> Come over the hill of Parley,"

and anything more like the wording of some legal documents I could not wish to see,' he added.

'You cannot,' said the Rector, taking or rather almost snatching the book from his guest, 'claim Mother Goose entirely for your profession, Colin. She was well read in history and hagiography. Where is it? Yes, I have it. Look at this footnote on Old King Cole, whom she describes as having reigned in England in the third century A.D. and being the father of St Helena. I daresay she was right.'

'But she wasn't always truthful,' said Eleanor, wresting the book with unfilial violence from her father. 'She says,

> "Go to bed first, a golden purse,
> Go to bed second, a golden pheasant,
> Go to bed third, a golden bird,"

and I know it isn't true, because I tried them all when I was little.'

Tom said better not ask what folk poems meant because it was always something quite awful.

'I know,' said Grace. 'Like the Bible, only most of that's pretty clear. I mean Sodom and Gomorrah and things like that.'

Her brother Henry, who was still young enough to be nervous about his family in public, said to Grace to shut up, and the chicken hot-pot announcing itself stopped one of the aimless quarrels in which, though conducted without rancour, their parents felt their younger children indulged far too often.

After supper during which Tom had given to anyone who didn't much want to listen some valuable information about potato clamps, Colin said he really ought to be getting home, on hearing which words Grace hung upon his arm with all her not inconsiderable weight and said he mustn't.

'In that case,' said Colin, unwinding her from him and getting on the other side of Henry, 'I certainly won't.'

Mrs Grantly said to Grace That was quite enough and why, she added, didn't they all go to the coppice and see if the Bank Holiday trippers had done more harm than usual to the old oak, as they usually did.

'There I recognise the authentic Voice of Authority,' said Colin. 'Just like Nannie when we were small and she told us to run away and draw or chalk or something. I am all for seeing an old oak.'

This might have sounded impertinent from a guest to a hostess who could at a pinch have been his mother, but Mrs Grantly quite realised that Colin was on her side and merely wished to deliver her and her husband from the monstrous regiment of the next generation, so she smiled at him in a kindly way and Colin suddenly felt quite sentimental and as if he were a schoolboy at Northbridge Manor again, with his mother glad to get rid of her adored younger son.

Those of our readers who skipped the first few pages of this book to see if anything more interesting was going to happen, may not remember that in the remains of what used to be Chaldicotes Chase there was one very old oak, half its trunk rotted or burnt away (not without the aid of children, tramps and trippers) and gaunt silvery branches sticking up like antlers among the few green boughs. The Rectory children had always believed it to be the identical oak under which Anne Page met Master Fenton and Falstaff was bewitched, and still held to the tradition though geography proved it baseless.

The drive from Barchester to Edgewood had been so pleasant, the supper so friendly and easy that Eleanor looked forward to their walk to the oak, but she had not reckoned with her sister Grace who in her usual artless and boring way began to attach herself to Colin, or rather to any portion of him that was handy, for, as Colin remarked, so long as she was hanging onto something she didn't seem to notice what it was.

'No, Grace,' he said, as that young woman pushed herself up against him. 'Certainly not. I am going to walk with Eleanor and discuss housekeepers. I think she might find one for me.'

'Race you to the oak, wish you'll die if you don't,' said Henry, using a formula consecrated by nursery tradition, which made it a point of honour for the person addressed to do what was asked at once, however difficult or dangerous. Grace at once responded and pushing past Colin with considerable violence sped along the grass walk after Henry, who was making straight for the end of the ha-ha. The three elders walked more calmly through the kitchen garden, at the far end of which was a wooden door opening upon the coppice. When they came to the door Tom stopped and looked at the fig tree which grew along the wall.

'Lord!' he said, 'the wasps are at the figs already. Do you mind if I go back and get my bags?' and he went quickly towards the tool shed.

'He doesn't mean trousers,' said Eleanor. 'Mother always makes a lot of muslin bags to put the figs in when they are getting ripe. We've had to use the old ones for ages, but luckily when Tom came back from India he brought some hideous India muslin for a present, so she has been cutting it up. We thought Tom might mind, but he has become so horticultural that he was quite pleased. Do you think he will be really good on the land, Colin?'

As she spoke she unlocked the wooden door and they went out. Before them lay a strip of rough meadow land where a few ponies and donkeys were grazing and beyond it the last remains of the great hunting forest, a little wood or coppice of mixed timber, the old oak raising its grey antlers above the other trees.

'Gypsies,' said Eleanor. 'They usually come about harvest time. They've got their caravans over there. Father christens all the last-year babies and Edna and Doris get their fortunes told, so they don't steal our stuff. This way.'

She led him by a path through a blackberry hedge and among the undergrowth for a hundred yards to where the old oak stood in a small and rather shabby clearing, littered with paper and tins.

'Beasts!' said Eleanor.

'I have always maintained,' said Colin, 'that printing was the first step towards decivilization. If it hadn't been for Gutenberg or whoever it was we wouldn't see these sights. But all the same it is very lovely and makes me feel romantic about it.'

As he spoke he was looking at Eleanor, though not with any special meaning, and to his surprise she turned red in the face and looked unhappy. Was she afraid that the romance was for her? This time he was going to get to the bottom of things.

'That's the hole,' said Eleanor in an uncertain voice, 'where people used to put messages in the oak. They say that if you write what you want and put it in the hole and shut your eyes the time it takes to say the Lord's prayer backwards, you will get it.'

'I don't think I could say it backwards,' said Colin. 'It would take a great deal of practice. And anyway I wouldn't like to. Did I say anything to annoy you, Eleanor?'

'No, no,' said Eleanor. 'It was only that something made me think of something,' and her eyes looked damp.

'Well, you'd better tell me,' said Colin. 'Probably I can make it better,' which nursery expression made her laugh through her hardly repressed tears.

'It's nothing to tell,' said Eleanor. 'Only you said about being romantic and something rather awful happened at the Towers which was rather my fault and I ought to have said I was there and then I wouldn't have heard.'

'That,' said Colin patiently, 'makes it all perfectly clear. Listen, Eleanor. I have got you alone and propose to make the best of my opportunities, Tom is being horticultural and I should think Henry and Grace are having an all-in unarmed combat in the ha-ha. I still require a housekeeper-receptionist. Any comments?'

'Do you mean me?' said Eleanor, blowing her nose most unromantically.

'I do,' said Colin, 'as well you know.'

'Would you want anything else?' said Eleanor.

'Certainly. A wife,' said Colin.

He took out a pocket book, tore a page from it, wrote something in it and pushed it into the hole. He then shut his eyes and repeated the first four stanzas of Horatius.

'I am more an antique Roman than a Dane,' he explained, 'and I think I have given it time to work. What do I do now? No, I don't want any kettle mending, or bawlor drabbing, or dukkerin telling, thank you,' which unexpected words were addressed to a gypsy who had silently approached them.

'You remember Jasper, young lady,' said the gypsy. 'You saw the little lord was frightened of the gypsy's pony and you found the words to take the fear out of the little lord. Jasper knows you did. And Jasper knows what the handsome gentleman has put on the paper.'

This sudden irruption of pure Romany Rye into an already overcharged atmosphere was almost too much for Eleanor, who felt she would either cry or have unseemly giggles in a moment.

'Look here,' said Colin, 'if I cross your hand with silver, will you go away? Six and sixpence is the best I can do,' he added, looking through his loose change.

'If the handsome gentleman writes on paper he will cross Jasper's hand with paper,' said the gypsy.

'I haven't got a cheque-book with me,' said Colin, 'but if ten shillings will meet the case it will be cheap at the price.'

'What you wished you have wrote; what you have wrote you will get,' said Jasper, accepting the ten-shilling note. 'And now Jasper will give the letter to the lady that knew the words to take the fear out of the little lord,' with which words he took Colin's paper from the oak, gave it to Eleanor, and with a look of secret amusement vanished among the undergrowth.

'Good lord, what a marvellous impostor,' said Colin. 'Give it to me, darling.'

'I won't,' said Eleanor, rapidly retreating a pace and opening the letter. 'I mean I will,' she added.

'Do you mean you will give me the letter?' said Colin.

'Of course not,' said Eleanor. 'I mean I will marry you if you really mean it.'

'Really mean it,' said Colin indignantly. 'Haven't I been asking you for at least a month, not counting the fortnight I was away, and you ask if I mean it. Come here, Charlotte, and I'll kiss yer,' and Eleanor, being as we know well read, took this invitation as it was given and if Jasper had been looking, which having got his ten shillings we do not think he was, he would have been quite justified in his prophecy.

'And now, no more nonsense about helping Lord Pomfret,' said Colin wondering how he could ever have been jealous of what so obviously could never have been.

'Poor Lord Pomfret,' said Eleanor, quite forgetting her misery and shame. 'He is always so tired. But the children are darlings.'

'Nothing to what ours will be,' said Colin firmly. 'How pleased Lydia will be. The one thing she has against me is that I am only an uncle. Now I shall be a husband and a father in due time. Would you mind being kissed again?'

'I say! You're engaged,' said Grace, who had just come up breathless after a prolonged tussle with Henry.

'Isn't it heavenly?' said Eleanor. 'Let's go home and tell mother and father,' so they walked back, Grace as a future sister-in-law hanging on Colin's arm even more heavily and affectionately than before. When they reached the Rectory they found Mr and Mrs Grantly doing some mild gardening outside the south front.

'Mr and Mrs John Browdie with the bridesmaid Miss Fanny Squeers, if you don't mind,' said Colin.

'I say, are you engaged?' said Henry. 'I'll come to the wedding only I hope my calling-up papers will have come and then of course I can't.'

15

Mr Adams had been away for ten days or more, during which time Lucy Marling worked very hard at Adamsfield and brought all her driving power to bear on Mr Spadger who, not without a grudging admiration for Lucy's determination, got out his plans. Word came through from Hogglestock, via the excellent secretary Miss Pickthorn, that Mr Adams said it was all O.K. about the permits and Miss Marling was to go full steam ahead.

'Though really, Miss Marling, it isn't the way I would put it as I am sure you will understand,' said Miss Pickthorn, 'but those were Mr Adams's words on the phone. Gentlemen have funny ideas sometimes,' to which Lucy replied that she quite understood and hoped Miss Pickthorn's mother was better. For among the many forms of blackmail that we have to pay not the least tiring is the pretence of taking an interest in other people's incredibly dull private affairs and remembering which is which. It all comes back to us in one way or another, but we sometimes wonder whether it is worth it.

'Oh, thank you, Miss Marling, mother is wonderfully better,' said Miss Pickthorn. 'I was only up with her three nights last week and if she does get a little touchy at times, well, as I was saying to Miss Cowshay in the Costing, it's hardly to be wondered at, poor old soul.'

'Well, I think you're splendid, Miss Pickthorn,' said Lucy, 'and I wish you and your mother were boiled in a pot,' she added when she had put the receiver up, for all occasions seemed to conspire against her and she felt very low. Her dear Oliver was making heavy weather of Jessica's marriage, though it did not prevent him seeing a great deal of her. He often stayed in town when he might have been down at Marling and Lucy missed him more than she chose to admit. Mr Adams had been away for nearly a fortnight. He had, it is true, left her a free hand to do as she thought best about the cowsheds and she felt certain he would trust her on a subject she knew and he didn't, but all the time she wondered if he had taken her advice about being careful over the permit as a hint that she distrusted his methods and for the first time in her life she slept badly. To Oliver whose nights were always broken this would not have seemed very dreadful, though boring, but to Lucy it was like a kind of bitter exile. But she was paid to do a job, so she gave herself a kind of angry shake and went on with it.

Under her ferocious supervision Tom Grantly was becoming quite useful, high praise from Lucy; and as Emmy turned up two or three times a week and Tom had been over to Rushwater every Sunday, his cow-education was making very good progress.

'I say,' said Emmy, who had brought her lunch with her and was sitting ungracefully on an upturned wheelbarrow, eating bacon sandwiches from a Rushwater pig, 'is it true about your sister getting engaged to Colin Keith? Mr Wickham told Martin at the Northbridge Flower Show.'

Tom said it was quite true and it would be in *The Times* the next day he supposed.

'She's jolly lucky,' said Emmy. 'They've got a very decent herd at Northbridge and Mr Wickham knows a bit about cows. I thought I'd give her one of Rushwater Churchill's calves when we get him going,' after which the conversation became too technical for our modest and ignorant pen to record it.

'Anyway,' said Lucy, 'a calf wouldn't be much use to her in London.'

'Good Lord! is she going to live in *London*?' said Emmy. 'How awful.'

'Well, she'll have to if Colin lives there,' said Tom.

'Catch me marrying anyone that lives in London,' said Emmy, wiping the bacon off her hands on a tuft of grass. 'I say, Tom, what do you think Martin is doing?'

'Not putting Parson's Corner under grass?' said Tom anxiously.

'No, we've stopped him doing that all right. It's about Macpherson's cottage. Dr Ford says he can't go on much longer,' said Emmy, who took a farmer's view of life and death as being merely the seasons of a greater year. 'So Martin said he and Sylvia wanted to give me a lease of the cottage for my own. I mean I'll have it like Macpherson does as long as I work at Rushwater. It's most awfully decent of them and as I'm always going to work for Rushwater it will suit me down to the ground. Of course I hope Macpherson won't die for ages, but if he did I'd get Conque to come and do for me. She cooks awfully well and she can go and quarrel with Mrs Siddon whenever she likes. I'll get father to let me have a couple of pigs and a horse from Holdings.'

Lucy, trampling on a slight feeling of envy for Emmy who was so young and was to have independence and pigs and a horse, congratulated her and said she would come over and have a look at the kitchen garden sometime, only not if Mr Macpherson minded.

'He won't mind,' said Emmy confidently. 'He thinks it's an awfully good idea and he's quite keen about dying. I think that's a good thing, because when people want to die they never do, like old Mrs Hubback. Probably he'll live for another twenty years now. Anyway it's all great fun, isn't it, Tom?'

Tom, roused from some train of thought, said it was splendid and he was frightfully glad, to which Emmy replied that if she was glad she'd sound gladder than that and Tom withdrew into what we hardly like to call the sulks and went back to his vegetables, of which the ladies took no notice at all, discussing the future arrangements of Emmy's bachelor establishment. Emmy then got up, gave her breeches a hitch and said she must be getting back, at which moment a car was heard and Mr Adams came into the farmyard accompanied by Sir Edmund Pridham. Lucy felt unaccountably sick, but she was not paid to have unaccountable feelings so she got up to welcome Sir Edmund who had known her people for more years than Lucy could remember.

'Well, young lady,' said Sir Edmund, giving Lucy the great-avuncular kiss which elderly gentlemen are far too apt to force upon even not very young ladies. 'Adams here tells me you're doing a fine job, so I said I'd come and look. Now, who are you?' he continued, looking at Emmy. 'No, stop, I know. You are Agnes Graham's girl. You're working at Rushwater. Sensible young woman. All these girls wanting office jobs. Pshaw,' he said, quite distinctly, to the joy of his younger hearers, 'if I had a girl I'd put her under a good farmer and then I'd buy a farm and let her have her head.'

'No you wouldn't, Sir Edmund,' said Lucy. 'You'd interfere all the time,' at which Sir Edmund, again to the great joy of his audience, slapped his riding breeches and laughed.

'I wouldn't interfere with *you*, young lady,' said Sir Edmund. 'How is that man of yours, the half wit?' in which description Lucy at once recognised Ed Pollett whom Sir Edmund had rescued from the army at the beginning of the war and quite rightly, for though the doctor who examined the men had passed him as A1 it quite escaped his notice that Ed, who had always been immune to education, was far below even the standard set by the B.B.C. in its broadcasts to the Forces. Had not Sir Edmund with the immense weight of his age and county authority intervened, Ed would probably have found himself almost at once in the Barsetshire Regiment, where he would certainly have become really insane through fright and homesickness.

'Hi! Ed!' said Lucy directing her powerful voice towards a shed from which Ed Pollett emerged and to the great joy of all his friends pulled his front hair to Sir Edmund, who enquired after his wife and family.

'Millie she's expecting again,' said Ed, 'and if it's a boy we're going to call him Adams,' at which news the wealthy ironmaster looked entirely at a loss probably for the first time in his life. 'And if it's a girl we're going to call her Beedle.'

'You mean Beetle,' said Sir Edmund. 'Not that I'd call a girl Beetle myself.'

'No, Sir Edmund, it's Beedle, Millie said, after young Beedle like.'

At this point Mr Adams, who had raised himself by sheer brains and doggedness and a trust in his own star from a poor labourer's boy to a rich ironmaster and Member of Parliament for Barchester, was entirely flummoxed, the more so as Sir Edmund burst into a laugh which would not have disgraced Sir Tunbelly Clumsy.

'Come on over here, Henry,' said Ed, speaking towards the shed, and young Henry Beedle came forward and gave a kind of military salute to Sir Edmund.

'Now I know you,' said Sir Edmund. 'Don't tell me. You're

young Beedle. Your father was station-master at Winter Overcotes till this lot of damned meddling old women and Welshmen and foreigners murdered the railways. How's your father?'

'Nicely, Sir Edmund,' said young Beedle. 'His heart's fair broke about The Line, but he's making a model railway in the garden and he's going to call it after Our Line, Sir Edmund.'

'You were in the Barsetshires,' said Sir Edmund. 'And a prisoner of war after Dunkirk.'

'That's right, Sir Edmund,' said young Beedle. 'And I worked on the land there. Miss Lucy she's a fine farmer, Sir Edmund. It's a pleasure to serve under her.'

At this moment Tom Grantly appeared from behind the barn carrying a large sack of vegetables which he put into the Ford van.

'Who are you, young man?' said Sir Edmund.

'It's Tom Grantly,' said Lucy. 'His father is—'

'Now stop a moment, young lady,' said Sir Edmund. 'Wait. I know. Your father is old Major Grantly's grandson and your mother was a daughter of old – I'll be forgetting my own name next, but you know whom I mean – he used to hunt three days a week over Gatherum way and understood barley. People don't understand barley nowadays. You working for Lucy?'

'Well it's really for Mr Adams,' said Lucy, who wished to be fair. 'He's quite good, Sir Edmund, and Emmy's showing him about cows.'

'Cows eh?' said Sir Edmund. 'Stoke's the man for cows.'

'Lord Stoke's all right,' said Emmy, her sun-burnt arms akimbo, 'but he doesn't do bulls. We've got a champion, Sir Edmund. Rushwater Churchill. Come and see him.'

'Churchill, eh?' said Sir Edmund. 'I thought all the Rushwater bulls had names beginning with R.'

'So they do,' said Emmy. 'But we called this one Churchill just to cheer Mr Churchill up after the General Election.'

'Quite right, quite right,' said Sir Edmund gravely and Tom said if that was the idea he hoped the 1950 bull calf would be Rushwater Attlee, at which there was dead silence till the joke went home and a kind of hum of applause rose from the party, except from Mr Adams who though he was sure they meant well was getting further and further out of his depth, and also felt slightly uneasy under his manager's gaze. This was an entirely new experience for him. By sheer force of character, good-natured determination, and ruthlessness when required he had come to be first in most places where he was known and even in the House was treated with a certain amount of deference by both sides; for nothing causes more alarm and anxiety to the Government whips, nor more pleasing anxiety to the Opposition whips than a man who forms his own opinions, knows his own mind and votes as he wishes. We do not imply that such men make the best politicians, but as Mr Adams had said to Mr Gresham, the member for East Barchester, you can't keep all the people guessing all the time, but you can make the front benches sit up and pay attention to you. But now, here, on land owned by him, financed by him, a position which he had never thought to reach and indeed had only reached by the chance of Miss Lucy Marling coming into his office at Hogglestock to ask his opinion of fertilisers, he found himself entirely out of it and as nought, while people who, except for Sir Edmund Pridham, were all young enough to be his children, talked a language he didn't quite understand and what was more gave him no loophole by which to get back into the conversation.

Lucy, we think, saw his perplexity and half of her was sorry for him, but the other half was almost glad to make him feel small; a double point of view which we may explain as we can, or wish.

'Great gormed fool,' said an unpleasant voice, and from behind a sunny wall came old Nandy, scenting possible advantage to himself, 'Putting cowsheds down the three-acre where it's been flooded every year since my old grandfather's grandfather lived at Adamsfield. Nice mucky cowsheds they'll be, and a fine fool old Spadger will look coming all the way from Winter Overcotes with his yardstick and all,' and old Mr Nandy cleared his throat horribly.

'What do you know about it, Nandy?' said Sir Edmund, who had known Mr Nandy from the bench for a great many years.

'Calls himself Adams,' said old Mr Nandy contemptuously, 'and doesn't know that Adamsfield's flooded every February. I've seen cattle drown there with their legs rotted off and their horns too.'

This sudden irruption of Cold Comfort Farm made everyone speechless, some with surprise, some with annoyance. Sir Edmund with great difficulty controlled himself, for old Nandy lived on Marling land though Mr Adams had bought the home of his disreputable putative ancestors, and he would no more dream of putting down a fellow landowner's man than he would have allowed any fellow landowner to put down a man of his. Mr Adams would have had no such scruples, but river floods were not in his line.

'That's all rot,' said the manager of Mr Adams's market garden, the future manager of his cows and pigs. 'There's never been a flood in the three-acre since father had that bend in the river altered just above Naunton Hatches and the river conservancy board dredged the bed and planted the willows along the right bank.'

'Are you sure?' said Mr Adams, quite humbly.

'Of course Lucy's sure,' said Sir Edmund. 'I've never known her anything else. But what's more she's right.'

Young Beedle said he dessaid Mr Nandy was thinking of the old days and who was the gormed fool now.

'You didn't had ought to talk like that, Henry,' said Ed reproachfully. 'My Millie she'd say something to you if you talked like that when the kids were about.'

'Well I'm off to the Hop Pole,' said old Mr Nandy spitting horribly, and with a malevolent look at the whole company he hobbled off muttering that they ordered these things better in Russia; or words to that effect.

'I must be off,' said Sir Edmund, looking at his large old-fashioned almost spherical watch. 'Can you drop me in Barchester, Adams?'

Possibly Mr Adams would like to have stayed and had a word with his manager. Possibly Lucy would have liked to have a talk with her employer and ease her mind of the weight that had been oppressing it. But Sir Edmund in virtue of his great age and long service to the county ranked in the county's estimation higher than the Lord Lieutenant and even Mr Adams had recognised this. So the two went away together while Lucy went back to her work in the office and Emmy helped Tom in a friendly way to load the rest of the vegetables.

'I say,' said Tom. 'I was glad *really*. It will be splendid for you to have a house of your own.'

'It's a pity you can't come as a lodger,' said Emmy. 'We could do an awful lot about the cows if we had more time to talk. Why don't you?'

To this offer, made with downright good faith, Tom did not know what to reply. To him it was obvious enough that he could not very well be a lodger with Sir Robert and Lady Graham's eldest daughter. It was also very obvious that Emmy's mind was free from any suspicion that such a thing would be unusual. Brought up in a large family with many friends she was apt to look upon anyone she liked as a kind of relation, and as she liked Tom and thought highly of him as a promising pupil, it seemed reasonable to her to extend hospitality to him. Tom's silence must have surprised her, for she was evidently reflecting upon it and her sunburned face assumed a hue rather like the sun through a fog and unconsciously she moved away from Tom, as if from something she did not quite understand and was not trying to understand.

'It's all right, Emmy,' said Tom. 'I'll come as lodger with Mrs Hubback and throw pebbles up at your window at three o'clock on a cold winter morning because the Jersey has had a Siamese calf.'

Emmy's face slowly reassumed its natural complexion and after a few words with Ed she drove away with a parting smile at Tom that left him not ill content. So Lucy went on with her work alone and dealt with all the forms and documents required and saw Tom about one thing and Ed about another and then went home. But her mind was uneasy. Mr Adams had come to Adamsfield. It was the first time she had seen him for nearly a fortnight, since the day when she had said over the telephone words she would have given anything to have unsaid, and he had made no attempt to talk to her. He did not seem to be angry, for she had once or twice seen him lose his temper, though never with her; but there was a perplexed feeling of unreality about everything that her downright nature could not bear. If he thought ill of her she must have it out with him. But she had not thought ill of him, so why should he think it. The result of her wearying, recurring self-tormenting was that she sent Henry Beedle and Ed away at their usual hour, told Tom not to wait unless he wanted to and did a tedious and tiring piece of work down in the water-meadows that there was no need for her to do. When she got home, just in time for dinner, her father said Mr Adams had rung up.

'What about?' said Lucy.

'Didn't ask,' said her father. 'I don't ask what people want. He wanted to speak to you I suppose.'

Suppressing an impulse to plunge the poultry carving knife, worn by long use to a very fine and slender blade, into her father's heart, she said was there any message.

'Message?' said her father. 'I don't know about messages. Adams said they were cleanin' out the old well in Miss Sowerby's garden to-morrow and he wants you to come over and see if they're doin' the work properly. There's only one man who understands wells and that's old Bodger over at Harefield and he's dead.'

'There's Percy Bodger,' said Lucy.

'I said he was dead,' said Mr Marling.

'I know you did,' said Lucy. 'But. His. Son. Percy. Bodger. Knows. About. Wells.'

'Percy Bodger? That's what Adams said,' said Mr Marling. 'Any time to-morrow afternoon, he said. I remember a man fell down a well on Pomfret's land, not this Pomfret, his uncle. No. He didn't *fall* down. He knocked his old uncle and aunt on the head with a billet and then threw himself down the well. Old Bodger helped to get him up. Tidden, that was his name. Horace Tidden, old Ned Tidden's son. His mother was a love-child. I believe she's still alive. Ford sees her in the County Asylum.'

But this interesting story, worthy of the late Reverend George

Crabbe, was hardly heard by Lucy whose whole mind was given to reflection on Mr Adams's message. He wanted her to see that Percy did his work properly, that was clear. But did he want her as her employer, or as the kind and friendly person she had come to know during the last year? She could not drive from her thoughts and her dreams the memory of their last telephone conversation and how abruptly it had ended. Had she offended him mortally? If so, why did he keep her on at the market garden? And the answer seemed to her to be that she was worth her pay and that was all. Through her own folly and over-zealousness she had lost the very happy and comfortable feeling that she used to have with her employer. It was all her own fault. But she would go to Edgewood. One didn't let one's employer down.

At the Old Bank House Mr Adams and his daughter Heather were talking about her wedding which was to take place as we know in Hogglestock. Clarissa had promised to do the flowers. The reception would be at the Hogglestock house and to that house Heather and her husband would return after the honeymoon; while Mr Adams would live at the Old Bank House and go in to work every day, or as many days as he thought necessary, for he was planning some alterations in his way of living, as he could now well afford to do.

'If it weren't for Ted I wouldn't get married at all, dad,' said Heather.

Her father said she probably wouldn't since, so far as he knew, no one else had asked her.

'You know I don't mean that, dad,' said Heather, seating herself on the arm of her father's chair, for they were in the back room behind the staircase and here Mr Adams had arranged solid comfort more than beauty. 'Ted's one of the best, in fact he's the very best, but I'm afraid you'll be lonely,' to which her father said she should have thought of that before and he would probably marry Miss Hoggett; and in any case what with the works and his other business commitments and Parliament he wouldn't have time to be lonely.

'Bodger is coming to clear the well to-morrow,' he said. 'Sooner he than I. I'd rather work in a Government office than go down a well. I suppose he knows his job. It's going to cost me a bit.'

'You'd better ask Lucy over, dad,' said Heather. 'She knows everything.'

'I wouldn't say that,' said Mr Adams, 'but what she does know she knows and that's more than you can say of most these days. I saw her at Adamsfield to-day. She looked a bit off colour. I expect she's been overdoing it. You girls are all alike, you get bitten by a thing and you don't know where to stop. I'll ring her up. It'll do her good to have a change. I'd go melancholy mad if I lived her life. Her father's a fine old gentleman but he'd try the patience of a saint. She ought to be among young people,' and he rang up the exchange and asked for the Marling Hall number.

Heather watching him thought how like daddy it was to call Lucy a girl, who must be quite thirty. Dear old dad, he always saw the best in everyone, which judgment would have very much surprised Mr Adams who rather flattered himself, and not without reason, on sizing any new acquaintance up pretty accurately and sheering off from those who were in any way doubtful. But Heather's thoughts were quickly recalled to the present by her father's voice trying to make Mr Marling hear on the telephone.

'I've done my best, girlie,' he said. 'But there's none so deaf as those who can't hear.'

Heather asked if Lucy were coming.

'I hope so,' said her father. 'I gave the old gentleman the message.'

'Why don't you ask Lucy to come here for a few days while Ted and I are on our honeymoon?' said Heather. 'It would be company for you and she could have a go at the kitchen garden. Miss Hoggett could chaperone you,' at which suggestion Mr Adams laughed good-humouredly and said he was old enough to do without a chaperone.

'So's Lucy,' said Heather, who although she treated Lucy as a contemporary secretly thought of her as what we can only describe as a semi-aunt. And then she settled herself to write letters, for presents had begun to come and she liked to acknowledge each one in an orderly way as soon as possible. Mr Adams did some telephoning and made notes of letters to be dictated next day, for he very rarely wrote a letter himself, giving as a reason the old and we must say very poor joke Do right and fear no man; don't write and fear no woman. Then he lit his pipe and thought about Heather and how Mother, for his wife was still always Mother to him, would have enjoyed the fuss and excitement, so that when Heather spoke she almost startled him.

'Penny for your thoughts, dad,' she said.

'I was thinking of Mother, Heth,' said her father. 'How she would have enjoyed your wedding, poor soul. And a poor little thing you were, Heth, and the trouble I had with housekeepers no one would credit not if I swore to it. She was only thirty when she died, or maybe a year older. It's funny how one forgets.'

'About as old as Lucy,' said Heather. 'Well, good-night, dad,' and she kissed her father affectionately and went upstairs.

Mr Adams re-lit his pipe and sat alone in the dusk thinking of the past and the lonely difficult years while he was building up the Hogglestock works and laying the foundation of his other businesses and keeping a sharp eye on the housekeepers that had charge of his motherless Heather; his decision at last to send Heather to the Hosiers' Girls' Foundation School and the meeting with the Beltons that had so altered and, he gratefully acknowledged, improved his life and Heather's. And now Heather was marrying Ted Pilward, a nice boy and almost good enough for her, and after all the years of trying to be father and mother to her he would again be alone. Still, there was always work to be done, especially if the Government were going to nationalize steel, and he had been making the best arrangements he could with this blow to industry in view.

'Mother would have understood,' he said half aloud. 'Only thirty, or thereabouts, poor soul. And Miss Marling must be about thirty. You're a lucky man, Sam Adams, to have that young woman working for you. Stainless steel right through and then some,' and he thought of his visit to Adamsfield that morning and how Lucy had seemed a little strange, a little remote. Perhaps it was that young Grantly. He was a nice lad and a hard worker, but not good enough for Miss Marling. However that was none of his business.

It is hardly necessary to say that Mr Percy Bodger's visit was looked forward to eagerly by the whole of Edgewood. How it had got about we cannot exactly say, but as Mrs Belton had rung up Lady Waring at Beliers Priory she may have mentioned among other county gossip that old Bodger the rat-catcher at Harefield had told her old maid Wheeler that his grandson Percy was going to clean Mr Adams's well at Edgewood. And if Miss Palmyra Phipps at the exchange had been listening, as she always did and was in consequence a mine of useful information besides being always ready to oblige anyone, the news would undoubtedly have percolated to such strategic points as other telephone exchanges and local post offices.

Henry Grantly, sauntering carelessly down the street for perhaps the two hundredth time since he had come home for the holidays and dropping in, much to his own surprise, at the post office to enquire whether there were any letters for him, found Mrs Goble of the Post Office at the telephone and tried to look as if he had only come in by mistake.

'Nice doings at the Old Bank House,' said Mrs Goble coming back behind the counter. 'Mr Adams he's having Percy Bodger over to clean the well. I don't hold with cleaning wells. You never know what you'll find. My old auntie she had twenty cats and she threw all the kittens down the well except the one, every time she did. And I never heard of no one coming to any harm.'

Henry said there might be buried treasure.

'If there'd been as much as the sniff of a brass farthing down that well old Mr Sowerby he'd have had it out,' said Mrs Goble. 'Old Miss Sowerby's father that was. He was as poor as a church mouse that's trying to live on the cheese ration. Gambled it all away he did, same as his uncle. They was a great gambling family the Sowerbys.'

Or Roman remains, said Henry, putting off in a cowardly way the moment when Mrs Goble would tell him that there were no letters for him. To which Mrs Goble replied that if Percy Bodger had any sense he'd leave them alone, nasty bits of brick and what not, same as you'd find anywhere.

'There was a lady came to lecture the Women's Institute about Roman remains,' said Mrs Goble, 'with slides, and all I can say is they looked as if old Hitler had been having a smack at them. If that's Roman remains, I said to my niece that was with me, I don't see the sense in building things all broken like that. Now,

Mr Henry, don't say you've come bothering about your young lady's letter again. Well, we're only young but once, and thank the Lord for it too,' said Mrs Goble piously, 'and the letters were late this morning so Bob hasn't taken them round yet. Nothing for you, Mr Henry. Only one of them nasty dirty-looking long honverlopes. The Taxes I'll be bound. And one more, but it's a gentleman's hand. Never you mind. She'll write some day.'

Henry, who had seen the magic letters O.H.M.S. on the buff envelope, said in as careless a voice as he could assume, though it sounded uncommonly like the first symptoms of a seizure, that he might as well take it and thank Mrs Goble awfully and stumbled into the street like Mrs Gamp in a kind of walking swoon. Instead of going straight home he went by a back way that came out at the far side of the churchyard. Here, screened by a friendly yew hedge, he opened the buff envelope and when his emotions allowed his eyes to work in connection with his brain he read that His Majesty, speaking through the typewriter of the War Office wished Henry Arabin Grantly to proceed to Sparrowhill Camp.

As Dean Swift, or rather Lord Sparkish speaking for him, says in his Polite Conversations, One Shoulder of Mutton drives down another. Having at last got his heart's desire Henry was for perhaps fifty-five seconds in pure bliss. After which it suddenly occurred to him that he might be kept in England for his term of service and never go abroad, which was his secret dream, which piece of self-tormenting so depressed him that he put the official letter back in its buff envelope and decided not to tell his parents for the present. Not that he had any particular objection to their knowing, nor did he despise nor mistrust them, but he felt that to have his deepest feelings exposed to the atmosphere of the home would be for the present more than a fellow could be expected to bear, with the not surprising result that his parents wished with all their hearts that Henry could be called up at once if he was going to behave like that at breakfast.

When Mr Adams had decided on Miss Sowerby's recommendation and the advice of his builders to have the well cleaned he naturally expected a good deal of mess for a day. But what he had not expected was the intense interest of the whole county, or at any rate of all those and they were numerous who had heard directly or indirectly of his undertaking. Miss Sowerby, who we are glad to say, was enjoying Worthing much more than she had expected as there was a very nice church round the corner with a clergyman who saw eye to eye with her about all proposed changes in the Prayer Book, had written to Mr Adams practically ordering him to provide transport for her to and from Edgewood, which Mr Adams had been delighted to do. The Grantlys all considered it a friendly action to go down and see what was happening, especially as there was a baseless rumour that the churchyard drained into the well and the Rector felt this rumour should be officially quashed. Though why quashed, he said to his wife, and not squashed, he did not know. Emmy, who had heard about it from Tom, decided to join the Grantly party, hoping we think to find either a dead calf with two heads or the original germ of contagious abortion, and Mr Wickham who had of course heard of it from Colin Keith via Eleanor said cleaning a well was thirsty work and he'd bring a dozen bottles of beer in case Bodger needed them. All of which was flattering to Mr Adams as showing a neighbourly spirit, but as he said to his daughter Heather it seemed a rum thing if a man couldn't clean his well without all his friends coming to look.

'It's all your fault, daddy,' said Heather. 'You would buy the Old Bank House and you've bought the people with it. It's the Old Bank House they're interested in, not you,' which may have been partly true, but most of the self-invited guests also liked Mr Adams.

The proceedings were opened soon after breakfast by the arrival of Percy Bodger and a labourer who was as far as anybody knew well over seventy and commonly alluded to as The Boy, in a very shaky old Ford from the back of which they extracted what looked like several hundred yards of rope and a kind of portable windlass.

'What about a ladder?' said Mr Adams, who had taken the whole Saturday off and was showing the deepest interest in the whole business. Percy Bodger replied that where there was a church there was a ladder and he dessaid the Reverend wouldn't mind his having a loan of it if it was wanted.

'Shall I ring him up and ask?' said Mr Adams.

'Don't you trouble trouble till trouble troubles you, sir,' said Percy Bodger in his pleasant, slow Wessex voice. 'Isn't likely a ladder'd be any use, not unless there was something to put it on, say a ledge or what not, inside the well. You leave it to me and my boy, sir, and you'll not go far wrong.'

'He means don't interfere, dad,' said Heather. 'Now you're a country gentleman you've got to learn your place.'

'Well, you can't make stainless steel out of pig-iron in a day,' said Mr Adams good-humouredly, 'and we live and learn. Did you tell Miss Hoggett, girlie?'

Heather said there was no need to tell her, as Miss Hoggett's mother's half-brother was a cousin of old Bodger the ratcatcher at Harefield and Miss Hoggett had been preparing refreshments for the kitchen on a serious and solid scale, to which Mr Adams replied that so long as Miss Hoggett looked after Heth and him she was welcome to feed all the Bodgers in Barsetshire and he would go and see what the men were doing. Accordingly he and Heather went into the garden and through a door in a brick wall into a kind of courtyard behind the old stables paved with moss and weed-covered cobblestones, in the middle of which was a well. A couple of rotting stumps, one on each side of the well, showed where once the roller for the rope had been, with its little wooden penthouse above it and its iron handle to lower or raise the bucket. The brickwork round the mouth of the well was in fairly good condition, and Percy Bodger was testing it carefully before he began his operations. At the sight of his employer his face became studiously vacant.

'Well, Bodger, how's it going?' said Mr Adams.

Percy Bodger said, very respectfully, that he couldn't tell how she was faring to shape, till he'd given her the works; by which mingling of the old and new style Mr Adams quite clearly understood two things; one that Percy Bodger was not going to commit himself to anything and the other that the less Percy Bodger saw of him, Mr Adams, during the early stages of the work, the better pleased he would be.

'You'd better leave him alone, dad,' said Heather. 'It's like you with a big casting. You'd be furious if anyone that wasn't on the job came to look at you. Ted's dad is just the same. Ted says he's fit to kill anyone when the vats are cooling. Come along, daddy.'

Recognising his daughter's superior wisdom and commonsense Mr Adams went back with her into the garden. To his horror he saw Miss Sowerby, whom he had not expected till the afternoon, coming down the path towards him.

'A surprise visit, Mr Adams,' said Miss Sowerby. 'I felt quite certain that Percy Bodger – it is Bodger who is doing the well,

I suppose. He is the only man who understands wells now that his father is dead – would not know about the drain from the churchyard, so I took the liberty of ringing your housekeeper up and asking her to have the car sent early, which she most obligingly did. I did not wish to disturb you, as I know how every moment is precious to business gentlemen. Where is Bodger?'

Had Mr Adams ever seen the Beggar's Opera he might have expressed his feelings by saying that he was bubbled and troubled, bamboozled and bit. He had thought that he owned the Old Bank House by right of purchase; but his well-expert had twice as good as told him to keep out of the way and now the former owner of the house, to whom he had paid a good round sum for it, had made free with his car and his chauffeur in a way that he would not have done with any business friend and what was more had descended upon him for, as far as he knew, the next twelve hours, for he felt convinced that even if Percy Bodger worked till ten o'clock that night, and it was warm weather and there was a full moon, Miss Sowerby would insist on watching him and telling him what he ought to do. And what was more, he felt it in his bones that Percy Bodger would pay attention to a penniless old lady and no attention at all, though in a very civil and unattackable way, to himself. And what made him even more uncomfortable was that his daughter had realised this before he did and had been trying to protect him against his own folly. Well, Heth had a head on her shoulders which was a good thing and at the moment Mr Adams was inclined to doubt whether he had a head on his shoulders, or indeed any status at all in his own house and garden except as the wage-payer. Now if only it had been Miss Marling he thought, in the few seconds during which Miss Sowerby was speaking, he would have felt safe. She never made a man feel he had done the wrong thing. Still, she was coming later and to this sheet anchor he must cling.

Thoughts are swift and all those thoughts had passed through Mr Adams's mind almost as Miss Sowerby spoke, but he gave his thoughts no tongue, nor any unproportioned thought his act, and with great self-restraint said he was pleased to see Miss Sowerby at any time and Percy Bodger was in the well yard if Miss Sowerby wanted to talk to him.

'Which I certainly do,' said Miss Sowerby and pursued her course towards the well yard, followed by Mr Adams who did not really wish to follow her at all, but did not wish to seem uncivil. Heather, who had been watching and listening quietly, said aloud to herself 'Poor daddy, he does need someone to look after him,' and went back to the house to go on with her thank letters.

'Good morning, Percy,' said Miss Sowerby, surveying the well and the workers through her face-à-main. 'How is your grandfather?'

Percy Bodger, touching his cap, said grandfather was fine and if he lived till Michaelmas he hoped to have killed near on fifteen thousand rats, at which figure even Miss Sowerby's calm was shaken.

'Grandfather he began ratting when he was ten year old with his father,' said Percy Bodger, 'and he's seventy-five come Michaelmas, and he reckons he's killed between two and three hundred rats every year. Some years they weren't so good and other years they were. There was the year Mr Pilward had them in the brewery, miss, grandfather reckoned he killed near on two hundred there. He says if he had five shillings for every rat he killed he wouldn't need no Old Age Pension, miss.'

'A very fine record,' said Miss Sowerby with an unconscious patronage which Percy Bodger accepted from her as a matter of course, though from say, Mr Adams, he would have mutely resented it. 'And now what are you doing, Percy?'

Percy Bodger said he and the Boy were trying the brickwork before he went down. It needed some repointing, he said, here and there, but it wasn't too bad, and could wait till the well was cleaned.

'Now, Percy,' said Miss Sowerby, taking a seat on a stone horse-block, 'do you know about the churchyard drain?'

Percy Bodger said he had heard his father say there was no one knew with them old churchyards where they drained into.

'I don't know either,' said Miss Sowerby. 'But my dear father, who disliked the Rector intensely, always said he was certain the drainage from the east side of the church came out somewhere on his property and it was probably into the well. I think we had better have this looked into, Mr Adams.'

Mr Adams, overawed as he had not been for a great many years, started nervously and said he supposed so, but who would really know.

Mr Grantly should, said Miss Sowerby, in a way that showed how poor her opinion of the Rector would be if he could not produce a half-inch map of the churchyard drains. 'Could you ring him up, Mr Adams?'

But Mr Adams did not need to do this, though he was by now ready to do anything Miss Sowerby commanded, as the Rector himself came into the yard.

'I heard you were here, Miss Sowerby,' said he, 'and felt I must come down and see you. I know our friend Adams will allow me to claim this privilege of an old friend.'

Mr Adams, who liked all the Grantlys, was about to say how glad he was to see the Rector, but Miss Sowerby as he said afterwards to Heather tanked right over him.

'It is a question of the churchyard drain,' said Miss Sowerby. 'My dear father was morally certain that the drainage from the east side came out into, or much too near our well.'

'Did he have the water tested?' said Mr Grantly.

'Certainly not,' said Miss Sowerby. 'We had always drunk the water. But since then a great many people have been buried, more than were ever buried before,' said Miss Sowerby, eyeing the Rector as if he were responsible for the deaths in his parish. 'Not that it really matters. If one corpse doesn't poison you, twenty won't. But if Percy finds the outlet of the drain it would be most desirable that steps should be taken.'

Mr Grantly, who felt his friendship for Miss Sowerby disintegrating in his hands, asked what steps.

'I do not know,' said Miss Sowerby.

Percy Bodger, who with the Boy had been rigging up the apparatus for going down the well, said his father said he'd sooner have three dead men in a well than one dead rat, but the rest of what he said was drowned in a loud clanking and roaring as of a very old Ford being pulled up short on its haunches outside and Mr Wickham came through from the stable yard into the well yard, carrying two large covered baskets which he set down on the cobbles.

'Good morning everyone,' he said comprehensively. 'I heard you were having the well cleaned, Adams, so I thought I'd drop in. I've given Percy a hand before now, haven't I, Percy?'

'That's right, sir,' said Percy Bodger. 'That was a nice day, sir, at Northbridge when Mrs Twicker's cat got down the well.'

'Poor Nanny Twicker, she was fit to bind,' said Mr Wickham. 'And how are you, Miss Sowerby?'

Miss Sowerby, who approved of Mr Wickham because his people were of good yeoman farmer stock on what used to be the Chaldicotes estate in her great-uncle's time, said she found Worthing quite bracing.

'But the real question at the moment,' she said, 'is whether the churchyard drains into the well, because if it does and my dear father always said it did, steps should be taken.'

'All in good order and one thing at a time,' said Mr Wickham. 'There's nothing makes a man so thirsty as going down a well, except a lot of other things, so I brought over a few bottles of beer,' and he opened his two panniers and exposed twelve quart bottles of beer in each.

'No offence, Adams,' said Mr Wickham. 'What about you, Miss Sowerby? Adams, you'll join us, and the Rector?'

As no one refused, nor indeed did Mr Wickham leave them time to do so, he took four tin mugs out of the pockets of his shooting coat, filled them and passed them round. He then gave a bottle each to Percy Bodger and the Boy and saying, 'More and better corpses in the well' drank his mug off in one breath.

Mr Adams, who now knew that he had gone mad and was rather enjoying the sensation, pledged the health with great good-humour.

'I've seen nothing like this since there was that row at a political meeting before the General Election and my Works Choir sang Annie Laurie in parts,' said Mr Adams.

'And now, what's all this about churchyard drains?' said Mr Wickham. 'You first, Rector. They're your drains.'

'And it was my dear father's well,' said Miss Sowerby rebelliously.

'Unfortunately,' said Mr Grantly, ignoring Miss Sowerby's remark, 'I cannot lay my hands on the plan of the drains. I know my predecessor had them, for he specifically mentioned them to me when I first came here. He said he had lent them for some kind of survey of this part of the county and I was under the impression that they were back in the church, but they are not. And I know they are not in the Rectory. It is most awkward.'

Miss Sowerby said nothing, but her silence was of a quality which showed all too plainly her opinion of Rectors and of Rectors' predecessors who were such careless shepherds.

Even Mr Wickham noticed that something was wrong and favoured Mr Adams with a wink. To this sign of friendship Mr Adams did not respond in kind, but his eyes met Mr Wickham's and both men felt the better for it. Then, and not a moment too soon, Heather Adams came into the yard with Lucy Marling in breeches and a bright blue short-sleeved shirt, her face very hot and red through its brown.

'Hullo, Mr Adams,' said Lucy. 'Oh, hullo Miss Sowerby and everyone. I'm sorry I'm late. I had to go to Barchester first.'

'Market day?' said Mr Adams.

'Really, dad! You ought to know Saturday isn't market day by now,' said Heather affectionately.

'You're right, girlie,' said Mr Adams. 'Your old dad ought to know, but what with wells and drains and one thing and another, he wasn't using his brains. And now Miss Marling's here we'll get on a bit.'

'It was those drains you said about,' said Lucy to her employer. 'I knew I'd heard something about the church drains only I couldn't remember what it was till I saw Octavia Needham and she was talking about her father writing something about the parish of Edgewood for something or other. So I went to the Deanery and Dr Crawley was awfully pleased because the cesspool under the Palace isn't finished yet and the Bishop says he can't stay away any longer so Dr Crawley hoped he and the Bishopess would get spotted fever and die, so I asked about

Edgewood and he said he ought to have sent the map back to you ages ago, Mr Grantly, only he forgot. So I said I'd take it. I hope it's all right.'

As she finished speaking she pulled an envelope out of her breeches pocket and gave it to the Rector, who opened it and examined it with great interest and obviously growing perplexity.

'Is it what you wanted?' said Lucy.

'Exactly,' said the Rector, 'only I don't quite understand it. Here is the churchyard and I suppose that red line is the drain, but I can't make out where it goes.'

'Into my father's well,' said Miss Sowerby, speaking to an unseen hearer a few feet above the level of her friends' heads.

'Not into the Old Bank House well,' said the Rector at the same moment.

'Let's take our bearings,' said Mr Wickham, looking over the Rector's shoulder. 'There you are, Grantly. Down the east side of the churchyard, under the village street and south east into what was the recreation ground.'

'It is allotments now,' said the Rector.

'All the better,' said Mr Wickham. 'Make the potatoes fatten. So that's that.'

'But,' said Miss Sowerby, who unable to resist her curiosity had got up and was looking over the map which the Rector held, 'it goes straight across the allotments as far as the middle and then it stops. Where did it go next?'

Mr Wickham, rather tired of lay ignorance, said it just didn't.

'Cesspool,' he added. 'Same as under the Palace and good luck to it. So everybody's right and nobody's wrong and now Percy, you'd better get on a bit, or we'll all be here till dinnertime. More beer, anyone? Then we'll shut the bar for the present. Help yourself Percy when you feel like it and give the Boy some. I've booked a table at the Chaldicote Arms. May I have the honour of giving you lunch, Miss Sowerby?'

'Thank you, Mr Wickham, I should be delighted,' said Miss Sowerby. 'And afterwards, Mr Adams, if you will be so kind, I should like to go back to Worthing. I am an old woman and a stupid one. I thought I could manage a whole day's outing, but I can't.'

Mr Adams said she must say when she wanted the car and it would be at her disposal, and to tell the truth was rather relieved, for he felt that nothing would be safe from her inquisitorial eye and she might in an excess of zeal require him to rip up all the floor boards to look for rats and he would not be able to refuse.

'Half past one then, if it is convenient and many thanks for your kindness,' said Miss Sowerby and was turning to leave when Mrs Grantly came into the yard.

'I heard you were at the Post Office,' said Mrs Grantly to Miss Sowerby, 'and I came along at once. Oh, Mr Adams, how are you, and Mr Wickham. Please excuse this interruption, but I thought Miss Sowerby ought to know Palafox Borealis is coming into flower, so we ought to have some seeds this autumn.'

'I thought it would when I saw it in your kitchen,' said Miss Sowerby. 'Warmth and companionship were what it needed. Well, we all need them. This will be most annoying to Victoria Norton and I wouldn't mind now if I dropped down dead on the spot. Don't forget to let the Secretary of the Royal Horticultural know. Good-bye, Mr Adams. Remember, the Old Bank House must have a mistress. I think I will go now, Mr Wickham, if you will be so good,' and taking Mr Wickham's arm she made a stately exit.

'And a very fine old lady,' said Mr Adams when the wooden door had shut behind her. 'But a Tartar. I shan't be sorry to have lunch myself. And you will have it with Heth and me I hope, Miss Marling.'

Lucy said she thanked him awfully, but she had brought sandwiches with her so that she could give Percy Bodger a hand and Emmy Graham was coming to join her.

'I say, you won't mind or anything?' she added.

Mr Adams said he would like Miss Marling to feel exactly as she would at home and if she would excuse him he would come back again later. Heather looked from one to the other, not unkindly, but said nothing and went away with her father.

Shortly afterwards Emmy turned up, escorted by Tom Grantly. Freed from the presence of the older gentry Percy Bodger became delightfully communicative about what he had found in wells, including the whole story of the rescue of Horace Tidden's body and what it looked like, and warmed by the sound of his own voice and Mr Wickham's beer, consented to let Lucy, Emmy and Tom go down the well one at a time.

'Horrible,' said Tom, when they were all safely back in the light of day. 'I thought a great hairy hand would come out of a crack in the wall and drag me in like something in the Ghost Stories of an Antiquary.'

'I hoped there'd suddenly be a great hole in the wall and I'd look through it and see a lot of people conspiring like M. Jackal in *Les Mohicans de Paris*,' said Emmy, who was a fervent addict of Dumas père.

Lucy said people said you could see the stars at midday when you were down a well, but you jolly well couldn't.

'And I'll tell you for why,' said Tom, 'because it's half past two. I hope old Adams won't come out in a hurry. It's much more fun when we're alone,' with which Emmy agreed.

Lucy did not quite agree but she wished, though blaming

herself for cowardice, that his arrival might be postponed, because she felt she must clear away the shadow that was between them and yet was afraid she might fail. But the afternoon was passing. Percy Bodger and the Boy had between them removed many pailfuls of rubbish and slime and Percy Bodger's voice, like St John the Baptist in the opera *Salome*, came up at intervals, though not to chide them for their ways but to announce that he had got down to the sand and the water was beginning to come sweetly.

'Lucky it isn't chalky,' said Emmy. 'Ours is as hard as nails and leaves the most awful rims round the bath.'

And then at last Mr Adams did come and praised their labours and said tea was ready and would they come in.

'We're a bit mucky,' said Emmy, 'but here goes.'

'I thought you would be,' said Mr Adams, 'so Heth is having tea in the garden. Come along.'

He went away with Emmy, and Lucy and Tom after promising Percy Bodger they would come back followed their hosts though Tom seemed strangely reluctant to hurry.

'Come on,' said Lucy. 'We'll miss Miss Hoggett's cake. She makes marvellous cakes.'

'I say, Lucy,' said Tom, stopping at the door between the yard and the garden. 'Am I good or not? Don't stop to think.'

'Very good in some ways, not so good in others,' said Lucy. 'Emmy can knock spots off you with cows, but then she would knock spots off anyone. But you'll beat her at market gardening any day before long. And I give you top marks for onions. What's the matter?'

'That's what Macpherson said,' said Tom. 'I don't mean he said what was the matter, but about the onions. I say, Lucy, can I tell you something?'

'Don't be too long then,' said Lucy, 'or they'll come to look for us. What's the matter?'

'Look here, I'm serious,' said Tom. 'I know I sound awfully silly but it's deadly serious. Emmy has an idea that we could farm together at Rushwater. I mean run a lot of the Home Farm and the plantations and things and take some of the work off Martin. You know she's to have Macpherson's cottage when he dies.'

'Well, why not?' said Lucy. 'Jolly good idea. Emmy can do the animals and you do the kitchen garden and the plantations.'

'But I ought to go to an Agricultural College and learn about the business side,' said Tom. 'And if I do, I'll go mad. Chaps do go mad you know after the war. Most of us have got it coming to us one way or another, sooner or later. Going back to Oxford was ghastly though I love the place, but an agricultural place would be hell. I want to be with real ordinary people.'

'Well, why not?' said Lucy. 'Sylvia never went to an Agricultural College, nor did Martin, nor Emmy. Nor did I, for that matter. You're a farmer's grandson just as I'm a farmer's daughter. Don't listen to everything everyone tells you.'

'Thanks *awfully*,' said Tom. 'Emmy's awfully keen on me being at Rushwater.'

'Well, you'd better marry her,' said Lucy. 'Or anyway get engaged now and get married presently. She'll have a house, so you ought to do very nicely. Come on. Mr Adams will think we've forgotten him.'

'Thanks *most* awfully,' said Tom. 'I say, you are an awfully good sort, Lucy. I'll tell Emmy.'

'Then mind you tell her out of your own head and don't say I told you,' said Lucy. 'That would be enough to put any girl off. Anyway good luck and I hope you'll be awfully happy. Come on.'

They reached the tea-table just in time to stop Heather

coming to look for them, but not in time to prevent Mr Adams thinking about them. His thoughts were not of the happiest. Something had gone wrong between his market-garden manager and himself. He could not put a name to it, but there was a rift, a shadow. If Tom Grantly had anything to do with this change, well Lucy Marling was old enough to know her own mind and whatever decision she had made he wished her joy with all his heart. Later he would try to get her alone and ask if he had in any way hurt her, said or done something that in her world was not done or said. But he would not hurry, for in his experience opportunities came when they chose and the only hurry needed was the quick decision to seize them.

Miss Hoggett's cakes were appreciatively devoured. Emmy told the story of their descent into the well and Mr Adams looked serious.

'It's no good crying over spilt milk,' he said, 'but don't you ever do it again. If anything had happened to you, what would Percy Bodger have done? People don't want a well-man who lets his employer's friends drown themselves.'

The admonition was addressed to no one in particular, but Lucy felt it was for her and for the one hundredth time she felt the sick inward dread which would mean another restless night and sat back in weariness of spirit.

'Front door bell,' said Heather. 'Hoggett's gone down the street. I'll go.'

She went indoors and came back with Mr and Mrs Grantly, Henry and Grace.

'I feel it is quite disgraceful to intrude upon you twice in one day,' said Mrs Grantly, 'and so does my husband. But we have two pieces of news that we would like you, as neighbours, to know before other people.'

Mr Adams thanked her and indeed looked sensible of the kind thought.

'One is Eleanor's engagement to Colin Keith,' said Mrs Grantly. 'It will be in *The Times* on Monday, but you have been so kind to the children that we thought you would like to know. They will live in London, but I hope they will be down here sometimes and luckily lawyers have very long holidays. The date of the wedding isn't settled, but we hope you will come and Mrs Pilward as she will be then,' said Mrs Grantly smiling to Heather.

The pleasant buzz of congratulations having subsided Mr Adams asked what the other piece of news was.

'Quite different, but quite as exciting in its own way,' said Mrs Grantly. 'Grace has passed that stupid examination with six credits.'

'I can't say I see any sense in making them all study themselves silly,' said Mr Adams. 'But that's the way the world is and soon I won't be able to have a job myself seeing as I never passed an examination in my life. But I'm glad and Heth and I congratulate you, young lady, don't we, Heth?'

Heather joined warmly in his congratulations, as did Lucy.

'It's three bits of news,' said Henry, who had for some time been looking as if he had something inside him that was much too large and must be got rid of. 'I didn't tell you, father, because – oh well anyway I'll tell you now.'

He took from his pocket a long buff envelope and pulled out a form and an envelope.

'There,' he said. 'They've come. I'm to report to Sparrowhill Camp. And here's my railway warrant.'

It was not exactly a surprise and his parents had of late come to wish as fervently for the paper as Henry himself. Nor did it mean imminent danger, for danger may be anywhere now. But a faint chill struck to their hearts all the same.

'Oh Lord,' said Henry, 'I hadn't opened this letter. I must have put it in the envelope with the calling-up papers by mistake. It's from Gerry. Oh, *good* old Gerry! You know Gerry, father, Gerry Farquhar that made fifty-nine not out against Southbridge School. He's in the Barsetshires and he says it is pretty generally known that they're going to the Far East and they think our lot are going to get a quick course and go out with the next draft. Oh golly, golly!'

Henry was almost overwhelmed by the congratulations he received from Mr Adams and Heather and Lucy Marling and, though less interested, from his brother and sister. In fact so enthusiastic were the Adamses and Lucy Marling that he did not notice his parents' efforts to express a joy they did not feel; which perhaps was the effect the others had intended. In a few seconds Mrs Grantly collected herself and was able to say what fun it would be for Henry to see Gerry Farquhar, and he must bring him over to Edgewood when he got some leave; and then the Rector said much the same. We do not think that Mr Adams was taken in, but Heather and Lucy were, and the young people made a lot of happy, excited noise till Mrs Grantly said they had already given Mr Adams quite enough trouble what with the churchyard drain and all these congratulations and must be going home. Mr Adams accompanied them to the door.

'Thank you for your sympathy,' said Mrs Grantly, lingering for a moment when her husband with Tom and Henry and Grace had taken their leave.

'I never had a boy,' said Mr Adams, 'but believe me, Mrs Grantly, I admired your pluck, if I may say so.'

'It's not the army. That's good for young men,' said Mrs

Grantly. 'It's the Far East. I don't know a man or a boy who was out there during the war who isn't the worse for it in some way. Sometimes it hits them sooner, sometimes later; but it never fails to leave its poison somewhere. To help the Empire one would give anything, but what we are giving our young for now, I don't know. They have killed our Empire and They will kill what They call our Commonwealth if They can. No good talking about it. How handsome Heather looks. Good-bye.'

She hurried after her family and Mr Adams shut the front door. Heather was clearing away the tea-things and said she would wash up as Miss Hoggett was still out, so Mr Adams walked into his garden in the cool of the late afternoon, and went through the wooden door into the stable yard. Here Percy Bodger and the Boy were packing their hauling apparatus into the car while Lucy, extremely dirty, was cleaning the margin of the well.

'Thank you, my men,' said Mr Adams. 'It's a fine job and I hope they treated you all right.'

'Not too bad, sir,' said Percy Bodger. 'Miss Hoggett she give us a nice tea before she went out. She's a great hand at cakes the old lady. The Boy and me we rinsed our cups and things and left them on the draining board in the scullery, sir. And Mr Wickham he came in and said he didn't want the beer, sir, only the baskets. It's over there, sir,' and Percy Bodger pointed to a fine phalanx of bottles. 'He took the empties away, sir, but he don't want these.'

'Then you men had better take them,' said Mr Adams. 'And here's your pay and a bit over.'

'Thank you, sir,' said Percy Bodger. 'It's a pleasure to work in some places, sir, and with some people. Now Miss Marling she's a rare one to work with. My old grandfather says she's as good with a terrier as anyone he knows when he's ratting in a rick-yard or a barn. Good-night, sir.'

Peace fell upon the stable yard as Percy Bodger and the Boy drove away and Mr Adams went over to the well.

'I'm just re-pointing the last bricks and then your well ought to be all right for ages,' said Lucy, slapping Percy Bodger's mortar onto his mortar-board with his trowel in a most professional way. She worked in silence for a few more moments, then straightened herself and set down the tools.

'A nice job,' she said. 'Thanks awfully for letting me come, Mr Adams. I'll be off now. Oh, could you come over on Tuesday or Wednesday to see Spadger about those permits. We've got them through, haven't we?'

'We have,' said Mr Adams, thinking that we was a better word than I.

'I'll tell you what,' said Lucy. 'When you rang up about those permits I was awfully stupid.'

She paused, collecting all her courage to confess her own stupidity; her breeches and shirt dirty and in places damp from her descent of the well, her hands and arms covered with mortar, even her hair spattered with it, her face very red, with a large smudge which she had acquired while greasing Percy Bodger's pulley.

'I wanted to talk to you about that too, Miss Marling,' said Mr Adams. 'I was very stupid myself. In fact I can't forgive myself until you forgive me.'

'But there isn't anything to forgive,' said Lucy. 'When you rang up and said it would be all right I said were you sure, because what I meant was you had to be quite sure it was all right, because if you weren't awfully careful now people are *beasts* and say you're cheating. And then I thought perhaps you thought I thought, I mean I meant, that you might be cheating a bit and I wouldn't think that if I were a hundred years old, only it is so difficult to say what one wants to say sometimes. *Please*, Mr Adams, this is true. I couldn't *ever* have thought you would cheat.'

More than anything she would have liked to burst into tears, or jump into her car and drive away to some ultimate dim Thule. But she had confessed her fault and must await judgment.

'I'm old enough to be your father, Miss Marling,' said Mr Adams, 'that is,' he added, 'if I'd married a good bit earlier than I did, though that was pretty early, but that didn't stop me making a fine fool of myself. I did take your words the way you said you were afraid I'd take them. But as soon as I came to think it over I knew that I was a fool. Sam Adams, I said to myself, you are a fool and you might as well know it. Miss Marling is the best stainless steel and she couldn't say, let alone think, what you are thinking she meant. I could have kicked myself, Miss Marling and I meant to make my apologies to you on the Monday. Then I had to go to London, where I may say I've been arranging things so that the Government I helped to put in won't do me quite as much harm as it will do to some, and I didn't like to ring you up because the telephone hadn't been much of a success before. I've been waiting all day to have a chance to tell you Sam Adams is downright ashamed and if going down on my knees could help, down I'd go: and a fine figure of fun I'd look,' said Mr Adams reflectively.

'Then it's all right?' said Lucy.

'If it's all right for you, it's all right for me, every time,' said Mr Adams.

'Oh!' said Lucy and sat down on the kerb of the well.

'I can give you my word of honour such a thing won't ever happen again,' said Mr Adams. 'I'd rather put my hand in the rolling mills than hurt you.'

'You didn't hurt me,' said Lucy. 'It was all the telephone. I hate telephones. I must get along now. It's been a splendid day and thanks most awfully. And can you come to see Spadger soon?'

'There's something more important than Spadger,' said Mr Adams. 'I'm going in for farming in a bigger way now and I'm thinking of buying some land round Edgewood. I'd need a manager. Can you take it on?'

'Rather,' said Lucy. 'Would you want me to run the market garden, or the farm, or both?'

'I was thinking of a living-in job,' said Mr Adams.

'I'd love that,' said Lucy. 'Like what Emmy does at Rushwater. Only I don't know if my people would mind. I'm the only one at home now.'

'Then it's high time you weren't,' said Mr Adams. 'Look here, Miss Marling. Heather is getting married. I shall be alone here. I know what I am and what I have to offer. It isn't much, but I would like to offer it you and with my whole heart.'

There was complete silence. If Lucy's face could have been more crimson than it already was it would have been so, but this was impossible.

'Do you mean you want me to live *here*?' said Lucy, incredulous and strangely breathless, not sure who or where she was.

'If you will honour me by marrying me, yes,' said Mr Adams. 'If not we will ever be the best of friends; that is if you will honour me with your friendship.'

'But I do. I have,' said Lucy.

'Does that mean that friendship is all?' said Mr Adams. 'If so, God bless you, and we'll carry on with Adamsfield and forget the rest.'

'But what would Mrs Adams say?' said Lucy.

For a moment Mr Adams did not take her meaning. Then he laughed, though very kindly.

'The one thing Mother studied was my happiness,' said Mr Adams. 'And when she died, poor soul, she told me I must study Heather's happiness. I've done my best and it's not always been easy. Now my girlie's going to be married and to a very good fellow, and I am going to be alone. If Mother was here, Miss Marling, I'll tell you what she'd say. She'd say, Don't you live alone because of me, Sam. Marry someone that will make a home for you and someone you can study and think for, because what you need, she would say, is someone to care for.'

There was another silence while Lucy painfully thought of all her employer had said.

'Well,' she said at last. 'I'll tell you what. If you are sure Mrs Adams would be pleased, I will marry you. Thank you very much.'

There seemed to be nothing else to say. The light was fading from the air. Venus shone chill in a green sky.

'I'll go home,' said Lucy. 'I expect Papa will be furious for a bit, but that's all right. I'll see you at Adamsfield on Monday then, with Spadger.'

Mr Adams walked with her to her car.

'I say,' said Lucy, pausing inelegantly with one leg in the car and one on the ground, 'What about children and all that rot?' and had she been facing the western sky Mr Adams might have seen her colour grow even deeper than before.

'Don't worry about that,' said Mr Adams, 'you're not married yet. We'll see about it all later. You're only a child yourself.'

Lucy got the other leg in and pressed the self-starter. Mr Adams shut the door of the car. Lucy quickly bent her head and rubbed her face against his hand and as swiftly drove away.

'Mother would say I'd done right,' said Mr Adams. 'And now I must tell Heather.'

As he went back to the house he saw Heather, in the lighted room, talking to someone on the telephone.

'Young Ted, I'll be bound,' he said to himself.

'I must ring off now, darling,' Heather was saying. 'From what I've just seen in the yard daddy is going to give me a step-mother. I expect I'll have to break the news for him, poor darling. Well, I couldn't have a nicer one. I thought daddy would never come to the point. Good-bye, darling.'

'And now,' said Heather, as her father came into the room with a faintly sheepish look on his face, 'I'll tell you what. Miss Sowerby was right.'

'How do you mean right, girlie?' said Mr Adams.

'The Old Bank House needed a mistress,' said Heather.

VIRAGO MODERN CLASSICS

The first Virago Modern Classic, *Frost in May* by Antonia White, was published in 1978. It launched a list dedicated to the celebration of women writers and to the rediscovery and reprinting of their works. Its aim was, and is, to demonstrate the existence of a female tradition in literature, and to broaden the sometimes narrow definition of a 'classic'. Published with new introductions by some of today's best writers, the books are chosen for many reasons: they may be great works of literature; they may be wonderful period pieces; they may reveal particular aspects of women's lives; they may be classics of comedy, storytelling, letter-writing or autobiography.

'The Virago Modern Classics list contains some of the greatest fiction and non-fiction of the modern age, by authors whose lives were frequently as significant as their writing. Still captivating, still memorable, still utterly essential reading' SARAH WATERS

'The Virago Modern Classics list is wonderful. It's quite simply one of the best and most essential things that has happened in publishing in our time. I hate to think where we'd be without it' ALI SMITH

'The Virago Modern Classics have reshaped literary history and enriched the reading of us all. No library is complete without them' MARGARET DRABBLE

'The writers are formidable, the production handsome. The whole enterprise is thoroughly grand' LOUISE ERDRICH

'Good news for everyone writing and reading today' HILARY MANTEL

VIRAGO MODERN CLASSICS

AUTHORS INCLUDE:

Elizabeth von Arnim, Beryl Bainbridge, Pat Barker, Nina Bawden, Vera Brittain, Angela Carter, Willa Cather, Barbara Comyns, E. M. Delafield, Polly Devlin, Monica Dickens, Elaine Dundy, Nell Dunn, Nora Ephron, Janet Flanner, Janet Frame, Miles Franklin, Marilyn French, Stella Gibbons, Charlotte Perkins Gilman, Rumer Godden, Radclyffe Hall, Helene Hanff, Josephine Hart, Shirley Hazzard, Bessie Head, Patricia Highsmith, Winifred Holtby, Attia Hosain, Zora Neale Hurston, Elizabeth Jenkins, Molly Keane, Rosamond Lehmann, Anne Lister, Rose Macaulay, Shena Mackay, Beryl Markham, Daphne du Maurier, Mary McCarthy, Kate O'Brien, Grace Paley, Ann Petry, Barbara Pym, Mary Renault, Stevie Smith, Muriel Spark, Elizabeth Taylor, Angela Thirkell, Mary Webb, Eudora Welty, Rebecca West, Edith Wharton, Antonia White

CHILDREN'S CLASSICS INCLUDE:

Joan Aiken, Nina Bawden, Frances Hodgson Burnett, Susan Coolidge, Rumer Godden, L. M. Montgomery, Edith Nesbit, Noel Streatfeild, P. L. Travers